What They're Saying

"One of the delights of *The Chemist* is that there are no clear boundaries of black and white or good and evil. Instead, it places the protagonist on a tightrope of tension as he tries to figure out his place within a tale of stunning plot twists that builds into something much more than just another obvious effort to save the world."

—*Midwest Book Review*

"Far and away one of the most original and just flat-out interesting and crazy thriller/suspense fiction novels I've read in forever."

—Jhonni Parker, *Goodreads.com*

"Field brings a fresh attitude and literary style and makes it all his own and doesn't just rehash the same old plot lines we've seen a million times before which makes this book wholly unique."

—Steph Coleman, *Goodreads.com*

"An easy and exciting read, this book brings together science, big business, terrorism, espionage and special operations."

—Katrina, *Amazon.com*

"Try and be bored reading this… just try. I dare ya!"

—Claire Middleton, *Goodreads.com*

THE CHEMIST

Alan J. Field

ThrillRide Media

The Chemist
A ThrillRide Media Book

This is a work of fiction. All of the characters, organizations and events portrayed in this novel are either products of author's imagination or are used fictitiously. Any similarity to real persons, living or dead, is coincidental and not intended by the author.

ISBN: 978-0-9980508-2-9
ASIN: B01J0KFN5M

Print Formatting: By Your Side Self-Publishing
www.ByYourSideSelfPub.com

PUBLISHED IN THE UNITED STATES OF AMERICA

To Leah, whose encouragement made this book possible. And to Sharon, my partner in life and the better writer, who keeps me young at heart.

"I am proud of the fact that I have never invented weapons that kill."

—Thomas A. Edison

PART I

"It is a profound and necessary truth that the deep things in science are not found because they are useful; they are found because it was possible to find them."

—Robert Oppenheimer

Chapter 1

April 17th, 7:45 p.m.
Beirut, Lebanon

Sabir Al-Dahar-Essa tightened his grasp around the concealed item he had stuffed in a paper bag. He advanced along Bir Hassen Street like a revenant Barbary lion ready to pounce on its prey—head low, gaze focused on his destination. To onlookers, he was like any other 34 year old man amidst the din of sidewalk market peddlers packing it in for the day. The setting sun silhouetted buckling clotheslines and satellite dishes.

Like a lab rat slithering through a contrived maze, he was aware of the men following him who made no attempt to hide. This would be Sabir's first test of unequivocal loyalty, the first of many, and they would watch his every move.

He left the bustling boulevard behind as he turned onto a forgettable side street. Latif's flat was just ahead. He looked up as he walked into the rustic courtyard with crumbling stone benches and overgrown bushes. A flickering light filtered through Latif's curtains as the hum of LBCI soccer match highlights bled through the walls.

Sabir would end this quickly.

He climbed the stairs up to the flat. After three hard knocks, the door creaked open.

Latif appeared in the doorway. Dispensing with a Salaam Alaikum embrace, Sabir stepped back and motioned for his friend to follow him out to the balcony. Latif stepped out, his rawboned body looking slightly plumper, and closed the door, silently waiting.

"Are the four chickens inside?" Sabir spat out as he handed him the paper bag enshrouding the oblong-shaped object.

Latif gave him a questioning look.

"It is a gift," Sabir said.

Latif frowned. "They are not cowards. They will do as they are told."

"There is a difference between blind obedience and achieving glory in the eyes of Allah. Are they competent?"

"As much as they need to be."

Sabir glanced over the edge of the balcony. The last man following him had disappeared, choosing not to enter the courtyard. Nevertheless, omnipresent ears listened. "They are young," Sabir said. "Young men are reckless."

"But, they are eager to see you."

"Fine. Let me see them." Sabir followed Latif inside to the one bedroom apartment.

Four empty-headed recruits—none looking older than twenty—were sprawled out on a brown sofa, their eyes transfixed on a shiny new flat screen. The announcer of the soccer match declared a goal, and the four young men cheered and clapped. Empty, overturned Maltina bottles mixed with the garbage scattered on the floor and coffee table. Shisha smoke filled the air.

Sabir stood near the couch and waited, but the young men took no notice. Latif slammed the front door to get their attention. When they finally bothered to look up at Sabir standing there with hands clasped behind his back, they scrambled to their feet. They did not dare approach him.

There would be no pleasantries.

Four machine guns were angled up against the window sill behind them, recently opened boxes torn and crumpled on the floor. Sabir resisted the urge to shake his head at the pitiful scene. He gave Latif a disapproving glance. "I thought you told them not to bring weapons."

Latif cleared his throat. "They brought them so you could see they are ready for Jannah. They are eager and ready to do what is necessary."

Sabir grinned inwardly. His ultimate task was all too easy, especially with these cretins. He narrowed his eyes at the young men in counterpoint. "You are to leave these weapons behind. I don't care where you got them or how much you spent. Understood?"

They nodded like mindless bobble-heads.

He stroked his scraggly beard that he knew would be shaved off soon. "I am not here to ask you how the family is, or how the girlfriend is, unless she is sitting on my lap."

One of them sat back down and stretched as if in his own living room.

Sabir took a step toward the boy. "How old are you?"

"Nineteen."

"Are you a virgin?"

"I save myself for Allah."

Without warning, Sabir raised his arm as he bent over the cluttered coffee table and swept it clear in one fluid motion. Bottles clattered to the floor.

The young man leapt back to his feet. The others flinched and held their breath. Sabir motioned to Latif to place the paper bag on the table. This time, he wouldn't hold back a disapproving shake of his head. "How can we expect to defeat the enemy if you carry yourselves in this way? It is shameful. What kind of way is this to live for a warrior of Islam?"

The young men stared at him attentively.

"The time is now," Sabir continued. "We must act quickly, my brothers." He had changed his tone to one of stoic deliberation. He considered himself a devout atheist from Palestine. The boys in the room hailed from Saudi Arabia and Syria. The last thing he considered them to be were his brothers. He knew how to forge camaraderie with such hollow words.

He motioned at the door. "If you want to leave now, then go. You will not get another chance to save yourself." None of them moved. Satisfied by their collective silence, he continued. "The weapon needed to destroy the infidels will soon be ours, and Allah is counting on each of you to fulfill your roles to secure it."

As they gazed at him with hopeful eyes like docile puppies, Sabir thought of the unwavering goal that had consumed his whole life up to that point; the destruction of the bastard State. The young men on the other hand, sought to extend their brand of terror to a worldwide scale.

What fools. Terror was not something to create for no reason—it must have a purpose and an end result.

Latif spoke up. "But you have not told us where we can find the weapon, Sabir."

"In America."

"But, how can we gain access to American military installations? Our appearance—"

"It is not within the military," Sabir interrupted. "A private company in New York City developed it, so it remains there for us to acquire as our own."

Latif bowed his head slightly. "What will you have us do, Sabir?"

He looked upon them with a demonic glare. "We will go to this company and learn how it is made. Then we will bring what we know back here. And when I—," he paused. "When *we* do, we will elevate terror upon the West unlike anything seen before." He couldn't tell if they even understood the urgency of the matter. The ignorant hypocrites. If not imbibing was a way to respect Allah, then why spit on Allah's legacy? They would justify it through the doctrine of Taqiyya, all the while knowing their knowledge applied only under threat or duress amongst infidels. They had become the true infidels.

Sabir wanted Israel. He wanted it to become an everlasting hellfire. Stooges like the ones before him could have the West for themselves.

He studied the young men. What a waste they were. "By now," he said, "you have all heard about me and what I will demand of you. The company who made the weapon will require some persuasion. You will assist me with that."

"You can count on us," Latif said, eyes beaming. The others nodded.

"Good. We leave tomorrow." He allowed himself a plastic smile, to put them at ease, then he stood. "My brothers." He paused, the words sour in his mouth. "My brothers, the hour is late and I need to secure our passports. Come morning, we shall alter our appearances. It will be a long journey." He motioned at the paper bag on the table. "Enjoy my gift. I only wish I could revel in celebration with you."

Sabir embraced Latif, who he'd known since their days in the Bakkah Valley. He would miss him. Latif would be a small sacrifice in reaching his ultimate goal.

He opened the door before turning back to the group one last time. "Enjoy your celebration. The work ahead has only just begun."

Latif slid the object out of the paper bag and smiled. "Thank you, Sabir." It was a large bottle of Taybeh wine direct from the West Bank.

Sabir walked out quickly and shut the door behind him.

He had been an ambitious terrorist and had tortured more Israeli soldiers than he could recall. How much more terror could the world take?

As much as it deserved.

Disappearing into the milieu of the bustling thoroughfare, he pondered what his place in history would be. Hero of the Palestinian people? Jannah, the so-called eternal place for Muslims, was for illiterates with misguided ideals. He would live to see the day Israel would crumble to dust.

He felt the presence again of the men who had been following him. As he turned off the forgotten side street and stepped onto Bir Hassan Street, the ground rumbled and he heard the explosion of fire and broken glass behind him. His gift had been opened.

He thought of the five million Riyal sitting in his bank account, courtesy of his new friends. That was incentive enough to throw away the life he had known and pursue their presumptuous vision of a new world order—for the time being. But most of all, he thought of the one woman who made his life worth the risk he was about to take.

My habibti, soon we will be together.

Chapter 2

April 17th, 1:30 p.m.
The South Bronx, New York City

They came here through no fault of their own. That's what they told Daniel Strong, when he started working here. He'd just led a group session for teen addicts at the Caring Sanctuary of New York Rehab Center in the Bronx.

The Center insisted the staff call them clients, but Danny thought more of them than that. He was one of the few counselors who had made it a point to speak with any of the teens in one-on-one sessions he had scheduled, which they more often than not blew off. The office was a cramped, windowless space he shared with five others. Governmental issue metallic desks and chairs were arranged into pint-sized cubicles with weathered and ripped gray plastic dividers. A 1990s desktop computer that still took floppy disks sat on a vacant desk.

Almost three years to the day had passed since Danny had moved to New York City. He eked out a living both as a drug rehabilitation counselor and as a personal trainer for a gaggle of uptown fitness clubs. He once told himself that he needed a change in his life, to move away from his familiar southern roots. The job seemed like a natural progression; helping others overcome the demons that had almost devoured him in the wake of depression, a consequence of grieving the death of a loved one.

On his way out, Danny noticed that everyone else had left for the day. Walking five blocks to the Fordham Road bus stop, he passed two boarded up *bodegas*, rows of walk-ups and some multifamily buildings. The City never got around to paving this section of street or replacing the crumbling and uneven sidewalks. In a word, it was desolate, making it that much easier to hear the hurried and uneven footsteps that followed about forty feet behind him.

He turned to look back and thought he caught a glimpse of someone darting behind a stairwell of one of the walk-ups. The sound of the footsteps vanished, but started again when he resumed his journey, so he quickened his pace. The footsteps sped up in time. When he got to the corner, Danny stopped again. He started to turn back, but froze, eyes darting to his right. Again the footsteps stopped. The block ahead was covered with scaffolding, a green dumpster parked about midway against the curb. The sidewalk was blocked off and rerouted along the street side of the dumpster.

Danny crossed the street and followed the makeshift path, then made the sharp right that led back to the original sidewalk along the short end of the dumpster. The sound of footsteps still moved toward him. When Danny made the turn, he paused, and waited.

When he heard the footsteps approach, he pounced, grabbing his pursuer by a dark gray sweat jacket and pushing him against the dumpster. A red polyester book bag landed on the ground with a thud. Danny released his grip when he realized who it was. “Why are you following me?” he said, pinning the assailant against the dumpster.

Darryl, one of Danny’s clients, straightened quickly for someone who had just been slammed into solid metal. “Hey, Mr. Strong. I never meant to do nothin’ to you.”

“Oh yeah, what then? Something you want to tell me?”

Darryl looked away.

“Look at me, Darryl.” Danny noticed at his feet a thick wad of twenty dollar bills held together with a rubber band. It had jarred loose when he grabbed Darryl. He judged the wad to amount to about two grand.

He reached down and held the wad up to Darryl’s face. “You’ve been doing more than smokin’ the bottles.”

He knew there had to be a reason Darryl had wanted to follow him. A bit more coaxing was necessary. “I can’t help you unless you’re straight with me now.”

“Mekhi, man.”

“Who’s that?

“My friend. In the projects.”

“Was Mekhi dealing too?”

“He’s fucked up bad. In the hospital.”

Darryl’s fidgeting hands and clipped words told him there was more to the story.

Danny recalled Darryl mentioning the name of his longtime friend from the same project apartment building. He’d already figured Darryl was dealing, selling the product from the wooden benches in front of his building. Entry level peddlers, boys as young as ten, kept a 24/7 vigil in the projects. The busiest times were from dusk to well after midnight daily. Dealers lured susceptible boys into the trade by paying for Nike high tops, cool haircuts, and hand-held computer games, then feeding them some unattainable dream of becoming the next, black Donald Trump with the profits they would earn. The police patrolled the area and even sent in narcs to chase them out, but the dealers always came out again when the coast was clear.

“He was taking a cut off the top or buying from someone else. Right?”

Darryl answered with a nod as he shut his eyes.

“How long have you two been working for them?”

Darryl’s eyes were stone cold, but the pullback of his upper lip belied the heartlessness he was trying to project. “Four, five months.”

“So why’d they hurt him?”

Darryl looked down again.

He grabbed Darryl’s chin and tugged it forward. “Look at me, Darryl.”

“They didn’t do nothin'. I… I did it to him.”

Though Danny showed no reaction, inside he might have been standing over a three-eyed mutant. They'd done more than make Darryl sell, they'd made him a heavy. Danny understood this to be a common career move. Upseller sends a message to Mekhi through Darryl with the promise of a bigger cut in the future. It didn't seem to matter that the boys had grown up in the same building. Business was business.

"So Mekhi was taking a cut off the top or buying from someone else. Right?"

"Yeah. I don't know. Both. I don't wanna get got. I do what I got to for the big man, you know?"

"They have you in a headlock."

"They told me to take him out from behind but I couldn't do it. I wacked him in the head and ran. They say I fucked up just like Mekhi, 'cept they gonna take me out and my mom—tonight. I dunno, I thought—."

The kid's eyes moistened before he shut them both hard. Danny was also raised by a single mother in the Smoky Mountain foothills of North Carolina. "You want my help? Then tell me who they are."

What did Darryl expect him to do, *talk* to the man? He'd be a proverbial fish out of water, and that analogy went well beyond skin color. Besides, there was the rule: keep off-hours contact to a minimum. When he'd served in Delta Force, Danny had accomplished several rescue missions, but they always took place in windblown deserts, foothills and jungles. Maybe some small villages, but not inner city environs.

"Ramon. The guy goes by Ramon. That's it. He comes 'round tonight, yo."

"You know I can't just…." Danny shut his eyes for a moment, resisting the temptation to slap him across the bow. He already knew it would take more than just words to solve this. Yet the kid had the guts to reach out to him, even if he had to coax it out of him. It had been a long time since Danny answered the call of duty to help someone in need. Perhaps he had something left in him. Still, the doubts of accomplishing anything raced through his mind. "I'll think about it and call you. Now get outta' here and take your bag with you. And don't ever follow me again."

Without another word, Darryl quickly stuck the wad into his pocket, then scampered down the block.

Talking heads debated the repercussions of the latest ecological contagion: a tanker oil spill in the Sea of Japan.

Forearm over eyes in darkness, Danny tried in vain to put Darryl's plight out of mind. When one of his clients beckoned, he wasn't one to turn away.

Flat on his back, he reached down to the floor to grab the remote. When his hand found it, he pointed and pressed, resulting in an eerie silence. Only the Dyckman Street traffic noise found its way through the lone cracked window.

When he'd finally succeeded in pushing Darryl away, Kelly appeared. His mind had no safe harbor.

The memories beckoned from his doorless closet. Sitting up, he turned on the table lamp resting on the nightstand. The tattoos adorning his shirtless torso and shoulders revealed his special ops history, but he bore no identification insignias, which were specifically discouraged. One was a green dragon slithering down his backbone. His proudest was a Brothers-in-Arms design of a soldier with the body of an M-4 rifle, an American flag flying overhead.

He reached for the opened cardboard boxes. One contained holiday cards, handwritten letters and Kelly's DVDs. The other, a pristine wedding album enshrouded in a smooth light blue material with gold trim. He couldn't bring himself to revisit any of it, except for the one photo of her he kept in his wallet. The other smaller box was his CIA get-out-of-Dodge kit. It had multiple passports, visas, and residency papers from several countries where he'd been stationed. He'd wondered why no one bothered to confiscate the stash, yet he'd never returned any of it.

Once a spy, always a spy.

His mind drifted off to the last time they had slept together. She was on furlough from the battlefront in Afghanistan, and he was between assignments but still living in Prague. They reunited at the Israeli beach town of Eilat. The love they shared remained strong, despite the extended separations. Their walks along the beach were halcyon, the Israeli food delectable, but pleasures of the flesh between them took precedence. With her arms wrapped around him in spooning position, he had no inkling that would be their last morning together.

"This sucks," he whispered.

"What?" she said at the tail end of an extended yawn, and then narrowed her eyes at him as she turned over to face him.

"I mean being away from each other so much."

"I know," she said.

Wincing, Danny wished he could stop what he'd just started. Seconds before, his face had been buried in the peppermint-scented, tawny shaded buzz cut hair. But he persisted anyway, having opened the door. "After your next tour of duty, let's go stateside."

"Are you kidding?" she asked.

"No, I'm not. The assignments don't mean as much to me as they once did. I can't go back to Special Forces, but I could get reassigned to Langley and you could transfer to Virginia or North Carolina, so that we could settle down and finally have a family." He couldn't look at her now, knowing what assignments he actually did for the Agency. Danny squeezed her harder. Too hard, in fact.

"Are you gonna be okay?"

Danny didn't have to answer. His hesitation said it all.

He was relieved to hear the answer he had hoped for. "After this tour ends, we'll see, okay?" She stretched out, then rolled over on top of him, straddling his washboard torso.

The pit in his stomach had swelled at the prospect of losing Darryl. It would be the closest he had ever been to raising his own child.

He needed a plan. If he confronted Ramon head-on and didn't send a strong enough message, then he would have only succeeded in putting Darryl and his mother in grave danger. It had to be dynamic enough to convince them that to approach Darryl would reap too high a cost.

After an hour or so, his plan took shape. It would come down to execution. If anything his special ops training taught him, it was imperative to have in place viable alternatives if the plan of action went bad.

He picked up his cell phone from its cradle on the nightstand and punched in Darryl's number.

"Mr. Strong?"

Darryl's voice was all he needed to hear. "I'll help you tonight, but listen up. This is what I want you to do."

Chapter 3

April 17th, 1:45 p.m.
Langley, Virginia

"Mommy, when are you coming back?"

Even on the phone, Joanne Dawson's seven year old daughter's plaintive cry tugged at her heart, but she had to focus on her work.

A wall of six high resolution life-sized television screens illuminated the subterranean surveillance room. A satellite feed showed Sabir standing on a Beirut street. A console flickered before her. Joanne was transfixed on her laptop, reviewing dossiers of all key players involved in her latest assignment.

Her two surveillance men on this assignment, Phil Farrat and Jeff Parneau, were hunched over their consoles beside her, headsets on, listening intently. Phil, a competent surveillance expert with short blond hair and bulbous cheeks on a face only a mother could love barely fit under the console, his lank legs folded under his too-close-to-the-floor chair. Jeff was a matchstick. Wire framed eyeglasses and smooth brown hair parted down the center exuded 'geek'.

"Mommy!" Latisha repeated to seemingly deaf ears.

Mesmerized by the current dossier, Joanne perused a surveillance photo of a slight young woman exiting a New York City taxi. The blonde wore thick black rimmed glasses. The description read:

Age: 23
IQ: 163
College: Massachusetts Institute of Technology
Major: PhD Bio-Chemistry
Honors: Phi Beta Kappa
Class Rank: 1
Annual Salary: $180,000

"Mommy!" Latisha pleaded once again.

Her trance broken, Joanne brushed away a few strands of wavy dark hair and leaned back in her swivel chair. She spoke in a sotto voce whisper, "Mommy has to work, and sometimes her work is somewhere faraway." Joanne thought that maybe it was time she stop speaking in the third person to a second grader, but the habit was hard to break. "Daddy will be there while I'm away."

"When are you coming back?" Latisha repeated, as if Joanne had said nothing at all.

"I don't know when, baby. I'll call you as soon as I learn."

"Mommy, why do you have to leave us?"

Another nervous breath followed before Joanne resorted to an impromptu speech, not unlike one would give on an elementary school career day. "Mommy's job keeps everyone safe, especially you and your brothers." She inhaled deeply. "And keeping everyone safe is hard!" The corners of her lips pinched, making an exaggerated smile, as if Latisha could somehow see her through the phone.

Gary Dawson came on the line. "How long before you come home, you think?"

"Between you and me, three weeks. I hope less."

"Please be careful. The kids want their mother back in one piece."

"You know how to keep things together. Tell them I love them."

"You bet. I love you."

Latisha and her brothers were screaming at each other in the background. "Gotta go," she heard. "Talk to you later." The line disconnected.

I love you, too.

Joanne refocused her attention on the last dossier. The photo showed a smartly dressed woman in her 50s in the foreground, a man with a familiar face following behind. She shuddered.

Geneva.

She'd just as soon forget *that* one. It had nearly derailed her career. Up to then, she'd been a rising star, having been station chief there until her office had been implicated in the death of a Russian embassy employee.

They reassigned her to Afghanistan, to do what she'd been trained for since she'd left the armed forces for the CIA. She'd been assigned to PSYOP, the Army's Psychological Operations Group during Desert Storm and Enduring Freedom. That unit's goal was to break the will of the enemy by using local Islamic teachings and superstitions. She eventually was reassigned to a covert public relations function for their Propaganda Management team in the Afghanistan conflict to ensure that any bad press caused by Coalition Forces would be 'handled' effectively. They'd presented it as a promotion, but she knew it was the Agency's way of saying, 'lay low and maybe someday we'll trust you to run another operation'.

The chemist's psychological profile was as depressing as her credentials were stellar: a sordid history of child abuse, drug addiction since adolescence, and a bi-polar disorder to boot. *A certified genius, a real savant, but self-destructive. Scary combination.* A PSYOP component, Joanne concluded, would make sense and produce the desired result.

Joanne's shoulders tensed when she heard the door behind her fly open to the sound of the corridor ambience.

She swiveled around in her chair to see Trae Dixon, a well-built man with a jovial demeanor. "The man's looking for you."

Joanne exhaled and rolled her eyes. "Didn't you tell him I'd already left?"

"I couldn't."

She knew the Agency kept tabs on each employee's whereabouts, so it would have been futile to lie about it.

"Did he deliver his package?" he asked.

"Uh-huh. We see and hear all," Joanne shot a glance over to Phil and Jeff, who had removed their head phones.

Jeff spoke up. "What's the plan now, coach?"

Joanne stood and turned to them. "Pack your bags, guys. It's on to New York tomorrow." She walked past Trae to the door speaking low. "Walk with me. I need some fresh air anyway."

Joanne led him down the elevator to the cavernous lobby of the original building with the gray and white checkerboard floor with blue columns. They stopped in front of the north wall commemorating CIA employees who died in the line of service.

"Impressive, isn't it?" she said. The Wall bore the inscription 'IN HONOR OF THOSE MEMBERS OF THE CENTRAL INTELLIGENCE AGENCY WHO GAVE THEIR LIVES IN THE SERVICE OF THEIR COUNTRY' in gold block letters. All that denoted them were blue stars without names.

Trae stared up at it too. "Sad. Heroes without stories to tell."

"True, but I've got to wonder how many of them were conflicted about whether what they were doing was right when their time came."

For six years, she was a paper pusher for the Operations Directorate while raising three children. Now she had a chance to prove her worth and do what was necessary to save the planet—from a 23 year old brat.

They took the elevator back upstairs and walked to Scuro's office.

"Slippery bastard," he said, shaking his head.

"We'll have to keep Sabir in our crosshairs 24/7."

"Roger that," the former Army Ranger responded. "Heard back from Javi?"

"Oh yeah. Already up there.

"Has he…?"

"No, but he'll reel him in. Scuro's jones-ing on this. Never seen anything like it. Our own chemists can't even deconstruct it."

"You really think the guy'll bite? I mean, it's been years."

"I'd bet my life on it. It's in his DNA."

Scuro's office walls displayed the trappings of lifetime government service and high-up connections. There were framed Agency citations for exemplary service, black and white photos with him accepting an award from William Webster and photo ops with other CIA and FBI directors of yesteryears.

After the last election, the President, with the Director's blessing, appointed him as DDI. Yale educated, he left the Agency for the Bureau after 17 years, only to return, causing increased tension within the Agency ranks as some looked upon him as a turncoat looking for a reprieve. He also brought over his Bureau mindset with a 'don't-move-without-hard-evidence' stance.

But Joanne thought Agency Operations didn't have the luxury of waiting. Many of her colleagues believed, as she did, that it was the Agency's job to connect the dots and move forward without waiting for that mythical piece of hard evidence. When or if it ever surfaced, it would be too late. Innocents would die.

Scuro shifted his eyes from his computer monitor on his otherwise spotless desk to Joanne. "I saw your work-up on this Tri-methyl Phosphofloramine. This is high priority, straight from the DCI."

She thought the man to be a pernicious prick, sitting there behind his desk with his silvery hair and over-tanned skin. "I know sir, but I thought the Bureau was working this already."

He harrumphed and shook his head in mild frustration. "They've done shit. Even with a man inside. Idiots."

Joanne knew one point of contention was turf. FBI was domestic, CIA was everything but. In reality though, it all overlapped, especially since 9/11. The CIA no longer saw itself as beholden to such directive—unofficially, anyway.

She also saw it as her duty to raise the other elephant in the room: that the operation would be limited to New York City, a clear violation of the ban against domestic CIA operations. "Yes sir, but don't you think that domestic missions like this—"

"—are sometimes warranted," he interrupted flatly. "Especially when it comes to weapons of mass destruction. I shouldn't have to tell you that."

Joanne knew this mission was multi-pronged: Find it, contain it, and then secure its creator. The cryptic verbiage of the last goal was what gave Joanne pause from the start.

When Scuro first presented her with the assignment, its importance was unsubstantiated. She knew it was common knowledge that for less than two-hundred dollars, any terrorist organization or rogue nation could order the components of such a weapon from the Internet. *Hell, even a chemistry nerd could make one if he wanted to.* But after perusing the file and its multiple dossiers, she learned why this wasn't just your average under-the-kitchen-sink neurotoxin. First, its unprecedented potency, and second, its chemical formula and individual elements could not be deconstructed by a mass spectrometry, making it undetectable.

Still, she wanted her objection on the record. "But the Charter states—"

"Screw the Charter," Scuro growled as the dark lines in his forehead deepened. "Off the record, of course. Being that the stakes here may have emergent international consequences if the planned auction is carried out, we can't let the Bureau's inability to get the job done prevent our intelligence apparatus from moving in. They're a good two steps behind us and this just can't wait." He returned his gaze to the computer monitor.

She gathered this was about Scuro needing to protect his former employer.

"This NOC you want read in. Four years out because of a drug problem?"

She straightened. "I can vouch for him, Sir. Worked for me on several operations, mostly in Europe.

"Yes, I see that. Not all of them went our way. So excuse me if I'm not head-over-heels."

She wanted him to look at her, but his paucity of eye contact made her defensive. "He's the best there is, especially under the tight deadline we're dealing with here and the fact that he's living up in New York right now. He's been through a lot. A good man who deserves a second shot."

"*You* only have *one* shot."

"Noted." Joanne expected as much from this man who clearly knew her story. For the last six years, she never doubted that someday the opportunity would present itself to get her back in the field. Perhaps he'd also figured out to push her buttons. Regardless, her loyalty to the Agency was unwavering. When Scuro dismissed her, she brought up the one issue that still gnawed at her conscience.

"But, assuming we achieve containment, this WMD could be reproduced at anytime, anywhere, to anyone, if the chemist so chooses. How does the Agency propose to deal with that eventuality?"

She finally got the eye contact she so craved.

"We both know there's only one way."

Chapter 4

April 17th, 11:45 p.m.
The Bronx, New York

Danny wore his gray hoodie set tight around his face, both hands in the warmer concealing the knuckle knife as he strutted erect on the sidewalk, never looking down. A row of forgotten parking meters stood guard over the crumbling sidewalk along the rear of Darryl's building. No one suspected the Kevlar vest he'd donned underneath. His strident gait projected that of someone who owned the sidewalk underneath him, while his thoughts focused on any escape routes he could use at the first signs of trouble.

Parkchester Houses, a city-block sized plot with twenty three six-story buildings was always at the top of the city's worst projects list. It was a place where, Danny had been told, the Devil himself wouldn't set foot in. This particular section had been dubbed, 'Siberia', by local law enforcement.

Approaching the expansive courtyard, he could hear the unmistakable clamber of residents and buyers congregating across from Building 4's front entrance. A driveway curved around the building, between it and a small playground. The benches were lined with young men, with lines forming in front of them like patrons waiting to enter a rock concert. The entire scene had the aura of a dysfunctional block party, except no one was dancing. Three boys popped off sounds with makeshift percussive objects. One sat with a pair of drumsticks rattling away against the bottom of a plastic overturned industrial sized paint can.

After a preliminary scan of the area, he realized he wasn't the only Caucasian paying a visit to the projects tonight. He noticed several high school and college kids, either too brazen or too stupid to care about their own safety, lined up for their fair share of crack and heroin, the drugs du jour.

The undercover cops Darryl had described were conspicuously absent, but Danny assumed they were watching from above, laying in waiting for someone to make a mistake.

Danny stood in line and watched how the system ran seamlessly, like a play wherein everyone performed their part to perfection. Without a word, a customer stopped at the bench and extended a hand as if to shake, except he had held a folded deck of money which the seller palmed, then raised his left hand and waved it back at the front entrance of the building, three middle fingers curled down with pinkie and thumb extended in a Tai-Chi-like move. The seller palmed the money to one of the others, who walked to the front entrance, stooped down at the three boys banging away and stuck the wad of bills under the overturned bucket. Then, another boy walked out of the building through the solid metal door and likewise palmed the vials to the customer.

Every third bench had a teenaged boy sitting up on its back ready to sell. One group huddled up ogling a Gameboy.

He closed in on Darryl, surrounded by three others and looked straight into his eyes. "Where's Mekhi?"

"He sick, man. I doing his stash tonight." The other boys looked on in bewilderment.

"I want to see him. Now," Danny repeated as he stepped closer. "What he sold me last time was shit."

One of the other boys stepped in. "Hey Mister, my boy just said he sick."

"He must be deaf or something," the second boy said, followed by muffled snickering.

"Then I want to see whoever he got this stash from. Tell me where he is."

"Don't know where. He come whenever he want to." The kid shrugged, followed by backup laughter from the group.

They all looked at each other, except for Darryl, who stared blankly back at Danny, playing the part.

"I'm not going anywhere until then," Danny said.

"No one get to see *him*," the first boy said, sounding all-important.

Then Darryl spoke. "He right, Mister. So take a walk and go somewhere else."

Almost on cue, Darryl's cell phone vibrated.

"That's the man, isn't?" Danny demanded.

"Like I said, he—"

In mid-sentence, Danny charged Darryl and pummeled him with ease to the ground. Then he pulled out the knuckle knife and pressed it to Darryl's throat, eying the two other boys. "You tell me where he is or I'll kill this kid."

Darryl's voice came out high-pitched. "Don't tell him!"

Frozen in place, the two boys were too scared to confront Danny.

One of the boys blurted, "He out front right now."

Danny grabbed Darryl's cell phone like a spoil of victory, then released tension on the knife. "If any of you follow me out there, I carve you up."

As he walked away, the two boys helped Darryl up.

"What?" the first kid said. "You had to tell him where Ramon at? You should'a lied about where he is. Ramon just gonna' smoke him, is all."

The second boy, nodding rapidly, said, "That dude's gonna' get got. Believe."

As Danny approached the curb, he saw the Grand Torino double parked, engine growling, tendrils of smoke curling out from the cracked open passenger side tinted window. One of Ramon's lieutenants, stocky with a muscular build but less than intimidating, was smoking a joint, leaning against the rear car door fender.

"I want to see Ramon," Danny said, stalking up.

"Yeah?" the lieutenant said. "He not here, so fuck off."

"Look, I know he's in the car, so just step aside."

The man acted as a human wall, barring access to the passenger side door. "Hey. What'd you want with him, man?"

"I need to work out a deal I did with Mekhi last week."

"What about it? Ramon too busy, man. Any problem you got, you talk to me."

Unfazed, Danny stepped up and put his face directly in front of the lieutenant's, chin protruding forward. "Listen up. I heard Mekhi's not doing any dealing right now and I think I know why," he said, flicking up an eyebrow and registering a snarl. The lieutenant didn't react. "He was selling bad stash. I want my money back. Now."

"Looks like you gotta find your stash someplace else," the lieutenant said, inhaling another breath of smoke and exhaling through his nostrils.

Danny slouched in apparent defeat, "Yeah, okay. I guess you're right."

He turned to walk away, then wheeled around in a crouch. Danny shot upward, his forehead making contact with the man's face, smashing it and knocking him back onto the trunk of the car. The lieutenant rolled off the back of the trunk and fell onto the street, groaning while his bloody fingers clamped his recently acquired broken nose.

The rear passenger side door swung open. Another young man vaulted out of the car and held a gun straight at Danny. The driver's side door opened and the driver, Marco, emerged. Had it not been for him, Danny would have sidestepped and kicked the door back in his face.

"You feel like lyin' dead out here on the sidewalk, man?" he asked. "Don't even think about it."

"I want to see Ramon," Danny said.

"Oh you gonna see him now, awright."

Danny heard the sound of the passenger side automatic window lower. He remained aware of the man with the gun, careful not to break his gaze.

"I'm right here. Say what you want to say." The figure in the front seat turned, his face still ensconced in the shadow of the car's interior."

"No. Not here," Danny said with chilled conviction.

"Hey, get a load of this guy, Ramon. He telling us what to do," said the man with the gun, ready to pull the trigger on the order.

Danny wouldn't retreat, although he took account of all possible escape routes.

Gun still pointed at his head, the front passenger side door clicked and swung open. Ramon stood up, although not a bigger-than-life figure, his eyes displayed a seductive depth and sheen that indicated he'd killed a man or two in his lifetime with his bare hands—and laughed at the thought of it.

Danny thought it ironic that the only thing that saved him was his skin color. An open air execution of a white man would embolden the NYPD to crack down on the "activities" at Parkchester.

"Let's take a walk," Ramon said. Both the gunman and the driver followed along the sidewalk

"Look, I didn't come here to—"

"Turn around muchacho," the gunman said.

Silent, Danny complied. The gunman jabbed the pistol into Danny's lower back.

"Pedro ain't too happy these days," Ramon said. "Follow me."

Ramon led them to a wide alleyway halfway down the block with a half full dumpster on one side. "You pretty cool for a customer, man."

Marco spoke. "Hey, man, he gotta be some narc, right?"

"I don't know, are you?" Ramon pressed.

"I want to know what happened to Mekhi."

Ramon sneered. "Like I said, that none of your business."

"If you're gonna' drop me, then those boys in the yard are gonna know about it. They'll all know."

Danny saw Ramon wave off Pedro, but the gun still trained on him.

"I don't know what you're talkin' about man," Ramon said. Then he looked at the other two and asked, "Any of you know what he talking about?" They both shook their heads and shrugged.

"I'm no cop. I'm your worst nightmare, so stop acting like you don't know what really went down."

"You just talking shit, man," Ramon said.

Danny stepped up to Ramon, ignoring the twitch of Pedro's shoulders and the ever present gun aimed his way. "If I ever hear that you hurt one of these kids again, I'll rip your face off," he said, staring hard into Ramon's eyes. A thin layer of sweat formed on his temples; he hoped the thugs wouldn't notice it.

Brows furrowed, Ramon stared back at him, ready to lunge. He unsheathed a switch blade from his belt then laughed as the other two joined in.

In an instant, Danny pivoted on his right foot and moved counterclockwise around as his left hand swept around and caught Pedro's arm, sweeping it outward, separating the gun from his hand. As it hit the concrete, Danny powered the webbing of his right hand against Pedro's throat, crushing the thug's trachea.

Unarmed, Marco stood frozen in time, too shocked to do anything except watch the scene unfold.

Ramon pulled out his own gun. By the time he got off a shot, Danny had tackled him to the ground. Danny tried to pin down Ramon's gun hand, but found himself in a stalemate against Ramon's formidable strength. He reached inside his sweat jacket's hand warmer and grabbed the knuckle knife, burying it into Ramon's left eye.

Ramon grabbed what was left of his eye and wailed with pain. Danny slammed down on Ramon's chest with his knees. The cracking sound of breaking ribs shot into the air.

"If I *ever* see you here again, I'll rip your fucking face off all over again," Danny growled into Ramon's ear.

Marco finally snapped back into reality. He turned and ran from the alley onto the sidewalk, he was racing for the safety of the car. Danny left Ramon on the ground and tackled Marco from behind. Danny pulled Marco to his feet by his hair and proceeded to slam his head into a parking meter. Danny pulled Marco's head back and forth like a hinge, causing it to make repeated contact with the meter until Marco withered and crumpled to the ground. A gathering crowd of people from the courtyard started to pour out onto the street a few yards away, drawn by Ramon's gunshot.

Danny made certain not to run, moving with the deliberate strides of a soldier who had just returned from a successful mission. He walked to the end of the block, across the street, and was out of sight before anyone thought to chase after him. All he could think about was the verbal dance he'd have to perform if—no, when—the Center ever found out.

Chapter 5

April 18th, 8:45 a.m.
The Upper West Side, New York City

"Oh, baby. Oh, God. Oh, baby, you're so good. So good." Dr. Katelyn Carrie was doing her best to feel the moment, but nothing came of it.

Nothing except lab work. Take the necessary precautions—face mask, hairnet. I have all the chemicals I need. I see the rounded flask, mounted to a ring stand, boiling over a heating mantle. Affixed to the flask is a cold water condenser tube running vertical for a few inches, then curling downward to a collection flask. The solution is dripping in there nicely. Careful with those tongs. Nice and steady. Secure those pincers around the flask. Now just pour the solution into the test tube. Yeah, just the right amount. Now repeat.

They kissed as Jared bore down. He gently brushed his fingers through her lemony hued hair. Kate's blouse, bra, and underwear clumped together on the Berber carpet. His lips, brushing across the hollow of her neck and over the rise of her breasts, sparked a slight tingle within her, but nothing more. His hand caressing the smooth inside of her thigh was warm, knowing and patient.

Now grasp that syringe gingerly. Pull the plunger down, then up. Only halfway now. Empty it into the vial. Repeat.

She was as thrilled to hold him as she would a sopping wet wash cloth. Even as her nipples grew hard against his darting tongue, her mind was elsewhere.

One more to go. Steady. God, it's hot in here. Why is my hand shaking? Oh shit, the fucking tongs can't hold it. It's all over the counter and over my other hand. I'm so fucked! No! Only five seconds left, then I'm history. Where are my gloves?

Her iPhone vibrated from the nightstand. Turning her head sideways, she saw the iPhone standing at attention on its base, next to two spent syringes and a pair of folded jet black horn-rimmed glasses. The caller ID displayed the name 'V Carrie', but she had no intention of answering it.

"Oh, Kate," Jared whispered as his lips undulated gently against her skin.

She stared up past Jared's sweat-dampened hair at the white ceiling, while his fingers massaged her below.

She ignored the recurrent buzz of the iPhone, but it made her convulse. Giving it one last chance, she expressed the stress she felt over the iPhone as a last gasp at an invitation. "Oh, baby, come to me. Come to me," she moaned. "Don't stop, Jared. Oh, yes, baby, yes. Don't stop."

But it was not to be. Her hope for any sort of arousal derailed, she extended her left arm to the nightstand and grabbed the glasses with her bony fingers and put them on. She thought Jared's muscular physique and alluring dimples when he smiled were nothing to sneeze at, but she'd long ago accepted the reality that he was hardly a Don Juan. Yet she had to give him kudos for the heroin and coke he had provided since they had met each other at work not one month ago. It complemented the supply her dealer provided quite nicely, thank you.

Maybe it's about time I take a shower to wash away this indignity. Unable to keep up the charade any longer, she spoke in a hard count. "Jared."

"Hold me, Kate. Don't stop." Still, Jared wasn't getting it, so gentle force was required.

She reached up and pressed her right palm against his chest. He pulled out with reluctance. "Jared, I… just can't." The unbearable urge screamed out within her to scratch away the incessant itch that blazed over every inch of her.

He sat up, wearing a protruded lower lip. Then he squinted. "Are you okay?"

The damned iPhone vibrated yet again, and this time she rolled her eyes so Jared could see.

"The boss lady on your back?"

"Yeah. I have to go in today. You?"

He rolled off her and reached for his pants at the foot of the bed. Buckling his belt, he said, "Call you later, okay?"

"Okay," she said after a pregnant pause. "Not coming in?"

"Nah. I just came down with a case of rejection." He punctuated the slight with an awkward smirk.

Focused on the ceiling, she said, "Oh yeah, money's on the table. Thanks, again What a ride last night, right?" she asked, giggling, as her small chin and cheek bones protruded through her pale sallow-hued skin.

"For sure. Anytime. I gotta' run."

She noted his sudden urge to get out of Dodge as he walked out, followed by an unceremonious slam of the apartment door.

When the iPhone buzzed one too many times, she grabbed the offending item from the night stand and heaved it across the room as she screamed. She watched the phone meet the bureau mirror, shattering on the left hand side and leaving a spider-webbed design, glass shards falling off onto the bureau and carpet. *Take that Vanessa! H*er moment of satisfaction was short-lived. The iPhone merely bounced back onto the carpet, unscathed, save for a noticeable crack across the front of the outer case.

And it was still buzzing.

Looking out of the window of the cab she took to work daily, she cleared her sinuses with two quick sniffs, and then subconsciously pinched the base of her septum to wipe away any white residue from her nostrils. Scrawny and pale at twenty-three, Kate easily could have been mistaken from behind for a teenager, yet her drawn face indicated someone at least fifteen years her senior. Stray tendrils of hair peeked out from a makeshift chignon. The glasses that corrected farsightedness since age eight didn't hide the dark eye circles. For that, she used concealer and brightener. By 4 p.m., her application would wear thin and the deep sockets returned. The glasses were both a security blanket and a protective wall that allowed her to focus on her work.

Her taxi pulled over to the curb before the glass and steel edifice that was the Frugeré. The company was well past its prime, but its corporate headquarters belied that reality. Its offices were renovated in the early 1990s to impress. Frugeré Real Estate Corporation owned the fifty-five story high building, but only occupied floors forty-eight through fifty-two.

Wearing a button down blouse, blue jeans and flats, Kate stepped out of the elevator on forty-eight into the marble-floored reception area that led to an atrium. On three sides, four floors of glass offices stood behind parapets. Forty-eight was the research floor where a staff of twelve chemists and assistants worked on developing new cosmetics for all of the vain people of the world. Although almost every other beauty firm located their color labs miles away from Manhattan, Floor 52 was reserved for the queen, CEO Vanessa Carrie, who had always insisted her chemists be in-house. That cut into Frugeré's bottom line, yet cosmetic industry profits were immense, especially when one considered it cost less than three dollars to produce a hundred and fifty dollar bottle of perfume.

Kate entered the lab area from a door adjacent to the elevator bank with her employee ID card. She walked down an uncarpeted hallway with white walls and three separate enclosed labs on each side. As these labs were used to mix pigments for various cosmetic products, they liked to call themselves 'color chemists'. They might as well have been finger painting, with color palettes lying within each lab room. Each lab had a windowed door and a frosted windowed wall skirting the hallway. Beyond was an open employee area with three circular tables and chairs. She headed to the perimeter for the mini-kitchen.

Continuing straight through that room was another hallway that passed another group of frosted fishbowl labs used for fragrance creation. Those chemists liked to call themselves 'aroma scientists'.

Three colleagues took up one table, enjoying an extended coffee break. Brief, muffled 'hellos' were thrown at her, but she ignored them as she headed for the Keurig. In a hissy fit, she quickly opened and shut cabinets, finding no more K-cups.

The fuckers used the last ones!

Hearing whispered laughter behind her, she muttered barely audible oaths under her breath, gave up the search, then turned to leave, bumping into an employee she'd never noticed before. The heightened resentment began when Vanessa had moved her to the only private lab on the floor to work on 'special' product development assignments. But it had been there from the very first day she arrived less than two years ago. After all, she was the boss's daughter and kept to herself. It didn't help that she habitually came in late, high as a satellite and left earlier than anyone else.

Only eight full time chemists remained after the last layoff and most of those remaining were under thirty-five. The young chemist who she bowled into made the most grievous error of approaching her. Worse, he decided to ask her a question.

"Sorry, Kate. My name's Peter, I just started here last week. Good morning," he said like a hyperactive puppy dog.

Visibly irritated that her private world was invaded, she inflected a disinterested 'good morning', then started to turn away, eyes forward.

Although a head taller than her, his diffidence flagged him as nothing more than a lame peon. Apparently, this guy hadn't been read in on what she was about and chatted away. "Do you know about color combos? Could you help me?" he asked, eyes wide like he was consulting the great chemistry god.

"Sure," she answered robotically.

"I was just wondering. Whit has me working on a new dye color for this season's mascara line, and I can't get it to the color I need it to be."

Eyes rolling, she exhaled to control herself. "What color would that be?"

"Well, I need it to be purple, but it's more blue than purple, ya know? What am I doing wrong?"

"Did you check the pH level?"

His jaw dropped. "Uh, no, I didn't. Should I have?"

She wanted to smack the guy. When an opportunity to exude arrogance presented itself, she just couldn't help herself. "You're kidding, right? Anyone who knows anything about color combos knows to check the pH level. I can tell already that you need to adjust the combo to a more acidic level. Did you even check that with the meter?" she asked sharply.

He looked like he was about to cry as she heard muttered laughter from other chemists. It was a rough work environment, to say the least. "I'm sorry, I guess I should have. But, how can I adjust it?"

Shutting her eyes for a moment, this was getting too much for her. "You didn't even use HCL, did you?" she said. When his face froze up, she prompted him like a school child. "You know, the Hydrochloric Acid?

His catatonic stare caused her to rail. "Do you even know what HCL is?"

"Sure, but—"

Before he could piece another sentence together, she shook her head and stormed off to her lab.

Her white lab coat, which she grabbed from the rack outside of her lab, cloaked her as it stretched down all the way to her knees. Today, she needed to focus because she was to mix the last batch of Tri-Methyl Phosphofloramine, or as Vanessa coined it, the 'Tri-Meth'.

She accessed the lab at the end of the hallway behind another door by inserting a key card and a numerical access code. Having punched in the proper numeric sequence, she walked through an unfinished section of the floor that had been stripped down to its pillars. Against the near wall was her enclosed lab. One small double-paned window was cut out on the door. Inside was everything she needed.

It was nothing more than a ten-by-twelve room, was equipped with state-of-the-art safety precautions such as an overhead hood and a fire extinguisher. A wash basin eliminated potential eye contamination, but she knew it wouldn't do any good to prevent this toxin from ravaging the human ecosystem. What really protected her were her Nitrile gloves, white lab coat and most importantly, an aspirator.

On the soap stone counter where she did her work, there were three inlaid heating mantles. The necessary distillation equipment took up half the space. Test tubes, beakers, flasks and vials sparkled in a glass menagerie before her in the bright overhead lights.

At the age of twenty-three, she had developed the molecular structure that caused irreversible nerve damage. No known antidote would save a potential victim. Not only that, its diffusion factor, or 'spread range', was such that its strength was maintained for a greater distance that any other known chemical weapon. The chemical compound also contained, in addition to the typical chemicals one would find in such toxins, a few others that she incorporated in to increase its range and concentration, significantly enhancing its lethal effects.

Nice to know I'm putting my MIT degree to good use.

She inserted one subdivided vial into a rack where several others she'd already prepared were resting. One end of each vial housed powder, the other half a liquid, aligned so that once the seal between them was broken, it created the byproduct—a deadly gas. She was halfway through the process, but only needed one more afternoon to finish up the ten vials required for the auction. Kate noticed something was off as she counted them. One was missing: the test vial.

Her eyes scanned the counter and shelves for the missing item just as the lab phone rang. Vexed by the disconcerting ring, she picked up the receiver, already knowing who it was. "Hello?" she answered in the most glacial monotone she could muster.

She could tell Vanessa was not pleased. "You're late!" she barked.

"And?"

Scoff ignored, Vanessa ticked up her volume level a few notches. "Kate, I need to see you in my office, now!"

"I haven't even started yet, why?"

"Just come up here now," Vanessa ordered with parental finality. "This can't wait. There's a security matter we need to discuss. I want all loose ends to be tied up before the auction."

"Okay." Kate detested when *anyone* interrupted her concentration and lately, only Vanessa had that dubious honor. But this was new. Vanessa hadn't involved her in security matters before.

My, how this is shaping up to be a real shitty day.

Chapter 6

April 18th, 10:15 a.m.
The Bronx, New York

Danny was at the indoor court playing one-on-one with one of his clients, a fifteen-year-old drug addict in recovery. James was one of the residents at the center and had worked up a good sweat, whereas Danny had barely broken one.

When the boy attempted an ill-executed sky hook, Danny swatted it away at the point of release. The ball rolled across the sideline as it stopped under the weight of a brown boot. Partially obscured by some wooden bleachers, the owner of the boot emerged.

Danny recognized him instantly. The man, dressed in jeans, a sweat shirt and a sleeveless windbreaker, approached. Danny dismissed James with a 'see you tomorrow' slap on the shoulders, and resumed his guarded stare at this apparition from the past. The other man spoke first.

"Hey bro, it's been how long?"

Danny's guarded demeanor melted on the spot. "Well I be. The doctor himself." The other man hadn't changed a bit, his crew cut and dark complexion accenting his rounded eyes and light mustache. "Javier Marquez in the flesh." He walked up to Javi as they embraced in man hug formation.

"Great thing you're doing. Helping these kids."

Danny answered with a question. "You? Let me guess—still with the Agency?"

Javi just smiled back at him. "Hey, you disappeared off the face of the earth."

"It's not like anyone came looking for me, either," he said, shaking off Javi's gaze. Danny bounce passed the ball to Javi, harder than he normally would have. "Anyway, I'm doin' fine now. I needed the reboot."

"We need to catch up."

Danny picked up on Javi's clumsy attempt at a solicitation. "C'mon. Who are you talking to? You wouldn't just show up out of the blue unless… No."

"Straight up? We need you. Something's up right here and we thought you'd be the best man for the job."

"Just tell her 'm done. That's it."

"Who are *you* talking to?" Javi said, bounce passing the ball back at him.

He caught it, shrugged, shook his head and looked up at the ceiling as if he was trapped in a boomerang vortex. "Unbelievable."

"It'll be a short term assignment. Three weeks tops. I wasn't messing with you. I do want to catch up. I'm only in town until this thing ends."

"What do you know about it?" Danny asked.

"Can't say. Haven't been read in."

"Okay, so now what?"

"She wants to see you tonight."

Danny racked his brain for a moment. The call of government service rang in his ears, and based on what just happened at Park Chester, he figured it might be the perfect time for a leave of absence. He couldn't help but trust his fellow Delta Force comrade. He had to give Joanne kudos for sending Javi out to make contact. Before he knew it, Javi had turned to walk out.

"Hey, where am I going?"

"Read your text, bro."

When Danny grabbed his phone from the bleacher, he found his answer. His voice echoed of the walls of the reverberant gym. "Don't I even get car service to this place?"

Javi turned back with a smile and said, "You're on your own, man. You know, budget cuts." Danny threw up some foul shots, mulling over the possibilities.

Chapter 7

April 18th, 10:30 a.m.
Midtown, New York City

"Have a seat, dear. This is important."

Vanessa Carrie inhaled a puff from the cigarette she'd been cradling between her fore and middle fingers. The soft olive shaded eyes that Kate knew all too well belied her true persona. A weeping willow of dirty blond hair flowed downward just below the shoulders of her turtleneck knit blouse. It shouldn't have been remarkable that Vanessa had tried to maintain her radiant features well into her fifties, having undergone several nip/tuck adjustments over the past decade. Even so, her face had a rubbery look to it, accentuated especially when she scowled, which she'd been doing quite a bit of lately.

To Vanessa's left, was company Kate already loathed: Frugere's corporate security chief, Gunther McGore, or resident spook, as she preferred. An imposing man whether sitting or standing, Gunther's wavy rust-hued hair and well-groomed beard hid most of his pockmarked face.

Kate had made up her mind that she would have no interest in what Vanessa was about to say, but Gunther spoke first.

"We need you to end it with Jared Darmanian. Immediately."

"He doesn't belong here," Vanessa added.

Her breathing stopped short for a moment. "Why?"

"Halle Ruse cosmetics sent him to spy on us," Gunther answered as his Leonid Brezhnev eyebrows slanted downward to the bridge of his nose. "Having him here puts our trade secrets at risk and we can't have that."

Kate pursed her lips as if she'd just sucked a lemon. A snarky retort was all she could muster. "And what secrets would that be?"

Gunther answered. "He's been on Sid Barnett's payroll for more than a year. We've caught him trying to access our R&D files, asking questions."

"That can't be."

"You seem so sure of that," Gunther said. "Let me ask you something. Has he seen your lab?"

She looked down for a moment as she recalled the times they had indulged in the pleasurable opiate experience. Not something that would look good on her resume.

"Please answer him, sweetie," Vanessa pressed, ever so gingerly.

"Yes. Yes he has, but it was only to help me clean up a couple of times."

Vanessa crushed the spent cigarette butt into her ashtray. "Very bad, Kate! You knew that only the three of us have access. Everything we've worked for, the life I have provided for you, he wants to destroy," Vanessa admonished with the disciplinary timbre of a first grade teacher.

Whenever Vanessa said 'us', Kate heard it as 'me'. "You're wrong! He's a good guy." Kate knew full well it was his portable medicine cabinet that was appealing, but that was beside the point.

"Don't you get it?" the twice-divorced executive growled. "You're being played and you don't even see it."

Having survived the gut punch, Kate tried to look away, but Vanessa's assessment finally sunk in.

Leaning back in her chair, Vanessa continued, "But fortunately, this is easily fixed." She nodded to Gunther.

He reached down to the floor beside his chair to pick up a gift box and placed it on the desk in front of Kate. "Arrange a time to meet after work and break it to him. Then give him this.

Vanessa's hardened eyes suddenly glistened. They looked as though they were about to well up. "I really need you, now," she said, "like you needed me."

Oh, brother. Kate groped for inner strength and found none, just more snarkiness. "You can't make me 'not' see him again. And why should I give it to him? Just fire him."

Vanessa handled this one. "We think a token gift will soften the blow for him while not tipping off Halle Ruse that we know about his true intentions."

Vanessa nodded to Gunther to take his leave.

Kate tried to dig in as she seethed inside. How she loved these little mentor-protégé chats. They always ended up being one-way conversations with Vanessa getting the last word in. This was no different. "He's still my boyfriend," she answered, but it wasn't for the reason she tried to project.

"This month," Vanessa snapped, shaking her head with disbelieving superiority. "You've been buying drugs from him, haven't you?"

Kate couldn't help but stare down at the floor, reluctantly acknowledging guilt.

Vanessa looked down as she shook her head in disbelief. "I thought you would be stronger, like the way I raised you."

"I… just want to be happy, for however short a time. I don't want to be alone. Unlike you."

"I'd rather be alone than be with a man who doesn't know me." Vanessa then transformed into a concerned mother as she stood up and walked over to Kate, taking a seat in a chair next to her. "It's like I've told you before, you don't need a man to do that. Wanting a man is one thing. It's when you think you need a man that you get taken advantage of."

"My little golden girl. That's what I always liked to call you, from the very first day I first saw you at… that place. Remember?"

"Zion," Kate said. She knew Vanessa was playing her, knowing exactly what buttons to press. And she knew it was working. It was there, at the Zion Rehabilitative Center for Girls that Vanessa took an interest in her, just an orphan barely eleven years old.

On the way up to the top, Vanessa chose not to raise children of her own, believing that being a role model for young women in the industry would take the place of that, but it didn't. Not really. Vanessa looked at Kate as a way to raise a girl in her image—strong, self-sufficient and smart. So about fifteen years ago, Vanessa decided to take a more active role in donating to organizations that helped less fortunate girls. Donating grew into participating in community service projects in the city and surrounding area. Every so often, Vanessa would visit local female-only halfway houses on the weekends and speak with some of the residents. For a time, she really thought she could make a difference.

Vanessa moved in close and whispered, "When this is over, you'll be able to pursue whatever you want."

You mean, like you? Kate retracted her hand. "I'm sorry. I want to make you happy, too," she groveled. I'm really confused about everything right now."

"I know sweetie, and thank you for being such a dear. The next time you feel unhappy with me, I want you to think about where you would be if I hadn't been there for you."

And that was the dagger. The weight of gratitude borne out of guilt was simply too great. "I'll handle it," she said after a forlorn sigh.

Chapter 8

April 18th, 1:00 p.m.
The Upper West Side, New York City

Sabir entered through the grand wrought-iron, lion-clad gates of the west entrance of the Columbia University campus and made his way to Dodge Hall, which housed the School of Fine Arts. He didn't need to walk inside because he spotted Adalet. She wore etched blue jeans and a light blue Columbia sweatshirt on the lawn in front of the building with two of her friends.

He stood on the lawn about thirty feet from her, then she caught his gaze. At first, she did not recognize the man staring at her and held a confused look on her face for a moment, then she nodded in recognition. Adalet excused herself and ran to him for a kiss and long embrace. He had long since eschewed the Arabic aversion to public displays of affection with the opposite sex. By traditional standards, an enlightened terrorist, indeed. *And besides, this is America where the women dress like whores.* He had to admit he did not dislike it, in spite of the cultural inhibition against exposed female flesh. When he was a teen, he and his friends would spend time after school bragging of their sexual exploits that never occurred.

In English, she said, "It has been too long. Are we safe?"

Her warmth was a welcome sensation that conjured up the memory of prior encounters with her. "I took care of my friends back home. Not to worry, my beloved."

"They said—" she spoke with wide eyed excitement when he pressed his two fingers against her lips.

"In the mother tongue," he said in Arabic.

They were never supposed to be together, but fate had another plan in mind. Like him, Adalet grew up on the West Bank, but they never knew each other until the tragic chain of events that had brought them together. Adalet's father, Sidayim Ramli, a man of stocky build with hair graying at the temples, was a teacher at Sha'ar Bin Salehl high school in Bil'n, a village twenty miles northwest of Jerusalem. An impassioned anti-Semite who conducted his classes as a recruitment tool to further the resistance, he was instrumental in supporting Abdullah Abu Rahmah in leading protests against the Israeli government years ago. He taught in a dimly lit undersized classroom with oversized school desks and deteriorating walls that leaked water during the rains, and pontificated on why the Jews were not only impure but that Mohammed's curse put upon them would condemn them to a fiery death. It was ironic that Sidayim's rhetoric was tame when measured against the like-minded politicians and terrorists of the day.

Sabir came to understand that the Arabic language was rife with wicked hyperbole. Frighteningly real to the outsider, but strangely comforting to his people—a way of keeping the dream alive. All the Arab leaders knew this. Sidayim did not follow through with actions but Sabir had forgiven him for it. In fact, he respected Sidayim because his rhetoric was directed solely toward Israel, the only true enemy in their shared opinion.

At only sixteen years of age, after having been taken in by Sidayim's charismatic rants, Sabir, like several of his classmates, yearned to join the Islamic Jihad. He never knew his father, who died of tuberculosis in the camps when Sabir was only two. Sidayim was the perfect paternal replacement.

Adalet, like most other Palestinian girls of the day, dressed in traditional clothing, more ornate and colorful than that of the women of their more prosperous neighbors. They did not need to cover their faces, thereby calling themselves 'progressive'. Yet, young women still were not permitted to work outside the home and needed escorts when traveling alone.

Sabir first laid eyes on Adalet during a lecture given by her father at a local community college. Five years his junior and still in high school, she had come with a couple of her friends. Her honey shaded skin and almond shaped eyes drew his attention. Knowing he could not publicly approach her, he had to find a more clandestine way of doing so. The cultural divide between their families was steep but as far as Sabir saw it, not insurmountable.

Adalet, through Sidayim's exalted position, was able to live in a one-story single family home made of white stone. Although not considered luxurious by western standards, the fact that they had their own kitchen, sitting room, bathing room, and small bedrooms, denoted the *Ramli*'s enhanced social status. Sabir and his family were camp rats, whose home consisted of small cement-block huts with corrugated metal doors and roofing. Their 'kitchen' consisted of a metal grate placed over a charcoal pit, and thin mats for beds. As for bathing and washing clothes, a large metal drum was used.

He knew early on that the quickest way to Adalet's heart was through Sidayim, who called sporadic nighttime meetings with his former 'students' to discuss strategies for beating back the uninvited West Bankers, as he put it. Now seen as a dutiful soldier at only nineteen in the Palestinian struggle to evict and destroy these Jews, Sabir and Sidayim's respect for each other grew stronger.

One night after other boys dispersed following one of their meetings, Sabir made his appeal.

"Adalet is not taken, is she?" he asked.

Sidayim was quick to recognize where this was going, but opted to challenge him, his black mustache twitching with mock annoyance. "Now, why would you want to know about that?" he said with a gentle smile.

Sabir said, "I only asked because…"

"You like her, eh?" Sidayim asked, wearing a crooked grin and a raised eyebrow.

Sabir nodded repeatedly without a word, accepting that his feelings for Adalet were no longer secret.

"You do realize that she has lofty aspirations that you do not have?" Sidayim asked in mock accusatory fashion. "And that she may not be interested in such a camp rat of the likes of you?

"I did not mean—"

Sidayim stopped the charade. "No need to say it, Sabir. You have my permission to see her, in the customary way and places. We do understand each other?"

"Of course. I have never felt this way about a girl before."

"You must promise me one thing—that you will look after her. She is my only one."

The political tension in the West Bank had risen to an all-time high. Some within the PA wanted to work with the Israelis. Sidayim, of course, would have none of it. His position in the Palestinian Authority enabled him to expose those people and his speeches had promised no less. It was known that the West Bankers despised him. So on the day he was abducted and found dead the following day floating in the Jordan River with a bullet through his brain, the press assumed that the Israelis killed him, although it was never proven. Sabir wept for the first time.

Adalet was forced to work part time while going to school to help support the family. Her older brothers were imprisoned for terrorist activities, so the onus was on her and her mother to run the household. It was only a matter of time before they lost their home and thus their social status. The only hope for her was the college savings Sidayim had stashed away for her.

That was not the end of it. Israeli settlers broke into her home while she was alone studying 'to finish the job'. It infuriated Sabir that a Jew had so brutally violated her when he had never gotten the chance to bare his soul to her. So with the help of his brothers, he and his friends tracked down each of those responsible and beat them to a pulp.

Sabir was now her hero and had been ever since.

In English, she said, "You should know that your new friends already called me. They will call me if they need me."

"Let us hope it won't come to that. But if it does, I'm sure that you will put on the performance of a lifetime for them, my *habibti.*"

Jared waited just inside the Central Park entrance on West 72nd Street, now closed to vehicular traffic. He wore a casual button down shirt and jeans, with a shoulder bag. The entrance was flanked by two wooden trellises, looking like natural covered bridges adorned only with twig sized vines, it being too early in the season for any ivy to show. He got Kate's attention with a wave as she arrived with the gift box clenched in her hand. He walked toward her and when he leaned in to hug her, she tensed up and pulled back, sensing the apprehension as she pulled back both lips.

"We really need to talk." Her quivering jaw and labored breathing were something

Jared hadn't noticed before.

"Hey, I have your stuff," he said, pulling out a paper bag that contained several small baggies of gold tinted powder.

She grabbed it out of his hand and quickly stuffed into her purse. Kate eyed him with incredulity, with the glowering eyes of admonishment. "Not here, Jared. Jesus, what is wrong with you?"

Wishing he hadn't been so careless as to ignore her discomfort, he said, "I'm sorry. My bad."

Kate stammered. "Jared, I think… that we should… go our separate ways. You know?"

Frowning, he pressed her for a reason. "Hey, where is this coming from? I know you're stressed, but—"

"I really want to be with you but I don't think that you really want to be with me. I mean, our relationship so far is based on these." She grasped her purse.

"But I really want to see you. That's what you want, right?"

Flinching as if he'd poked her on the forehead, she replied, "Is that what *you* want, Jared? I just can't believe you."

The information he'd been tasked to retrieve would still be locked away in Frugeré's confidential lab notes and most probably in Kate's head. His only option was to save face. "Kate, don't let Vanessa tell you what to do with your life," he said in the most serious tone he'd ever taken with her. "I can only imagine what burden you must be carrying right now. I can see it in your face."

For a moment, he thought she might cave, hoping that she'd finally realize that her priorities and allegiance to Vanessa had to change. He noticed her hands were quivering, seemingly not knowing what to do with them.

Kate shook her head. "We just can't continue this 'thing' that we have. Whatever 'this' is," she said, holding up her arm and rocking her wrist to and fro between them, index finger extended. "I'm sorry, I just can't." Her jittery voice was struggling to spit out the words.

After a moment, she composed herself. "I appreciate what you shared with me. That's why I thought you might like this," she said, glancing down to her purse as she pulled out the box. She leaned forward and gave him a harmless peck on the cheek, then whispered as she drew close to his left ear, "You still have my number when you have more stuff for me, okay?"

He had to acknowledge her honesty, their relationship *was* a sham, even if Kate didn't know the truth of it. Yet, he would be damned if Kate would be drawn into Vanessa's disease.

"You don't have to put up with her," he repeated, sounding less like a jilted boyfriend or even a jaded social worker, but rather as a concerned sibling.

"I gotta go. Good luck, Jared," she said with a chilled edge.

"No, wait!" he started, but Kate had already turned away and headed for the sidewalk. He wanted to run after her but didn't want to make a scene. Her gait turned into a steady saunter until she reached the curb to hail an approaching cab. After she entered and closed the door, the taxi started off. Through the window, he saw her throw a quick glance back at him, then turned forward as she punched a number on a burner phone before bringing it up to her ear.

Jared found himself standing alone with nothing he could report back to his contact. He couldn't help but sense that Kate had wanted to impart something to him. She may have been too frightened to share the information in a public place. Perhaps the answer, he thought, was wrapped inside the box.

He sat on a nearby park bench, removed his shoulder bag and then unwrapped his gift. When he opened the unmarked white box, he saw a folded piece of white lined paper wrapped in dark blue crumpled tissue. Jared carefully unfolded it, only to find that it was completely blank. Holding the sheet in his hand, his fingers ran over what seemed like a thin film of dust on it, only then realizing that the white powdered substance had stained his fingertips, like flour. Before he knew it, his fingers turned beet red. Jared didn't know what was happening.

Jared, overcome with panic, stood up and started to run toward Central Park West, dropping the box as the deadly sheet of paper flew out, blowing away in the swirling spring time wind. He broke out into a sweat and became extremely nauseous. He lost his sense of balance as he stumbled forward to the curb, his run deteriorating into a drunken stumble. When he started crossing the street, he lost all sense of reality and reason, and finally his balance. Then his heart jolted to a painful, sudden halt. The last thing he heard was the earsplitting sound of screeching brakes of the oncoming truck right before his corpse struck the blacktop.

Chapter 9

April 18th, 4:15 p.m.
The Lower East Side, New York City

The call from the taxi was a "heads-up" to Kate's dealer. It was time to restock. Sure, Jared had just supplied her with some, but she knew that would only get her to next Thursday. Once a month, she would receive an envelope with a scrap of paper and a scrawled phone number jotted on it.

She took her downtown jaunts in stride, they were the most exciting activity she had going on in her life. It was an adventure, a walk on the wild side for a well-to-do white girl from the Upper West Side. She grew up believing subways were beneath her, with Vanessa always dragging her along in taxis, car services or limos. Today she preferred them, if nothing else, as another rebellion against authority.

The Donnybrook tavern at the corner of Clinton and Stanton wore a gray sandstone façade with an engraved welcome that read 'Home to lively debate and raucous revelry,' though neither was going on at the time, being an hour or so before the after-work flood of patrons. The place had dark brown wooden tables and chairs, matching the bar and stools. Kate took up residence at a table against the far wall adjacent to the bar, the darkest spot in the place and stared at the brick wall. A few minutes later, a woman slid in across from her.

Her birth name was Jennifer Elizabeth Anna Marie Depietrio-Andonio, but Kate knew her only as Jen D. She wore a black penny dress, her hair and lips equally jet black. She also had that nose ring and cross bar thing going on. Kate thought the silver one impaling her right nostril to be a nice touch, too. She no doubt had put her fashion merchandizing degree from LIM College to good use. Her olive complexion exuded an understated sensuousness about her, like a wild provincial gypsy who had been instantly transported to the big city.

Kate appreciated the contrast: Upper West Side chic meets Lower East Side Goth. The place was upscale, but her new booth companion reeked of cigarette smoke and cheap shampoo. "You look cheery, as usual."

The brooding Catholic School drop-out from Valley Stream, Long Island returned fire with glib artillery. "Thanks, you look like shit… as usual." They both looked up at the distraction that was their overly-solicitous waitress and ordered lattes.

Kate had first contacted Jen through one of her short term affairs when she moved back to New York after graduate school. At that time, Jen was operating her business out of her mother's home in Long Island. Both traded catty looks with each other, but Jen's was more suspicious. Kate would lose more weight and add more years to her own face each time they met. The cover up under the eyes by now had long since worn off, her face gaunt and peaked.

Ignoring the jibe, Kate changed the subject. "So, you moved out, huh?"

Jen chortled. "Kicked out is more like it." Her arms outstretched, she rocked back and forth. "My mom just couldn't take it anymore. Threatened to burn my clothes if I didn't leave."

"Uh-oh. What'd ya do?" Kate asked with the tone a mother uses when she knows her child crapped in his pants.

"Real funny, actually," Jen answered, followed by another chortle. "One of my ex-customers somehow got a hold of my house number and spoke with my mom about when the next batch would be ready. Can you believe that shit?" Jen asked with an eye roll. "So what've you got for me?"

She caught Jen gazing at her Louis Vuitton purse, from which she removed a white envelope filled with cash. Kate plucked it from her purse and slid it to Jen across the wooden shellacked table.

Jen's signature poker face took a holiday for a few moments. She was used to nickel and dime deals, but Kate had figured Jen looked forward to providing happiness to a pathetic trust fund baby. Jen opened it up to find a healthy sum of cash—eight-thousand dollars-worth—for her month supply of heroin and cocaine, and had found her annuity at last. Jen's brown eyes widened and her nostrils flared.

The waitress returned with their lattes.

"And it gives me great pleasure to make you happy," Kate said.

"Fuck you," Jen said. "You know, I have to ask myself, what's an attractive one like you doing this shit for? And I always come up with the same answer: because you need some excitement in your boring uptown life."

"Well, maybe my life's not as boring as you think," she said, cocking her head to the side.

"If you say so." Jen sipped her latte, put the cup aside and leaned in. Kate used her best *sotto voce.* She scuttled Jen's Amway-like success story speech, bursting with adolescent anticipation, "So, can we do this thing, already? I thought we came here to do the thing."

Jen met her gaze with her soft endearing brown eyes. She smiled and said, "I don't know what you're talking about, girl. We're just a couple of chicks enjoying our lattes."

Kate grinned and said nothing.

Jen slid out of the booth. Then tapped her on the shoulder as she passed, then walked out.

The grin turned sour when she realized their coffees were unpaid for. Shaking her head, Kate tossed a twenty on the table before walking outside.

She took a left on Essex Street, spotted Jen up ahead, and caught up alongside.

"So, how are you doing?" she asked.

"Oh, business is pretty good. Right now, you're one of my best customers, though." After a few moments of silence, Jen asked, "Why do you always take it raw, anyway?"

"I prepare it all myself. Always have." She thought it strange Jen couldn't fathom why a customer wouldn't want to justify a hefty discount.

"Modest to a fault, aren't we?" Another eye roll followed. Ever the ambitious one, soon she recruited enough of her buyers to become pushers themselves as she rose in stature to a mid-level supplier. Jen had not too long ago set up a heroin mill in her apartment with a couple of her local pushers. Her inventory came from upper-level suppliers of a Dominican cartel, which advocated a business policy of discipline and quality control. "You got me thinking. I'm expanding and well, could make a fortune together if…" Jen cut herself short.

"Sorry, I'm just a woman of science, not Walter White."

Before she knew it, Jen pulled out a cute strawberry print gift bag from her purse and stuffed it into Kate's.

She tried to recover Jen's train of thought. "But let's say for the sake of argument that I wanted to—"

Jen raised her hand palm out. "On second thought, just forget it. I'd sooner tell you to do it with one of your friends anyway… except you don't seem to have any."

She threw back a proud smirk before descending into the subway station, leaving Jen with nothing to do except return to her day job.

Kate wanted to burst out of her own skin. The unbearable itching was God's way of telling her it was time for another hit. *God, I need it, NOW!*

Outfitted with hardwood floors and decorative moldings, her apartment was what every young single 23-year-old woman would want, but most could only yearn for. But it was far from pristine. Kate kicked a half empty Lo Mein container through her living room littered with several other take-out containers. Scattered mounds of white dust dotted the table.

She walked into her kitchen and dropped her mail on the table that shared space with a Bunsen burner, singed spoons, and new and used syringes. Her nose crinkled as she shut her eyes, then she inhaled the rancid scent of processed heroin.

After separating the junk mail, she saw the letter she had been waiting for. The return address was from the State of Rhode Island Department of Health. She set herself down at the table and scanned the envelope with suspicion, like it was set to explode upon opening it. Then the torturous itching barged in and accosted her attention.

It was time.

The antidote was in her purse, the contents of which she emptied along with the paper bag of tiny, plastic, tan powder-filled baggies on the kitchen table. She set the envelope down and grabbed one of the spoons from the kitchen, heated up the powder, and added water, all within less than five minutes. Grabbing a fresh syringe, she submerged its plunger down into the solution, then retracted it. A deliberate jab into her left elbow was all that was required.

Uhmm.

She strolled into her spacious bedroom, kicked off her shoes, then stripped down to her panties. She started scratching herself wherever sweat had formed under her clothes. Red welts were already present where she had scratched herself raw on several occasions. She only stopped when her fingernails dug up blood, as an open wound sting replaced the itching. Sleeveless, she glanced down on both of her arms near her elbows. Her veins were almost completely blown out. She'd have to start injecting in her big toe. Looking at her wardrobe, she thought to herself that being on Frugeré's payroll sure had its advantages.

Before she retreated to her bathroom and reached in the drawer under the sink to find a stash of sterile syringes.

At least I'm a responsible junkie!

Having filled the syringe with the contents of the spoon, she then grabbed the rubber band resting on the towel rack and wrapped it tightly around her forearm. She took the syringe and gave her left arm a good stab, seeing blood briefly back up into the vessel, before pressing down on the plunger. *Liquid Nirvana has arrived, thank God.* Then she punctuated the high with her customary sugar rush appetizer by grabbing a bunch of gummy bears from an open bag lying on the kitchen table and stuffing them in her mouth, swallowing them whole without chewing. Dinner tonight would consist of a well-balanced diet of Wheat Thins and Sea Salt Caramel ice cream straight from the container.

Her schedule for the rest of the evening included watching *Castle* reruns on TBS—the-all Castle-all-the-time channel—maybe read a journal or two, then sleep. She admired Detective Beckett conducting all of those intense criminal interrogations. Kate didn't know why, but she was awed by the way Beckett worked the suspect over: the questions, the chase and the search for the truth. *Just plain cool,* she thought. Sleeping, on the other hand, was something she couldn't do, both because of the drug and because of the fear of experiencing horrible nightmares and hallucinations.

There she was, sitting in her living room chair while the drug coursed through her, alone together with none other than Kate Beckett.

Chapter 10

April 18th, 11:00 p.m.
The Bronx, New York City

Safe houses were typically dark, dank and musty places with high ceilings where on occasion, certain unnamed activities occurred that would call into question American Intelligence's adherence to due process. Danny stood across the street opposite the entrance to the location he was given—131 Claremont Avenue in the Bronx. When he received the text, he walked through the warped and smudged double glass doors which looked as if they hadn't been wiped down in over twenty years. They slammed shut behind him like a vault.

The chance to cut and run was no longer available. The deserted lobby's black and white checkerboard linoleum floor was littered with garbage and lit by two red exit signs over metal doors on opposite sides. It was dingy, dust-covered and deserted. The scent of an unidentifiable mold found his nostrils and made him wince. Toward the rear, he saw one tarnished elevator door. Beyond that was a wall with a heavy metal door. The only modern piece of equipment he could identify was the camera protruding from the ceiling, its glassy, black semi-globe panned back and forth, and its blinking red light unceasing.

After about five minutes, the door opened and a fair skinned woman with flaming red hair tied back into a ponytail and wearing jeans and button down collared shirt motioned him inside. With a bright smile, as if she was shepherding around a celebrity, she said, "Hi, I'm Lindsey. We've been expecting you, Mr. Strong."

He entered into a cavernous warehouse room that was totally empty save for some folding chairs and a lone table. Four long rows of spotlight racks sat high above, indicating prior industrial use. On the right side of the room from where he stood, two small offices with windows faced out onto the main floor. An enclosed office hovered above them on a mezzanine with two elongated picture windows, not unlike those of a maternity ward.

"Hey! Do you know you have the same name as that guy who was on—"

"*Buffy the Vampire Slayer*. Yeah, I get that a lot," he said. "But I'm a bit taller."

She chuckled. “Wait here, Mr. Strong,” she instructed and walked through an inner door and out of sight.

Really? Like I have a choice?

Actually he did but the calling to serve his country that had lain dormant for so long had reemerged, guiding his decisions. Within a minute, she entered through a door from one of the lit offices and approached him, walking tall, wearing navy blue pants and a white blouse with the customary matching blazer. Behind her followed Javi and Lindsey.

“It’s good to see you again, Danny.”

“Good to see you again, too,” he said with guarded interest. “So, what’s this all about? You know I haven’t been in the game for a long time.”

“True. We all thought we’d lost you.”

And no one thought to look me up. “Joanne,” he started. He really wanted to say, *Fuck you* but professionalism won out.

Joanne extended her arm, palm facing out to silence him. “We need to keep moving, just you and me.” She motioned to the exit door.

She shuttled him out of the warehouse where a black Cadillac SUV with tinted windows was waiting for them. Lindsey and Javi entered in the front, Joanne and Danny the rear. As the car made its way out to the street, they sat in the back seat, both looking straight ahead, both silent.

Joanne broke the uneasy lull. “I know it’s been a long time since we’ve been in touch.”

He stared out the window at more warehouses lying silent and vacant in the night.

“To the point, this assignment’s timetable is extremely aggressive,” she said. “We really need someone with your profile on a NOC basis. You do understand, don’t you?”

“NOC?” he asked, expressing reservation at his non-official cover status in his tone. It would mean being a ghost for the Agency.

“Yup. Based on what happened to you, they…”

“Don’t want me back on the books. Expendable. I get it.” After Kelly died in what had been deemed an act of Fratricide during a reconnaissance mission in Afghanistan, he spiraled into a depression, spending days on end in his apartment, sometimes in nothing but his underwear, watching television. Soon after that, Danny turned to pain killers, which led to heroin. Within six months, he was relieved of his duties at the Agency without so much as a 'Thank you', just a 'Don’t call us, we’ll call you' letter of disengagement. He internalized his separation as an unofficial disavowment from what transpired in Geneva, rather than a reprimand for his descent into drug induced depression. Either way, his pariah status was undeniable, having not received communications from any of his colleagues or superiors.

Joanne nodded and said, “Take it as a stepping stone, before making you official again. That’s all.”

He had second thoughts about buying into whatever Joanne had in mind, but recalled that she was good at her job. Too good, in fact. She could be very crafty when she had to be, like his first assignment in Geneva where Joanne was station chief. They had since worked together in various assignments for the Agency before Kelly died. One could never tell what Joanne was holding back at any particular time.

"I may be interested," he said, pursing his lips.

"Good, because this assignment was ready made for you. We need someone who is available with a delicate touch."

"Meaning?"

"It'll involve someone with your *expertise*."

Danny couldn't help but smile inwardly. His role with the Agency had been, to put it bluntly, that of a Lothario for foreign embassy employees with access to top secret information. *My God, if Kelly had ever known.* "I have obligations, Joanne."

"Please. You *had* obligations. We know all about what happened at Parkchester. So, I think you'll have the time for this assignment. Not only that, we'll use your ready-made personal trainer work to draw the subject in."

Danny relented. She's thought it all through.

Joanne briefed him about how they learned about the proposed auction through surveillance of hand-picked international weapons dealers who were invited to participate.

Danny sat back. "So what's so special about this chemical weapon, anyway? I thought it was always the delivery system of the weapon that was the roadblock."

"What Dr. Carrie was able to accomplish has yet to be achieved by any known government or terrorist group on earth. From what we've been able to piece together, the molecular structure of this neurotoxin duplicates itself like a virus over a coverage area previously unheard of. With only 8ml of the substance, an entire city's population could be wiped clean within an hour or two before the chemical reaction dissipates from its epicenter. It's the chemical equivalent of the Neutron bomb."

"All this from a recent grad student hooked on heroin?" Danny asked. "I remember from briefings that chemical agents couldn't compete with nuclear technology when it came to mass destruction."

"She found a way," Joanne replied. "That auction can never take place but there's something else you need to know." She drew a breath. "This afternoon in Central Park, the FBI agent assigned to the subject was killed."

"Shit," he said, resisting the urge to scratch the hair on the back of his neck.

"He last reported that he was to meet the subject there, so we tracked them. Our surveillance photos show her giving him a small package shortly before he died—run over by a truck on Central Park West. But when we commandeered the body, we found red discolorations on his fingertips, indicating that he'd been poisoned, we think by the nerve agent."

Danny's mind raced with the thought of the diabolical irony of a gift-wrapped box of poison. He cleared his throat, swallowed hard and said, "So, this chemist's a killer, too?"

"You make your own conclusions. I already have. As far as we know, the only other person who has access to the toxin is her mother and security personnel."

Nothing like a family show to make things interesting.

"I'm in." There was nothing else to look forward to. The thrilling rush of the spy game coursed through his veins like a pulsing electrical charge.

Chapter 11

April 19th, 10:00 a.m.
The Upper West Side, New York City

Kate woke up in her living room shirtless, with the TV still humming. She began the day with a scalding hot shower, but that did nothing to quell away the heroin induced itching nor wash away the self-loathing and anguish. In spite of the impressive cache of clothes, she stuck to basic outfits. Long sleeves were a must, probably a knit turtleneck today and a skirt.

Although she couldn't recall the last time she had slept through the night, she was certain it had been at least a month. Today, she'd finish up her work for Vanessa, but would require another hit by mid-afternoon.

She walked to the kitchen for a drink of water, then saw the envelope, then tore it open with her fingers. The initial anticipation of its contents as she read the return address met with apprehensive hesitation. She stuffed it in her purse.

Before leaving, she made the obligatory visit to the bathroom for a snort of cocaine up each nostril, her daily pick-me-up. She slipped on her kids-sized six shoes and sauntered down the steps onto the sidewalk, unaware of interested eyes.

She ordered the cabbie to take her to Fifty-eighth and Park. *No small talk, please.*

As the taxi crawled along Broadway, she removed the envelope from her purse, ripping it open with fingernails laced with powdery residue. Inside were two sheets of paper—one a cover letter, the other a name, address and phone number. She read it:

Dear Ms. Carrie,

Thank you for your inquiry.

You will be happy to know that our office has located your biological mother.

We have provided her address in the attachment, and you are free to make contact at any time.

Please understand that the Department of Health can never guarantee that a biological parent will be receptive to an adoptee's inquiry.

We wish you good luck in your search.

Sincerely,
Evelyn Wilson

For moment Kate's eyes welled, but the cocaine's effects kept her 'on'. As the taxi pulled to stop along the curb, she abruptly stuffed the envelope in her purse. Yesterday's memories effectively suppressed, she was ready to charge ahead. As the taxi pulled away, she stood before the edifice that was Frugeré headquarters. The coke high made her punchy as a bull in the ring.

When the elevator doors opened onto the lab floor, she noticed a few of her colleagues talking, one sobbing into a tissue. Usually everyone kept to themselves lest they become unfocused in their work, but today, they called her over.

"Kate," one of them said. "Have you heard?"

"What happened?" she responded, as if she didn't want to be bothered.

"Jared's dead. Run over by a truck outside the park yesterday! So awful."

This can't be happening. Her head swayed as if a brick had fallen on her, and she thought she might double over. Instead, rage quickly built up as she recalled yesterday's chain of events.

I'm such a fucking fool.

"Kate, did you hear what I said?" her colleague asked.

Outwardly vacant to others, she seethed within.

Vanessa!

"Are you okay?" Her fellow chemists looked at each other, wearing fearful expressions, trying to guess what she might do next.

This was more than she knew how to handle. Her stomach twisted in multiple rope knots. Her head throbbing, she had disassociated from the group.

"I gotta go," she croaked, dropping her purse to the floor and bolted for the elevator bank. She was determined, wearing a nothing-can-stop-me-now look on her face. One set of elevator doors opened as she got there. Without so much as an 'excuse me', she shouldered her way into the car and shouted sternly, "fifty-two."

What had happened was so obvious, that she cursed under her breath on the way up.

All self-control had evaporated when she crossed the elevator threshold and stormed straight into Vanessa's waiting area, making a beeline for the double doors.

Without extending so much as a 'good morning' to Vanessa's secretary, she demanded, "Where is she?"

"She's here Kate, but—"

Hearing all she needed, she pushed open the double doors. Behind, she heard, "Don't go in there!"

She saw Vanessa sitting at her desk with two Frugeré company men sitting opposite. They didn't register in her world.

"Kate, I didn't ask you to—"

Her groundswell of rage had Vanessa in its crosshairs. Marching up to Vanessa's desk, she shouted, "How could you do that to him?"

She leaned over the desk and was inches from Vanessa's face. "Break it off! That's what you said! I fucking hate you!" She stretched across the desk as both hands grasped Vanessa's neck and squeezed. The two men quickly grabbed Kate, holding her back.

One of the men said, "Get her off!" Pulling back her fingers, they separated the two women.

Arms flailing and tears of frustration running down her cheeks, Kate continued. "Let me go!"

Her temper reached its crescendo. She was a living, breathing tempest that even two able-bodied men couldn't handle. Gunther, whom the secretary had summoned, ran in to help restrain her. With an ugly grunt, he pulled her backward with such force that she lost her balance and fell to the salmon pink carpeted floor.

"Are you all right?" Gunther asked of Vanessa, straightening his jacket.

Kate looked through her own blurry eyes at Vanessa rubbing her throat, breathless and coughing. When Vanessa reassumed her composure, she calmly stood, straightened her blouse and hovered over the pathetic creature. Finally, she spoke. "Gentlemen, I'm sorry you had to see this, really I am."

Gunther asked, "Would you like me to escort her out of the building?"

Oh, you'd so like that, wouldn't you!

"No," Vanessa answered him, then addressed her company. "Forgive me, gentlemen. Please step outside. We need a moment."

She felt the rage evaporate into depression. The high was over and she crashed, curling on the floor in an almost fetal position, writhing through sobs.

As the door shut, Vanessa stepped closer, hovering over Kate, and said, "Get up! Now!" Her trumpet-like voice reverted to the Brooklyn accent that reappeared during periods of strong emotion.

Vanessa hoisted her up by the armpits with the force of a backhoe and dropped her in one of the chairs in front of the desk. She then slapped Kate across the face. She may as well have been hitting a block of ice.

Kate pleaded, "No. He can't be dead."

"You're all doped up again, aren't you?"

"No, I…"

"Don't lie to me!" Vanessa slapped her again, so hard this time, Kate fell off the chair. She knelt down on the carpet, glaring into Kate's eyes, hands firmly on her shoulders, pinning them against the chair. "Look at yourself. I'll be damned if I'm going to let you screw this whole thing up. My reputation is on the line and you're a… pitiful mess." Vanessa released her hold momentarily.

"It was the toxin, wasn't it?" Kate mumbled, fighting back tears.

Vanessa ignored her.

"I know you're lying," she continued in full voice. "The test vial was missing."

Vanessa exhaled heavily. "Dear, no one said that Jared was poisoned, so I don't know where this is coming from."

Kate wasn't mollified in the least. "You used the vial to put some toxin inside that box."

Vanessa's silence told Kate all she needed to know. "You had no right!"

"I have as much right to those vials as you have. More, in fact."

"But that's not what we agreed!" Kate shouted.

"Agreed?" Vanessa moved slowly toward her again. "*I'll* tell you what we agreed. We agreed that you were to do as you're told. That's what we agreed. You'd better learn how to control yourself, or you'll be no use to me or anyone else."

"I don't want to be a part of this anymore!" she proclaimed, then coughed out sputum, the stinging bile creeping up into her throat.

Vanessa grabbed her shoulders harder than before and pinned her against the back of the chair. After a teeth gnashing, she said, "Now you listen to me and repeat." Vanessa's eyes narrowed on her, as she tried to catch her breath under the pressure of Vanessa's shoulder holds. "I, Katelyn Carrie, promise to follow Vanessa Carrie's instructions to the letter."

Kate could only shake her head, trying to break her gaze.

"Say it!" Vanessa shook her with violent ferocity.

When she could breathe again, Kate said, "I, Katelyn Carrie, promise to follow Vanessa Carrie's instructions."

"To maintain composure at all times."

"To maintain composure at all times."

"And to respect Vanessa Carrie, my sole savior, so help me God."

"And to respect Vanessa Carrie, my sole savior, so help me God."

Then Vanessa, true to form, let her go and stepped back to grab a cigarette, lit it, took in a puff and stared lovingly at her. Those hardened eyes gave way to a soft and rounded motherly gentleness. She brought her voice down. "I just don't know what to do with you anymore. You make me look bad when you act like this. You can't imagine how much you've hurt me right now. I'm so disappointed in you."

Kate regained some composure and rose from her chair as Vanessa moved to embrace her. She shook her head in disbelief and pushed Vanessa away. "You know what? I can't take this anymore! I really can't. Up to now I have done everything you've wanted. No questions asked, but this…" Her fist clenched by her side. "I'm sorry, I can't. *I won't*! I'm tired of smiling for you, laughing for you in front of people,"—*killing for you!*—"pretending that everything is all just so lovely, when clearly, it's not! Until now, I'd never given a shit about how many could die from my Tri-Meth and yeah, it's *mine*. But now, I'm starting to think about it, a lot. I just don't want this on my head anymore. I just want to go home," she concluded ruefully.

Vanessa regarded her. "Well, we can't put the genie back in the bottle, now, can we? It's out there and nothing can change that. Two more weeks. That's all I ask. So please, dear, finish mixing the last of the vials today, then, you're free to take some time off. Can you do that for me, my golden girl?" Vanessa's endearing sweetness was hypnotic.

God damn her!

"Don't call me that anymore," she protested, but the ensuing silence broke her, retreating to obstinate acquiescence. "Fine, I'll finish up, go home and come to your meeting."

"*Our* meeting, dear."

"What-evs," Kate said with her face crinkled up in a bitter lemon look. Then she turned around and marched out.

She rode the elevator down to the lab one last time, barely controlling intermittent sobs. She wouldn't have to imagine as the others stared at her pitiful dishevelment, the sound of chuckling and muttered quips of 'lemonhead' trailing behind her as she returned to the lab. She spent the afternoon completing the last vial, finding it difficult to work and control her anger. Yet she was able to do it; quite the high functioning addict. The fact that she put in all of the research drove her to prevent relinquishing any of it.

Kate kicked off her flats for Uggs, then went to work.

She conducted the distillation procedure. Next, she carefully poured the contents of a tiny amount of the liquid into each vial, which had two compartments separated by a rubber seal. She then sealed the vial, upended it, then reached over and gently opened a container of white powder, the consistency of confectioner's sugar, although this substance was far from edible. Her powder reduced the time it took to reach the bloodstream from what was normally minutes to a few seconds. She proceeded to fill the other end of the vial with the powdery substance. The seal prevented the two chemical compounds from combining, but once broken, the toxin would turn deadly active, the liquid causing the powder to vaporize and disperse, killing any living thing that happened to come in contact with it, either by breathing it in or touching it; a gaseous cloud of death.

Before she left for the day, her anger towards Vanessa only intensified. *I have to take things into my own hands,* she thought.

She knew Vanessa wanted the chemical compound and would pay dearly for it when the time came. But why not go all the way and control the inventory as well? Trust between them was at an all-time low, she so wanted to control something in her life. So in one spontaneous act, she stuffed the vial case into her purse, not knowing that by doing that, everything was about to change. It didn't fit all the way in, but she didn't care.

On her way out, she stopped in the ladies room. Repulsed at the thought of seeing her reflection in the mirror these days, she sauntered straight into a stall, closed the door, dropped to kneel over the porcelain goddess and wretched into the bowl. Voided, she pulled herself up off the tiled floor, sat on the toilet and gave herself another hit.

Then Kate left the building, hoping she'd never return.

Chapter 12

April 19th, 1:45 p.m.
Midtown, New York City

Vanessa waited for her two o'clock while her fingers drum rolled on the table. A morning rain shower left a thin cloak of humid air in its wake, saturating the bones of millions of New Yorkers. By the time she arrived at BG's entry, the sun had burned away much of the overcast sky. She had reserved a table overlooking the Pulitzer Fountain across from the Plaza Hotel and beyond that was the Grand Army Plaza with the Sherman Statue. The Wollman Rink was an icy aberration in the vast green oasis that was Central Park to the North and East.

Vanessa acknowledged the Rosehips with Hibiscus tea the server set before her with a nod. With a nonchalant smile and sharp glance, she intimated that no further conversation was necessary or desired. Deep in thought over what had transpired that morning, she glided the thumb of her right hand repeatedly over each of her fingers one by one.

Her visitor arrived, wearing a sleeveless, fitted, royal blue sheath dress and pumps for their prearranged tête-à-tête. Without a word, the other woman sat across from Vanessa. The elegant chairs with enclosed, mustard-hued backs seemed to envelope each chair's occupant.

"Everything set up on your end?" Brooke Sato asked with prosecutorial forthrightness.

Vanessa had met Brooke when she worked for The Axis Group seven years ago, arranging one of what was to be several financing vehicles for Frugeré. An investment banker with an eidetic memory, her vast experience with cross border transactions was impressive. Having been managing partner for twelve years running with Pan Asian Bankers Trust, at forty-one, she was one of two female partners, and the only Japanese woman within the company. Her straight, jet black hair rested on her shoulders; pencil thin eyebrows and perfectly proportioned lips completed the image. A light grouping of freckles lay just below her right eye.

"Kate's preparing the last vial today," Vanessa responded as she looked out through the window at the park.

Brooke's icy demeanor warmed. She placed both arms on the table, palms upturned. "Good. Just so you know, the buyers are lining up nicely. All their deposits are in escrow. May 4th is the day. Midnight."

"I would prefer if the date was moved up," said Vanessa, clenching her fists under the table. "The creditors keep knocking. I'm running out of time."

"I would if I could, but a video conference is out of the question. Cyber security concerns." Five bidders—infamous weapons dealers representing various anonymous foreign governments—would be serving as discrete proxies for foreign governments. "Low tech is the way to go on this deal."

"Should Kate attend?"

"I've contracted an independent chemist to verify it, but it'd still be good to have her there."

Brooke had presented the idea of an auction to rescue Frugeré from its dreadful financial position. Although Vanessa had been reluctant to engage in such 'unseemly' transactions, Brooke convinced her that it was all legal and that chemists within Vanessa's company could be utilized to conduct research and development so long as the project was kept off the books.

The toxin would be awarded to the highest bidder. Anyone who wanted to 'play' was required to place a substantial down payment into a Cayman Islands escrow account, one that only Brooke could access. Brooke had developed relationships worldwide with governments looking to get in the weapons game, as well as private acquisition companies who acted as brokers. Resale of weapons was a huge market. These brokers justified proliferation on an international scale. They wanted the most effective product on the market to sell to their customers, and were willing to pay dearly to get it. The profit was simply too large to ignore. So what if a terrorist group or two got hold of a weapon of mass destruction and used it. That was just collateral damage.

Vanessa drifted into her own thoughts as Brooke reached across the table and gently stroked the back of her hand.

Vanessa shuddered as Brooke gently rubbed her leg against hers in a slow but deliberate circular motion.

"You know how I feel about you, Vee," Brooke said, leaning in closer.

Vanessa tensed but didn't cringe away. "Not here, please. I can't… hold back when you do that." She was honest for the first time today.

"I don't care," Brooke responded, continuing to rub her leg against Vanessa's, validating their unique bond. After a few seconds that seemed to last a lifetime, she moved her leg away slowly.

Brooke withdrew her hand as she frowned, eyes shimmering with longing. "I'm sorry. I wish you wouldn't be so sensitive about it." Before Vanessa could respond, Brooke asked, "Does Kate know?"

Vanessa's face tightened as she hesitated but Brooke was persistent.

"Vee, does she know?" Brooke repeated.

All Vanessa could muster was a silent head shake, eyes glistening, before she whispered, "After this is behind us, it'll be different. I promise." Vanessa's hand quivered.

"I know, but for now, just save those tears."

Chapter 13

April 19th, 2:30 p.m.
The Upper West Side, New York City

Kate knew Vanessa would have Gunther come after her once they discovered the vials were missing. Creeping guilt led to buyer's remorse before she remembered their last encounter. Her resolve firmed.

After ruminating in her unkempt apartment for four hours, watching another block of *Castle* episodes, Kate decided to solve her little dilemma by hiding the vials. *Maybe they deserved a proper, decent burial somewhere.* She walked eastward to Central Park, which she knew well, having spent her teen years in the City.

The perfect place dawned on her. *The Ramble.*

It lay in the Park's southern midsection, bordered by 73rd Street in the South to 79th Street in the north, a heavily forested area with several rock formations that remained untouched since the park was developed in the nineteenth century. A park within a park, The Ramble was a perennial favorite of birdwatchers, but also was known for private, homosexual encounters. Straight couples could join in the fun, too, of course. It was not uncommon to find used condoms lying around on the dirt or in the brush.

Kate knew the precise spot, but she'd left out one minor detail. She had no shovel and she wasn't about to dirty her hands and clothes in the mud. In Manhattan, no one had reason to buy them and the few hardware stores that sold them were sparse. A quick search on her cell phone revealed one on 72nd Street. Hey, who knew?

Gartner's was only two blocks away but she sauntered there. Out of breath, she asked the clerk if he could help her pick out a shovel, which he did. Kate eyed a large one she liked, even though he had tried to sell her a smaller, 'lady-sized' shovel, as he liked to call it.

"No, this one's fine," she snapped at him, as if he had just tried to make a pass at her. "Thank you." Walking to the cashier and realized after the fact how rude she must have sounded.

In the Park, Kate steered clear of the 72nd Street entrance and instead entered at 77th Street, and then walked eastward toward Belvedere Castle. When she crossed south on a bridge overlooking the 79th Street Traverse with the sound of moving traffic below, she found it—a rock adjacent to the fence overlooking the Traverse in the shadow of the castle. After finding the short winding dirt path that led to a rock face in an ensconced clearing, she dropped to her knees and started digging a hole against the base of the rock. When she thought it was deep enough, she placed the case in the hole and covered it over with dirt, patting it down with the shovel.

Kate was emboldened to give her gym a go, a place she hadn't attended in well over a month. She had taken to jogging while in college and graduate school, before the heroin took hold. As her drug intake skyrocketed, her stamina went south.

She wore long sleeved workout shirts and sweatpants to cover the unseemly black and blue tracks marring her skin. It didn't take but five minutes on the treadmill before her labored breathing made her give up the ghost, the techno pop music pulsating through the room and through her own head in an uncomfortable way. She took a huge swig from her water bottle and limped off.

So much for getting back on that horse.

"Are you okay?" asked an unfamiliar voice. When she looked up, she saw before her a handsome figure in long rust colored hair and blue eyes wearing a tank top and guy shorts, who could have passed for the Son of God as far as she was concerned.

"I saw you huffing and puffing all the way from over there," he said with an endearing smile.

"I'm fine, but thanks for asking," she said.

"Hey, didn't I just see you on the cover of Women's Health?"

"Are you always this obnoxious?" she answered with another question, too winded to react to the lame attempt at a pick up line from a muscle head. On second thought, his physique was worth admiring, at least.

"I'm Eric. I do personal training here."

"You're not from around here, are you?" she said, noting his accent.

"No, I'm not. But thanks for the compliment."

"Oh, that wasn't a compliment," she said with off-putting glibness.

He shrugged. "You know, I could really help you improve your stamina. If you didn't work out in heavy clothing like that, you wouldn't overheat like you just did."

"Thanks for the tip. I'll have to remember that next time."

"And *you* are?"

"Kate," was all she gave him.

He extended his hand more than halfway, which left little choice for her but to shake it.

"I can schedule you in. We'll work out a payment plan. How about ten sessions?"

"I'm not up for it right now, but maybe some other time, okay… Eric, is it? I really appreciate it, I do. But I'm *really* okay now." She noticed faint needle scars on his left arm.

"No problem. Whenever you're ready, let me know."

I just want to be happy, for however short a time. Her own words to Vanessa startled her. I don't care what she said. Wanting a man isn't a bad thing. Even not knowing who he was, she couldn't deny that he looked hot.

All her relationships had ended up in the garbage pile. Either guys were put off by her drug use and bi-polar weirdness or her constant banter about chemistry, or her recoil with premature advances. To her, seeking love for drugs was a full time job. *I wonder what he takes. Does he deal, too? Should I risk asking? God, I'm such a whore!*

Her interest piqued, she decided to hang around a little longer and do some stretching.

As Eric was leaving for the night, she went for it. She ran up from behind. "Hey, I see what you're about!" she said with a frisky lilt. She even thought it uncanny how extraverted she became when it came to drug-seeking activities.

"What?" he asked, barely turning to look at her.

"Oh, you can't fool me. I think you have something I want."

"Okay… well, see you later," he said, sounding as if he thought of her as a stalker to be avoided.

"Quitter!" she said as she blocked his path in front of the glass door leading out to the street.

"Well, damn, you made me forget my pick up line!" he responded.

"I know what you've been into. Why do you think I wear long sleeves?"

His eyes motioned to the exit. "Just walk with me," he said. "That is, if you don't mind if I walk you home."

They took a wordless stroll along Broadway, then turned onto 74th Street nearing her apartment when Eric finally broke the silence. "You know, I may not know what you're talking about, so follow me on this, alright?" he said, looking straight ahead and speaking low. "I take it you want new *experiences*, right?"

"Yeah and I'm good for it too," she said eagerly.

"You already buy from others?"

"Yeah. Why?"

"Then you wouldn't be interested and neither would I."

"What's it to you who I buy from?"

Eric smirked. "Look, I just need to know that you'll be a steady customer."

"I just said I'm good for it.

"So, what makes you so special?"

She gave him a sheepish grin.

"Great, so we're both special," he said. "Tell you what, if you're so interested, let's meet—."

As they approached her apartment's front stoop, a man who'd been lurking around the adjacent building closed in from behind and pushed Eric toward the curb. She screamed as the mugger grabbed for her purse, but struggled to hold onto it. When the mugger let go, she fell to the ground. Eric charged the mugger and punched the other man in the face, knocking him to the pavement. Before Eric could pin him down, the attacker pulled out a switchblade and swung it for Eric's face, grazing Eric's right temple. Eric stepped in and grabbed the mugger's knife-wielding arm, applying pressure on the mugger's wrist and forcing the knife out. Eric shoved the mugger to the ground. As Eric paused to wipe the blood from his face, the mugger sprang up and ran, empty handed, down the street and around the corner, disappearing into the night.

Eric crouched over her, still on the pavement, wincing. “Are you okay?”

Looking up at him, she said, “Oh my God. You’re bleeding!”

“I’m fine,” he responded, breaths coming slow and steady as the adrenaline tapered off. Blood smeared his fingers.

“No you’re not! You need a hospital.”

“It’ll stop on its own. I can handle it.” He paused to think it over, “but I could use some gauze or a band aid or something if you have one.”

“In my apartment,” she said, directing him up the steps.

Once inside, while Eric lay on her sofa, she rummaged around for some gauze and found a roll under the bathroom sink. “That guy could have killed you. You should have let him take my purse.” She tore off a piece, sprayed some Bacitracin on it and covered the wound with it. “Now hold still.”

“Bullshit. Ow!” he groaned as she applied the gauze. She had him hold the pad not having any tape to hold it down. “Thanks, Kate. I’m such an idiot.”

“Yeah, you sure are, but if it’s all just the same, thank you for hitting that jerk.”

Eric sighed. “Look, I should go. I’ve had a long day and I’m worn out. But like I was saying, if you think you’ll want more than that junk you’re into, let me know, okay?”

“Maybe but I just bought some, so I’m set for a while.”

“You prepare your own bundles?” he asked.

She saw him glance over at the table with the burnt spoon, white powder residue and plastic baggie collection. It wasn't like she ever thought to hide her drug paraphernalia before, she didn't get many visitors. Kate thought not to answer. The picture was worth a thousand words.

“All by myself.”

“Nice, but like I said, if you think you’ll need more product, drop by the gym. I’m there all the time. I guarantee it’s better than the junk you’re buying now.”

“Right. I’ll remember that.”

Kate saw him to the door and he walked out. It took less than two hours and she was smitten, but she didn’t know if it was because of his good looks or access to 'new experiences'. Either way, he was on her mind and she couldn’t sleep.

Time to get to work.

She spent the better part of an hour preparing more heroin and placed containers of the liquid in her refrigerator. Save for her steady diet of gummy bears and yogurt, she didn’t eat much these days, which explained the absence of any solid food in the apartment. She ended the day by taking yet another hit, another mouth full of gummys and flicking on the flat screen to the all-*Castle*-all-the-time channel. She leaned forward at the glow of the TV, hypnotized by the light emanating from the screen and then leaned back onto her sofa, falling into another dreamless sleep two and a half episodes later.

Chapter 14

April 19, 4:00 p.m.
Jersey City, New Jersey

The Masjid Muhammed Mosque wasn't a traditional structure. As long as one was among brothers, that was all that mattered. A brick facade with a European influenced entrance led to a large room with high windows and an imam standing in one of the far corners.

Approaching *Asr*, Sabir unfurled his *sajjada* against the back wall of the room, and proceeded to prostrate himself East, facing Mecca, behind twenty or so other men. Even though he prayed, he wasn't here to satisfy any devotion toward Islam. When he rose, he sensed a man's presence to his right, but maintained his vision straight ahead. An African-American male knelt down on his prayer mat and began speaking in Arabic.

"We can meet outside when you've finished," the man said. "It's not my intention to disrespect the sanctity of this place."

You already have, he scoffed inwardly. "No. You may speak to me now. Here, or not at all."

He heard the man's breath pause for just a moment. "As we agreed, *Ummu* delivered your present two hours ago," he said. "A delivery was made to your brothers this morning. We thought you would appreciate it. It's your call as to how to dispose of it."

"Yes. It is appreciated," Sabir said.

"Okay, then. Before you can go back home, *Ummu* expects you to make a shopping list for her." The man paused, then placed a post-it-note on Sabir's mat. The only sound that broke the chilly, dead air between them was the murmur of men in prayer.

"And when I return from shopping, what then?"

"*Ummu* will give you more books to study. She loves you for passing the first test, but passing the next one would make her very happy."

"Anything to please her." Sabir finished his prayers, noting when the man had left, along with his mat. When he finished, he slipped on his shoes and walked out.

Jaffa was waiting out front on the sidewalk. “They made a delivery this morning.”
“Yes. So they said. Is our friend comfortable?” Sabir asked.

“I’ve given him ‘special’ treatment with the tools you have provided.”

“Good. You are free to make him comfortable but make sure he is still alive when I pay him a visit tomorrow.

“He is and he eagerly awaits Mohammed, Allah… and you.”

Vanessa sat on her queen size bed in her doorman duplex apartment at 53rd Park Avenue and 69th Street barking over the phone to one of her managers. “I want that shoot to go as scheduled. The NuYou commercials need to make the media-buying deadline… that’s right, and tell them it better go as planned this time… for your sake, it better be.” She disconnected her cell phone and rested it on the nightstand, then disrobed, showing off her pink tank top.

The apartment was a duplex of modern design, a remnant of Vanessa's second marriage to fashion designer Frederich Allon. A very public affair followed by the New York tabloids and industry papers, it was occasional dinners out between his frenetic travel schedule and her time devoted to building their respective businesses. The divorce settlement involved the apartment and a modest seven figure settlement.

She had a first love; a neighborhood kid and high school classmate. Although motivated by an immature need to achieve some degree of conformity, Vanessa dumped him after two and a half years, confiding in girlfriends that he just had no ambition whatsoever to be as successful as she wanted to be.

Her apartment had a specious living room with an open wooden staircase that led to a mezzanine with two bedrooms. Clear glass sliding doors and a window above it looked out onto a balcony with a western view of the fading sunset.

Brooke walked in from the bathroom donning a light pink satin pajama tank top, Vanessa was wrapped in a burgundy velour robe and they both snuggled under the covers. Brooke wrapped her arms around her. Vanessa tensed up. She hadn’t moved on from what had happened that morning.

“It’s Kate again, isn’t it?”

“I can’t control her anymore. You told me I should give her the benefit of a doubt but she’s not well and I’m ill-equipped to help her,” Vanessa confessed.

Brooke craned her neck and kissed her on the cheek. “It’s not your fault,” she said, turning a blind eye to any responsibility Vanessa may have had in perpetuating Kate’s current condition.

“I’ve fed her, clothed her, educated her, given her a roof over her head. I’ve given her a life. Yet she shows no gratitude at all.”

“You did good, Vee,” Brooke said with assurance. “Do *not* beat yourself up over it.” She reached over and pulled off Vanessa’s tank top.

Nude, Vanessa read Brooke’s eyes perfectly. Her self-pity was suppressed by the urge to lash out. “It was you who convinced me to trust her.”

Brooke pouted like a child whose favorite pet had died. “I never meant for your relationship to suffer.”

Vanessa’s tone dropped another degree. “Because of you, my business is on the brink. Because of you, Kate's morose and miserable. She's become an embarrassment and you know how I feel about that." It had never crossed her mind that she had perhaps cared more about the business than Kate's welfare.

"I'm sorry." Vanessa thought she saw fear in Brooke's eyes.

"I can't relate to what you two have, but I-I know what we have here," Brooke whispered, then kissed Vanessa's smooth, elongated belly. "And I won't let you go."

In the moment, Brooke's entreaties allayed Vanessa's apprehensions. They tittered like school girls. Their lips met, then parted.

"I love you," Brooke said as she lowered herself over Vanessa. She trailed downward, only stopping when she had reached Vanessa's soft spot.

Brooke's deliciously gentle touch was enough to tame Vanessa's frustration. She could no longer resist the impulse to raise her legs and wrap around Brooke's back. "I love you, too," she mumbled before a euphoric moan took her.

Tracing delicate kisses along her jaw line and down her neck, Vanessa didn't stop until Brooke's moan confirmed that her partner was just as ready as she was. Their bodies entangled as they both drove each other to impossible heights.

Shudder after shudder ran through Vanessa until Brooke's undulating cry broke the heated moment. "Oh, God, your power intoxicates me," were her last words before she drifted off into a contented slumber.

"Yes, dear. I know."

Chapter 15

April 20th, 11:00 a.m.
The Upper West Side, New York City

The outstretched fingers of morning sunlight through the blinds illuminated her weathered face. Aroused from her not-so-sound sleep, Kate raised them all the way, allowing the sunlight to flood the apartment. The overcast that had cloaked the City had lifted. In the light, her weight loss definitely showed. She had scratched the crooks of her elbows and knees raw during the night. Her nails looked ragged. She hadn't eaten anything with real nutritional value in weeks. Her face had that unmistakable emaciated look to it, cheek bones poking out through her skin. *Why drink coffee when I can snort cocaine instead?* And she did just that; two deliberate snorts, one up each nostril.

Her physical condition notwithstanding, Kate took the time to stretch. She allowed herself to enjoy the respite away from Vanessa and the time to pursue her new project that was Eric Stone. *Didn't a knight in shining armor actually rescue me last night?* She decided to find out, leaving the Vanessa issue by the wayside for the time being. She took a pleasant stroll to the gym, with no intention whatsoever of working out.

She wasn't disappointed. Walking in, she spotted Eric instantly. He was spotting a balding, middle aged man with a barbell, helping him with reps. She found herself staring at him again, caught herself and charged ahead as she walked up to him. "Hey, stranger," she said.

"Just a sec'." He excused himself from his portly client. "Well, don't you look as pretty as a peach today," he said, charmed by her beaming smile.

"Hey, you said if I wanted something more from you, I should stop by… and you never gave me your number."

He led her to the door to the stairwell.

"I didn't think you'd stop in so soon. That's all. I'll give you my number then. How's that?" he said with a reassuring wink.

"Hey, I like you and I want to know if what you have is real."

"Sure. I can arrange something tonight. Ever been to the Dance Factory?"

"It's on my to-do list."

"I can meet you in front of the club, or…?"

"You know where I live," she said, sparing him the discomfort of having to ask.

"Sounds good. I'll be by around 9. Just remember to bring cash."

"Just remember to bring cash," he instructed before leaving her to wonder whether he was really into her or not.

Some like to build model airplanes or do needlepoint but Kate liked doing science experiments to pass the time by preparing cool chemical reactions of the kind that high school science nerds would die for.

When she let Danny in, she hadn't even bothered to get ready for her 'night out', playing the familiar role of absentminded professor.

"Sorry, Eric. I was working on something in the kitchen. I still gotta' change. Feel free," she said, motioning to the sofa, unaccustomed as she was at being an ever-so-gracious hostess. "I'd offer you something, but… here," she said, tossing a bag of gummy bears at him before she walked into her bedroom.

Danny's detailed dossier on her described her continuous drug use through college, finding friends who perpetuated her habit but eventually, her habit escalated to such a level that it drove them away while they matured and settled into high profile jobs. The constant search for the next high and subsequent low exceeded her desire to maintain meaningful friendships. They saw what heroin was doing to her but no one had been willing to pull her out of the abyss.

Kate left him alone to breathe in the burnt metal and tobacco aroma amongst the collection of take-out containers at his feet. She emerged from the bedroom wearing a clubbing outfit consisting of one black Ali Ro stretch jersey, a long sleeve drape dress and a pair of black Tory Burch ballet flats. Her recent, dramatic weight loss made the dress look billowy on her, yet still attractive. Her pale skin was in stark contrast to her black dress, shoes and glasses.

"Been working hard?" he asked, glancing over toward the kitchen as she came out.

"Oh, sorry. Yeah. Wanna see?"

When Danny saw her set-up out in the open, it confirmed she was the type of person who went all out.

The set up on the kitchen table consisted of a lone heating pad with a beaker held up on a base. Inside the beaker were fine crystals.

"What is that?"

"Just watch," she said, turning up the heat of the pad. When the crystals turned to liquid and started to boil, she grabbed a few gummy bears from an open bag on the table and dropped them in. A fiery light shot upward.

"Whoa."

"Cool, right? That is if you ever want to impress your friends."

"Nerd alert. Nerd alert," he said with a tightened throat, his half clenched fist covering his mouth as a makeshift megaphone.

"Shut up! It's heated potassium chlorate with added sugar, you jerk! A redux reaction."

"A what?" he asked, like a dumbfounded muscle head.

"A redux—just forget it and let's go," she said. "Lesson's over."

She'd just made it known she would run the show tonight.

Dance Factory was one of a hand full of hot dance clubs on the West Side on 27th Street. From the entrance, Kate and Danny could feel the vibrations of the thumping bass from the floor as it shook the sidewalks. Danny paid Kate's cover as they walked through the strobe-lighted dance floor, packed with twenty-somethings. He held Kate's hand to guide her through the crowd on the main floor to the rear of the building. They took the stairs down to the basement level restrooms.

"I gotta pee," she said.

Before he knew it, Kate came out more alert than he had seen her. A dimly lit narrow hallway led past the men's room to an exit door that opened to a brightly lit alleyway below street level. Three other couples were present, one of them in mid-embrace, the other two sets exchanging drags. No one paid attention to them as they continued downward.

At the bottom of the stairwell, Shannon, a towering broad shouldered CIA agent with short blond hair was waiting.

"This is her?" Shannon muttered.

Danny nodded.

"I think you're gonna' like this. It's up-market, very pure."

Shannon palmed a glass vial of the heroin into Danny's hand. He looked at it up close and nodded to Kate. "It's real," he said."

Kate reached down, removed her left shoe and withdrew a wad of cash.

After counting it, Shannon grabbed it unceremoniously and jogged up the stairwell without another word.

Danny reached into his left pant pocket and pulled out a glass vial filed with water that Joanne had given him. "Me first," he said, emptying its contents into a syringe, quickly tossing the plastic vial to the ground. He injected himself with the inactive solution, quickly grabbing another vial from his right pant pocket and filling it about half way.

Danny saw that that ruffled her feathers, as intended.

"Hey, mister, I want my fair share! I paid for it!" she shouted.

"Sure and you're also about eighty pounds lighter than I am."

"Fuck you!" she snarled. She grabbed the syringe and vial away from him and pulled the plunger all the way out. "I'm a chemist. I know what I can handle," she proclaimed, sounding like the spoiled brat that she was.

"No." Danny knew he should have stopped her but thought about how blowing his cover here could jeopardize the grand plan. It was too late.

After Kate emptied the brew into her bloated veins, she tossed the syringe and vial to the floor.

He saw Kate smile with euphoric glee like a proud daredevil who'd just survived a death defying leap. When the concoction that should have calmed her down didn't, he grew alarmed and knew something was off.

"Let's go!" Kate yelled, grabbing his hand and leading him out of the stairwell out onto the main dance floor with the music still pounding while strobe lights manically flashed. Kate hit the floor and started dancing in contorted gyrations while laughing like a deranged hyena. She was oblivious to him and everyone one else in the world.

"Whoo-hoo! I wanna' dance all night!" she yelled through the noise. She grabbed his arms and tried to twirl him around with reckless abandon. Danny played along reluctantly.

"Take it easy!" he shouted. "I'm not gonna take it easy! I'm floating on air!"

Then Kate's energy appeared to plateau as she stopped in her tracks. Her pupils rolled upward to the back of her head. Multicolored flashing lights swirled around them as her breathing faltered. She went limp.

"Kate!" he said, catching her mid-fall. She had lost consciousness. Danny lowered her to the floor flat on her back.

He fell to his knees and shook Kate's diminutive body in desperation. "Please stay with me, Kate, stay with me!" No chest movement told him her breathing had stopped. When an intermittent strobe shined onto her face, that's when Danny spotted the white residue in both of her nostrils.

Oh, God.

He couldn't believe he'd missed it. She'd obviously snorted in the ladies room before the injection.

A club bouncer appeared and knelt down next to Danny. "What happened? He shouted amidst the din. What's wrong with her?"

"Don't know. Too much to drink," Danny lied, hoping he could somehow carry her out without creating more of a scene.

Fortunately for Kate, this particular bouncer was a registered nurse by day. When he pulled out his pen-sized flashlight, he too noticed the residue, shook his head and then lifted an eyelid to find dilated pupils no larger than pin pricks. Moving quickly, he grabbed firm hold of the cuff on her right sleeve and ripped it apart lengthwise upwards past the elbow. He saw the long dark tracks that stretched from elbows to wrists. "Oh, Shit!" He turned to Danny and said, "Dude, you better call 911, now!"

PART II

"I need physics more than friends."

—Robert Oppenheimer

Chapter 16

April 20th, 8:30 p.m.
Midtown, New York City

There has always been a fine line between an acolyte and sycophant. One absorbs what she can from her superiors in order to learn the ropes of her job and the business, while the other learns the ropes in order to surpass the superior. Neither of them are mindless, but the acolyte, looking upon the superior with starry eyed naïveté, has yet to learn how to use treachery to her advantage. So it was with Vanessa's latest class of three up-and-coming Frugeré hopefuls who surrounded her like bodyguards sans the dark sunglasses, wearing sheath dresses of varying designs.

Tonight, the cosmetic trade association was holding their annual Spring industry awards event at the Waldorf-Astoria Hotel and Vanessa was to be one of its recipients this evening. All the key industry players were in attendance and many of the up-and-comers, too. Vanessa had grown to detest these events in light of her current position. What she loathed most was the press and especially, those fashion groupies; the pasty faced Eurotrash reporters who seemed to succeed every year in crashing the event. *But they've never actually created anything in their pathetic lives!*

CEO Vanessa Joy Carrie had proven, as others before her, that people will pay for that special look or scent that will distinguish them from others. After all, her company had been the height of "chic" a mere twenty years ago. Styles had changed, yet Frugeré hadn't, at least not in step with current trends enough to maintain its heretofore meteoric rise in the industry.

What's a woman to do if she wants to transform her life? To Vanessa Carrie, the answer was simple—run like hell to the cosmetics counter. Be it lotions, mascara, rouge, fragrances, creams, you name it, beauty business is armed and ready to help anyone make any life changing transition at any time.

To satisfy that need, Vanessa Carrie had been there for over the past thirty years. Following in the steps of Elizabeth Arden, Estée Lauder, Helena Rubenstein and Bobbie Brown, Vanessa Carrie had started Frugeré from nothing. All a woman need to do was take a trip to any department store make-up counter, ground zero for the beauty industry. In fact, anyone can start a cosmetics company on a shoe string. Anyone, that is, with samples and a song. But it takes a skilled and talented marketer to grow the business and Vanessa had proven many times over that she was both. What you didn't know could be made up along the way. Because of her, eyeliner pencils were now 'cosmetic writing instruments'.

"Sell the story the customer wants to hear," Vanessa was once quoted as saying. "That's what women get when they visit the make-up counter."

Vanessa didn't come from money, but she learned quickly how to create her own license. As if taken right out of a Horatio Alger novel, her humble beginning began in relative obscurity in Brooklyn, back when she was Vanessa Cohen. Working behind the fragrance counters of Kossoff's and Bloomingdales, she honed her ability to sell. And sell she did. Though she had no formal college education to speak of, she read voraciously and paid attention to the latest trends. She endured the biannual jaunts to the much anticipated Premiere Vision textile trade show in Villepinte, just outside of Paris, where industry trendsetters learn about what people would be wearing, applying and spraying on them the following spring and fall.

Vanessa was unabashedly honest about her secret to success. "A woman is attracted to cosmetics by stories, promises and possibilities. Just create the illusion that this season's hottest color will be sold out soon, so rush to your nearest cosmetics counter to snatch up the product before it's too late." In other words, customers will buy something no one actually needs, but everybody wants.

Continued success meant throwing more parties, acquiring more couture and art, and donating to more charities. Her reputation was well earned—an aggressive marketer and perfectionist who answered to no one. Although tyrannical towards her employees, she knew how to charm all the industry high fliers and even the press. She became an industry leader and role model for women in the business community, ascending to the industry throne through unapologetic determination.

The present was a different story. Over the previous decade, Frugeré had struggled to keep pace with a dynamic industry. So much so, that the balance sheets showed a company on the verge of collapse. Her license to print money had eventually expired. Suddenly, any competitor's ill will that had been building up throughout was about to boil over. The dream had turned into a nightmare for Vanessa, so she needed a game-changing product to turn the tide.

Vanessa was in full evening gown regalia. For a woman, Vanessa was tall at 5'11". Add to that the fact that she eschewed her signature boots for three-inch high heels on this night, she was an imposing figure. Her imperious demeanor emanated from her very skin. To her, cutthroat ambition was a moral imperative. "I don't meet competition. I crush it!" she once said in an interview.

After Vanessa stepped out of her Crown Victoria, one of many lined up on Fifth Avenue, her three assistants followed. A few reporters stepped up and started asking questions about her business, "Is it true Frugeré will be filing for bankruptcy at the end of this month?" one reporter asked. "Will you be laying off more employees?" another one asked. "Can you comment on the rumor that Frugeré will be on the market for a suitor?" from someone else.

Always gracious to a fault in public, she responded radiantly, "I assure everyone that Frugeré is a financially healthy company and will be one for as long as I'm around. My new product line will be coming out this June, and it will be eye opening."

Having successfully assuaged the interrogation, she continued inside.

The main hall was enclosed in what appeared to be a glass dome. Attendees and the press had already poured in. The grand art-deco design with off-white walls and beige trim harkened back to a bygone era of Guy Lombardo at New Year's Eve. The polished parquet dance floor shined bright, surrounded by a crimson carpet's checkerboard design. A mezzanine encircled the hall's perimeter giving the venue an opera house feel. Above the mezzanine rested railed sky boxes.

Vanessa, her entourage in tow, entered the hall and was immediately greeted by young admirers hoping to hear words of inspiration from the Queen. For tonight, she was to receive her lifetime achievement award. It was nice to see that young crowds still adored her.

Over the din of clattering flatware and the tingling sounds wine flutes, servers snaked through the crowd with hors d'oeuvres of risotto balls with white truffle and teriyaki chicken bites on toothpicks. Nothing was more prevalent than talk of the sexy looks and the hot colors of the summer ahead. The color this year? Mauve. Last year, it was Char-gold. The year before that? Gray.

As she approached table six, she met three of her contemporaries with hugs and kisses. There sat Harlow Odette, herself a prominent industry executive, as was Miranda Korda. All of them divorcees. Although her three assistants had taken their seats, Vanessa didn't bother to introduce them.

"It's so good to see you, Vanessa," said Harlow. With her dark complexion and willowy hairstyle, she could have been mistaken for Vanessa's twin, except that she had managed to keep her age in check much better. "Congratulations on your award, darling."

Miranda, sporting a perm of brunette hair the size of Manhattan knew just where to probe for weakness. "So, we were wondering why Frugeré hadn't issued its press releases yet to the buyers about your fall line."

Friendly, but competitors just the same, the conversation turned from cordial to discomforting in the flick of an eyelash. Vanessa wasn't from as cultured a background as the other three, but she was easily the toughest.

"It's all part of the grand strategy, girls," Vanessa said, managing a forced smile and a barely audible laugh, shoulders tensed. "The anticipation factor this season is intended to add a little spice to the buzz."

"Vee," Francesca, alabaster skinned, with short brown hair and was the thinnest of the bunch, wore a patterned sheath dress, entered the fray. "I just hired six of your former employees. I do hope all is well over at Frugeré."

Vanessa cursed inside but maintained her endearing smile. "No worries, dear. Frugeré's just as strong as ever. We all know how challenging it is to market our products year after year. I dare say that each of us have experienced down years at one time or another."

Her statement brought a sudden chill to the table. The arrows successfully redirected, Vanessa started talking about general popular trends, avoiding any further shop talk discussion. After a catered dinner of garden salad and chicken Cordon Bleu, the award portion of the evening began as dessert was being served.

As the crowd settled down, the master of ceremonies thanked everyone, then started announcing the awards. Finally, it was Vanessa's turn. The emcee welcomed her as she approached the impressive, solid oak dais with an air of confidence. She adjusted the microphone upward as all eyes gazed upon her, and prefaced her speech by thanking the Association for the honor.

"Some say that a superior intellect is the key to success in this industry," she began. "Others say that to make it you have to appeal to people's good graces on the way up because you'll meet them on the way down. Still some others insist that appearances are everything. Well, I wasn't smart, I wasn't nice to people and, well, you all see what I'm wearing this evening."

A ripple of laughter filled the room for a few moments before she continued. "The business world has two kinds of people: you are either a mouse or a lioness. A mouse gets the crumbs, but a lioness fights tooth and claw for what she needs to survive. To make it, you have to be selling all the time, yourself, your products. To achieve greater success, you must believe in yourself. You must let go of the opinions of others and find the greatness that lies within you."

She continued with her speech and accepted her award with her signature Vanessa Carrie smile and grace.

The evening would have ended on a high note, but for the fact that she had decided to remain in the hall a bit longer. It was then that she eyed Sid approaching her and expected one of his signature jibes, but instead was greeted with, "Wonderful speech, Vanessa."

Sid, whom she thought to be a rat-faced bastard of a man, was wearing a conservative gray pinstriped suit with a red tie. His once black curly hair extended slightly over his forehead, giving way to a distinguishing salt and pepper look on the sides.

Vanessa's eyelashes flitted. "Always a pleasure, Sid." *So I could throw you into a vat of piping hot oil.*

"A word?" he said with the terseness of an order, not a request. "This won't take long." He motioned her to follow him outside to the hallway which led out to the main lobby.

Alone, Sid turned toward her, speaking in *sotto voce*. "A proposition. Everyone knows that Frugeré's on the ropes. Your product line's old and tired. I can offer you a way out. A merger, we'll call it, to save face. It's the right move for you."

"No sale." she answered with a dark forced smile.

"Didn't you hear what I said? I'm offering you a chance to preserve your precious legacy—before it goes down the shitter."

"I said no, Sid. Not to anybody and especially not to you. Now if you'll excuse me—"

"Face it, Vanessa, Frugeré has run its course and everyone here knows it," he proclaimed, like an argumentative lawyer cross examining a hostile witness.

"Everyone in there just validated my reputation this evening. Which is something I can't say about yours," she responded, while forcing a polite smile.

"That was a retirement dinner for you. A send off. Nothing more. If you don't take my deal, your precious empire will crumble and no one will be around to pick up the crumbs."

Prick. For the first time in as long as she could remember, Vanessa was speechless.

Her dead glassy eyes narrowed in on his, both white knuckled fists clenched with fury.

Then sweet as maple syrup, she said, smiling and forcing a laugh "I repeat. No deal. Now or ever. Have a good night, Sid."

Vanessa spun away and began marching out, saying nothing.

In a full voice so that everyone could hear, he said, "Damn shame, we were all so looking forward to kicking your ass again this year." Sid continued to taunt her. "That's right. Just run away, you pathetic bitch!"

She knew it was time to gather the girls and make an exit but Sid was about to cross the line. "So that's what you do when someone pushes you too hard, is it?

"No, this is." She then walked to the center of the floor, as if on a soap box and said, "Excuse me everyone, I have an announcement to make. Sid Barnett just made a most gracious offer to merge with Frugeré."

The sound of muted laughter from some attendees who were in earshot was lost on the two, as bewildered guests in the lobby turned. A small crowd had started to form around them.

Sid said nothing, but one could see him grit his teeth and mouth the word 'Bitch'.

"Oh, Sid. Surely, you'd like to share it with all of us here. Tell us how Halle Ruse has been selling your watered down garbage to the public for years. And I'm sure they'd love to hear about how your legal department routinely gives the FDA the runaround by paying off the inspectors!"

Losing composure, he approached her shouting, "You're through, Vanessa! You'll be crawling back to me for a job in no time, when no one else will hire you."

Confident she'd have the last word, she wheeled around and said, "The only one of us who'll be crawling is you, when we all find out what a fraud you are."

Vanessa left Sid shouting obscenities at her, leaving her adversary in the dust as she walked away into the proverbial sunset.

Her three handmaidens finally caught up. One of them said, "Wow! You were brilliant. I can't believe he said those things to you."

Vanessa adjusted her blouse and then told them to leave her.

As she got in her waiting car, her cell phone beckoned. It was Gunther. "Vanessa, you'd better get over here right away. It's urgent."

"No, tell me now. What happened?"

Gunther's uncomfortable silence on the other end on the line was telling. 'It's the Tri-Meth vials. They're… gone."

Chapter 17

April 20th, 10:30 p.m.
Chelsea-Clinton, New York City

The paramedics arrived at the club within five minutes after the 911 call. One removed a Naloxone syringe-like container and inserted its plastic atomizer tip through one of Kate's nostrils, still ringed with powdery residue. Weak, Kate started breathing. More doses would be required to maintain a steady rhythm until they reached the hospital to access the damage to her brain and respiratory system. Danny knew that although she'd just earned a reprieve, the paramedics still had to find the correct dosage. Too little would mean repeated doses; too much could mean violent withdrawal-like side effects.

Danny rode along with her in the ambulance headed to Roosevelt Hospital while Monique and Shannon trailed behind, briefing Joanne on the evening's events. A light rain fell as the ambulance rolled up Tenth Avenue. Inside Danny brooded, wanting to help but powerless to do anything. Joanne had given him the syringe to encourage Kate's penchant for drug seeking activity. The pure form was supposed to be just enough to impress Kate, but that plan went terribly wrong when she added cocaine to the equation.

One paramedic motioned Danny to remain seated as they continued to monitor her vital signs. As the ambulance pulled up to the emergency room entrance an excruciating seven minutes later, Kate's breathing stopped, causing one paramedic to administer another burst of Naproxen. Amidst a flurry of voices, they wheeled the stretcher out onto the ground. Danny saw Kate's torso convulse upward, back arched, body held in place only by the straps tightened around her chest. Her body suddenly went limp. She expelled a sickening wheeze. The heart monitor's *blip-blip* pulse turned into a long, high-pitched drone.

"Code!" shouted the ER doctor on the receiving team. He and a nurse at his side accompanied Kate and the paramedics through the double doors.

Danny was told to stay in the waiting area, which was almost filled to capacity and the cries of infants. Having taken a seat, he opened his wallet and stared at Kelly's photo, looking for answers.

After she died, he withdrew and was no longer viewed as a reliable government agent, being a no-show at briefings on a consistent basis while wallowing in despair. The investigation into the tragedy resulted in an inconclusive report. It all happened in a distant Afghan mountain village during the dark of night, a 50-pound bomb dropped from an F-16 fighter jet, killing most of her platoon, having mistaken them for hostiles. The rumor was that the friendly fire was caused by the ineptitude or corruption of a private mercenary contractor, yet no one was implicated, let alone court marshaled. His relationship with the CIA severed, unresolved grief led to a depression and pain killer dependency, then heroin addiction. He could thank a former Delta force buddy for that. He was too ashamed to admit to the habit and retreated inward. Only through the generosity of an anonymous source was he able to join a rehab program in the Smoky Mountain foothills of North Carolina—near his original home. Last he'd heard, his mother still lived in a trailer park. He never knew his father, who—he'd been told—perished in a training accident while serving in the army.

The tap on Danny's shoulder returned him back to the present. He flinched and quickly shut his wallet.

"Come," the familiar voice beckoned. Joanne led Danny to a hallway leading to a mezzanine overlooking the front entrance of the hospital. "How is she doing?" she asked, more, he thought, out of concern for the operation than for Kate. "Did they say anything about her condition?"

"Nothing yet. She crashed when they brought her in."

"What happened? The dosage shouldn't have been strong enough to do this."

"She was speed-balling and I missed it. She stopped breathing at the club."

He knew Kate needed counseling, but this assignment counted on furthering her addiction. "I'm okay. She's a mark," he said with stolid resolve meant more to placate Joanne. "But how long do I need to…?" he started, but his voice sounded like he'd just swallowed a toad.

"We just confirmed the time frame. We monitored Vanessa Carrie and her investment banker having lunch the other day. Put it on your calendar—May 4th at midnight."

She drew closer, her voice even and soft. "Once this is over, we'll do everything we can to get her what she needs. But now, I need you focused and committed."

"*If* she pulls through, you mean," he said with a sullen breath, burying his face again under both hands.

When Danny finally looked up, she was gone.

He sat in the waiting area for another hour. A nurse eventually came to find him, calling out, "Eric Stone." Danny stood up and approached her. "Are you Eric Stone, the one who came in with Ms. Carrie?"

He nodded and followed her inside.

The emergency room hallway was lined with closed curtains and murmured with the drone of beeping machines. They stopped just outside of Kate's room, the doctor speaking low.

"She had a close call. We had to resuscitate her and put her on a ventilator for a while until she could breathe on her own again." The doctor stopped to read the expression on Danny's face, gauging his reaction, but found none. He continued. "She had traces of cocaine and opiates in her system. That's like playing Russian Roulette while diving off a diving board into an empty swimming pool.

"She's as strong a patient as I have ever seen, but I have to warn you that her apparent addiction to heroin is causing rapid deterioration of her bodily functions. Even if she were to stop now, she'll most likely develop severe liver damage at a very young age. If you like, I can direct you to places that will help her."

"No, Doctor, that won't be necessary. We'll handle this in our own way."

They reached the examination room. "You are free to see her now if you like, but she's still very groggy," the resident said, as he drew open the light green curtain.

When Danny pushed it aside, he saw Kate lying there with her head slightly raised. She was conscious but slow to react.

"Can you hear me?"

With eyes shut, she said, "I'm so stupid. I should have listened to you."

"Get some rest, Kate," Danny murmured.

After another minute, she opened her eyes and found his. "I'm so glad you were there with me. I guess I owe you a big 'thank you'."

He knew that it was a lie, hoping his expression wouldn't indicate his suffocating guilt. "I need the high all the time. It's better than the shit life I'm leading now." Kate's dreary voice was outdone only by her ashen face.

"Don't say that."

"But it's true."

Incredibly, her fear of death at the hands of the drug still lost out to the desire to continue the habit. He couldn't fathom that someone as brilliant as Kate could be so self-destructive. Maybe her brilliance was a burden, even a curse.

He saw her eyelids grow heavier.

"You'll get out of here. But now, stay right here until you get your strength back."

Kate didn't hear him because she'd already drifted off to sleep.

This woman can be saved. She must be saved, Danny thought.

He pondered whether she served as just a 'project' for him. He found himself identifying with her plight, seeing his reflection in her. Then he became so disgusted, his stomach churned.

This is so wrong.

Thinking about her only raised more questions. He'd been in faux-relationships with other women on several assignments without all this angst, solely to secure vital information, so why would this assignment feel any different. He'd rationalized his motives by convincing himself none of them were really hurt, but thought about how he would have had any clue as to what they felt. A flash of memory placed itself front and center, the one assignment that stuck in his craw from long ago, before Kelly had departed. The one he'd rather forget. The one where an innocent subject paid for her attraction to him with her life.

Returning to the present, Danny leaned forward and kissed Kate on the forehead. *Rest now. You'll need everything you've got to get through this.*

Chapter 18

April 20, 10:45 p.m.
Midtown, New York City

Vanessa found herself in the basement level security room viewing the console monitor. The room contained no fewer than twenty separate monitors, each connected to various cameras stationed throughout every floor of the company.

Gunther pointed to the monitor only used to review prior surveillance tapes. "This occurred at 2:30 p.m. two days ago. Take a look."

It showed Kate walking out of the lab, slamming the door behind her carrying her purse, trying to cover something inside it.

Vanessa recognized it instantly as the case that held the Tri-Meth containers. "My God. She took them all," Vanessa shouted, banging both fists on the console. "You just let her walk right out of here with it in broad daylight." She turned to Gunther, eyes full of searing anger. "And I hold *you* fully responsible for this!"

He acknowledged to himself that this was an inexcusable professional failure. Up until now, his record protecting clandestine information had been perfect. Vanessa brought him on because his skill set dovetailed well with the cosmetic industry, where perfume formulas were kept top secret from competitors. His British military and MI-6 surveillance expertise proved valuable to Vanessa. She also delegated all the dirty work for her with aplomb, never shying away from employing blatant harassment and bullying tactics for problem employees.

Knowing he had to repair the damage to save his job, he offered Vanessa a silver lining. "We still have the test vial."

"Not good enough! The bidders want to see all of them. That's what they are buying"

"Not to worry, I'll retrieve all of them from her and get that formula out of that pretty little head of hers, too."

Vanessa wrung her hands and scowled. "It's whenever someone tells me not to worry that I start to worry."

Gunther let her comment sink in for a moment, then pressed on with new information in an attempt to deflect her anger. "There is something else you need to know that I just discovered through my surveillance."

"What?"

"Another agent has approached her and is fishing for what she knows. They met at her gym. A personal trainer."

"After what I said to her the other day? God, it never stops."

"Is this another one we have to worry about?"

"I believe so. Yes."

"How can you be so sure?

"Because I know him."

Vanessa's jaw froze as she wanted to hear more. Gunther obliged with a tale of his own.

He explained to her it had been in Geneva, twelve years ago. An operation gone wrong. Gunther was the seasoned professional MI-6 operations leader, Danny the CIA upstart. Both had a Special Forces commonality that just didn't seem to mesh with the intelligence operation. As he told it, Danny had been accused of murdering a young woman and had to flee. Danny and Gunther had never seen each other again. That was when Gunther 'retired' from MI-6 for greener pastures as the CEO of his Private Military Corporation, entering into contracts in Iraq and Afghanistan.

Gunther concluded, "I'd heard they'd discharged him when his drug addiction was disclosed a number of years ago. Apparently, he'd been reactivated."

"Whoever he is, I want him out of her life."

"That can be arranged."

"Good, because I have *nothing* more to say to that little shit!"

Gunther nimbly stepped forward and offered his counsel. "I know we are pressed for time, but I would advise that we wait a few more days before I turn the screws on either one of them. If we let them think we're not on to them, they'll lead us right to where the Tri-Meth is located. In the meantime, I'd let them feel comfortable."

"Oh, yes. You'll pay her a visit alright. Do you think you could handle *that?"*

"I look forward to it."

Chapter 19

April 20th, 11:30 p.m.
Elizabeth, New Jersey

Under the shadow of the Goethals Bridge, behind a gentleman's club and liquor store, stood a modest sized warehouse. From all appearances, it was abandoned. It had been a textile factory at one time. Corrugated metal surrounded the property, with a rusted gate the only way in or out. The building itself was made of darkened gray cinderblock with a flat, dilapidated tar rooftop.

The entryway was a stripped-down room that was once an office. Behind the inner door was a long, darkened corridor, illuminated overhead with Klieg lights. It did nothing to improve the ambience of the place, which reeked of mold and damp. The corridor had several doors. The one at the end led to the abandoned factory, to the right was a separate office and a small restroom. To the left were two more doors. One led to an old office, the other was the one Sabir would enter.

"In there," Jaffa said with a glance.

"I see they've been true to their word," Sabir said. Wasting no time, he pushed open the door, startling its occupant.

The man, wearing nothing except for his underwear, was hung by his arms behind his head, his legs tied together as a rope, looped over a pipe was tied to an iron rod, just long enough so his toes separated from the dusty floor. This was known as a Palestinian Hanging, but its history went back to the early Renaissance. Left alone a few hours more and his arms would be slowly wrenched from the shoulder sockets, causing his body to fall forward, making breathing excruciatingly painful. The Americans tortured Mandel al-Jamdi in this way too, before he died in captivity. Sabir's expertise was using torture techniques. As a young man, he was recruited by PLO functionaries, but soon joined the PFLP, which went its separate way when Arafat shook hands with Rabin. He received his training in Lebanon and Syria, the heart of PFLP's political leadership, where he learned the rudiments of both physical and psychological torture methods.

Sabir had long been a 'cat' lover. The prisoner's back had several marks, grouped in red parallel blotches of nine. The result of Jaffa having used a nine-pronged whip, the infamous cat o'nine tails. The ends of each prong had tiny metal balls with spikes on them, another torture device, this one going back to the ancient Egyptians.

When Sabir caught the prisoner's eye, the man shuddered in horror and tried to look away. Covered with sweat, he broke his silence with a plea for his life.

"Sabir. I beg you! I have done nothing wrong!" he screamed in Arabic.

Sabir knew better.

Rahfeek was far from innocent. His darkened skin was covered in perspiration that dripped from his forehead and three-day old beard. He appeared remarkably young with no gray evident in his hair even after all this time. It took nearly twenty years but Sabir's men had finally tracked Rahfeek down, thanks to some new American 'friends'. This was personal. An old score would finally be settled.

"You were never my friend," Sabir intoned.

They had grown up together and attended the same high school where Sidayim taught. But Sabir had come to learn that it was Rahfeek who betrayed Sidayim as an informant for the Israelis. They had paid him well for the trouble—sanctuary and passage to America, free to abandon his Palestinian roots and resettling there, under an assumed name with the help of the Americans.

"What do you want, Sabir? I'll do anything!" Rahfeek said, his voice several octaves higher than it usually was.

"You will die. It is Allah's will. But before that, you will confess what you did here and now. Do not expect mercy."

"No! No! *Alahu Akbar! Alahu Akbar*!" Rahfeek shouted.

Stepping closer, Sabir unsheathed a small knife from his belt. "Allah will never embrace you."

Convulsing in panic, Rahfeek screamed, "Wait! Wait! I have money! I have lots of money!"

"It is time," was all Sabir had to say. Rahfeek's eyes bulged. The knife shimmered in the light as it sliced through Rahfeek's left ear.

Blood flowed from the wound to his shoulder and down his chest, yet Rahfeek did not appear to register pain. Rahfeek forced a grin, willing himself to regain a modicum of self-control, relieved that he was still breathing the sweet smell of life. "I did nothing," he said.

"Liar!" Sabir's voice cut through the rancid air. Then he spoke, softly. "Now."

Hearing no response, Sabir moved in closer, resting the point of the knife just below Rahfeek's Adam's Apple.

In tears, Rahfeek fought to justify his sin, "Sidayim was to betray us! To betray you!"

"No. The Jews made you one of them and you broke my heart because of it." Sabir stood face to face with Rahfeek. Close enough to smell the stink of the captive's breath.

"You are not our true savior, Sabir!"

Satisfied, Sabir whispered, "Allah awaits," as his knife pierced Rahfeek's skin, finding the windpipe. Blood seeped out from the puncture. Air wheezed free and a sick gurgling sound followed. Drowning in his own blood, Rahfeek's pleas for mercy were reduced to a pathetic series of wet gasps.

One minute later, Rahfeek's corpse was left hanging, motionless. Sabir relished the sight, finally getting vengeance that was long overdue.

He walked out of the room, as if he'd just finished his spring cleaning. "It is done," he said to Jaffa. "Did you purchase the items we will need?

"Yes. They're in the back, under the tarp. We loaded them on while you were inside."

As they stepped outside, Jaffa asked, "So when will the time be right?"

"Patience my friend. Patience. Our friends need more time before we are needed."

They reached the van. Sabir opened the door and inspected several items: an iron, a car battery, a grappling hook with chain, a crank with pulleys, handcuffs and some oversized pliers. He nodded his approval. "With their list and these items, we will soon have our answer."

Jaffa closed the door and started the engine. "This girl. She has no idea the hell she is to endure, does she?"

"No matter. It will go quickly."

Chapter 20

April 21st, 11:30 a.m.
The Upper West Side, New York City

The resident released Kate from the hospital the following day after having advised her of the drug rehab programs available. As the cab rolled to a halt in front of her apartment, she leaned over and pecked Danny on the cheek.

"Wait," he said. "I'll walk you inside."

Though her reflex was to reject his offer, she relented.

He guided her up the stoop to her apartment with a gentle touch to the small of her back. "Just hang out today and get some rest." She shuddered as she guided his hand away. "I'll give you a call this afternoon."

Pushing him away was the safe option for her. "You don't have to. I'll be fine." She unlocked the front door and stepped inside.

When she entered the apartment, she turned on the TV for her next *Castle* fix. She'd seen them all before. Many times, in fact, but never grew tired of them. She even mouthed the lines along with the characters on occasion.

Three and a half episodes later, she fell into a dreamless sleep. Deep-rooted memories resurfaced this time. When she opened her eyes, Kate was no longer in her apartment, but rather lying in her first foster parents' home, on a toddler bed and five years old again. The gray stucco ceiling looked down on her with a dim overhead light, eclipsed only by the off white walls of peeling paint. A lone window was half covered with a shade, the few sun rays peering through not reaching her.

Wearing a filthy nightgown, Kate couldn't evade the odor of old vomit and urine. She realized that her mother, Felicia, had left her completely alone in the pre-war ranch house in Pawtucket, Rhode Island. She ran into the living room to the front door, opened it and cried out, "Mommy! Mommy!" but no one answered. Felicia and her boyfriend, Ted, had gone out to score drugs this morning. Like so many others.

Kate passed the time alone spinning the spokes of a bicycle left in the kitchen by the back door leading to the garage, where she tiptoed around shards of glass from a broken spaghetti sauce jar. The toddler Kate screamed, tears rolling down both cheeks as she hobbled out to the living room sofa, where she sat down to dig a piece of glass from her bleeding foot. Crimson spots followed behind her on the tan, low-grade wool carpet. She wept in silence, biting her lip, and squinted her eyes shut until the tears stopped falling.

Looking out of the window, Kate saw her mother standing on the sidewalk in front of the home in pink fuzzy slippers, helping Ted inject something into his arm.

They entered laughing, ignoring Kate, until she yelled, “Mommy, I’m hungry!” She hadn’t eaten in two days.

“Shut up!” her mother hissed. “Don’t bother me today, okay? Go play.” Felicia's disheveled, shoulder-length hair bobbed around her weathered face indicative of her drug use. Her raspy voice was typical of chain smokers.

When a shard of guilt overcame her, Felicia tossed Kate a bag of Gummy Bears. The appreciative little girl, in an attempt to show some gratitude, tried to cuddle up alongside her saying, “I love you Mommy,” extending her tiny hand that was summarily swatted away.

“I don’t want to hold your hand!” Felicia snapped. “Leave me the fuck alone!”

The lone bathroom in the house was littered with empty syringes overflowing from a waste paper basket. Two Colt 45 malt liquor cans lay discarded and empty on the floor. A row of Kate’s underpants were hanging over the shower rod. The toilet was filthy and unflushed from its last usage. The bath tub was coated with green mold, flies and dank water. Each time Felicia gave her a bath, which could be weeks apart, she had to bribe her with new underwear.

The interesting days were when Felicia used her as a prop to beg for money at local gas stations and convenience stores. When most kindergartners were home sleeping, Felicia exploited Kate's charms; with her tiny pink plastic folding chair, wearing a cute frilly sun dress, sitting near the pumps so that drivers could see her, little Kate got plenty of attention. Each time a car stopped at the pumps, Felicia offered to pump gas for chump change. After the driver left, Kate would always ask, “Did he say yes, Mommy?” To keep her occupied, Felicia would buy her Chips Ahoy cookie packs.

Kate lived in a world devoid of lasting affection and meaningful friendship. She became her own best playmate.

Her first attempt to run away from home happened at age six when Ted punched her in the face. It was the first time Kate would wind up in a juvenile halfway house, one of several she would encounter in her childhood. And this was just the first of five foster homes until Vanessa found her.

When Kate awoke back in her apartment, she helped herself to another hit and then stripped down to a tank top and pajama shorts. She lay flat on her bed, staring up at the ceiling.

Then without warning, *they* came.

Orange speckled lights skittered across her bedroom ceiling. She scoured the apartment, looking for an answer. Her tortured bi-polar mind told her to look for something that would stop the streaming lights. She didn’t know what it was she was looking for, but anything to stop *them* would do.

Kate grabbed any objects that weren’t tied down and hurled them to the floor. The kitchen came first, as she opened drawers and cabinets, emptying the contents, plates and glassware shattering on the floor. She picked up the largest kitchen knife she saw and ran into the living room, leaving blood stained footprints wherever she stepped, then ripped open all the sofa and chair cushions in the living room. She made deep knife cuts in her mattress and bed pillows, hacking in random directions as down feathers floated aimlessly across the room like windblown snow.

Kate dropped to the floor and huddled in a corner of her bedroom, quivering with inexplicable fear. She remained there for what to her seemed like hours. Her iPhone chirped several times. Not knowing or caring who it could be, she refused to answer it.

Again, perceived hours later, the apartment buzzer sounded off several times. Sufficiently self-aware that her mania had ceased, she picked herself off the carpet to answer the summons. Her wounds had clotted, but burned with each step.

"Who is it?" she said, speaking to the intercom and catching scent of her own rancid breath.

"Kate, it's Eric. Is everything okay?" the voice asked. "I tried calling you several times tonight."

Relieved to hear his voice, she buzzed him in. When Kate heard him knock, she brushed back her disheveled hair to no effect. As soon as she saw him in the doorway, she resisted the temptation to collapse onto his shoulders. Before she could catch his gaze, he was scanning the carnage behind her.

"My God, what happened? The place looks like the aftermath of a frat house party that's been burglarized." Books were scattered pell-mell on the wooden floor, furniture overturned or askew, cushions destroyed, glass shattered.

"I saw some bright lights and had to… make them stop," she said, knowing it sounded ridiculous.

He offered to help her clean up. "No!" she said before he could start. "Don't touch anything. I don't want the lights to come back!"

"What lights, Kate?" he asked, placing his hands on each of her shoulders.

A tidal wave of paranoia flooded her mind as she backed away from him. "Stay away from me, asshole!" She ran into her bedroom, emerging with the kitchen knife gripped in both hands, charging straight toward him.

Kate would have stabbed him right in the stomach if he hadn't evaded to his right with a swivel of his hips. Kate lost her balance and dropped the knife, but the blade caught him, the tip slicing through his shirt just below his right shoulder. Blood trickled through the ripped sleeve, but he was able to duck under her next swing and tackle her to the ground, slamming her wrist into the floor. The knife bounced free from her grasp. He grabbed it and flung it across the room.

She flailed her arms out and threw weak haymaker punches at his sides that didn't register at all, while pleading with him through tears. "No! No! I'm sorry! Please!"

With Danny straddling her, the tide ebbed.

"It's okay, I'm here," Danny said in a calm but measured voice. "There's nothing to be afraid of."

When she calmed down, Danny released his grip and helped her up. This time she didn't resist. He pulled off his shirt and grabbed a bathroom rag to stop his bleeding and helped her remove glass shards from her feet before bandaging them up. There were no uncut chairs except in the kitchen, seeing the floor littered with broken glass and porcelain. He brought two kitchen chairs out to the living room.

He sat himself in the chair across the table from her. Both of them had to catch their collective breaths.

"Help me to understand. What did you see?" he asked.

"I saw… lights. Orangey-yellow ones. They tell me what I have to do," Kate said, waving her arms in opposite directions.

"How often do you see them?"

"I mostly dream about them. Except sometimes they come when I'm watching TV."

"Listen, I think we should get out for a while. What'd you think? Get some fresh air or something and maybe some dinner. Think you're up for it?"

She was receptive as her breaths evened out. "Yeah, I guess that'd be good, but I have to change first." She couldn't understand why he was still here, why he hadn't run away from her.

She dressed in Navy blue cropped pants, a sweatshirt and flats. On the way out of the bedroom, she grabbed several vials of heroin, syringes and bags of cocaine, and stuffed them in her purse, thinking that he couldn't possibly know when she would need to shoot up again. When she came out, she saw that he was still shirtless, his rippling muscles in full view. She also noticed quite a few scars and tattoos covering his back and shoulders.

Kate said, "Hang on, I've got something for you." She shuffled back in for but a moment and when she came out, she threw him a winter green-colored sweatshirt. It had been Jared's or some other guy's. She couldn't recall, exactly. Although a tight fit, Danny would have to suffer through it or go without.

They left the apartment and made their way eastward toward Riverside Park. *The Boat Basin* restaurant seemed as good a place as any to take in the urban scenery.

"How's your arm?" she asked as they walked side by side.

"I'm fine," he responded. "So, how much do you remember doing what you did back there?"

"I don't know," Kate said. "It seems like they come and go, days, weeks, even months at a time, and come back when I least expect it."

"You really scared the heck out of me," Danny confessed.

"I know, I'm sorry. I didn't mean to hurt you."

"It just occurred to me that hanging out with you is a hazardous activity."

She couldn't help but giggle inside at the jibe because she thought he could not have been more dead-on. *Toxic activities happen to be my specialty.*

The Boat Basin Café was an open air restaurant, operating under a traffic circle that guided cars off of the southbound West Side Highway at 79th Street.

After Kate and Danny were seated, the initial discomfort of a first date set in. The wind from the Hudson River brought a slight chill to the air as dusk settled across the New Jersey sky, a pink arch imprinting itself on the heavens. Every square inch of the restaurant was stone masonry, causing the echoes of passing cars above them to reverberate off the walls.

Their waitress stopped by to take drink orders. Danny ordered a Pepsi; Kate, a shimmering glass of Prosecco. She broke the silence first by asking about his job. As she predicted, like most guys, he started talking about himself. "I've been doing personal training here for about three years, but I just started at your gym last week."

When the waitress returned, Danny ordered the Chicken Parmesan. Kate had zero appetite, which was common these days. Nevertheless, she ordered a goat cheese salad.

"So how long have you been in the City?" Danny asked.

"Since I was eleven." Kate saw his eyes widen with astonishment. She did not elaborate. You?" She had no interest being in the spotlight and took a healthy swig of her Prosecco.

"Two years now. Came from North Carolina."

"What did you do before?

"Typical army brat. My Dad was a staff sergeant. We traveled around Germany, Japan, San Diego, Fort Benning, Fort Hood, Fort Myer and ended up in Fort Bragg."

Ah, the tattoos, she realized. "Fort Myer. That's in Florida, right?" she asked.

"That's in Virginia. Sorry." Danny tried to wrest control of the conversation before she could probe more. "So, what does a chemist do all day?"

"Experiments." She recalled that her present, now like her past, was also something she abhorred, but managed to eke out answers in such a way as to be flat and expressionless.

Thankfully, Danny took the hint and continued to talk about himself while Kate drank. "Well, you saw that I work with people all day long who are in serious need of physical activity. And when I don't, I work out. Now I'm just a gym rat."

"And sell drugs," Kate pointed out.

"Hey, you could handle it, too."

He could see this ticked her off. "I wish people would stop telling me that."

Danny gave it a rest for a minute while Kate imbibed more of her drink. Her mouth formed a brooding frown. "I think I really hate people, sometimes."

"That's pretty final."

"Okay, so maybe hate is too strong a word. How about, 'I just seem to feel a whole hell of a lot better when they're not around'."

After a quiet moment, Danny posed a question. "Was it always like that for you?"

"Yeah. Kinda. I was adopted. Few friends. Those I had drifted away when I—." Kate expelled an unceremonious burp. "If it were me locked in a lab all day, I think I'd go crazy."

"I've always felt at home there. I guess I'm just your typical anti-claustrophobic." She started slurring her words. "Call it Zhen. Call it anti-claustrophobic. It tuned out whatever shit was going on in my life at the time. Even when I was a kid, I was into it. My adopted mom even set up a lab in the basement of her summer home."

Another tandem chuckle followed. It dawned on her that the son-of-a-bitch got her talking about her past when she really hadn't wanted to. "Even when I was a kid, I was into it. My adopted mom even set up a lab in the basement of her summer home."

"Summer home?" he said as if a boyhood friend had just informed him his parents had bought him a trampoline.

"Yeah. Upstate. The lab was always a place I had control. I found I could control chemical reactions but not people. At least I don't know how, anyway." She slurped another sip of Prosecco.

"Hey, I'm no chemistry genius—"

"Obviously."

"But aren't we all made up of chemicals, or molecules, or atoms, or whatever?"

Interesting comment from a gym rat. "I guess," she said as she pondered the comment for a moment. "But people are more complex than that."

The stress of talking about people she wanted nothing to do with anymore triggered another episode. It manifested itself as unprovoked sarcasm. "Hey, I know what we could do," she proposed, raising her voice to that of someone in a drunken stupor, loud enough for other tables to hear. "What if all of our inhibitions would just melt away so people attracted to each other wouldn't have to go through all this preliminary bullshit? This meaningless small talk, the dating. Just let it happen, like how molecules do it. And what if someone figured out how to do it painlessly?" Then she reflected for a moment and recoiled to despair. "But there's not."

"Yeah, I guess New York is kind of like that. But there are other places where it's not. Here, in the big city, they want to us to be isolated, so they can control us better. I mean, look at all the cell phone apps. You never have to look away from the screen to talk with anyone. It's isolation through technology. Christ, they want to turn all of us into cyborgs or something."

"Just toss the iPhone, right?" She laughed nervously, thinking of the broken mirror. "Yeah, I know what you mean. I have all of the technology in front of me, but lately, I couldn't care less about it most of the time. I'm just a fucking nihilist."

The waitress brought the food to them and Kate pecked at her salad, while Danny dug in.

Even though her brain was engulfed in a murky cloud, all Kate could think of was Danny standing in her living room, shirtless and had been convinced that this guy seemed like he was genuinely concerned about her. But now, she wasn't so sure, resentment and suspicion taking hold. *Sure, he said he dealt drugs, but something was off about him. He's gotta' have a dark secret? We all have one, right? Shit. Guys like him had a knack for making smart girls dumb! All these years of women fighting for equality, and still we fall for* them*! Still, am I not allowed to have a good time?*

The waitress asked if they wanted dessert. Danny ordered the molten chocolate cake while Kate refused, ordering another Prosecco instead.

Dessert never came.

But she got her drink which was enough to send her reeling. The evening turned sour from there.

Some of her drink spilled out of the cup on her shirt as she sipped. "Shit."

"Easy on the drink, alright?" Danny said, his smile dropping to a dead-serious frown.

Within her, the reversion back to the rage was complete "Hey, I don't need you to tell me how much I can drink, smoke, snort or fuck," she hissed, loud enough so the couples sitting on adjacent tables couldn't help but hear her.

In a concerned low voice, he answered, "So, what happened at the Dance Factory didn't count? I guess you didn't need me to tell you anything then, either."

"Said by the man who sells drugs to kids." she charged. Then she turned to the couple on her right and leaned in, saying, "Hey, this gym rat thinks he can tell me what to do." Then she eyed him. "You're just like all the rest."

"Kate, that's enough," Danny said, but she steamrolled over him, speaking in full voice. "My mom's right. I don't need you to make me happy. I was fucking happy without you!"

Before the hostess could rush over, Danny threw three twenties down on the table, stood up, and tried to guide Kate out, pressing his hand against the small of her back. "It's time to go, Kate."

Earlier that day, she had welcomed his touch there, but her present state of mind told her 'no way.' "No, it's not. I need chemistry more than fucking friends like you!" She heaved the Prosecco, shattering it on the floor to the shock of the other patrons.

"Just tell me all about it outside, Kate. Let's go."

The hostess motioned to Danny for them to leave, now. "Maybe another night?" she said as polite as could be.

In an effort to save face, he said, "Sorry folks, she's very tired and needs to turn in early tonight."

Kate had had enough of his patronizing behavior. "Oh, you all suck shit! This place is shit! God is shit! Everything is all shit!" Without his help, she stormed out in a tirade, marching north along the river.

Danny followed and caught up with her. He grasped her arm gently. "You're scared. I get it, but I don't want you to let go of me."

Kate wrenched away from him.

"No, *you* let go of *me*!" she said before slapping him hard across the face and planted her shoe square into his shin that made him halt with a groan. Satisfied she inflicted maximum pain, she stormed off in a maddening fury as the hue of the night sky approached midnight blue.

Chapter 21

April 21st, 10:00 p.m.
The Upper West Side, New York City

Trailing at a safe distance, Danny followed Kate through the darkened and now silent park, the only sounds the din of traffic from the West Side Highway. She'd walked about a mile before resting at a deserted playground called the Dinosaur Park, surrounded by a wrought iron fence. She was keeping company with a swing set and the faux dinosaurs, Triceratops and Hadrosaur, standing up on its hind legs. Though officially closed after sunset, the entrance gate had been left unlocked, so she walked inside and sat on one of the benches.

He waited a good fifteen minutes before walking inside. When he approached her bench, she said, "Just leave me alone. Please."

"It's just a hand, Kate," Danny said as he reached out to her. He held his ground. He knew she was frustrated with life and people and all the baggage they carry with them. "Just give people a chance. Give me a chance."

Before his eyes, Ms. Hyde, for the second time today, transformed back to Dr. Jekyll. He sat down beside her, but looked straight ahead, avoiding eye contact.

"Those things I said… I couldn't control myself," she said, apologetically.

"Don't worry about it. You need more time."

He half expected her to tell him to go to hell, but knew she had nowhere to go after having ransacked her own apartment. He thought it prudent to take the leap. "You are welcome to crash at my place. Then we'll figure out what you should do in the morning." Treading lightly, he said, "There's a sofa."

She didn't have the strength to protest. Without a word, she accepted the offer with a slight nod. He saw her shiver as a nighttime wind kicked up from the Hudson River. She wrapped herself in her own arms, recoiling into a ball of tension.

Danny's apartment—the one Kate was supposed to see on West 71st Street and Broadway—was set up by the Agency. He thought they had gone a tad overboard. Sure, it was a nice sized loft with brand new, modern conveniences typical of a bachelor's apartment… for someone who worked on Wall Street. There was a wide screen television, a bar, Frank Sinatra's arrest photo accusing him of 'Seduction'. It even had the most up to date kitchen appliances. Worst of all, the place was too darned clean for a bachelor.

When Danny turned on the soft glow of the back lighting, Kate's blue eyes widened at the sight. She immediately challenged him. "Wow. All this on a personal trainer's salary?"

He wanted to take a match to the Berber carpet but he kept in character. "You already know what I do."

"People think I could do it too, but I'll always be a purchaser."

"When I started, it was good. It paid for my college tuition. It paid for this place and I'm not ashamed of that. But once I got hooked on my own product, I had to get out. Now I just deal on the side."

"I'd met people who put themselves through school like that," she said. "But I didn't need to do it. Mom paid for everything. Besides, how many women you know of who deal?" she asked, thinking of her last conversation with Jen.

Danny shrugged. "Good for you. For me, it got pretty dark for a while. It took everything I had to fight the addiction. I don't want to see that happen to you, either. You're brilliant and passionate about what you do." When he looked at her in the soft but direct light, the straight light, hair line, her cheekbones and fair skin reminded him of Kelly. He paused. The sudden thought that this had to be more than a reclamation project entered his mind.

"When you collapsed on that dance floor, it made me think about what I'd never had to face—that the drugs I supplied killed many of my buyers. I'd only heard about it through second- and third-hand knowledge, so it was easy to shrug it off. But you…" A warm rush swelled from his chest.

"I can handle it. Really," she said, resisting his offer.

"I think you want to stop, but can't do it on your own. No one in your life is there to support you."

"But you can't even know how hard it is for me," she said. "The things I've had to deal with in my life."

Yes, I do, Kate. There was a moment when he thought she may come clean about her project, but it passed. Her eyes glistened as he said, "It's not too late. I'm here for you and willing to help." He moved closer and spoke soft and low. "Just try to say the words, 'I… need… help. I… need… help.'"

"Please stop. I can't do this right now."

He leaned in, ever so close, when he saw her will to resist was slipping.

"I'm going through hell at work right now. You can't even imagine," she said, trying to hold onto the defiance within her.

Danny leaned in just a little more. "Believe in yourself. Whatever it is, there's a way out. You don't have to be afraid anymore, Kate." His own inhibitions started to evaporate.

"I'm not," she answered, her eyes saying otherwise. She tried to look away. "No. Please. I'm not for you. I'm damaged. Can't you see that?"

"The words," Danny repeated in a whisper.

Kate shut her eyes and nodded repeatedly. He felt the barrier between crumble. She said, "I need help! Oh God, I need help! Please help me, Eric." Tears crawled down her cheeks.

"You deserve to be loved and you are capable of loving." His face was inches away from hers.

"But, I… d-don't… know h-how to d-do that!" She started to hyperventilate.

"I think you do," he whispered. He raised both his hands up to her face, gently removing her glasses as if he thought her body would break apart at the slightest touch. "You don't need to hide anymore." Her warm tears dampened his fingertips as they caressed her left cheek. He brought his lips a hair's breadth from hers.

She whispered, "I didn't want to feel… but I do." The connection was now complete. "Oh God," she moaned.

Their lips connected, two warm souls joining as he wrapped his arms around her waist and lifted her against him. His hard length pressed against her, as his body weight pinned her against the wall. His hands stroked her hair as they kissed. Her chignon unraveled, along with any last trace of inhibitions. He knew at that instant he was hooked.

He carried her to the bedroom and drove her onto the bed. He undid the button on her slacks and pulled them down with her panties so he could stroke her thighs. Then he leaned forward to bury his mouth in forbidden territory. Her undulating moans became short staccato howls, her arms reaching up and around, digging her nails into his shoulders.

He reached behind her, unhooking her bra with his left hand as the fingers of his right hand made back and forth movements over her left nipple. She slid her own hands down his body and let him enter her. All too quickly her inner pulsations overtook him. *This was not supposed to happen.*

Danny's heart pounded with a sensation of floating in space. There was no up, no down; no right, no left. Finally he understood why he was drawn to Kate. *I don't want to hurt her. I want to save her,* he marveled, his body continuing to rock in and out of her. Without warning, he reached climax. Kate moaned in crisp, repeated bursts, holding him tighter as she quivered in his arms. They were chest to chest, laughing.

As she lay on top of him, he kissed the back of her neck. She purred, then drifted off to sleep. He lay there, caressing her body, wanting to fall asleep yet hypnotized by her comforting warmth. He found his thoughts swirling in haphazard directions. The groundswell of passion had bubbled over within him, but there would be a cost. *No, just stick to the plan. Focus on what you have to do,* he told himself. He'd done this all before, when it had been part of his job.

But she is…

Rolling onto his back, Danny stared at the recessed light fixture. He knew the choice he just made would make his job that much harder, if not impossible.

Chapter 22

April 28th, 2:00 p.m.
Central Park, New York City

A week had passed since the connection. They spent every moment since then together. Danny helped her bring some of her spring and summer clothes over to his apartment. His walk-in closet was even larger that hers, but she never questioned the fact that it was sparsely filled. Kate picked outfits that had hung in her closet for months, but that she hadn't bothered trying on, tags still hanging on them. She still wore long sleeved shirts and blouses.

They relished the honeymoon mode they were in; Danny took Kate out every night and led her on nice walks in the City, especially in Central Park. As they strolled, he recalled that when he wasn't with someone, every couple he saw held hands. Now that he was with her, no one else seemed to be holding hands.

They walked past Belvedere Castle, through the Ramble, along the path above the location of the buried vials. They came upon a clearing, shielded by dogwood trees and other foliage. She turned and hugged him, head cuddled against his chest. She looked up, beaming into his eyes, as if to say, 'I'm yours'. He fell backward onto the ground and took her with him, rolling around and laughing in the dirt.

"I want to be with you, Eric," she murmured. "I don't think I'll ever want to sleep again if it means missing time with you."

"Wow," he said, shaking his head. "You know, they say that you know you're in love when reality is better than your dreams."

"I don't give a shit what they say. I just want to freeze this moment."

Danny rolled her over, lowering her to the ground, kissing her neck. Left alone for a minute longer, they would have delved into some more tender pleasures of the flesh, but they were rudely interrupted by an elderly couple who also strayed from the path. The two lovebirds sprung up, but not before the couple had seen their activity.

"Don't mind us," the woman said, charmed by her discovery.

Danny's sheepish grin acknowledged the newcomers. He apologized, then led Kate away back onto the path.

He would have suggested they head out for some lunch, when he felt the buzz from his cell phone indicating a text. "Oh, shit," he said after reading the encrypted text message.

"What is it? What's wrong?"

"Nothing, I have to head back to the gym. I had scheduled a work out session with a client that I totally forgot about."

When they reached Broadway, they split up, Kate heading south to Danny's apartment, he heading north, but not to the gym. On the way, Danny glanced at the text again. It was from Joanne, directing him to meet her on the rooftop of 335 West 81st Street. When he got there, he took the elevator to the top floor, then the stairwell up to the rooftop.

When he opened the bulkhead door and stepped outside, he saw Joanne. She was turned away, looking out over the parapet westward, past the Hudson River at New Jersey. He walked up to her, avoiding eye contact as they continued to enjoy the view.

Joanne spoke first. "You reviewed what I'd sent you?"

"Yeah," he replied.

"The next phase won't involve you. But I may need you for Phase III, should it come to that.

"Won't I be read in on that?"

"When the time comes," she said as if he'd just pried into her own sexual proclivities.

He shook his head with a disapproving throat clearing.

Joanne turned to face him. "You have a problem with that, Danny?"

He was about to rail about how this mission was screwing Kate up. Joanne's apathy toward Kate's wellbeing had stuck in his craw since the hospital. No one cared that what heroin, the CIA, and Vanessa were doing to Kate would destroy her.

"No," he said but the lump in his throat made the single word excruciating to say.

"I didn't think so."

"But," he said, posing a philosophical position, "just for the sake of argument, say that she really needed help overcoming her problem."

"We've already been over this," Joanne answered. "Once we have the information from her and put a stop to the auction, then we'll talk about helping her. But right now, we need to exploit her weaknesses. This is a national security issue, Danny."

His backbone stiffened and he turned to view Joanne's profile. "You don't have to tell me that the Agency doesn't always take care of it assets." He knew it was common knowledge that agents routinely exploited a person's weaknesses to convince them to spy for Uncle Sam, then tossed them aside when their information was no longer needed or valued.

She turned toward him and glared. "Oh, please don't tell me you're in love with her."

He returned his gaze to New Jersey.

"You are, aren't you," she said, pointing an accusatory finger at him. "This is no different from any other operation you've ever worked on. I seem to recall you didn't seem to have any problem walking away from *those* women." She tapped his shoulder indicating that she wanted his full attention. He turned to face her again. "I just want you to be prepared for the fact that she may be too far gone to help. Her profile…"

He'd wished he could reach down Joanne's throat and rip out her tongue as their professional exchange grew clipped. “Drop it,” he growled. He wanted to tell Joanne that *this* mark was different from all the others, that Kate didn't deserve any of this.

Joanne put her left hand on his shoulder and said, “Let me remind you of a few things, in case your love lust has clouded your vision. For starters, she made her deal with the devil the day she created the Tri-Meth. Second, you knew from the get-go she was unpredictable.” She paused to gauge Danny's reaction, then removed her hand from his shoulder. “For Christ's sake Danny, she almost killed you with a kitchen knife! How do you know she won't wake up one night and slice your throat wide open while you sleep?”

“I haven't seen anything since then that tells me she's a murderer. Vanessa Carrie had to have set her up. It makes perfect sense.”

“No?” Joanne's eyebrows peaked. “We have surveillance photos of her handing the neurotoxin laced package to the informant. Vanessa Carrie didn't help her make the Tri-Meth. Your pure, sweet, innocent, Ph.D. victim did that all on her own.”

“I'm in control here. Katelyn Carrie has the psychological constitution of a paper bag.”

“Good, which is why it'll be that much easier to get it from her in the next phase.”

Danny was through with her. He turned and walked away to the bulkhead exit without a word.

Reaching the handle on the metal door, he heard Joanne call out to him. “Oh, and Danny, just remember to wear your protection when you get the word, okay?”

Stopped dead in his tracks, he didn't dare turn around, blood now boiling. “So, when is this supposed to happen?”

“Sooner than you think.”

Kate returned to Danny's apartment. After unlocking and opening the front door, she saw her purse upended on the floor, empty, with its contents spread out over the living room carpet. She walked over and was about to bend over to gather the items, but as she did, she heard footsteps from behind and a thin wire flash down over her face and bit into her neck, jerking her back into the person's warm shoulder, cheek against her ear.

Gunther had her in a death grip with his Garrote wire. “Hello, Katelyn,” his warm breath blowing on her left ear in a soothing voice. “Do you know why I fancy death by strangulation so much?”

She tried to grab the wire in futility, it being too taut to grab. Incomprehensible gurgling came out of her throat instead of screams for help which she would have preferred.

“It's because it is so satisfying to be able to look your victim in the eye and experience the true terror there as they think their last thoughts.” Her legs and feet dangled as she writhed. Gunther pulled her head back farther, having her look up at the ceiling. “And so long as a man has a firm grip on the victim's neck, the blood flow through the carotid arteries to the brain stops, death is guaranteed in less than thirty seconds. And then… *Snap*!”

Just as her world turned to black, Gunther released the wire and threw her to the floor. Her hands grabbed at her neck while her lungs filled with sweet air, still in too much shock to scream or cry. All she could do was look up at his towering presence.

"I see that you've been enjoying yourself these past few days," Gunther said with an unsettling drollness.

Coughing and gasping for air, Kate rubbed her throat where a thin red line had formed. She croaked, "What do you want?"

"I have to say I am disappointed. For a so-called genius, you really are very, very stupid," he said, shaking his head like a schoolmaster proud of insulting his student.

Kate struggled to regain her composure and stiffened, fighting back tears. "Fucking asshole!" she spit out. "Get out of here!"

"Oh, I'd like nothing better that to kill you where you lie," Gunther sneered, "but your employer, *our* employer, would like you very much alive. So don't try to insult my intelligence."

"They're hidden. From you. From everybody," she said, wishing her words could kill him where he stood.

"I know. As for your precious compound, we searched your flat before you destroyed it and found nothing. Even on your laptop."

"Fuck you! You had no right to enter my apartment."

"Oh, *your* apartment is it?" he responded. "Really? You mean the one Vanessa *bought* for you?"

He wasn't wrong; she broke eye contact. It was time to state her claim. "It's *my* creation. In my own head and you can't have it," she said, pounding her fist against her chest. "Now get out!"

"Don't be an idiot," Gunther said. "Fine, I'll be on my way, but know this. Your new friend, Eric, he didn't even exist before last week. He's a CIA agent sent to get the toxin from you, just like your beloved Jared before him. My, you do seem to attract them like flies, don't you?" he said with sing-song detachment.

"What makes you think I'd just give it to him or anyone else?"

"Because you're weak," he growled. "Because you're just another pathetic junkie who's living for her next high. The CIA doesn't bollocks around. Others will come looking for you. Some may wish to silence you permanently after they have it. I loathe you but Vanessa doesn't want you hurt in anyway."

"Until I give it up," she blurted out like a spiteful teen, coughing up more sputum.

"The CIA knows how to get information from anyone, whether you give it to them willingly or not." Opening the door to leave, he turned back. "Just remember, Katelyn. I'll be watching."

Once the door slammed shut, the rush of terror charged through her. She pounded her fist on the floor like a spoiled child, whimpering. The lingering disorientation from Gunther's chokehold stung.

Too frightened to stand, she crawled across the floor into the bathroom, climbed into the bathtub, and turned on the shower fully clothed. She wanted to wash away the misery that had enshrouded her life, wash away the anguish, wash away the despair, wash away the guilt she felt for having not fought back. As the steady stream of warm droplets pelted her, Kate pulled her shins tight and buried her face between her knees. She stomped her feet against the tiles, continuing her childish tantrum by splashing water everywhere. A keening wail of anguish ripped from her raw throat under the warm spray of the glistening showerhead, the moist white steam enveloping her.

Chapter 23

April 28, 3:30 p.m.
Midtown, New York City

The man entered the intimidating environs of Brooke Sato's office. She was admonishing a poor sap on the other end of a call.

"I don't care if his investors are skittish on the deal," she said, her steely cold voice making her stance very clear. "His investor group already signed the Memorandum of Agreement." After a muddled response came a pause. Brooke eyed the impressive looking Katana mounted on the opposite wall next to her door. A memento from her original home. "Then he should have thought of that before".

After a short pause, she said, "You tell him that if he's changed his mind, it's not my problem that he was brain dead when he signed the MOA, it's his!"

Brooke's office had a good sized conference table with a wireless Polycom VoiceStation in the center. The Katana mounted high over the doorway was encased in glass. Its hand-carved ebony handle and gold mount secured the sleek water stone sharpened silver, curved blade, its black sheath mounted above it.

Brooke collected various Japanese artifacts like the Katana. She saw herself as the family's cultural standard bearer, the one who would further her family's heritage. A *Sansei,* she made it a point to delve into her own family history, as well as the culture at large. Brooke had also earned and maintained a black belt in Judo and donated money to several cultural museums. Her grandparents were laid to rest at the Heart Mountain internment facility in Wyoming during the Second World War. Like many others, they were arrested for 'un-American' activities, a moniker for espionage. Her grandfather was exonerated posthumously years later. Her grandmother, also exonerated, carried the shame with her the rest of her life, dying of cancer well before they got the official 'apology'.

Farai Mubenga was a dark complexioned, expertly dressed man sporting a multicolored Madiba shirt and expensive looking shoes, with short black wiry hair and a full faced salt and pepper beard. Despite his leisurely appearance, without a noticeable swagger, put forth an air of getting down to business.

"So Mr. Mubenga, I understand that you would like to discuss a potential transaction to acquire various American energy assets, correct?"

He spoke in a moderately thick South African accent. "Yes, Ms. Sato, but please call me Farai. I have come before you because your reputation precedes itself."

She opened a manila-hued, pristine file folder prepared with his company's background information. "I hope your flight from Johannesburg was uneventful. I'm impressed you graduated Summa Cum Laude from the Hilton College of Michaelhouse, then business at Harvard."

"You studied at Stanford, I understand."

"Yes. It seems we both have stellar pedigrees," she said as the small talk drew to a close. "Your proposal intrigues me. Please walk me through it."

He explained. It involved the acquisition of several entities in the US through a handful of shell corporations to effectively mask his, as well as that of his domestic company's true identity from American investors. After he concluded his summary, she commented, "That is viable and something we would be more than happy to arrange for you, Farai. You do know our collateral requirement?"

"Of course," he acknowledged with a slight nod.

"Good. Based on the projected transaction value, you'll need to deposit $14.5 million into escrow."

"I possess such assets to cover that," he said with the slightest bit of irritation.

"Fine. When the funds are ready, let me know."

"I do not have the cash to contribute but rather something of more intrinsic value."

"Hummh," she inflected, reacting to Farai's riddle challenge like a tiger looking to move in for a kill. She reclined in her chair and shot him a coy look, milking the dry humor in the moment. "Because you insist on couching this asset in mystery, let me have a crack at it."

Farai grinned and leaned back in his chair.

She hypothesized as the fingers of both hands met, forming a steeple in front of her face that she flexed back and forth, middle finger touching her chin, while leaning back and swiveling in her chair. "Let me see… you hail from South Africa… have an asset that has more intrinsic value than money… something more durable, too. Well, that could only mean one thing." She paused for dramatic effect as if expecting a drumroll. "Diamonds!"

Farai gave a more gallant grin this time. "Correct."

They both chuckled for a moment, then Brooke took to her stone cold tone, bringing her fingers together in a pyramid and placed her elbows on her desk. "I can work with that."

"Good. In fact, I brought them here. He then pulled out a small, tan, suede bag with a pull string on it from his briefcase side pocket and tossed it nonchalantly on Brooke's desk. He then emptied the contents in front of her. Sparkling diamonds never looked so good, clattering on her glass top desk before her like petite hail stones.

Eyes widened and mouth agape for a noticeable nanosecond, she stiffened in a moment's time, leaning forward in attention. She said, "You do realize I'll need to have these examined."

"Of course, but I would like to give them to you now, for safekeeping."

She cleared her throat "However unorthodox this request is, I believe we can honor that, so long as you authorize this bank to be the official custodian of these assets. Will you consent to this?"

"Of course," he said.

"I will need you to sign our broker agreement," she said, fully engaged in Farai's unique way of doing business. "Do you have a few minutes?" Without waiting for his answer, she held up her index finger as she pressed the intercom call button. "Ellie, Mr. MuBenga would like to sign our brokerage agreement today. Please prepare one, now."

"Will do," Ellie responded.

"Brooke, I am sorry, but I just remembered that I am to meet the ambassador at the consulate for tea. Is it possible I may come back at some other time?"

"No." Brooke said as she lurched forward, raising her arm with palm out as if to say 'halt'. Then she relaxed and took a quick breath. "I'll expedite this personally, if you'll excuse me." Then she stood up and walked swiftly from her office.

The man known as Farai proceeded to take out another item from his brief case. This time it was a tiny zip drive. He knew Brooke Sato always brought her laptop and cell phone along with her everywhere she went, and today was no exception as they both lay on her desk. He plugged the drive into one of the ports as the laptop hard drive buzzed while he downloaded the installed app. He removed an even smaller drive from the briefcase and did the same with her cell phone. It was done in moments.

When Brooke returned with the custodian and broker agreements, he signed both of them in short order after quickly reviewing them. They shook hands and Farai left the office, the diamonds still sprawled out on her desk. She pushed the call button again and said, "Ellie, Mr. MuBenga wishes to make a deposit with us."

Farai walked out of the building after his meeting and approached the teal van across the street. He knocked on the door four times before it opened for him. Joanne was waiting to greet him. Agent Devon Wilson dropped the fake beard on the floor along with his well-rehearsed South African accent.

"Well?" Joanne asked.

He nodded to her confirming a completed assignment. "All I gotta' say is, Brooke Sato's gonna' shit a brick when it happens, if I say so myself."

Chapter 24

April 28th, 3:00 p.m.
The Upper West Side, New York City

Danny walked to the Starbucks on Broadway and West 81st to meet Javi. Several days had passed since the two men last saw one another.

He thought of why Kate was different from any other woman he had been assigned to. She was the smartest by a mile. Her drug addiction didn't seem to affect her ability to do her work. Rather, it got her through each day. Kate's self-medication and shyness masked a yearning for meaningful contact, all that more apparent once she shed her glasses.

Already seated, Javi raised his hand to get Danny's attention. The place was packed. One long line had formed almost out the door, and all the comfortable seats had been taken by people with laptops, or smartly dressed sales reps making a pitch to prospective clients.

Danny had to laugh inside about the incongruity of two rough and tumble Delta Force veterans sipping cappuccinos in a *bouj-ee* café.

"I met with Joanne today." He grabbed the cup of latte Javi had ordered for him.

"Did she tell you to focus?"

Danny smirked, then raised his arms up from the table, palms facing in. "She even accused me of being in love with her."

"So, *are* you?" Javi asked. His question stilled the air for a few tense seconds.

Danny shifted in his seat, as if he had been charged with unspeakable crimes. "No. All I said to her was that Katelyn Carrie's no murderer. It's clear to me, so why not to everybody else?"

They took healthy gulps of their watered-down lattes in silence amidst the din of mid-day customers.

Javi looked up at him and spoke, his words heavy with gravity. "I never told you about what happened."

"No."

"I think it's time you knew."

Knowing Javi was the last person to see Kelly alive, he said, "I don't."

"Hey, no one ever dropped a bomb on *you*." Javi was assigned to her platoon as one of three trained medics—and also one of three troops to survive the ordeal.

"Okay, so maybe I was in my own head about it, dealing with my own problems. You were in the middle of that shit show." Danny caught himself as his parched throat made him fight to clear it.

Without holding back, Javi said, "She was brave all the way." Javi had been the one who administered first aid to Kelly in those final moments. "She was doing the job she'd been assigned to do right when it happened."

Danny resisted the urge to reach across the table and slug him as Javi picked at an ugly scab. "They never found out who was responsible," he said, despondently at first, then the emotions lashed out, "But it makes no sense!" Javi's eyes darted around to see if anyone else had heard the outburst, but the din of the place was enough to mask his reaction.

"We both know that report was bullshit," Javi said, referring to the Army's rushed investigation of the Fratricide incident.

Javi leaned forward and dropped his head into his palms. "There wasn't any indication…" His voice broke before he could finish.

"Central Command knew something, but was either too afraid—or too embarrassed—to disclose what really went down. But no one knows why." "There were issues, like tension between the American and British forces, even though they were in it together, publicly at least."

"Yeah, I remember that came up on my European assignments too."

"But not just with the armed forces. It was also the PMCs. They were out for themselves. Fat contracts with upfront money from Uncle Sam. Same with the British."

"You really think British PMCs were backstabbing the coalition's efforts in the field?"

"No doubt. I'm serious. Things we'd witnessed on the way up to the village and testified about before the committee that never made it into the official report. Like the shotty workmanship on the culvert grating. Any hostile could've put an IED in there if they'd wanted to. Like that any PMCs had been anywhere near the village at all. The committee blew it off as if they didn't want certain facts to come out."

"I want to hear what happened, just not in this place." He wanted to hear every word. "I need to check on her," he said.

"You mean your mark, don't you?" Javi said with an informal wink.

He ignored the harmless intimation. "It's crazy with her, like the same thing that drove her to create the toxin makes her so unstable."

"Geniuses are like that, man. No one can stand 'em."

"You mean they're misunderstood, Javi."

Danny returned to the apartment and saw the upended contents of Kate's purse on the floor. An envelope from the Rhode Island Department of Health was folded like an accordion. When he picked it up, he noticed that it was empty.

When he heard the sound of running water from the master bathroom, he called out to her. With no response, he bolted for the bedroom. He found her huddled in the shower, fully clothed and completely drenched.

He cringed at the sight, knowing he'd have to tread lightly. "What are you doing?"

"Just go away, please."

He stooped down to meet her level. Danny had noticed the thin red line running across the front of her neck. "I can't help you if you don't tell me what happened."

"It was a man. He came from behind," she answered, still trembling.

He took his fingers and lightly brushed the back of his hand against her wet cheek. Kate shuddered and he quickly recoiled.

"How'd you get away?"

"I don't know. He… I blacked out. When I woke up, he was gone."

Danny knew that story was preposterous. He couldn't understand why a man who could have easily have strangled her to death suddenly would have had a change of heart. Then, if he believed she was dead, why nothing was stolen.

"I'll call the police."

Kate stood up, indignation plastered on her face. "No, don't. Just forget it, okay?"

He didn't know what to say that could breach the barrier she'd put up.

Kate finally regained some modicum of composure. "Just… I need to be alone. Please," she said, resolute.

"I'll check to see if the guy dropped anything on the way out."

He found nothing, so he decided to leave the apartment and maybe do some food shopping to give her the space she wanted. When he returned, Kate had dried out and was sitting in the living room sofa with knees folded into her chest with both arms wrapped around them as she stared at the flat screen, oblivious to all else around her.

Chapter 25

April 29th, 10:00 a.m.
The Upper West Side, New York City

The next morning, they both slept in. Danny awoke first this time. It turned out to be a warm and lovely day after the torrential downpour had drenched the City the night before.

He had never known anyone with such a fragile mental condition. Sure, he had friends who served in the military and had to deal with Post Traumatic Stress Disorder, but he never had to face someone who experienced psychotic breaks like Kate. No doubt this was a young woman trapped in her own being who desperately wanted to break out of her own skin. He didn't know Vanessa Carrie and hoped that he never would, but could only imagine what abuse she had doled out. Kate's burden no doubt drove her to the proverbial edge. He saw her wallow in despair and loneliness, especially because she had so much potential for success. That hidden beauty she possessed was corroding because of her addiction.

He pondered how she had to deal with her creation, the most deadly nerve gas on earth. He thought of all of those scientists who worked on the atomic bomb project and the excruciating inner conflict. Even the Russian officer who invented the AK-47, the first rapid fire machine gun, regretted on his deathbed that he invented it and that it had been used to gun down women and children. But there also were those who could separate themselves from their deadly discoveries. He imagined the hypothetical red button on a console that the operator was told would kill a million people who he didn't know each time he pushed it. It was vastly different from Special Forces training where Danny learned to kill a man with his bare hands, throwing his entire nervous system into the effort. Even the sound of an exploding grenade had had neurological effects on him, what with the periodic ringing in his ears he still experienced whenever he heard sirens, jackhammers, and other loud sounds. Maybe the inventors would think differently if they knew there was someone else out there in the world with their own red button to press, instantly killing a million people she didn't know. And they sure as hell didn't know Katelyn Carrie.

Behind her surly appearance, she made a noticeable impression on him in so short a time. *When did my own lust turn to love?* He pondered that one for a while, coming up with no discernible answer, but for him and maybe for many other men, he just had to learn to love the one he was attracted to.

He reached across her, embracing her from behind and kissing her softly on the neck.

"I'm hungry," she mumbled.

He took that as a good sign. "Good. I'll make you some eggs."

When he returned with the eggs, she said, "I want to leave this place. This city, I mean." She then told him about Vanessa's summer home up in the Catskills and that she wanted to take him there. Today.

Acting on her whim, he rented a Jeep Cherokee and the two of them drove up the Thruway until they turned west onto Route 17. For the first hour, they drove in silence. As they left the grit of the City behind, the suburbs turned to rolling hills with igneous rock formations. It was easy to appreciate the change of scenery.

"How are you?" he asked.

"Like a freight train ran over my head."

He reached over and held her left hand for a moment, finding it chilly.

From the county road, a seven-mile long macadam covered dirt road wound its way up to the property. The way was heavily forested on each side as they traveled over several small creeks. One, about a mile and a half in, channeled under the road by a stone masonry bridge. Although narrow, the creek ran under the bridge through a corrugated drainpipe.

They passed several homes along the way but Vanessa's property was at the terminus of the road near to the very top of the mountain. The home, set back at the midway point of a circular paved driveway, was a signature Frank Lloyd Wright split-level light box design a flagstone exterior with a pitched roof.

When they left the Jeep, they realized how cold the temperature was up so far north and at 2,800 feet. She beat him to the front door as the windy swells kicked up.

Safely inside, she warmed quickly. The baseboard heat had kept the home temperate through the winter. "Let me give you the grand tour," she said.

The vestibule led to a nice sized living room with a vaulted exposed wooden rafter ceiling, track lighting between each rafter. A prominent flagstone fireplace was on the right, covered by a mezzanine level walkway overhand with steps wrapping around the left side of the fireplace flume. To the left of the vestibule was a large living room suitable for large gatherings, with a glass coffee table surrounded by two burgundy cushioned, wooden armchairs, a white Ottoman, and a gray sofa. Against the far right wall was the kitchen, separated by a granite counter top and cabinets. Against the far wall were nice sized square windows extending from the ceiling down to the cushions of a long, built-in sofa.

On the second floor were four full-sized bedrooms and a den all the way on the left which rested over a three car garage. The windows on the second floor were floor-length to rear of the home, looking over the valley with vertical privacy shades. The wall facing the front had small salt box style windows.

The entire home's walls, floors and moldings were a golden shade of brown, as if one was sitting in an elegant log cabin amidst natural surroundings. The first floor living area had a high ceiling. Off to the right was the kitchen and breakfast bar area. The living area had sofas and area rugs looking out over several picturesque windows over a deck that extended over the precipice with a good three-hundred foot drop. A Mahjong set lay opened on a table, the dust on the case indicating it had not been used in some time.

Kate started the tour. "She took me up here for summers and some long weekends."

Danny thought he detected a hint of nostalgic longing in her voice.

She showed him the upstairs, where they peeked into each of the bedrooms, two of which overlooked the front of the home to the circular driveway and surrounding forest. Vanessa, of course, had used the master, but Kate's was only next door. It was carpeted and adorned with a fully made bed with four posts and a white curtain. There stood a large closet with folding doors and girlish double shelved dresser, but all other signs of any childhood were absent.

She led him across the hall to a spare bedroom and to the left of that, an enormous den, which was an intimidating room to be in if one had to face Vanessa. The walls were adorned with photographs of Vanessa with former colleagues and competitors at various functions. The style of the room was a direct counterpoint to the rest of the home. Its moldings and adornments spoke of a more classic style than rustic.

"I remember living up here when she would have industry people I'd never heard of show up to negotiate agreements between Frugeré and one of her competitors. I guess she thought that the mountain air was a calming influence on everyone."

"I think she's right," Danny said as he recalled his own memories of the Smokey Mountains.

On the far wall was yet another fireplace and a bookcase. Kate walked over to it. "Check this out."

He expected that Kate would show him some of the shelved books. Instead, she pushed aside the bookcase to reveal a hidden door leading to a bi-level stairwell. It led all the way down to an exit to the garage and down another level to the basement.

"The previous owner wanted to get to his precious cars without having to walk through the rest of the house," she said, eyes rolling upward.

"That's going to a lot of trouble just to save a few steps," Danny observed.

She led him down one flight past the garage entrance, then down another flight to the basement built into rocky precipice over the ravine, the view separated only by a sliding glass door leading to a balcony. Near the window were chairs and a coffee table facing a large flat screen TV. Behind the chairs lay a minibar. Separate from the near wall was a long rectangular island with a jet black Soapstone counter top that matched the shelving above it against the near wall. It could have been a kitchen, but it was Kate's very own chemistry lab. An array of beakers and test tubes stood like erect soldiers lined up on all of the counters. Two heating pads stood atop the island counter top.

"So, this is where you worked?" Danny commented, expecting a verbose explanation.

"Played, actually. It's basically been untouched since I graduated high school, but I used to read up on cool chemical reactions. You know, the stuff you can find online. Like what I showed you at my place."

He saw the thin shroud of dust that had settled on the counter top.

She continued. "I can do it again," she said, pointing over to the counter to a glass container holding a white crystalline substance.

"I probably would have gotten into a lot more trouble if I'd known how to do that as a kid," she said with a charming upturned lilt.

"Yeah. That was frightening actually, when you did that."

She smiled and resumed her focus as she scooped a tablespoon sized amount with a measuring spoon and emptied it into a beaker. She placed the beaker on the stand directly over the pad.

"It's not a fire hazard, really. Just don't look down into it, unless you want a charred face."

"I could use a shave," he quipped. Danny gazed at her with admiration. One could actually learn things from her. When Kate wasn't seeking out the next high, her mental dexterity and meticulousness made an impression.

She reached underneath the counter and switched on the heating pad.

"All I have to do is add sugar to the heated crystals, and… *voila*!"

Here we go again.

"Gummy bears."

"Right," she said, sounding satisfied her student was finally getting it.

He reached around her waist and he kissed the back of her neck, she bristled at first. "Eric," she protested

"It just occurred to me that you are a real pyromaniac."

"Everyone's got their own fetish. What can I tell you?" She guided his hands away. "I think I want to take a walk outside, now. I'll show you around the trails." She reached down to an old dial under the countertop and turned off the pad. She'd have to reschedule her master class for a later time.

She led him outside, into the wilderness, the home heavily forested on three sides. One trail led them south, back toward the main road. Another led north, hugging a ridge where they took in fantastic vistas. His attempt at initiating a playful conversation with her failed miserably again, as the talk devolved into deep introspection, "So, besides blowing things up, what turns you on?"

"Like besides being here with you?" she quipped. "How about a cool breeze? That's what I remember most."

They came upon a rocky overlook of the valley. The western sky overhead was robins-egg blue, with no clouds to be had. The wind kicked up against the ridge. They found a shady patch of grass to sit, leaning against a rock formation. Kate set her head against his shoulder.

"What's your mom like?" he asked.

"Please," she moaned. "She made me."

"And who might that be?" Danny inquired thoughtfully.

He thought she might say, 'a fucked up drug addicted mentally ill bitch', but instead had to field another question thrown back at him. "Let me ask you something. Have you ever accomplished making a big mistake? That you could have taken another path and done something else that now you could look back and be proud of?"

Taken aback by the mouthful of philosophical proposition, he answered, "No, but I also think that it's never too late to change paths."

"I guess, but what if your accomplishment affected other people in a bad way and there was no way you could undo it?

"I think I'd have to work hard at doing something with my life that would be something positive?" He saw her wear a sullen and serious look. "What's this about?"

She shook her head. "I don't know. Did you know boys didn't want to have anything to do with the science nerd with glasses?"

"Well, I think they were stupid to pass you up." He motioned her to sit between his legs then kissed the back of her neck and shoulders, ending all conversation. When he touched her, he found that her warmth had returned. The cool breeze was no match for the heat they generated. When she turned over on her back, she grabbed his hand at the index and middle fingers and guided them slowly to touch her. But something different happened this time. She took control, coming down on him, which he didn't mind at all, as the dappled sunlight shown through the trees.

Laying flat on their backs, they gazed up at the sky. The serene moment was interrupted by another buzz from his cell phone. At first surprised at the existing cell coverage, he read the incoming text, then rolled his head over to her. "That was a friend of mine. He and his girlfriend invited us out for dinner, tonight. Feel up to it?"

"Sure. Sounds great" Kate said with wide, bright blue eyes and a hopeful smile.

Phase II was on.

Chapter 26

April 29th, 7:30 p.m.
Brooklyn Heights, New York City

They strolled on the Brooklyn Heights Promenade as they admired the Manhattan's skyline set against the nighttime sky like stalagmites formations shimmering with speckled yellow lights, the sky glowing cobalt blue. The Empire State Building was lit in blue with a yellow streak in its halo, commemorating European Union Day.

They stopped and he took her hand. "See, now that *almost* makes me want to stay here."

"I love it, too, but I'd leave it in a second if I could. Maybe go somewhere where I could start over. I realize now that I definitely need a change."

"And just walk away from all this? Why the rush to leave? You still haven't told me why."

"I can't talk about it, really," she said, pulling her hand away. "I'm sorry. I didn't mean it like that."

"It's okay. I know it must be hard. When you're ready, I'm sure you'll face it head on."

When she didn't respond, they continued their walk. His 'friends' were waiting outside the restaurant and Danny introduced them as Sue and Dave. Danny knew them as Lindsey and Javi.

Javi said he was an accountant and Lindsey a registered nurse. Throughout the evening, Kate rolled with it, although her appetite was D.O.A.

"So, Eric didn't tell us much about you", Lindsey said.

"This guy never does," Javi said.

"So what do you do, Kate?"

She was done talking about her job but to her credit, played along. "I'm a chemist with Frugeré cosmetics," she said with a forced smile. *Do I really have to go through this again?* In this City, everyone sized up by conversation by how cool a job you had.

"Real glamorous, I bet."

"Not really, I spend most of my time in a boring lab. It's not like I'm invited to any gala events or anything like that. Besides, I have one of those killer bosses. *Really, I do,*" Kate added, nervous that she had been too literal in her assessment and relieved—so she thought—they didn't pick up on it.

"Don't we all," Javi said, laughing. The other two followed suit. "I never wanted to go corporate. That's why I went to med school, but you know what? I found out hospitals are corporate too. You know, bottom line, squeezing you to handle more patients."

"That's why I'm my own boss," Danny cut in.

"Ha!" Javi exclaimed. "Man, you think you are, but we're really all working for the same dude."

"Speak for yourself," said Danny.

The waitress brought their orders. Kate, having declined an entrée, was still picking at her salad while the others dug in.

Javi resumed the conversation, according to script. "Hey," he asked Danny, "Are you still into it?"

"Nope. I'm scaling back. Do other things like work for a living."

"We still like it, in moderation," Lindsey added.

Kate looked intrigued about where 'Dave' and 'Lindsey' were going with this.

Danny glowered at him. "Still walk on the wild side, do you? I don't think so. Not tonight, but thanks."

Javi talked over him and said, "We're gonna' meet our guy after dinner, off of Flushing Avenue."

"Wanna come?" Lindsey asked as a follow up.

Danny rolled his eyes, using the motion to sneak a glance at Kate. "That's a hike and it's walking through neighborhoods I'd rather not—"

All of a sudden, Kate emerged from her sulk. "No, it's fine. Really."

"I thought we agreed to cool it," he said, completely veering from the script. The plan was for them to lure her in and for him to gently attempt to protest but speaking directly to her was pushing it. Danny thought it was too late to recover until she reacted just like her profile told them she would.

"I know, but what's the harm in walking with them? I mean, just because I'm on a diet doesn't mean I can't look at a menu, right?" Kate responded.

Javi and Lindsey laughed.

"Fine but we leave right after," Danny said adamantly.

They walked east on Clark Street, then Tillary, turning north onto Jay Street. The hip restaurants, bars and well maintained brownstones gave way to a food mart and less attractive apartments, then on to abandoned vacant lots. The rush of traffic from the Brooklyn-Queens Expressway loomed overhead as they walked beneath it. The conversation digressed into talk of past drug experiences, with Danny remaining silent most of the way.

After about a twenty minute walk, they came upon a small parking lot, no larger than the size of a professional basketball court. Cars were parked but no one was manning the booth. A lone overhead street lamp illuminated the side where the closed check-in booth sat.

A man came out of the shadows holding a large knapsack, dressed rather shabbily in a jet black sweat jacket and gym pants. This was Devon, playing yet another role.

"Hey," Javi said to him.

"You brought friends tonight, huh."

"They're cool."

"All right."

Javi and Lindsey examined the virtual drug store selection of uppers, opiates and hallucinogens. Kate looked on. Danny just stared silently.

Devon, the dealer, started into his monologue about what he had to offer. Javi said, "Okay, we'll take these," pointing to some hallucinogen that even Danny couldn't recognize. "Kate, you want to ask him anything?"

As Devon was about to answer, the sound of screeching tires cut through the air as a van turned into the lot, heading straight for them. The glare of its headlights blinded the five unlucky souls as it abruptly stopped short, no more than twenty feet from where they were standing. Without warning, the back door flung open and two men stormed out brandishing submachine guns.

"Oh my God!" Kate screamed, frozen in place like the others.

The men charged at them, taking aim with their raised weapons. Instinctively, Danny moved in front of Kate, pushing her to the ground shouting, "Look out!" In an instant, a flash of gunfire struck all four of the undercover agents.

The men converged on Kate who was still on the blacktop as they approached. They took hold of her. Kate gasped when she glanced over at Danny; he lay motionless, blood spewing out from multiple bullet holes in his torso. The same for the others. "No!" she wailed in agony, reaching out but unable to touch him.

Two men pulled her up by her pony tail while another pressed the barrel of his gun against her cheek. She heard what she thought was a fourth man join the other two hovering above her. One of them spoke in a thick Middle Eastern accent, "if you want to live, come with us."

They flung her against the side of the van so hard she shrieked. Two of them pinned her against the sliding door while the third man violently stabbed a hypodermic needle it into her neck. Within seconds, her body went limp as she fell back against the side of the van, losing consciousness.

A man wearing a black bomber jacket had followed the group from the restaurant. Lurking behind the stairway, he observed the entire scene. He watched the men pick up and throw Kate in the back of the van like a sack of potatoes.

The man didn't recognize the leader, but heard him admonish his crew and slapped one hard across the face. "Be careful. You do not harm her. Leave that to me."

Doors shut, the driver peeled out of the lot and sped away from the bloody carnage, leaving four CIA agents dead or dying.

As soon as one van left the lot, another appeared on the street. This one drove up to the bodies in a dirge-like crawl. Two men left the vehicle and carried the bodies inside one by one while one woman stood by and watched. The van left the lot as quietly as it came, until it reached the end of the block, then the observer heard the engine rev.

When all was quiet, he took out his cell phone and dialed a number. As soon as the line connected, he said in King's English, "Hey gaffer, you won't believe what I just saw."

PART III

"I can honestly say I've never sold any arms to a repressive foreign regime while reassuring everyone at home that the weapons will be used for nice things."

—Jo Brand

Chapter 27

April 30th, 6:30 a.m.
Elizabeth, New Jersey

A horrific Super 8 home movie played out in her head; a sequence of grainy memories from the last few days. Her abductors pulling her to her feet by her hair, seeing what she'd believed to be Eric's lifeless blood-soaked body as she was thrust against the side of a van, then to Vanessa's office, being slapped repeatedly. Later it was Gunther trying to strangle her, his cruel laughter echoing in her ears. She found herself back in Central Park, by the rock, falling to her knees and digging frantically in the pouring rain where she had hidden the vials, to no avail.

Did they find the vials?

Moving a few feet away, she would dig another hole, and another and another, until the entire clearing was full of holes. No vials to be found, her hands, face, sleeves, pants, and shoes now caked in mud.

Depressive psychosis had found Katelyn Carrie again, but this time within the confines of a 10 by 10 by 20 foot high darkened cell in wherever-the-hell this place was. She lay on the floor in a corner. She recited unintelligible gibberish, non sequitur words of things, places and chemical compounds. *Triglyceride... Ocean... Popcorn... Freezer... Nitrate...*

Kate had left reality and lost her way back.

She stood in front of her bathroom mirror, nude. Her skin covered with tattoos of the secret formula from head to toe. Staring at herself in horror, she shrieked in her mind, succumbing to her skin's plaintive cry for relief. Her nails attacked her breasts and arms like sharp talons, cutting herself to shreds. Blood ran through her fingers and dripped into the sink. It was as if she was trying to peel away the formula from her exterior. Her nails moved to her face, ending in the same result. When the psychosis subsided, fear took its place as she awoke to the bright overhead lights, their heat bearing down on her and metallic smell filling the cell.

It took her eyes a moment to adjust to the intense brightness. "Hello?" she pleaded, "Is anybody there? Where am I? Please, someone help me." Her world was sideways, lying there on the floor, when she saw the cell door creak open. She looked up at a person wearing a charcoal balaclava. They stepped inside the cell and laid something on the floor next to Kate. Without a word, the man left as quickly as he had entered, the shutting of the metal door behind him echoing throughout the cell. Kate could hear the deadbolt sound of the lock.

She noticed a white Styrofoam container on the floor, along with an 8oz bottle of unopened spring water. She crawled over to open the container which contained Wonderbread slices with nothing between them but American cheese. She took one bite and spit it out, opting for the water instead.

Without warning, the lights shut off, returning her to utter darkness.

Alone again, she focused on her abductors. All she remembered were these masked figures rushing toward her, pointing rifles in her face after the bullets struck down Eric in cold blood. She had no idea whether she had been here for an hour, twelve hours, a day, or a week.

The lights turned on again, blaring brightness as Kate rubbed her eyes to adjust. The cell door creaked open once more. This time two men entered wearing masks, and without saying a word lifted her off the floor. She was too weak to put up much resistance. Grabbing each of her arms, they dragged her outside the cell to an empty, dimly lit hallway. They led her down the hall to a door with a small window. When they brought her in, the room was well lit with Klieg lighting, but completely bare save for a metal table and two metal folding chairs placed opposite each other on two sides of the table. They sat her down in the chair furthest from the door and left her in the room. Taahid and Moiz, Palestinian compatriots, stood sentry by the door behind her. Taahid was tall and slender, Moiz a bit shorter but looking more weather beaten in the face.

Another minute or two passed before she heard the door open behind her. She heard someone's footsteps circle around to the opposite side of the table. This was a man wearing no mask at all. He seemed gentle, but foreboding in an instant. He did not speak until he sat down.

"Good morning, Dr. Carrie. I hope that your accommodations were adequate last night," Sabir said.

Her face was haggard but her irascibility rose to the surface. That he seemed so cordial annoyed her even more. "What is this place? Why am I here?" she said, spitting out her words. "What did you do to Eric?"

"Your friend is dead," he said.

She said, "No" several times through tears.

"All we want is something that you already know," Sabir assured her. His calm, sickly sweet demeanor she found excruciatingly creepy. "Provide it, and you will be free to go."

Her skin was afire with pin prick tingling.

He then pulled from under his jacket a syringe and the heroin she assumed it contained, holding it in his right hand and displaying it flagrantly before her. "This shall be your reward when you do."

"No. I don't want to be responsible for it anymore, so please, just leave me alone and let me go."

"Nothing would please me more than to relieve the pain that I promise you will experience very soon," he said, sliding the syringe out in front of her.

"I-I can't live without that. It's all I've got now."

She lunged forward, but the chair restraints held her back.

"But," he continued as he slid it away from her with chilling calm, "if you don't tell us what it is, you will leave me no choice but to keep you here without this."

"I n-need it, please!"

Sabir stood before her, reached across and slapped her across the face.

"Fuck you! I didn't do anything," she squealed, then spit in his direction that fell short on the table. Sabir nodded to Zami who grabbed an oversized set of pliers from a side table and stood by her left hand side. Jamal grabbed her wrist, clamped the tool firmly at the tip of her index finger, then pulled as bloodcurdling howls flooded the room.

No one who cared was listening.

Chapter 28

April 30th, 2:00 p.m.
Midtown, New York City

Gunther described his man's account of the evening's events to Vanessa, beginning from Danny's first walk with Kate that night, dinner, the walk to the parking lot just before Kate's abduction and finally the shooting itself, leaving out just one not insignificant detail.

He had despised the American military over the years. Their bravado and imperious attitude against the world based on their military strength was certainly offensive to a lot of people.

The Special Forces modeled their methods of operation on our SAS, the bloody bastards.

But he knew despite their cooperative nature with Great Britain on the surface, they habitually spied on their political leaders with whom the President routinely shook hands with on countless photo ops, as well as on several other European allies. He knew this well before Eric Snowden appeared, the insufferable sod who'd exposed the entire scheme. *So why not return the favor?*

Gunther was the operations manager on the same joint CIA/MI-6 surveillance team that Danny had been assigned to, with Joanne Dawson as the CIA counterpart. It would be Gunther's last official intelligence operation. It went terribly wrong, as one man's intelligence career disintegrated in the process, while one Embassy employee lost her life.

Danny's assignment had been to infiltrate the Russian Embassy to access the files that listed the Russian informants and his assignment was to befriend an Embassy employee long enough so that another agent posing as a computer programmer could acquire the list from their mainframe computer. It was to be a quick in and out operation.

But Gunther took on the Geneva assignment to take care of some unfinished business—to tie up a loose end. It was nearing midnight and Lika, living in a Terra-Cotta style apartment building had just been escorted home by her date for the evening.

Gunther approached and easily breached the front door, making his way up the steps to the woman's apartment. He knocked on the door. Believing it to be her date who had left her not five minutes earlier, she opened it as Gunther bull rushed his way in, propelling her backward as she stumbled to the floor. She stood up immediately, recognizing him instantly. Slamming the door shut behind him, he effectively blocked her escape. "You leave now," she said in English with a Russian accent. "The walls are thin here."

He spoke fluent Russian. "You're a fool, you know. I just thought you should know that before I kill you, tonight. You've been very careless."

"The Americans are playing *you* for one. I wouldn't have expected that from someone with such formidable credentials as yourself."

"Your government would be very interested to know how you've been playing both sides," referring to Gunther's penchant for selling information back and forth between the superpowers, always careful never to tip the balance. She was working for the SVR but was sent abroad to protect such information.

"I learned very early on that the world's economy depends on hostility to perpetuate itself"

"I know who you are. Both sides respect you and revile you just the same."

"Very few people know who I am and when I take care of you, the list will be even smaller".

At that, she moved toward the lamp shade on the side table, where a gun awaited her. But before she could grasp it, he grabbed her wrist, snapping it, as the lamp fell to the carpet.

She couldn't scream because he'd grabbed her throat with his left hand, pinning her to the living room wall. When his right hand joined the left, she was gone.

Gunther called in the troops for a Long Island City meeting. It was a short cab ride from the office but he took the necessary precautions. When he hailed the cab, the driver turned around and said, "Where to, Sir?" This was Soren, the only one of the group he really cared about, their relationship going way back to SAS days. He smiled but said nothing. They drove over to the West Side, to the Gotham Cab Company garage, where they changed into different clothes, then drove out in a jet black limousine, the tinted glass masking the identity of its driver and passenger.

They all gathered inside the shuttered Amalgamated Paper building, soon to be renovated into high end cooperatives.

Two overhead fluorescent fixtures illuminated the room. A titanium-plated laptop lay on a folding table fit for poker. There were six metal folding chairs but no one was standing.

He and Soren were the last to arrive and surveyed the group, consisting of mercenaries of all walks of life: "Retired" American and SAS veterans, Euro trash mercenaries, two disillusioned Chicago gang members and even a Chechnyan sniper. The chattering and laughing among the crew ceased immediately as they entered. Apparently, his reputation preceded him. He was to divvy out assignments for the job.

"Alright you blokes, we haven't a moment to lose." This unruly cast of characters who gave the Star Wars bar scene a run for its money were all formidable mercenaries, some of whom had additional skills in surveillance. Gunther had himself nine trigger-happy mercenaries on his side, but thankfully, all were unarmed. "Keep your trigger fingers in your trousers. I'll need some of you for surveillance only tasks. "Our assignment just became more involved than originally anticipated." He paused, knowing he had to take care only to divulge just enough information to do their jobs. "I need you for security detail for an auction to sell off some very sensitive military hardware. "But, the scientist who created it made off with the entire lot of it and hid it in an undisclosed location."

One of the mutants spoke up, apparently the self-appointed representative of the group, Shane Vance, balding, sporting a Fu Manchu mustache extending down the sides of his mouth. He was in essence, the Michelin Man. He sported a distinguishing tattoo: that of an oversized black stenciled grenade extending from the bottom of his chin downward to the bottom of his neck. Even his burley chest hair couldn't detract from such a work of art. "When do we get paid? We'd all like to know."

"After the auction," Gunther responded. "Your living expenses will be covered by Frugeré up until then."

Gunther summed up the situation for them by recounting his surveillance efforts and providing Kate and Danny's profiles. "This chap left the CIA years ago when his wife perished in Afghanistan. He also had drug addiction issues, which put him out of service for a while. Now he's back with a full compliment of agents."

"But last night, the girl was abducted by what appeared to be four Middle Eastern blokes and was made to believe that Strong was killed along with three other agents."

Soren then gave his eye witness account. "The CIA set her up. I saw a group of Middle Eastern blokes machine gun them and make off with the girl in a van. But then I see them rise from the dead. Yes I did."

"It's obvious to me they're shagging with her head. We have to get her back before they break her. No one else can get the weapon". Gunther read the confused expressions on their faces, then continued. "And they'll do whatever it takes to make her talk and she will. She's a pathetic heroin addict, so right now, they probably have her locked away somewhere until she begs for mercy. That's what I'd do."

"How do we find her then?" asked Nils Bruenig, a burly and light haired German mercenary.

"Danny Strong will lead us right to her." Then came the kicker. "And once he does, we'll make sure he never existed."

Chapter 29

April 28th, 2:30 p.m.
Elizabeth, New Jersey

Kate found herself smack dab in the middle of 53rd and Fifth Avenue on a bright cloudless day. She wore the horn-rimmed beauties, the ones she'd worn since childhood. There were no cars, no people and no sound. Then two visages appeared. On the southeast corner stood Danny, looking affectionately at her. On the northwest corner stood Vanessa, glaring. Then the scene changed and they were in the courtyard of a gray Gothic style building. Kate recognized it as the psychiatric facility she stayed in for eight months when she was ten. Then all of a sudden, another figure appeared next to her left. It was a young girl, eight, looking up at her while tugging at her shirt sleeve. Then she recognized the girl as herself when she was that age. The girl simply said, "Tell them." To which she replied, "Tell them what?" The girl responded with, "You know," sheepishly.

A blur, then she whisked away to her seventh and last foster parents' home. She was eight. This was not an illusion. This was a real and palpable historical fact.

It all had the look and feel of a nurturing suburban home. In her new bedroom, she lay in a bed aglow with morning light filtering through pink lace curtains. There sat a brand new wooden blackboard easel, stuffed animals and dolls that crowded the top of her dresser. The room was painted in a light pink hue.

The Delmars, Trudy and Burt, appeared harmless enough at first but just like most of her prior foster homes, drugs had made their reappearance felt in Kate's life in a major way. Trudy and Burt, however, were both perpetual drug addicts.

"Don't be afraid," the voice said softly. I want to show you something."

Kate's nostrils flared at the unmistakable fetor of whiskey. She felt she was about to retch as bile filled her throat. Still enveloped by darkness, she heard him unzip his pants and pull them down as she could feel him hover over her. Then she started to shake.

"Feel me." His member hard and ready. "Go ahead. You can touch it." He gently grabbed her wrist and drew it closer. Kate had learned to be numb to insincere love and rejection, but unwanted sexual touching, especially for this nine year old, was new. At first, she had liked the sound of Burt's voice, but it soon took on a sickening dark timbre and trembled. This would end badly. When her hand made contact, she tried to pull away and started to scream but Burt's hand has already covered her mouth and pressed the back of her head into her pillow.

"I want you, angel," his sickening voice still in the air while he grabbed the elastic waist on her pajama bottoms and proceeded to pull them down, along with her underwear.

"You belong to me, angel," his voice turning edgy and vicious, teeth grinding.

Fully under his grasp and control, she couldn't even scream.

When Burt finally withdrew, he gently stroked his two fingers over her forehead and cheeks. "So sweet. This is our little secret, okay?" he said with a shaky voice of a madman.

The ceiling and four walls of the bedroom collapsed onto her and dissolved into more darkness. Her thighs reeked of urine.

I've fallen into hell and I can't get out!

She'd once read that after 30 days in an enclosed area with no light whatsoever, one could go completely blind. *And after 60 days, they'd go completely nuts.*

The cell door burst open and more food was thrown at her. This time, it was saltine crackers and water. The water was enough. She would have vomited if she tried the crackers. Then she thought of everything that heroin had taken from her; money, her job, her friends, her health… but soon the craving squeezed out those memories. The itching made her insane and depressed at once. *Maybe if I told them...* But then she understood the ramifications of that. She knew there was no guarantee they would let her walk out of here alive.

I just wanted to be a chemist.

Instead, because of her discovery, she'd be nothing more than a hired murderer.

That's why I buried them!

Without any product to sell or anyway to reproduce it, Vanessa had nothing and Kate would preserve what was left of her morality. She'd become just another one of those scientists, from Da Vinci to Goddard to Oppenheimer, who routinely proffered their inventions and discoveries to governments with military aspirations.

Eric! she moaned, then broke down sobbing again. *I'm the reason he's dead.*

The only man who'd ever cared about her was gone.

He didn't want to go with them. I did.

Chapter 30

April 29th, 10:30 p.m.
The Upper West Side, New York City

Danny had walked aimlessly about the Upper West Side for what seemed like hours and was returning home to his true apartment. The Agency had gotten what they wanted out of him. Now, he was supposed to move on. Officially, he was to be on radio silence unless Joanne contacted him for further instructions. Danny had no way of intervening on Kate's behalf, even if he had been read in on her location. He had even stopped by the gym but soon left, unable to maintain any focus.

When he came upon his walkup building, he glanced up at his third floor apartment window and noticed that the lights were on—and a shadow behind the drawn shades was moving between the windows. His Glock was in the apartment, in a box on the bedroom closet shelf. He feared that if the intruder had been there long enough, he may have already confiscated it. Bringing it with him to the gym would have been out of the question.

He looked to the alley, blocked by a black wrought iron gate, looked around to see if anyone was looking, then vaulted over it. When he reached the rear of the building, he saw the fire escape. Being that the ladder from the second floor to the ground was retracted, he had to climb up the wall to reach it. He saw a folded ladder on its side against the wall, apparently left by the super. He grabbed it, opened it and climbed to the fire escape. Four feet separated his outstretched arms from the fire escape. He decided to make leap for it, which he knew was a one shot deal. When he did, the ladder kicked out from under him onto the ground with a metal *klack*, but his right hand was able to grab one of the struts. With both arms, he was able to pull himself up. Moving slowly up the escape to avoid a sound, he made his way to his apartment window that led to his kitchen, which was actually just a corner of the studio consisting of an undersized refrigerator, stove, sink and overhead cupboard. This window didn't have drawn shades, so he stood just to the left of it. He peeked inside to see a man in the alcove leading to the living room opening cabinets.

He tapped the window hard. The intruder looked up, pulled out a gun and moved toward the window. The window opened and the barrel of the gun broke the plane. Seizing the opportunity, he kicked the gun out of his hand, then used the railing of the escape to push off and break the window, making contact with the man right in the chest. In virtual darkness, the two of them struggled on the floor. The man threw him off and charged toward the knife rack. But before he could reach it, Danny grabbed him and pushed his torso onto the countertop. The man grabbed some dishwashing liquid and tried squirting back in Danny's eyes, but missed and hit his mouth instead, making him release his grip on the man, who started running out of the kitchen. Danny then grabbed a knife, pulled the man from behind and pushed it into his groin. The man groaned. He had hit the target.

"Who do you work for?!" he shouted in the man's face, then buried his knees into the ribs with his full body weight.

The man didn't respond, Danny hearing him writhing in pain through the darkness.

Danny sprung up, turned on the lights and quickly bore down on him again, before the man could get up. He grabbed the man's bag, dumping its contents on the floor. They were several listening devices that Danny recognized. "Call your boss!" he ordered, but got nothing. "Call your boss, now!" The intruder was too scared to speak.

He grabbed the man's cell phone from his belt case, and threw it at his forehead. Danny got a good look at him, the bowl-shaped haired man's wallet lying on the floor. His ID said he was Aldus Wiggins, a British Subject.

Frustrated, he grabbed the phone and dialed the last number.

Before the first ring ended, the other line picked up.

"McGore," the voice said. His blood turned cold when he heard it.

"I take it my man had a bit of a row with you?"

"Tell your *man* that if he ever wants to pee again, he has to leave my apartment!"

He held the phone up to the man's mouth. "He stuck me in the willy!" 'Wiggy' as everyone called him. A useful surveillance man, yet inexperienced and dim-witted of the group in military expertise and ability.

"This one'll be out of action for a while."

"It would appear so," said Gunther, nonplussed by the screw-up.

"What do you want?"

"Same thing that you want. So it appears we're in competition, again."

"It would *appear* so," mocking McGore.

"Geneva will always be your cross to bear."

"You betrayed one of our own."

"Water under the bridge."

"Someone else got to her first, not me."

"Your word against the polizei."

"You won't find Katelyn because I don't know where she is."

"Katelyn is worthless without that formula swimming around in her head."

"Don't fuck with her."

"Pot calling kettle." Gunther's inner child came through. "What do you think *you've* been doing with her?" Gunther went for the kill, "Just another fish, eh? Get what you want and discard her like rubbish. Your M.O., I believe?" Gunther continued." Let me see, last time we spoke you were, what, shagging that woman in Geneva? But I've heard there were so many after that one. I've simply lost track."

The chill Danny had experienced only a moment ago warmed to a sizzle. “She got away from both of us,” acting as if nothing had ever happened between them.

“Cock off, Strong. You know where she is.”

Danny was silent. He didn't know, but he'd play along to find out what Gunther knew.

“Oh, yeah. I know all about that little stunt you chaps pulled in that parking lot. Did you really think I wouldn't figure that all out?”

Fully ‘made’, Danny rolled with the verbal joust, returning a thrust of his own. “By the time you find out where she is, it'll be too late.”

“Underestimating me would be the biggest mistake you'll ever make. Oh and tell my bloke he can leave.”

“Gladly,” he said long after the line had gone dead. He opened the apartment door, grabbed Wiggy's jacket in the back, lifting him off, throwing him outside before slamming the door shut.

Danny's mental journey had taken him in what was five minutes from a state-side army base to an operation in Geneva. It had been nearly twelve years since he had heard that voice. Its frosty undertone intimidated men as if he were the Grim Reaper.

The Geneva operation was the one he wished he could forget, but Gunther's reentry into his life crushed any chance of that happening. It was shortly after he had left the Special Forces, having been recruited by none other than Joanne Dawson, the then Geneva station chief.

Joanne, then station chief, brought him to Geneva a year earlier and introduced him to Gunther. Danny was impressed with both Gunther's military background and his surveillance know-how. With Gunther as the operations leader, Danny, under an assumed name of Swiss national computer programming consultant, Ulrich Maurer, was to upload a program that would make the Russians believe a virus had penetrated their firewall. When that occurred, he was to call in the true computer consultant who knew how to navigate through the Russian computer system and locate the files that contained a list of Russian informants working in the U.S. Once this was accomplished, he would befriend the lovely information manager there, by the name of Lika Kuznetsova. He had learned fluent Russian while in Special Forces and was prepped further by the Agency to speak it with a Swiss accent.

The legitimate consultant he brought in was fellow CIA operative and mainframe computer whiz, Jay Tremont, going by the name Sigmund Brunner, a fictitious Swiss national, professionally dressed with graying straight short hair and unremarkable features. The company they had “formed” was called Computech Solutions, a fictitious company created by the Agency, which now had verifiable backdated corporate documents and a well-endowed bank account.

They set up operations in the Hotel NH Rex some six blocks away from the Consulate off of Rue De Meryrin in downtown Geneva, where Gunther monitored Jay's work and Danny's progress with Lika.

That was the extent of the operation, but Jay, although able to breach the Russian computer's firewall with ease, was unable to locate the sought after files on the Russian system in short order.

Apparently, charm was the same in any language because a lunch date led to a dinner the following evening, which led to a visit to her apartment. She came on to him, but he graciously refused her advances.

When Danny couldn't get a hold of her at work the next day, he contacted the Consulate to learn that Lika had been found dead in her apartment and that a full investigation was under way. Langley arranged for Joanne and Danny's recall and were told not to attempt contact with Tremont in any way. When they reached out to Gunther, he agreed to notify him but never did because he too had arranged his exit strategy.

When the Russians couldn't find Danny, they approached Tremont and asked him questions about Mr. Brunner and what he was doing. When they checked the system, they discovered his scheme.

Chalked up as a failed operation, the CIA cut Tremont loose and he was disavowed, while he rotted in a Russian prison as a spy. He spent nearly four years there, until the Agency finally arranged a trade, spy for spy. Although he returned to the States, his government career was destroyed and he was no longer a desirable hire. He was a pariah to the private sector employers as well, having to explain four unaccounted-for years of his life. Unable to find steady work, and with no family to support him, he drifted between YMCA boarding houses, holding menial retail jobs across the South. He had disappeared off the grid from everyone Danny knew at the Agency.

It was painfully obvious why Joanne hadn't read him in on Gunther's involvement. Alone in his apartment, he began mulling over this new development. He could arrive at only one conclusion: Joanne knew what kind of man he was. She recruited Danny into the CIA and assigned him to the operation in the first place. Danny wanted to confront her about it but knew that he couldn't because of his need-to-know status. He vowed to fight that battle when the time came.

Chapter 31

April 30th, 8:30 p.m.
Elizabeth, New Jersey

Kate regained consciousness in an unfamiliar room. Although she was lying on the flo Kate regained consciousness in an unfamiliar room. She lay on the floor, flat on her back, both hands tied together with plastic cuffs attached to a metal chain ascending upward to a pulley. She was the embodiment of an ocean liner-sized anchor. The blood from both throbbing forefingers where Sabir had removed her nails had seeped through both bandages and had trickled down her hand before it dried in dark red splotches. A dull pain and throbbing remained.

The room, which was new to her, was completely dark, save for one dimly lit overhead lamp. The ceiling was ten feet high with pipes crisscrossing overhead, the floor laden with what sounded like sawdust, as she heard a crunch as she stepped, but were actually metal shavings. Combined with the stench of her own person, she recognized the scent of a copper and zinc compound. She then thrashed about, a heavy belt clasped around her bare stomach, from which 4 small wires extended upward, each taped to her torso, as if she was undergoing an EKG exam. They had removed her blouse so that her bra was exposed. Then she noticed two more wires protruding from the belt, like extended coils to a car battery.

A very big car battery.

Her raspy voice made it difficult to scream, all she could muster were unladylike guttural squeaks.

At that point, Sabir entered with his entire crew of four men.

"Good evening Kate," he said, then stared at her silently. "You see what's in store for you, now. Don't you?"

Jaffa stood in front of a crude console with sliding switch on it, like a miniature recording studio mixing board.

Her comprehension of what was to happen next turned her stomach, which triggered her retching reflex, but only bile came up, having not eaten anything in her recent memory.

Zami poured a bucket of water onto her head and torso. She coughed away whatever water that had found its way up her nose.

"Up," Sabir directed.

The ugly sound of scraping and squeaking of metal against metal penetrated her ears as she was pulled up, high enough so that her outstretched flats were just high enough to leave a noticeable and excruciating gap between her outstretched shoes and the floor. She feared her arms would separate from their sockets at any moment.

"The compound, please, Kate, or you know what will happen next." He sounded eager to get on with it.

The sadistic fuck!

"Begin," he said to Jaffa.

A low hum filled the air as the first charge was set to a very low voltage, just enough to feel like she was at a chiropractor's office. After a few seconds, Sabir nodded to Jaffa to stop.

"It will feel so much better when you tell me."

Sabir nodded again, Jaffa increased the voltage and moved the sliding switch again. This time, her body shuddered. She thought her eyes were going to pop out of their sockets at any second. Her arms were about to pull out of their sockets too. The low hum had changed to a sickening crackling buzz, drowned out by Kate's undulating scream.

"Stop, please!" she croaked.

"It will only get worse for you if you do not tell me, now."

Another stronger charge ripped through her with muted screams.

Then came an even stronger one, this time lasting for about twenty seconds. Now she was screaming at the top of her lungs. Once the switch was turned off, she accepted there was no escape from this. Sabir was about to nod approval for yet another stronger charge before she finally said the words they were waiting for."

Her voice giving out, she said, "Wait, please don't. Wait, wait, I'll tell you, I'll tell you."

Sabir told Muiz to release the chain. They eased her down gently until she hit the deck, remaining there cuddled in a ball, shivering.

"Now, what will you tell us?" he asked.

The pain had yet to subside for her to give a coherent answer.

"What will you tell us?" he repeated.

"The Tri-Meth! What you want…" she wheezed, then endured a coughing spell, her sore vocal chords flaming with each cough. "You promised…"

"Yes," Sabir responded, "You will have it if you tell us."

Kate nodded her head repeatedly. Sabir played savior by re-bandaging her nail-less fingers while she lay on the floor then stroking the back of her hands, as if to comfort her.

What kind of madman would do this to me?

Sabir had them disconnect the wires. Abra and Taahid, who had been guarding the door, lifted Kate up on her feet and guided her back to the first room where she met Sabir.

They sat her down again on the chair next to the table, but did not restrain her. Sabir followed and threw down a yellow note pad and pen before her. The top of the page had the word “Tri-Meth” printed in large letters. She still shook at the visceral memory of the electric charge.

“Leave us,” Sabir ordered and proceeded to sit in the chair opposite Kate. He drew closer to her and whispered into her left ear, “It will all be over soon, if you tell us.” He then sat down quietly in his chair and scanned her carefully.

Both fingers still throbbing, Kate capitulated as she picked up the pen and scrawled a molecular structure. Slowly at first, acting as if trying to remember it, but after a few seconds, more deliberately.

“There!” she cawed like a child who was manipulated into picking up a toy, pushing the pad away and dropping her head into her arms, clutching the pen.

Sabir looked at the scribbling that was unintelligible to him, then said with a sickly gentle calm, “Thank you so much, Katelyn. You will learn that I keep my promises.” He then pulled out a syringe containing heroin and placed it on the table, but it could have contained anything as far as she knew. He withdrew it once again from her reach and placed it on a stand next to the chair in front of him, “But first, we will make sure you have told us the truth.” If there was any time she really needed an opiate, it was now.

“Why would I lie to you? You’d just shock me again.” she posed to him, attempting to bargain with him from a hopeless position of weakness.

Sabir then said to Zami and Moiz, “Put her shirt back on and take her back.” Then he turned to her and said, “I will verify this before we let you go.” He ripped the page from the pad, took out his cell phone and took a photo of the scribbling.

“But I have to pee, now.” she pleaded as her throat felt like it was on fire. Sabir looked in her eyes, then sighed ruefully. “Very well, then. Take her to the toilet.”

They complied, leaving her shirt behind, dragging her into a tiny closet big enough for a toilet and small sink. The paint was peeling off the cinderblock walls and the floor was littered with garbage. Her hopes were dashed when she saw no windows, but only an exposed light bulb and a cabinet under the sink. First things first, she injected the syringe into the side of her big toe, then, relieved herself. When she opened it, she saw her way out. On the toilet, she looked up toward the light and saw a pipe enshrouded with aluminum tape insulation. She turned on the sink and splashed her face with cold water. Leaving it running, she opened the cabinet under the sink for anything that could help her and then she saw it.

Amongst dusty aerosol cans and plastic cleaners was a bottle of Drano. She opened it to see that it was filled with crystals. When she looked down, she saw an empty plastic Gatorade bottle with its orange cap screwed on. Looking up, she noticed a partially exposed water pipe, so she stood on the closed toilet bowl lid to reach it. She was able to rip out several strips of aluminum from the insulation with her middle and ring fingernails.

“Out now, bitch!” Zami rapped his fist on the door multiple times.

She curled the strips into balls and stuffed them in the empty bottle.

“I need my top back!” she yelled from behind the door. Thankful for the additional time, she pocketed the empty syringe for good measure.

A minute later, the door opened as Zami tossed it on the floor through the opening. After donning her blouse, she was able to conceal the bottle under her pants. As soon as she opened the door, they grabbed her and she hoped the bottle wouldn’t slip downward any further. She knew that once it shook enough, the incendiary event would occur. They led her back to the cell and threw her down to the floor. Moiz said "I want her. Go tell Sabir we're not done, yet.

He bore down on her. She screamed, but knew there was no one to help her, so she started flailing, looking away from his weather beaten face and avoiding his putrid breath. She wouldn't let him have a part of her. She would have scratched his eyes out with pleasure if her arms hadn't been immobilized. Zami pulled down her pants, the bottle now exposed.

But before he could grab it, she raised her legs upward so they met his shoulders, then squeezed them along the base of his neck as hard as she could, then twisted her entire body to her right in what seemed as one quick motion. She heard a crack and a sick groan, then felt his grip go limp. When she relaxed her legs, he fell to the floor.

She didn't know where Sabir was, but she would forever see him a monster, yet she also wanted to scream out *for* him. The hallway led to a door with a red neon Exit sign above it. Heart pumping, she ran to the door to see a stairwell only to see Muhid and Taahid below, stationed on the landing.

When they yelled for her to stop, she shook the bottle and tossed it on the steps as they approached, causing an explosive pop that drove the two men backwards.

She heard footsteps behind her, two, maybe three men, so she ran down the stairs past the bodies and hit the floor of a poorly lit corridor with another door, but this time, it was locked. Then she heard what she thought were gunshots from behind, then the falling bodies of the men who had chased her. When a door behind her suddenly opened, she felt a sharp pin-prick pierce the back of her neck. A brief dizzy spell made her fall to the ground.

Still conscious but dazed as she looked up, Kate thought she heard some more machine gun fire, men hovering over her in SWAT-type uniforms, and one looking over her shouting," That's her! Dr. Carrie, we need to get you out of here, now! But she couldn't sit up, let alone stand.

"Pick her up and carry her out if you have to!" commanded an unrecognizable female voice beyond her field of vision as Kate felt like someone entombed within the soothing warmth of a fleece blanket.

They placed her in a makeshift litter and carried her outside into the cool but comfortable outside air. She saw it was nighttime. The mind clouds around her had lifted—almost. Someone up ahead opened the back door of an ambulance and lifted her in, seeing only its ceiling and the heads of four people above as the jarring sound of shutting doors startled her.

"What happened?" she said in a soft whisper. Her mind slogged through the haze.

The woman with the unrecognizable voice appeared over her and spoke with comforting sweetness. "It's okay, honey, you're safe now."

Chapter 32

April 30, 9:00 p.m.
The Upper West Side, New York City

He texted Javi within minutes of the break-in and stand-down with Gunther.

This time, they met at the Gin Mill, an Upper West Side bar. Javi shared a text of his own.

"Looks like your girl gave it up."

He still wanted to get to know Kate on his own terms, rather than hide behind his bogus identity. *But it was all based on a lie, wasn't it?* The false name was the least of it. He'd been the one who'd encouraged her to inject at the club, which brought her to within an inch of her life. He'd been part of the scheme to make her believe he'd been brutally murdered.

"I guess that's it then," he said, only thinking about how challenging it would be for her to break the vicious cycle of addiction, but at least he could be there for her—that is *if* she wanted to enter a relationship with him after all that had happened.

"Hey, man, you said yourself that she's a smart cookie. She'll be smart enough to stay alive and get what she needs, now that Vanessa Carrie will be out of her life."

"C'mon Javi. I know the odds. If she won't let anyone help her, she'll probably end up dead in a dark alley somewhere with a needle in her arm. You know it."

As he shared what happened, Javi's face turned pale.

"Shit. It's the same guy."

"What?"

"Gunther's PMC in Afghanistan. A witness in the village told us they came in and killed everyone in that village, but nobody was ever called out for it."

Now Danny felt his chin twitch and chest constrict. It hadn't occurred to him that Javi wasn't read in on the man. "It's time you told me everything."

Kelly's 2nd Battalion unit stationed north of Kabul had the unenviable task of locating insurgents and their suspected hideouts. Commander Colonel McClarity had been cracking the whip on a consistent basis across the region. Kelly's platoon, the 28th, was assigned a reconnaissance mission to locate one insurgent named Shazir Kahn-Jin. Much to the chagrin of coalition commanders, air superiority was ineffectual in rooting out the Taliban hiding in splintered groups throughout the remote mountains to the north and east of Kabul. Reliable intelligence as to their locations was hard to come by. Insurgents routinely launched after-dark hit-and-run attacks. Every village had at least one Taliban informant to alert insurgents of approaching coalition incursions. As furtive as Osama Bin Laden once had been, his network of cave dwelling insurgents made it known that the Coalition Forces were not welcome in the region.

The platoon snaked its way through the hills and ridges, along precipices overlooking the northern extent of the Panjshir Valley. When they reached the plateau about five kilometers wide, the village of Khenj lay on the opposite end of it. It was a community nestled against the base of yet another mountain range that seemed to jut out of the earth like jagged moon rock, higher than the one they just passed through.

The surrounding area was a patchwork of small farms that grew turnips, carrots and the most profitable cash crop of all: opium. Being that the oldest trade route to Asia passed through here, there was ample opportunity for the locals to profit from the traffic.

As the caravan approached, save for the sound of stray goats, it was dead quiet when in mid-afternoon there should have been the sounds of market trading and women talking.

From a distance, all the structures appeared untouched by any violence. Nothing but grass and mud huts, some cinder block structures, most likely used by the village elders and village gatherings. It was as if space aliens kidnapped the entire village.

Platoon leader, Jim Breyer, a first lieutenant, had done tours of duty in Iraq. Though only 24, he looked and acted beyond his years and rank, thereby garnering respect from his men in short order. At 5' 9", his short dark brown hair and fresh face belied his experience in the field. Javi spoke from the rear as Kelly listened, "Sir, they could have all bugged out. Taliban insurgents could have looted the place and taken some villagers hostage."

As they approached the village center, they all encountered the raw iron-like scent of human decay. What they saw next turned their stomachs. There, in pell-mell fashion, lay dozens of men, women and children, who apparently had been riddled from head to toe with rapid fire machine gun rounds. It was a virtual ghost town in every sense of the word. There were no visible signs of life.

"Stand down," Breyer said.

It was not uncommon for the Taliban to kill their own people. Clan warfare between villages was a way of life and it had escalated in recent years because of the Taliban.

Twilight loomed and the deathly stench was overwhelming. They were supposed to cordon off the village so that reinforcements could move in and capture the Kahn-Jin, but that directive had changed.

Brenner was decisive. "This wasn't Taliban." Then he spoke into the radio alerting the platoon. "All right, listen up. Load up inside your vehicles before coming out.

There still may be insurgents up in the hills. But I want a full search of every building, every mud hut in this place for anyone still breathing."

The platoon moved out in pre-assigned pairs. All they found were more dead Afghanis.

Javi was teamed with John Crenshaw, another sergeant and Special Forces veteran. When they turned onto a small mud filled street, they saw three women shot to death surrounding a well, their buckets of water overturned beside them. It was then that Javi heard some faint groans emanating from a small mud and straw hut. They entered with guns raised. What they saw was an old man, apparently one of the elders, lying in a pronc position, thc cnd of his long white beard drenched with blood. Crenshaw turned him over, then Javi found a pillow and slipped it under the man's head. He had lost much blood and Javi didn't think he could save him. So he did what he could to make him comfortable.

Crenshaw radioed the platoon and in seconds, the others converged. Breyer entered first. "He was on the floor, Sir."

The man begged for mercy in Arabic. Breyer called out for Corporal Andy Sereno, the platoon's translator.

"Ask him who did this," Breyer directed.

The old man murmured a response that Sereno relayed back. "They wore uniforms. Guns. It happened so fast. I tried to run."

"What language did they speak?"

"I think English, but I don't understand most words."

"Did they say who they were?"

"No. No. They sounded like from Britannia."

"Are you certain?"

The old man was fading fast, but Breyer pressed him. "Did they say who they were?"

He only had three syllables left in him. "C – A –G," before he lost consciousness.

Breyer stormed out of the hut. "Fucking British mercs did this."

One private spoke out of turn. "Sir, we should call this in ASAP." "No shit, private!" he shot back. "Tell me again how to do my job and you'll be walking back to base!"

Having brushed him off, he then turned to Kelly. "Strong, contact the FOB. Now."

She, Breyer and Javi hustled back to the Humvee, grabbed the speaker, set the frequency and depressed the talk button. "This is Vulture E-4R. Come in FOB, over."

A voice responded within seconds, sooner, Javi thought, than it normally took to make contact with base.

"This is Vulture E-4R. Come in FOB. Over."

The crackled sound of a voice responded through the receiver. "This is FOB, Vulture E-4R, over."

"Need assistance. Platoon coordinates GS 179-23. Village of Khenj. Report to Major Hardin. Need assistance, over."

The line lay silent for a few seconds. "Major Hardin unavailable. This is Captain Thomason. What is your situation, over?"

"All Afghans dead on site. No apparent survivors, over."

"Roger that. We'll notify Provincial authority and have them take care of it, over."

Breyer grabbed the speaker from Kelly's hand. "Captain, we have reason to believe

British outfit, C.A.G., in the area may have done this, over."

"Affirmative. Will report it, Lieutenant. Have you notified anyone else? Over."

"Negative, over." Javi threw Kelly a look. The question was not one asked for something like this.

"Do you require airlift assistance, over?"

"Negative. We'll stay the night and return to base tomorrow, over."

"Understood, out." He signed off and looked to Kelly and Javi. "I want 24 hour watches. In case we get company."

That evening, Breyer took up residence under cover in what was the village post office. Everyone else slept under the stars in the village center. The stench was overwhelming.

They kept guard in four-hour shifts—eight at a time, surrounding the sleeping troops.

Kelly approached Javi, M-4 in hand. She wasn't trained in infantry but still cradled it as if she and it had been good friends. "I agree with the Lieutenant. This doesn't feel right."

"Yeah, but did it sound to you like the FOB dispatcher almost expected you to call in? Like someone else tipped him off about us?"

"No way. I'm the only one here with the call signs."

Javi shrugged as the two stood there looking into the darkness.

Kelly reflected, "I'm supposed to be tough around these guys but when I see this…"

"Hey sergeant," Javi said mockingly, having known Kelly since the night Danny met her. "You tellin' me you wanna' quit?

"I don't know. Danny and I talked about me retiring when my tour of duty ends. What do you think?"

"Fine with me. I agree this whole thing is soup sandwich. When you got outlaws who are supposed to be on our side running around killing innocents, maybe it's time to get out."

"Maybe it's time for us."

Then they heard the gunfire and rocket launchers up above them.

Chapter 33

April 30th, 9:30 p.m.
The Upper West Side, New York City

The van zipped through the Holland tunnel to Manhattan and made its way up 10th Avenue. "Who are you?" Kate asked in a low and creaky whisper.

"You're in good hands now. I'm Joanne and we're from the FBI."

Four other agents accompanied her in the ambulance.

The rescue was supposed to take out Sabir's men but Kate had beaten them to it. Sabir was conspicuously absent during the faux-raid, just as Joanne had planned it.

She held out a Styrofoam cup of hot tea and honey as Kate sat up, which she gladly accepted. When Joanne saw that Kate was lucid, she asked if she'd wanted a change of clothes.

"What do *you* think? I stink."

Joanne called up to the driver. "Hey Eddie, swing by Dr. Carrie's apartment." Eddie Markham, along with the others, rounded out the New York crew that joined in the operation once Phase 3 began. "Once you have changed and freshened up, we'll take you to a safe house for your protection."

"Thank you", she said, then added, "A really *big* thank you."

"It's our job, Kate. It must have been horrible for you in there."

After another minute or so of silence, she continued. "What did they do to you? We were afraid we wouldn't get there in time to extract you."

"Well, one tried to…," Kate froze, unable to express herself, but Joanne understood when she saw as Kate squirmed, disgust showed on her face. "I think… I don't know. He might be dead too. Then there were others…"

She held up her hand, acknowledging the stress Kate was under. "It's okay, honey. Just wait until we get to your apartment and we can talk about it."

With grim resignation, Kate bowed her head in memorial. "They killed my boyfriend"

She glanced at the others, then back to Kate. "Yes, we know. Eric was one of us."

Kate's jaw fell to the floor, "What? Oh, my God."

"Eric Stone was assigned to protect you from your abductors but he failed in his mission. We're all deeply upset about it. So tragic. He was a damned good agent."

Kate's eyes drifted downward, forlorn. "He treated me like no one else I'd ever… How could this happen to me? I don't even know what day it is."

She reached out to console Kate, while her Glock 22 was securely fastened, hidden from Kate's view in the small of her back.

When they reached the apartment building, Joanne let Kate out of the double parked ambulance. Once Joanne opened the apartment door, Kate ran inside to the bedroom's walk-in closet, Joanne trailing her, stopping just short of the closet doors.

She heard Kate rummaging around, sliding hangers back and forth. "Shit, I don't believe this. Someone took all of my clothes. Most of this is Eric's."

Sensing the opportunity, Joanne reached behind her back, grabbed the Glock, released the safety and slid it out of her waist band. "Keep looking. There's got to be something of yours." She heard more sliding hangers, "Kate, did they make you give it to them?"

Kate walked out of the closet empty handed. "They wouldn't let me go until I told them, so sure, I gave them something, but it wasn't' the Tri-Meth."

Joanne alertly stuffed the Glock back down under the small of her back and let it go.

"I was hoping that they wouldn't know the difference so they would let me go."

"Are you okay?"

"Thank God," Joanne acknowledged, free to exhale. "I don't have to tell you that if it got in terrorist hands, we'd be living in a much more dangerous place that it is now." She continued. "But if you didn't give up the Tri-Meth, what exactly *did* you give them?

"The formula for an inert gas," she responded as she cocked her head to one side, exuding a girlish satisfaction.

"We're so grateful for that. I don't have to tell you that to share it with terrorists would be catastrophic for everyone. We know that your mother wants to sell the entire Tri-Meth you created to the highest bidder in a few days. We don't want that to happen, either. Do you know where it will be?" Joanne caught herself in a ramble.

"No, I don't," Kate said with dejection, as if it was her fault she didn't know. "I'm really sorry. I wish I did. Vanessa was supposed to tell me where right before, but we… parted ways."

"That's okay. I'll contact headquarters to get the O-kay to move in to shut down Frugeré and retrieve the toxin."

"It's not there," Kate said. "Vanessa doesn't have it anymore. I took it. The whole world's supply."

"Where is it now?" she asked, perplexed with this new wrinkle.

She thought Kate was about to spill, until she said, "In a safe place."

Apparently, Katelyn Carrie could play games, too.

She realized she'd have to take another tact if she would have any hope of getting the information from her

"Kate, your country would be grateful if you shared the chemical compound with us and let us keep the inventory for safekeeping. We'll keep you safe, indefinitely," she lied.

"But I can't do that. I'm done with Vanessa." She narrowed her eyes directly at Joanne. "If I could trade the Tri-Meth for my ticket out of this hell hole that is my life, I'd do it. It's the only leverage I have to make that happen."

Joanne hid her frustration. She knew what had to come next. "I get it. I'll wait downstairs." She walked out into the living room, then sent out a text as she stood at the front door:

On the way out, she took Kate's purse and apartment keys that were hanging on a hook rack. Then she walked up the street to a Cadillac SUV and stepped inside. "Wait for my signal." No one dared say anything.

When Kate appeared in what she could only interpret as joyful saunter down the front steps as if to celebrate her new found freedom, Joanne nodded at Shannon who pressed a switch on a remote control.

A swoon of searing heat from an eruption before her knocked her backward onto the pavement. The ambulance was incinerated, leaving a smoldering shell of burned metal.

The SUV pulled away, as Joanne saw her splayed face down on the sidewalk. This time she addressed Brandon. "Tracker's on-line?"

Nodding, he said "Clear as a bell. She won't go anywhere we won't know about."

"Good, and neither will Sabir, if he knows what's good for him." As the SUV headed Bronx bound, she gave one more order. "Activate Strong and Marquez. She's ready."

Chapter 34

May 1, 12:30 a.m.
Afghanistan

Javi instantly recognized the sound of AK-47 gunfire, a perennial favorite of insurgents but wherever up in the hills they were, the artillery wasn't aimed at them. In fact, it was aimed upwards to the sky.

They heard Breyer shout from the village center. "Christ! Can anyone see anything up there?"

Kelly dropped her gun. "Call for fire!"

She and Javi bolted for the Humvee, its headlights illuminating the night. She activated the radio. "This is Vulture 8-R. Come in FOB, over." Static crackled from the speaker.

"No go?" Javi asked.

"Nothing. It was fine before. Nighttime reception should be even clearer."

"The mountains?"

"No way. We're line of site with base. It all white noise, Javi, on *all* frequencies. I better go tell the Lieutenant," she said, quickly disconnected the radio from the Humvee charger socket and carried it off with her to the village center.

Javi gathered all of the medical supplies he could stuff into his rucksack. Quick Clot powder pouches, tourniquets, souchers, travia pads and morphine injector Epipens. After Javi zippered up his pack, he heard the sound of an F-16 fighter plane approaching. When he looked up, he saw the tracers of an aircraft missile originate from the ridge just above the village and watched in horror as it looked like it was on a collision course with the jet, which continued onward north up the plateau. The missile narrowly missed the F-16 as it continued its course, but then only seconds later, circled back and headed back in the direction of the village. He heard the fighter jet as it flew overhead, the smoke having obscured Javi's view. The next thing he heard was a reverse sucking sound that he'd never heard before, then the sound of the explosion that rocked him so hard, he was thrown back against the Humvee. The sky toward the village center lit up for a split second, then the darkness returned, but this time, more heavy smoke from the explosion rose up and outward, cloaking him for a moment, causing him to choke and cough for a few seconds until he immediately fell to the ground, where the air was clear.

Javi cupped his ears, as if that would stop the ringing. After a few seconds that seemed to last an hour, he uncupped his ears and listened. He took in an eerie silence as he lay on the ground. Still alive, he wondered for how much longer, then he rose up, grabbed his rucksack and ran toward ground zero.

The horrifying seconds of utter silence were broken by the screams and groans of injured soldiers, many of whom in his assessment couldn't be saved. With his flashlight, Javi could identify body parts having been separated from unrecognizable bodies strewn every which way, as the overpowering stench of blood and sinew replaced the pure desert air.

The bomb had landed literally on top of fifteen soldiers, incinerating them instantly and pulverizing everything in its path for about fifty meters in all directions. Each and every structure in the village center had been reduced to rubble, including the one in which Breyer had occupied. He was entombed under a covering of bricks and mud.

They couldn't assess the carnage the bomb laid in its wake because of the darkness, broken only by the three remaining Humvees' headlights. The four other vehicles were reduced to smoldering charred frames.

Javi knew triage procedures would come into play. Along the perimeter of the blast were the critically wounded. He had to analyze the scene on a triage basis: Bleed outs took precedence, while lost limbs would have to wait. Better to save a life than a leg was the hard and fast rule. Using his flashlight, Javi saw several other men he wouldn't have been able to identify, had it not been for their dog tags.

But where was Kelly?

He started to backtrack. Using his flashlight, he came upon her. He shone it on her face, blackened by the blast. She was clearly alive, but her lucidity was wavering. He knelt down and turned the flashlight upward so that she could see his face.

"Kelly, talk to me!"

"Javi" she whispered, her face ashen from the shock of the blast. "I can't hear. Anything" she moaned. He knew then she'd gone completely deaf, the blast having blown out her eardrums. She looked up at him, then grabbed her stomach as she looked down at the gaping hole from a direct hit of shrapnel. Her entire midsection was soaked in blood. Though more than accustomed to his share of blood and gore, Javi still gagged at the sight but somehow held his bile in. A section of her entrails were lying in the dirt. He applied a morphine Epipen into her thigh, ripped open her blouse, then tore open the clot blocker packet and poured the gray powder over the wound, but it wasn't enough to halt the spew of blood.

Javi saw the radio she had carried on the ground beside her still intact, Kelly still clutching the receiver. Then he heard a voice from the speaker.

"Vulture 8R. What is your situation? Over." The voice repeated the same request.

Javi grabbed it and pushed the talk button. "This is Vulture 7. Sustained many casualties. Need assistance, now!"

"Affirmative Vulture 7. Rescue on the way. ETA twelve minutes. Out."

Shit! He knew that would be too late.

Kelly reached up and grasped his arm. "How bad, Javi? Tell me," she said in a monotone drug induced stupor, the morphine flowing through her.

"You'll make it. Just stay calm soldier," he lied, knowing it was a long shot proposition at best.

"Fuck you, Javi, I know that look." She said as she placed her hand over the wound, seemingly not caring that her blood bubbling up through her fingers. Then her face tightened, shutting her eyes to hold back tears. "Tell Danny…," followed by hollow laughter, delirium having taken over. It was all she could take as the tears started streaming down the side of her face. Within seconds after that, her hand released its grip on Javi, falling to her side as she slipped away.

Danny took in every word.

"We thought we'd reached someone from COAC but later found out they never got the message. There wasn't even a Captain Thomason but none of it ever came out in the report."

"Langley published a redacted report. They told me that officially, the unredacted report never existed."

"That means someone inside redacted it."

"When info's redacted, it never happened."

His new born obsession for the truth brought up all the anguish and frustration. He needed resolution. "I need the clean version. Could you help me get it from Langley?"

"I could try, bro but I'm thinking maybe Langley's the wrong approach to take."

"Meaning?"

"You know how cover-ups and the CIA are always one and the same these days, right? You gotta' find someone who could access military intelligence computers."

Danny's mind raced. "We already know Gunther's company had access in the region. All the mercs did. Isn't that enough, for Christ sake?" He slammed his fist down on the wooden table. "Goddammit, Javi. You were there. Think!" Ashamed, he was about to apologize for railing on him but Javi, to his credit, remained calm and collected.

"Like I told you, we were in the middle of an explosion with antiaircraft fire surrounding us. The report says the F-16 crew thought they were being attacked from the ground, and I remember seeing that. It's like the whole thing was staged. Someone was watching us and even fired an anti-aircraft missile at the plane. The screwed up thing was when the crew called CAOC about it, they were told it was most likely hostiles. But even if CAOC has screwed up by giving them bad intel, it should have come out that someone made a mistake, yet that never happened. They really believed the information they had was accurate."

"So whoever doctored the ACO, also intercepted the platoon's transmission to base? Who would do that for CAG? They would've had to have someone inside." The ACO was the Airspace Control Order list that contained detailed up-to-the-minute intel about the Afghanistan skies.

"It sounds crazy, I know, but to find out, you'd need a computer geek who can track whose fingerprints are all over that report on that day, at that time."

Danny's drowning mind needed to resurface. He could only come up with the one person who he might trust who could provide the answer. But where to find him? He had no idea.

Chapter 35

May 1, 1:00 a.m.
The Lower East Side, New York City

She took stock of her situation. Vanessa had dispatched Gunther & Company to watch her every move. The terrorists—whom she'd lost count of—were after her and so was the FBI, she thought. *Wait. Weren't they just blown to smithereens*?

So she headed south to the only one who she thought could help her. She reached the Lower East Side in less than four hours. Once a proverbial backwater, this neighborhood, like the rest of Manhattan, was almost completely gentrified. The original buildings were constructed over a century ago to house new immigrants. Just as it hit its nadir in the 1980s, artists and LGBT families moved into the neighborhood, spruced it up and made it a hip neighborhood. But Jen resided on one of those urban islands that gentrification hadn't touched.

After the walk, her toes, heels and ankles burned. Jen's place was a five floor walk-up, gray sooty brick, with a rusting wrought iron gate against the crumbling sidewalk. A "For Rent" sign was posted on the front door.

She pressed the buzzer for apartment 5B. No name identified the occupant. When no one answered, she pressed it repeatedly.

Finally, an agitated voice spoke through the rusted speaker, "What!"

"Jen, it's me. Please let me in."

"Who's me?" she said, sounding like she was guarding a top secret government facility.

Kate, in her head with all that self-loathing, forgot that perhaps Jen had at least one or two other customers. "It's Katelyn Carrie, Jen. I need your help, please."

"What the fu—. What is your problem, girl? Business hours are over. It's 3 fucking a.m.! Come back tomorrow, noon or later. G'bye."

"No, now! Please! We need to talk."

After about two minutes depressing the buzzer non-stop, she thought to try the door. Low and behold, it opened. The lock was broken. Relieved, she quickly stepped inside.

After trudging up the five flights, Kate stood before the 5B and banged repetitiously on the door, not caring if the entire block heard it. The door cracked opened, held fast only by the chain lock.

She saw a single brown eye with mascara peek through the opening. "How the fuck did you get in?

"Jen, please. I really need your help."

"Are you deaf or dense? I told you business hours are over."

"Please open up! It can't wait!"

"Whew!" Jen reacted with a crinkle and a nostril flare to Kate's aroma wafting through the door. "You smell like pee. Even from in here"

"Not funny. I need you to let me in."

"We can talk like this just fine."

She spoke in haphazard run-on. "There are people after me! The FBI… I mean my boss is looking for me and these terrorists tortured me by cutting off my nails and electrocuting me and then… the ambulance exploded and…"

Jen put the kibosh on Kate's rambling. "Kate!" Jen barked. "No, girl. It's the drugs! That's all. Now go home, get help. You won't find any here."

"No. No. No. Please, I need you! I need someone. I can't get back to my place." Kate tried to convince Jen that she wasn't on some kind of trip, that she wasn't having delusions, hallucinations, that she wasn't some kind of hopeless freak, but was doing a piss-poor job of it. "Sorry, but like I keep saying for the millionth time, I'm closed for the evening!" Jen said as she slammed the door shut.

She resorted to a murder-suicide tactic. "If you don't let me in, I'll stay out here until you come out!" Then she added, "I'm sure all your neighbors would want to know what you do!"

Her rant was followed by more pounding and stomping on walls from a few apartment walls and the ceiling, followed by a muffled 'shut-up' demand directly below, followed by more epithets.

The lock clicked and the door opened, Jen standing with a crow bar at her side and a vicious scowl. "You are fucking crazy, you know that? Jen stood before her in a black cropped tank, black pajama shorts and gray wool socks. "I never do this for anyone, got it?"

She rushed in like she's evaded mad rapist. Jen gestured her to sit, then turned and walked to the opposite corner, no doubt to evade her aroma. The apartment mirrored Jen's personality—dark and bare. Although a studio, it was larger than most with a high ten-foot ceiling with only one overhead light illuminating the apartment, which covered it. Next to the door was a small round table with a large lavender candle, a lame attempt to bring ambiance to the place. Off to the side wall were two rectangular folding tables littered with real estate brochures, coffee grinders, six scales and empty baggies for heroin hits. On the opposite side were an inset stove, puny countertop and refrigerator. In the center of it all was a large musty. Otherwise, it was barren except for the retracted Murphy bed from which she guessed Jen had just arisen. Above it on the wall was a recessed lee with a wooden crucifix mounted on it and a pull string dangling from the top of the wall by a nail. There was no closet space whatsoever, just open racks of clothes and a dresser.

"You can crash here if you want," Jen said, pointing to the pathetic looking couch.

"But tell me, when did you have your last hit?"

"Six hours ago, maybe. I need more, but it was in my apartment."

"So go back and get it.

"No. Someone took my purse and locked me out. I have no key."

"So get a locksmith."

"Okay. Number one, it's the middle of the night and number two, I have no money to get one. And number three, I don't know who the landlord is. I was staying with someone else."

"So 'tag', I'm it."

"It's not a trip, I swear." she said reaching under her blouse to scratch the sides of her torso, assuming it was okay that they weren't in mixed company. "Some terrorists tried to rape me!"

"Sounds deep. Are you sure you're not talking about that new boyfriend of yours, because…"

Accepting that Jen probably thought her nuttier than a chicken cashew combo, she held out both hands. "Look!" as if showing off an engagement ring, with nails missing from both index fingers.

"Eeww. Nasty. Whad'ya do to make them want to do that?"

She struggled to choose her words carefully. "It's about work. I'm working on a… project."

"Riiiight," she said with patronizing indifference. "You said your job wasn't boring. So?"

"Things got out of hand with my boss, and I kinda freaked out. Big time. So I, uh, took some time off," she explained. "They killed my boyfriend, then they took me to this… place!

Kate's rant had held Jen at bay until then. "Whoa! Dead boyfriend? What place? And who's 'they'."

"These Middle Eastern guys kept me in a cell for a couple of days, I think. I don't know how long. Anyway, I couldn't shoot up. It was awful."

"I'll bet, but how'd you get out? A get out of jail free card?" Jen's mouth turned up into a lighthearted grin.

Kate's eyes narrowed at her, truly vexed. She recounted her escape from Sabir's men, the FBI rescue, the ambulance going up in flames, ending with her downtown pilgrimage.

"Seriously?"

Kate really didn't know what else to say. "I don't know how long, but I have nothing, except for these clothes." "They took my cash, bank cards and my IDs. Everything."

She looked around and saw next to Jen's bed on a tiny night stand a silver and black semi-automatic pistol. It looked like something more than a basic girl gun.

"Your clothes. Now."

When she hesitated, Jen looked up and sighed. "Borrow some of mine.

Kate really wanted to push it. "Could I, maybe take a shower."

"Shower head doesn't work but if you want to take a bath, you'll have to take it up with Roary."

"Who?"

"My cat. She lives there and hates being evicted. Three's a crowd, if you know what I mean," Jen stepped into the bathroom that was slightly larger than a closet, just big enough for a toilet, mini sink with medicine cabinet and a white standalone tub. She emerged a moment later with a plastic bin filled with kitty litter and Roary, a light brown sugar striped tabby cat with diagonal white streaks running through it. She was fast asleep.

"Just so you know, staying at Hotel Jen will cost you. Since I know you prepare your own stuff, when you finish I've got raw stuff to "refine" and package. Just call it rent." Jen motioned her hand to the far table, where a mid-sized bowl of crushed Xanax lay. She then walked over to the oven and pulled out two 1000 gram bags of heroin and slapped them on the table. "One third Xanax for each bag, then bag 'em. Got it?"

Kate nodded, happy to do it. At least it was work she could focus on.

Jen stared at her for a few seconds before she opened the cabinet under the kitchen sink, grabbing a plastic bag with Chinese characters on it. "Stuff your clothes in here before I have to puke. Please."

"I promise to wash them tomorrow, first thing."

"You burn 'em, don't you?" said the LIM College fashion merchandizing graduate. "I'll put them out. You make them fit."

She had no doubt about that. Even Jen's small frame was larger than hers.

When she walked inside, she saw a filled syringe on the sink with a rubber band.

Compliments of the house. She figured Jen didn't want to have a deranged person she couldn't get rid of destroy her place.

The entry point of choice, having blown out both of her arm veins, was her big toe after she plopped down into the tub. She turned on the water, asquint in the comfortably hot water. As she lay there staring at the running faucet, she pondered through her drug induced haze on what options she had. *None.*

As her wet hair draped over the lip of the tub, she noticed some pink Lady Bic razors which made her think of slicing her wrists open in the tub. That, she thought, would be her final "screw you" to the world and to anyone who wanted to get the formula out of her. Vanessa had treated her as nothing more than a golden goose, a cash cow to be milked dry. All of her friends abandoned her, even the drugged out ones. Kate thought about the times she would run into them on the street or seeing them brunch on Broadway, only to have them offer her a patronizing cold shoulder comment. She thought of how much she wanted to look her best, but instead looked like some blond mop running around the place.

There must be a way to leave Vanessa.

After she bathed, Kate dressed in the clothes Jen left out and went to work.

At around 9:30 am, Kate awoke to the sound of wood scraping on wood. With one eye open, she could see Jen on the bed facing away from her, jiggering with a large wooden panel with the Crucifix affixed to it, above the open bed in the well where it folded into. She saw Jen walk through the opening that led to what looked like a very narrow closet. Jen disappeared as she turned right to the area that she could see had a standalone metal shelf with bags on it. Apparently, Jen had taken what she had processed and placed it in one of the large bags. Jen crawled out of the opening onto her bed as Kate quickly closed her eye, leaving her to hear the sound of the false wooden panel click into place.

"Wake up," Jen said, looking down upon her, then walked away to the kitchen sink, turning on the faucet.

Still groggy, she stretched her arms out above her. "What time is it?" Jen didn't even look at her but her voice resonated loud enough for her to hear it, "Time for you to leave."

"What?" Kate said rousing, not fully comprehending the sincerity of the request.

Jen turned and walked up to her. "You can't stay here anymore, okay?"

Kate sat up on the couch, now alert. "But I told you I had no place to go."

"I don't care," Jen said, sounding glacial.

Kate grasped at a last straw. "Don't you believe in… in the sisterhood of women?" realizing then how contrived she sounded.

"Yeah, sure. But I also believe in the Father, the Son and the Holy Ghost. I believe in Big Daddy Green. And yeah, I'd even believe in the tooth fairy before your sisterhood," Jen stopped and glanced over at table where Kate's finished product was just as she'd left it. Jen softened. "Look, I really appreciate you helping me out with that, but fact is I work alone. Always have."

At least we have something in common.

"If you let me, I could help you could improve efficiency of your production. You know I could," she said, hoping it would resurrect Jen's memory of their previous discussion.

Jen hissed, "Oh, just kiss my Sicilian ass, why don't you? You think your Ivy League degree will get you anything you want? Well, let me tell you something. I know it doesn't look like it, but I work very hard to supply my customers with the best 'whatever' drug there ever was on God's green earth, and I'll be damned if some smart ass trust fund baby tells me what to do."

"I can't beat my habit without help, Jen. I know that. I just need a place to stay to get my bearings back."

Jen instantly seized upon the absurd request. "Hold up. You're asking me, your pusher, to help you beat the habit?"

"No," she answered, having thought about this long and hard earlier in the bathtub, "I want to trade my freedom from my boss for the stuff I took from her, but I need your help to do it.

"So, what's the FBI got to do with this?"

"Something I'd been working on—for my mom."

That got Jen looking up again. "Say again? Your Mom works for Frugeré?"

"Jen, my Mom *is* Frugeré."

"Must be serious if terrorists and the FBI want to fuck with you."

Kate was reluctant to continue. "Hey, maybe *I'll* deprive you of your high if you don't tell me." "Okay. Okay. So, when I was in graduate school, I studied organic chemistry in the agribusiness industry." She saw Jen wasn't getting it. "You know, like pesticides. It's big business. Anyway, so I thought maybe it could lead to even bigger and better things."

"Meaning something to get you away from your mom?"

"Yeah, but she promised me that if I'd work for her, she'd take good care of me. She paid me a huge salary and got me a nice apartment and clothes."

"Tough life." Jen said, seemingly uninterested. "You know, seriously, I'm not really feeling your pain here."

"Fuck you! You have no idea what it's like to be me."

"Oh, please." Jen scoffed, then reflected. "Well, I guess you did come here first, so I see your point". So what'd you do, make a bomb or something?"

"Pretty close. My mom's friend got her into some international finance deals involving chemical nerve agents."

"Agents? You mean like spies?"

"No, Jen. Chemical agents. Poisons." She wanted to tell Jen exactly how she went about synthesizing the compound, isolating its components from their combined byproducts. She wanted to tell her how she tweaked the molecular structure of a pre-existing neurotoxin by manipulating the ion imbalance of individual elements. She wanted to tell her how one need only know how to isolate and manipulate existing elements in one concentrated mass. She wanted to tell her how she structured the new compound by adding a fluoride atom, thereby insuring the victims suffer irreversible dysfunctional nerve damage. Instead, she just said, "Think of it like pesticides on steroids."

"Sounds like some bad shit."

"Very bad. Just call me Dr. Death."

"I prefer the Devil in Tory Burch flats."

"So, your mom is selling this stuff?"

"And the chemical compound I used to make it. But it ain't leaving here," tapping the side of her head.

Jen's head cocked to one side as she scanned her through her squinty eyes.

"Believe me, if you'd met her, you'd know why I'd want to get out of this."

As she'd hoped, Jen's gears started turning and she sat down next to her. The exalted advisor imparted her wisdom, speaking in a professorial tone. "Just find a public place and tell her that you want to meet there or no deal. Tell her you'll give her what she wants, for a price. How much is what you've got worth to her?"

"Never thought about it, before. A million? She has the money and I know that she'll need what I have in a few days."

"Ah, good. That's called leverage," Jen's right index finger extended up in the air as she said it.

"I don't know. I just can't trust her anymore, so it'd be hard to face her."

The professor spoke, "So make it an introductory contact to discuss the terms—from a safe distance away, to feel her out, to see if you could trust her to do the deal."

She was getting it, but still needed Jen to draw a complete picture for her.

Jen exhaled with impatience. "Jesus. You know. Close enough for her to know you mean business, but far enough away that you can take off if she tries to pull anything," she said, her voice curling up at the end of her sentence as if waiting for Kate to complete it for her.

Her gears were turning along with Jen, now. "What about a subway station?"

"That'll work. I've made many deals there. It's busy enough. I like it."

"So you'll come with me, then?"

"Whoa! I never said I wanted in on your plan."

Kate thought it a good time to bring up Gunther. "There's this guy who works for her, some corporate security creep. He knows what everybody's doing. Listens in on phone calls, reads emails, keeps track of Internet URLs you've been to. He even broke into my apartment the other day and tried to choke me to death—as a joke." For the first time, she saw genuine shock on Jen's face, taking in every word. "He could have easily killed me if he'd wanted to. But he just wanted to scare me."

"No way! What an asshole," she cursed, sounding like a school girl trading gossip in front of her high school locker.

"I know, but that's who I'm dealing with. So you'll help me?" she asked with exuberant anticipation.

"Hey, I never said I would," she said, like the finality of an iron gate crashing down between them. "I don't know about this. I don't want to show my face too much around the City. You never know if one of my customers would recognize me out of my element. You know?"

She was learning to target what she thought was Jen's weakness. "Too bad, there'd be something in it for you, too, once I get the money."

And just like that, the gate reopened. "Oh, alright. Okay. I'll tag along," she said like making an apology for telling a crude joke.

It occurred to her that maybe Jen was more drawn into it for the thrill, rather than money.

Using one of Jen's burner phones, Kate texted Vanessa at 10:00 a.m. "Meet me at time sq. subway, dwtn 2 platform 4:30 p.m. We need to talk."

At 10:03, Vanessa responded, "So worried about you. See you then."

Chapter 36

May 1st, 11:00 a.m.
Midtown, New York City

He'd heard enough. It was bad enough getting burned by Vanessa's fire-breathing vitriol for allowing Kate to stroll out of the building with the vials in broad daylight or that he'd let her be taken by unknown Middle Eastern men holding her God knows where. He had worked for executives before who had expected no less than Godlike expectations of him. He couldn't monitor or track down anyone. His surveillance experience was invaluable to American companies looking to crack the whip on employees, who always knew to revile him.

Brooke had recommended him to Vanessa, having known of his reputation as a tough minded and loyal man who knew what CEOs wanted when it came to cutting costs: cut loose the dead weight and malcontents from the payroll.

In his prior lifetime, between MI 6 and Frugeré, CAG, his private military corporation, had been Gunther's baby. Having committed over 25 years of his adult life as a soldier and intelligence operative, he chose to rekindle his love for Special Ops by providing private military services with quasi-military objectives to British and American governments. It was the perfect situation for him. Having developed relationships from his SAS days from Operation Desert Storm and earlier, he was able to assemble a group of men willing to take the risk of working in a war zone. For his crew, it was the thrill of battle that drew them in.

His company not only provided security services for other contractors, it also provided construction contracts, paramilitary assignments that Special Forces were not apt to go and provided intelligence information to Coalition Forces in the region. They were even privy to the army's radio frequency call signs.

For him, the profits were too good to pass up. Often, he could negotiate huge upfront payments. It was also to manufacture faulty intelligence regarding the location of Taliban insurgents, just to prolong the conflict and increase CAG's coffers.

Some of CAG's assignments were to assist Coalition Forces in tracking down insurgents in the mountains and caves of northeastern Afghanistan, where they were thought to be hiding until they could arrange safe passage across the border into Pakistan. Special Forces had been doing most of this work, but became trigger shy when civilian casualties were reported. The PMCs provided welcome political cover to relieve the pressure on Coalition Forces and their respective governments.

His current problems brought up the incident in Afghanistan that made him reassess his choice to continue CAG.

The day before Kelly's platoon had arrived at the village, his crew had paid a visit to the village in the early morning as its seventy-eight inhabitants awoke to the high pitched clatter of machine guns fire, the roar of armored jeeps and shouts of soldiers ordering them to wake up and give up Shazir Kahn-Jin.

His group rumbled into Khenj like the drunk, trigger-happy interlopers that they were. Khenj was bustling with activity from its small market place.

Frightened, the villagers listened as Gunther announced through his bullhorn that "No one will make it to dinner if you do not tell us what happened to Kahn-Jin." The situation escalated when a young man tried to protest. His temple met the butt of one of Gunther's men's guns. Gunther fired his weapon upward as a warning shot.

Another one of his men spoke out of turn. "I say we mow them all down, boss," he said in King's English. "Let 'em know that no one fucks with C-A-G!"

Gunther wanted to shoot his own man on the spot, but before he could act on it, his men opened fire, mowing down several villagers in the back. Cries of pain, desperation were silenced when the other men started firing, each from their assigned section of the line of people, until each and every soul lay dead in the square.

Gunther cursed, spit in the dirt, then ordered all of his men to round up the women and anyone else who could be a witness to what they'd done. They scoured the entire village and rounded up the remaining residents, mostly women and children, then executed them too.

He then went about his plan to cover his tracks. They returned to their Humvees and continued on the main road and up into the mountains towering above them. On the way up, he identified a copse of underbrush on a ridge overlooking the village, then decamped for the night.

The next morning, his men brought up into the hills above the village, a Sergey, a Russian made ZU-23-2 anti-aircraft twin barreled auto cannon, powerful enough to take out an American jet. Typically manned on the ground, this Sergey had a unique remote firing device attached to its trigger. They aimed it up at the sky.

Gunther left the monitoring to his crew, taking shifts listening in through their portable satellite dish. One of his men finally found what he had been looking for. Kelly's platoon was heading up the ridge and was expected to reach the village by mid-day.

His appalling plan took shape. His crew doubled back to the village and planted well placed explosives surrounding the village before the Americans arrived to draw out the attention of Coalition jet fighters, who would instantly notify COAC, which monitored every square inch of airspace in the region. He hacked into their ACO records and listed the village as being occupied by hostile forces, so any Coalition F-16s flying overhead would be prone to attack it once it saw the antiaircraft fire.

When they intercepted Kelly's call about what her platoon had discovered, telling them to stay put sealed their fate.

When he'd learned from the CAOC that F-16s were dispatched to the area because of the doctored information he had provided, his radio operator called in a "call for fire" to the FOB, while men were firing their AK-47s in the background to simulate an ambush, then activated his white noise generator which blocked all communications to and from the area.

At 2:38 a.m., after the F-16s confirmed according to the ACO that, in fact, insurgents were reported in the area, the Sergey remote mechanism was activated, firing up toward the aircraft. After a quick confirmation of hostiles in the area, the wingman released the 500 pound bomb smack dab in the center of the village, onto Kelly's platoon.

However, there was one more thing he had to do. The investigative report, that was from a confidential American intelligence source, had implicated his company because his group had been active in that region and because of the old man's dying words to the troops that CAG was responsible.

His American intelligence source and CAOC made sure that his company's name in the report would never see the light of day. That was the moment he decided to cut and run into the open arms of corporate America.

In the here and now, he had to deal with the fact that as of four days ago, his primary target was missing, and he couldn't find her despite all his technical knowhow.

"Unacceptable for you to let this happen," Vanessa lashed out. "You know how important this is to me. For my company! For your job!"

"My instinct tells me that Mr. Strong was part of a government plan, possibly working alongside Kate's abductors, to make her talk." Then he added, "After he'd helped them arrange Kate's abduction, they killed him."

"I don't care. I need those vials."

Gunther knew he was screwed, having been outfoxed for the first time in as long as he could remember. The best he could come up with to assuage Vanessa was, "She will resurface."

Fortunately for him, some much needed luck smiled down on him from above at that very moment. Kate's text popped up on Vanessa's cell phone.

Vanessa frowned, then shook her head in disgust. "Unbelievable," she said as she looked up at him. "It's from Kate." She reread it just to make sure. "It looks like you've been given a stay of execution, Mr. McGore. Kate wants to meet me to discuss some kind of a deal in the Times Square station at 4:30 this afternoon."

Thinking on his feet and thanking the cosmos for a chance at redemption and job security, he quickly formulated a plan as she spoke. "I will deliver her to you using two of the chaps you had me hire, but," he continued, "It is critical that you come. Seeing you will draw her in so my men can move in to apprehend her."

Vanessa eyes narrowed on him. "So make it happen."

Chapter 37

May 1st, 3:45 p.m.
The Bronx, New York City

The once vacant warehouse was a hive of activity with the full team of agents pitching in as makeshift carpenters and electricians. Rows of two-by-fours, pressboard and sheet rock were lined up against the far wall. The piercing whine of automatic drills and the staccato sound of nail hammers filled the air. A pinewood scent filled the open space.

Sabir had played his role—he thought—to perfection. Yet the chemist had made a fool out of him and so had the CIA. Joanne had pulled the trigger on the faux-raid before the formula was verified. The woman infuriated him, ever since she had made the initial contact in Damascus. Posing as a network correspondent, she had tracked him down and lured him in, just as Assad had mounted his assault on the 'rebels', some of whom would join ISIL.

His carelessness gnawed at him.

Never again.

They had him on close watch ever since, but he saw himself as a master at playing the long game, confident that he would live to seize the opportunity to inflict maximum pain on Joanne and her associates. The only questions where how and when? Though unanswered, he would wait in the brush and pounce.

Two agents, Greg and Shannon, guarded him at all times. Shannon Michaels, a balding Delta alum standing at 6'5" and former FBI agent, Eddie Markham, a nimble and experienced former marine.

Shannon's cell phone chirped. "Come. Joanne wants to see you."

They led him inside a trailer filled with electronic equipment, including several monitors showing satellite feeds. Joanne was chatting on the phone with who he surmised was her husband.

"Just a couple more days," she said matter-of-factly. "I appreciate everything you're doing to keep things normal down there. You know that."

After a short silence, Joanne continued. "Yeah, it's been quite an assignment."

Sabir looked on at her smug stature. His shoulders and neck stiffened.

Joanne finally turned to the agents and held up her forefinger.

"Kiss them goodnight for me. I love you, too."

He also noticed an electronic map that displayed a lone white blip on the screen, that of Katelyn Carrie, courtesy of the uteral beacon implant his men had inserted before the raid.

Joanne waved off the agents, leaving her and Sabir alone in the make-shift control room.

"I just spoke with Adalet. She's ready to contribute, if necessary. Just like you said."

"Yes but if you had given me more time…"

"Face it, Sabir, she was too smart for both of us," appeasing and admonishing him at the same time. Then she qualified her opinion. "That is, of course, when she's fully aware of who she is," pursing her lips.

He thought it pointless to argue with her. He had no weapon or any of his 'tools'. He was a well-trained fighter, but he'd have to fight through eight agents to the exit door. Not only that, Joanne held over him the threat that should he disappear, his funds would be frozen solid and he'd never lay eyes on Adalet again.

"And you plan to change that?"

Joanne showed him a gentle smile, turned away and left the make-shift control room, leaving Sabir to wonder.

In the open warehouse, her agents continued their work. Most of them had extensive armed forces training in close quarters fighting. Joanne had planned ahead for a potential use of deadly force to secure the Tri-Meth, if necessary.

She called out to Danny and Javi when she saw them enter and flagged them over immediately. "Gentlemen, nice of you join us," she said with jocular sarcasm.

Groveling, Javi said, "We're sorry, Joanne."

"Please don't tell me you came together, did you?" Standard procedure is for agents to split up and take entirely different routes to the same destination.

Danny said, "No. We didn't hook up until just outside. I took three subways, a taxi and two bus transfers to get here."

Accepting his explanation and ignoring Javi completely, Joanne quickly moved on, offering her appreciation. "Masterful performance, Danny. Very commendable."

Sardonic, he said, "Thanks for the heads up. It would've been nice if you'd told me they'd be real bullets."

"We had to make it real. Besides, that Kevlar vest did the job." She paused for a moment, "You still worried about her?"

"I'd be lying if I said no."

"Look, we both know this whole assignment has been emotionally trying for you. I was ready to give you a well-deserved break from the action but there's been a wrinkle we need to deal with, so we'll need you here to assist."

"For what?"

"The final phase."

He looked around at the activity in the room. "Mind telling me what this is all about?"

"Sabir and his crew screwed up."

"What do you mean?"

"The good doctor gave up a bogus compound, so we had to change strategy and—"

"Mess with her head? As if we haven't done enough to her already? Please tell me you won't use PSYOP techniques."

Joanne served on the Army's Psychological Operations Group in Desert Storm and with Enduring Freedom, before transferring to Central Intelligence ten years ago as an OGA (Other Government Agency) employee. It was a change in name only. Although the stated purpose of US's psychological operations is to induce or reinforce attitudes and behaviors favorable to US objectives, the CIA's Special Activities Division, working under the Agency's National Clandestine Service not only included covert political influence, it also engaged in manipulative interrogation techniques on enemy combatants to extract tactical military initiatives against US forces. Creativity was encouraged. She once worked with a team that made an Afghani insurgent think he was being chased by a ghost before breaking him.

"Does that bother you? It's more humane than what Sabir did to her. She won't even realize what's happening. Absolutely painless."

"Physically, maybe, but the woman's mental state is hanging by a thread." He posed yet another objection, "Joanne, I have to ask. Why are you relying on a known terrorist? What could he possibly help us with now?'

"Actually, it's his girlfriend who'll be our star player. Both you and him will have *supporting* roles, too. Don't worry, we're keeping him close."

Just then, Jim Parneau walked up to them, holding a 9-by-12 manila envelope.

"Do you have the photos?"

"All set, the NYPD was very accommodating and so were the show's producers, by the way," he said, handing the folder to her.

She removed the color 8-by-10 glossies out of Danny and Javi's view and smiled. They were of the interior of an unidentified police precinct. "Nice. This ought to be convincing enough," she acknowledged. "I have someone I'd like you to meet." Joanne brought Danny to the control room. Sabir hadn't moved from where Joanne had left him, still fixated on the monitors and on the tracking screen.

"Sabir, this is the man you were surveilling for us, Danny Strong."

"My pleasure," Sabir said, extending his arm forward.

Danny didn't extend his. "I can't say the same," he said with a stone cold curtness.

The two men eyed each other for moment until Joanne broke the chill fest. She walked over to the door and opened it, motioning to Shannon and Eddie who were waiting outside. "Sabir, step outside and make yourself useful to the crew."

Once he left, Joanne said, "What is wrong with you. That wasn't very professional, was it?"

"How can you trust a man like that?"

"Because he's proven he can be turned and can lead us to even bigger fish in the Middle East terror network. He won't be able to fart without us knowing about it."

He asked about the white blip on the center monitor.

"That's our girl. She made her way downtown to her dealer's apartment early this morning."

"How long are you going to let her run around like this?

"As long as it takes and when that time comes, I'll need you and the others to be top performers."

He then asked her a question she'd hoped would never come up. "You recall the two days before the abduction?

She nodded with feigned interest and knew where this was going.

"Remember when I came back and found her in the shower, scared out of her mind from the strangler? It occurred to me that whoever it was, knew her. That the person had threatened her."

Joanne shrugged. "What does that have to do with anything?" she asked, knowing full well that Danny knew of the hidden cameras and the listening devices installed in the apartment that recorded Gunther's break-in and attack.

"I don't know, but I think there is someone else who is trying to get the same information. Did she receive any calls from Vanessa? Didn't the cameras get a good look at the guy?"

"No, he wore a mask" she lied. "He must have heard someone in the hallway. The camera recorded him rummaging around, then waiting behind the door for her to show up. He strangled her, let her go, threatened her to pay up, then left.

Danny maintained eye contact as she couldn't come up with a more convincing answer. "And the guy never took anything?"

"The guy sounded like one of her dealers sent him for not paying up. She's been known to run with that crowd." She deftly changed the focus before Danny could speak. "Look, we now know that's she's made of much stronger stuff than we anticipated. Her mental scars have built up a natural defense, which we had anticipated. "Have you ever done any carpentry work? We need all the hands we can get."

"That was a long time ago," he said, now distracted. "My body's aching all over." I guess taking those bullets really knocked the wind out of me."

Joanne eyed him. "I'm surprised, Danny. Really" She shook her head. "I see this whole assignment has taken an emotional toll on you, although frankly, I'd hoped you'd be more resilient." Then she let him off the hook. "So okay, take a day off to recharge but no more. I absolutely will need you here by 8 p.m. tomorrow. Got it?"

Not a minute passed after Danny left the room when he looked up to notice the white blip start to move, increasing speed uptown at a good clip, indicating she was riding the subway.

It looks like our girl is on the move.

Chapter 38

May 1st, 4:30 p.m.
Midtown, New York City

An uptown R train rolled into Times Square as the two of them stood on the platform. Kate wore one of Jen's gray pullover hoodie, black stretchy pants and flats. The oversized hood actually worked to her advantage, effectively covering the edges of her face, having pulled the drawstrings out tight, so that not even her hair was showing.

The cacophony of people at this time of day, midday shopping or returning from their lunch hour was only exceeded by the sound of a subway train entering the station, screeching to a halt. The opening doors gave way to the onslaught of riders exiting the cars. The dual electronic bell sound signaled an imminent door closing, as the hum of the squealing motor whined in the background.

"I'll stay here. You wait upstairs," Kate directed.

"So, what am I supposed to do, exactly?" Jen asked.

"How should I know, this was your idea?" she snapped. "That guy I told you about, the big guy with dirty blond hair and a beard. If he's here, keep him away from me."

"Okay," Jen acknowledged, knowing she couldn't follow it, given the vague description.

"If we get separated, I'll come back to your place. Okay?"

Again, Jen nodded acceptance, then palmed her some pepper spray. "Just in case." As she turned to climb up the steps, she mouthed the words, "Be careful." Kate sat on one of the benches on the uptown platform, facing the downtown platform across the station's expanse, the two track beds sunken like dry riverbeds in a darkened chasm.

As if on cue, the rumbling sound of the approaching uptown train swelled as it arrived, creating a suction of wind as it rushed by before screeching to a halt on the express track. The robotic voice announced another express train arriving on the downtown side, the two trains blocking Kate's view of the downtown platform.

After both trains pulled away, she had an unobstructed view of the downtown platform, this time eying Vanessa as she set herself down on another wooden bench, facing away from her. *Perfect.*

Thus, their texting war commenced.

Kate: "I'm here."

Vanessa: "Please let me help you."

Kate: "No"

Vanessa: "Why are you doing this?"

Kate: "u no y"

Vanessa: "Tell me where you are, dear. I want to see you"

Kate: "No"

Just then, the voice returned, this time announcing the arrival of an uptown local train.

Vanessa: "What do you want from me?"

Kate: $$$ for vials

Vanessa: "Excuse me??"

Kate: "u herd me"

Vanessa: "Don't be so foolish. Come home now"

Kate: "No"

Vanessa: "I am so worried about you. I love you."

Kate: "u don't give a shit"

Kate got no response, so she texted a follow-up message: "You give me $1 mil, I give you all vials"

Vanessa: "I need to see you. Please tell me where you are."

Kate: "look over ur left side."

As Vanessa stretched her head and left shoulder around, Kate raised her right arm. She turned back around.

Yet another downtown express train rumbled into the station, obstructing Kate's view.

When she hadn't heard back from Vanessa for several seconds, her generational short term attention span was about to get the best of her, but was interrupted by the voice announcing an uptown R express train would arrive at the station in three minutes.

When the downtown subway pulled away, Kate lost sight of Vanessa. She'd left once the train obstructed her view.

Shit.

She then thought Jen's well thought out plan to be a glorified crap shoot and was about the leave when, a police officer approached. This was Nils Bruenig, clean shaven with short blond hair parted down the middle. Kate tried to look away. "Excuse me, Miss, but you'll have to come with me," he said in a ridiculous American accent.

"Excuse me, Miss, but you'll have to come with me," he said in a ridiculous American accent.

This didn't make any sense to her and she was completely thrown off kilter. "Why? What have I done?" she challenged him.

"Drug possession."

Kate grew defensive, "Does it look like I have drugs?" remembering what was in the fanny pack still attached to her under the hoodie. "This is bullshit! I haven't done anything."

Nils, who thought it would be easier than this, started fumbling his words, "Miss, I'm afraid I'll have to write you up for resisting arrest, as well."

"What are you talking about?" she said, totally pissed, as Nils grabbed her forearm and tried to pull her up from the bench. "Hey, let go of me!" she shouted, but his grasp was firm.

That drew the attention of several onlookers, but they judged her as just another pathetic drug user.

Nils then jerked on her arm with such force, she slid off the bench onto her knees screaming, "Get away from me!"

Exasperated Nils repeated himself, "I'll have to take you in, Miss," he said, this time unable to cloak his German accent.

But he just swung her arm around and grabbed her wrist, twisting it and applying pressure toward her. Kate started screaming in pain, unable to resist for fear that he might break it.

The automated voice could be heard from the opposite platform that another downtown train, this one a local, would be in two minutes.

The both trains would converge at the state at about the same instant, the station echoing the electronic beeps of the incoming trains. The rumbling noise now deafening.

Before she knew it, Nils's hand started to shake her as she felt a tingling static electric spark run up through her arm that made him release his grip, screaming while falling to the platform.

"She said let go, creep!" Jen hissed, then reapplied the Taser to his shoulder for good measure. Although still conscious, he wasn't so eager to rise up off of the platform floor.

Few seemed to notice or care due to the rumbling of the incoming train. Enraged, Kate shouted, "Get on this train. I'll take the downtown," while eying the other platform, oblivious to the whoosh of the uptown train that just arrived before her.

Jen ignored her request to flee but instead said, "I'm not goin' anywhere!" then added, "This guy's no cop! His shoes are wrong." Referring to the fact that he was wearing brown loafers instead of shiny black tied shoes.

Again, the robotic voice echoed up to the concourse, "*An uptown R train will arrive at the station in one minute.*" Meanwhile, the downtown train hit the station a few seconds behind it.

As another uptown R rolled into the station in front of them, fellow riders were too shocked to do anything about what they had just witnessed.

Kate made for the stairs but found herself tailgating a large man. Gunther and Wiggy had just reached the top of the concourse steps, stopped and looked down, but neither Kate nor Gunther could see each other because of the crowd of riders who had just filed out of the open train doors up the stairs to the concourse. She followed the flow of people up the stairs leading up to the concourse as she pulled the hood strings tight, hiding as much of her face as was possible. In her haste, she ran up the left side of the hand rail grazing Gunther in the shoulder, but continued up the steps before she reflexively turned back to confirm his presence. Their eyes met briefly, but she quickly turned ahead, running right past the Wiggy.

She heard Gunther's voice from behind. "That's her! Go!" Kate had turned left to reach the downtown steps as three more high pitched buzzers signaled another downtown train's arrival.

Meanwhile, Jen gave Nils one last tase when he tried to sit up, then reinserted the gun into her purse before running up the steps right past Gunther.

Kate reached the downtown platform as Wiggy closed in. The rumble of the oncoming train shook the platform and it grew louder as all three were running alongside it, with only a few people standing in their way. Kate was running out of breath as the train halted and the doors opened. Then she stumbled and fell, then looked back at Wiggy, who had made an ill-advised decision to pull out his semiautomatic and point it at Kate, who instinctively took cover behind a green painted metal riveted column adjacent to another wooden bench. But Jen caught up to him and grabbed his arm, causing the gun to fire three rapid shots in Kate's direction, one ricocheting off of the column as green paint chipped off, the second striking a wooden bench and the third just missing Kate's left ear, deflecting off of the platform and landing harmlessly onto the opposite express track below.

Jen horse-collared him from behind and reached for his face with both sets of nails digging in, as they both started toppling back toward the moving train, still moving at a good clip. Jen lost her Taser and it clattered to the concrete—and her grip as they fell backward, but she fell to his left, away from the oncoming train, while he fell toward the train, he lost his balance and fell in one of the gaps between two of the cars dragging him forward, ripping both arms out of their sockets, followed by moans, groans and screams by horrified onlookers.

Kate dropped her head down to the platform in horror to avoid the gruesome scene.

"Fuck. Me." Jen said in a trance, before she got up and ran over to Kate helping her up.

"Are you shot? I thought…"

"Just go!" Kate shouted as Jen helped her up, then proceeded to run further down the platform to the second set of stairs as the train jolted to a stop. She ran right past Wiggy, who was groaning in pain, both arms having grown about six inches.

"Later." Jen yelled and sped back up the stairs from which they came, before anyone could ask any questions.

Kate glanced over the other platform to see Gunther charge for the adjacent set of stairs, he did the same on his side. Kate hit the concourse level first, but Gunther would catch up, fast. She confirmed his presence on the concourse with a quick backward glance. The only thing separating them being the hoard of people walking between them in all directions, but Gunther had no compunction about pushing them out of the way. She ran to the downtown 2 train platform as quickly as she could, gulping for air. *I have to make it.*

A downtown local train had just rolled alongside that platform, more crowded than the other one. The doors opened as straphangers poured out. As Gunther closed in, Kate resorted to weaving around exiting riders. Then she felt a burly hand grab her shoulder, but jerked it lose when more riders looking to board rudely pushed their way between them. Hoping Gunther was held up, she continued running up the platform as the robotic conductor warned the world to release the closing doors before the, familiar electronic high-low warning bells chimed.

With Gunther a full car length behind her, Kate scooted in just before the double doors started to close. She looked toward the rear of the car and saw no Gunther. She thought "I must have been locked out completely" as she caught her breath.

The train inched its way out of the station and reached full speed into the tunnel. Still winded, she glanced to the rear of the car again, but this time saw Gunther's torso through the glass, trying to turn the handle of the door connecting the two cars.

He just stared at her, with narrowed eyes and eyebrows angled inward in fury, with the look of someone ready to strangle another. She knew she had no escape route now, but realized the door was locked. Once again, he glowered at her in disgusted frustration.

Kate turned her head away, biting her lip to stop herself from screaming. She knew he'd be able to catch up to her at the next stop at 34th Street, so she had to think up something on the fly. She noticed two heavy set dark complexioned women standing at the far end of her car and walked over to them. She was out of Gunther's view as she spoke to them.

"Please help me!" Kate said to them, with an urgent whisper.

One of them asked, "Honey, what's the matter?" Unlike her world above, the universal sisterhood of women was at work down here in the New York City transit system.

She resisted the urge to glance back at Gunther, her back to him, who was still gazing at her through the locked door. "My ex, that guy staring at me in the next car, he's following me with a gun!"

"We see him, honey. Don't you worry 'bout him," was all Kate needed to hear as the train pulled into the station.

"Thank you," she mouthed a whisper back to them as she bolted out of the car toward the steps. The two women followed her out onto the platform.

Gunther had done the same, but when he turned to follow her, he found himself corralled by the two women. "Why don't you just leave that poor girl alone," one of them said. Kate turned around to watch the scene for a split second as she climbed the stairs, his eyes glaring at her. When he pushed his way in between the two women, one grabbed his jacket lapel, causing his gun to fall from his pocket. Before he could even bend down to pick it up, a New York City police officer—this time, an authentic one—approached and shouted, "Put your hands up and drop the gun, now!" his hand on his gun's holster.

Gunther would have to explain why he'd been carrying a concealed weapon.

The last thing Kate heard was the officer barking, "Sir, get on your knees and put your hands behind your head!"

Kate, driven by the adrenal fear, made her way through the concourse and up to the street level where she disappeared into the crowd.

PART IV

"Women can stand a beating except when it is with their own weapons."

—Samuel Butler

Chapter 39

May 2, 9:30 a.m.
Atlanta, Georgia

Javi texted his contacts at Langley about Jay Tremont's whereabouts and was able to trace him to Atlanta, Georgia. The CIA's Directorate of Administration akin to an enormous human resources department of a multinational corporation, kept track of all of its ex-employees and agents. It turned out that he was living under an assumed name. Upon learning the information, Danny took the first flight out of LaGuardia he could find. He wasn't the least bit surprised of the CIA's ability to track down its former employees, if one asked the right questions and knew who to ask.

Thomas Williams' last known address was a YMCA room on Pryor Avenue but when Danny arrived there, the administrator had told him he had stopped paying rent a few months earlier and became homeless. She told him that his personal effects had been transported over to a veteran's rehab center on Martin Luther King Jr. Drive not two weeks ago. Apparently, Tremont had hit rock bottom.

Danny introduced himself to the facilities manager, telling him that he had been an old friend from the army and wanted to reestablish contact with Mr. Williams. The short, squatty manager told him he was out on a supervised walk with other men to a nearby park and would be back shortly. It wasn't until after 11 am when the group returned.

He'd have to spend enough time with Tremont to reestablish a relationship that had been tenuous in the best case and wasn't even sure if Tremont would remember him. He found it hard to accept that Tremont would have forgotten anything about the shameless abandonment surrounding the failed Geneva affair.

He couldn't identify Tremont at first amongst the group and only spotted him when the manager spoke to him and pointed right at Danny. Tremont gazed at him from across the lobby, then turned around to go up to his room. He'd let his now gray knotty hair tied in a ponytail grow down below his shoulders. He was a mess. Expressionless, he had mostly salted scraggly beard and was balding.

It was going to take more than expected to move this mountain.

"I need to see Mr. Williams," he said in the best faux g-man voice he could muster.

"I'm sorry, he specifically told me that he didn't want to see you," the manager said. There's nothing I can do."

"I just need ten minutes. It's urgent," he pursued, "It's a matter of national security," he said while flashing his expired Central Intelligence ID card.

For a moment, the manager pondered on what'd he'd just told her. "Alright. Five minutes."

He knew people seemed to straighten up when they heard, 'national security' as a reason and graciously appreciated the invite.

Tremont shared his room with another occupant, who was nowhere in sight. He hadn't even unpacked his boxes, except one full of clothes and the other with Tremont's laptop, twisted mess of extension cords and other computer nerd hacking gear. Jay sat on his bed, about to lie down flat when the manager approached him and spoke low. "Mr. Williams, this gentleman says it's urgent that he speak with you. He says it's about some national security matter."

"Tell him to get the hell out!" he said gruffly. "I left that shit show years ago and I ain't never goin' back!"

Before the manager turned to lead Danny away, he crossed the threshold but then spoke soft but clear, "Listen up Jay. I know you remember me and how that all went down, and I'm sorry, but I need your help. Your country needs you."

Jay lay face up on his bed and addressed the manager, "Tell this S.O.B. to get his ass outta' here. He can't do shit for me."

He turned to the manager and whispered in her ear. "His name is really Jay Tremont. We've been trying to track him down for quite a while."

He had to find a way to calm Jay down quickly. "I know you don't want to go back there, Jay, but just so you know, you're not the only one who lost something. If you help me, maybe we can both recover what we lost back there."

Speaking outside of himself, he said, "I left that guy behind a long time ago. You won't find him anywhere."

"All I know is Jay Tremont was the brightest man I ever had the pleasure to work with." Tremont continued to stare up at the ceiling.

The manager gave Danny a perplexed look as they both waited on Jay's response.

Jay sat up and stared out of his window onto the courtyard, his eyes looking as if they bore a lifetime of pain and vitriol. Then he sighed. "Just tell me what you want and I'll tell you if I'm even interested in giving it to you."

Danny held his ground where he stood. "It's wrong what we did to you. You were the best, Jay."

"Listen, don't bullshit me with your sympathy. I don't need it. If that's all you're here for, don't waste my fucking time."

"I know it's too late for an apology but I swear if I'd known you'd been left behind, I would've helped you leave the country."

"I thought you all knew and just got out of dodge before the shit hit the fan."

"Jay, maybe you don't remember. It's been so long and you've been through so much, but Joanne Dawson had told me to leave because I was going to be arrested for the murder of that woman who worked at the consulate."

"Yeah, I remember hearing that that Russian lady from the embassy died, but I didn't know you were involved."

"I wasn't. Not with her dying, anyway. But whoever it was wanted to set me up. Why, I don't know."

"And no one ever found out who killed her, huh?"

"No, but the police were looking for me and Gunther McGore promised to warn you and arrange for your escape. I remember when I offered to handle it, but he said he'd take care of it, but…"

He shook his head ruefully. "I never heard squat from anybody. By the way, what's that piece of shit doing now?"

Danny seized upon the convenient transition Jay provided. "That's why I'm here. After he left MI-6, he ran a PMC in Afghanistan. I'm here because I need your hacking expertise to prove McGore was responsible for Kelly's death."

"Your wife?"

"I'm sorry, I thought you knew."

"It was just a job. Why would you think that, boy?"

"But don't you get it? The same guy who screwed up my life is the same guy who put you in prison."

"Shit, that guy really is toxic."

"But he also had to have help from the Agency to pull off what he did."

"What do you mean?"

"Gunther's people massacred a village in Afghanistan and Kelly's platoon found out who did it. But before they could tell anyone, an F-14 from out of the blue attacked them, I think, based on false information that insurgents were in the area."

Jay waxed philosophical. "Bad shit happens, Danny. You know, for bigger reasons than you and me. It'll never go public."

"You mean like the shit that Gunther pulled on you?"

That got his attention. Perhaps, the old dog had some fight left in him after all.

Danny continued, "Gunther McGore took away the person I'd loved most in this world. I dropped off the grid for a while and got hooked on heroin while you were in prison."

"How did you get out of it?"

He suspected Jay was searching for some inspiration as well at this time in his life. "Someone showed me the way."

Jay took it all in and stared out of his smudged crankshaft window.

"McGore's the one. I'm sure of it. Only now, he's working security for a corporation up in New York that's into making chemical weapons. I've been assigned to recover the inventory and the chemical compound used to make it."

Jay turned to him with a sly grin. "Is there a girl involved?"

He couldn't decide if he should be impressed with Jay's memory or his perceptiveness. "You could say that, but I want to nail Kelly's murderer and the one who put you away at the same time."

"So what do you want me to do?"

"I need you to hack in to the COAC mainframe and find out who altered the ACO database the day Kelly was killed. I think that somehow, his company prevented Kelly's platoon from notifying CENTCOM about a certain village massacre that McGore's mercs had carried out. I also believe that somehow he altered the database on that day to say that hostiles were in the village, not friendlies."

"You think he had help inside?"

"Had to."

Jay exhaled. "Tall order, Danny." He glanced at his box of equipment. "You know, hacking into the COAC's ACO historical database is no easy task for most people."

Danny got a better look at the tangle of wires under the wooden desk and the three laptops attached to them.

"Jay, I need to know. You remember how hostile McGore was to American armed forces, don't you? It was always about making us look bad. Well guess what, he's still at it."

He sounded like his life had purpose again. "When do you need it by?"

"As soon as you can. The operation will be over probably by tomorrow night. After that, McGore may disappear again. But if you need more time, I'll understand. It's no easy task, like you just said."

"I said, it's no easy task—for most people."

Danny looked confused.

"It so happens, Danny boy, that I was one of the original programmers who built COAC's mainframe. It'll all depend on how many modifications they've made since I'd left. I can breach any firewall they put in front of me."

Danny's eyes widened. A narrow grin followed.

Jay qualified his statement. "After that, it'll be a question of how quickly I can access the database history. I remember all the codes—unless they changed 'em."

"Thanks, Jay. How long do you think?"

"Don't know. But I'll start right now."

Danny noted the time and knew he'd be hard-pressed to make it back in time, unless he left immediately. "Sorry, Jay. I have to fly back to New York." He placed a burner phone on Jay's nightstand along with a scrap of paper with his number on it. "Call autodial one on this phone when you find out anything. And text me any hard evidence you find."

On the plane, Danny cringed at the thought of more mental anguish and misery Joanne had in store for Kate. All of a sudden, a deep seeded kernel of rage within him made his blood boil.

Enough.

Chapter 40

May 2, 6:35 p.m.
Midtown, New York City

Kate made the call from in front of the Pan-Asian Bank Building on 55th and 3rd Avenue.

"Brooke Sato's office," Ellie said.

"Yes, could you tell me if Ms. Sato is in, today?"

"Yes she is," she said with an up tilt in her voice. "Who may I ask who is calling?"

"Uh, do you know when she will be leaving for the day?"

"Who is calling, please?" Ellie pressed with mild irritation. "Hello?" she said as the click sounded at the other end of the line.

As she waited on a stone bench on the plaza in front of the building entrance, Kate thought about how little she knew about the financial component of the auction.

It wasn't until after 7 p.m. that she spotted Brooke walking out of the lobby. She met her under the overhang.

"Brooke, we need to talk."

Brooke gave her the look-over. "My God, you look awful. What happened to you?"

"I can't get into it right now. I just need your help."

"I don't understand. Why can't Vee help you?" speaking with guarded suspicion, looking as if she was being watched or recorded.

"That's… It's not possible. I… we had an argument last week."

"Are you kidding?" asking in rhetorical fashion, pursing her lips with irritation. "Just put that all aside until—."

"No," she urged, grabbing Brooke's arm. "I hate it all, Brooke. Didn't you ever stop to think about what we've done here? Millions of people could die!"

Her piercing exotic eyes locked in on Kate, effectively calming her down. Brooke spoke softly, "It's just business, Kate. You've been working on this since graduate school and only now it occurs to you? It's not about ending lives. Think of it as saving them. The balance of power in the world must be preserved. Once everyone has access to the same weapon—and they will—the balance of power will keep the players even and the global economy rolling."

"I don't need a geopolitics lecture. I need money. Right now. I need a place to stay. Bad things have happened to me because of what I know. I just can't take it anymore."

Brooke railed with admonishment "You of all people should be thankful for what Vee has done for you. And how do you repay her? By abusing drugs."

"Yeah, well maybe *you* can turn a blind eye to this whole thing, but I have to live with it for the rest of my life."

"If I were you, I wouldn't lose sleep over it," she said.

"Well, I guess that's big difference between you and me. *I* would," she said adamantly. "Please help me. Mom and I are done. She sent Gunther out to kill me in Times Square. Did you know that? A terrorist tortured me half to death and the FBI is involved in this. Did you know that too?"

She recognized Brooke's face of incredulity.

"Just shut it, Kate! What's wrong with you?" Brooke's icy delivery and hardened eyes deflated her resolve. "To thine own self be true. It's too late for you to back away from all this. But if you do, then I'd suggest you better start running as fast and as far away as you can." With that, Brooke gave her the shoulder and walked away.

Frozen, Kate shouted in desperation, "I have the toxin! All of it!"

Brooke stopped dead in her tracks, but never looked back.

"Last week, I stole all the vials from the lab and hid them. Vanessa knows all about it."

Brooke stiffened, then stalked away. She disappeared through the swarm of people as Kate's plaintive calls fell on deaf ears.

The last 30 hours had been brutal for Gunther McGore. He couldn't recall the last time he'd experienced this level of humiliation, frustration and helplessness. Once he'd presented his firearm license to the officer, he had to face Vanessa with the bad tidings. Patience and her confidence in him were worn to the bone.

"Get out!"

"She had help, I swear it."

"Do you think I care? Do your fucking job. You shouldn't have let her walk off with them in the first place," she admonished, pointing her enraged her finger at him. She drew a puff from her cigarette then crushed it violently into the ashtray.

Gunther wanted to mention that he *had* wanted remove Kate from the building, *before* she had the opportunity to access the lab but he held his tongue.

She continued with another of her signature tirades. "All that so-called technology at your fingertips and you still can't find her, or those vials. We've run out of time. By tomorrow night, if I don't present the Tri-Meth to the bidders…" Vanessa cut herself off, shuddering at the thought.

"I *will* track her down before the sun rises tomorrow morning."

"Good, because if you don't, I'll rip your balls off!" Vanessa said flat and stern, signaling his cue to make a quick exit.

After the lashing, with Zak's help, Gunther reviewed CCTV footage from the MTA databank with fellow Brit Zak Krueger, the scrawniest of the group. He was the honorary class clown of the group; one could laugh just by looking at the man. He had sunken eye sockets oversized ears, feminine lips, a perpetual smile and strung out wiry disheveled hair like Edward Scissorhands. Although diminutive, he was just as lethal with a gun as hacking into municipal security systems.

Also, thanks Zak's ability to hack digital video files, he was able to find a clear shot of Jen's face and cross check it with any criminal records. A match was found that showed her with two convictions involving possession during her college years. Jail time had been minimal compared to what it would have been had she been convicted of intent to distribute, which apparently never stuck.

If his treatment of Kate meant anything, this ruthlessly opportunistic soldier of fortune had zero tolerance for drug users, let alone drug dealers. He pyramided his fingers with sadistic gratification, formulating what was to happen next.

It was time to pay her a visit.

Gunther brought three cohorts with him: Soren, Turkish mercenary Sticks, Ozer, and Chechnyan Marina Proviskaya. 'Sticks' Ozer, the lone Turk in the delegation. He had short black hair and sported a huge brown blotch on his upper right temple, eyebrows with deep dark circles underneath, and bushy eyebrows that actually curved downward.

Marina, the lone female of Loohsan's package deal, was a sniper. Although the western military experts denied their existence, she was a member of the mythical White Tights, an elite group of biathlete sniper skiers who were utilized during the Chechnyan war. With long blond hair, fair skinned and diminutive frame, her shy demeanor belied her expert skills with a sniper rifle. Gunther also liked that she, too, had a spot-on American English accent.

Gunther's plan? He'd utilize her skills to gain access to Jen's apartment, then have Soren and Sticks apprehend Kate whenever she returned. He and Marina climbed the stairs of Jen's walkup, a TV show blared from a few doors on the way up. Picking the lock was a cinch as Gunther accomplished this undetected.

Backs against the wall on opposite sides of the door, they heard the sound of her TV. He gave Marina the nod to rap on the door in rapid succession. She spoke with a dead-on New York accent "Jen. Please, let me in. I need to talk to you."

Jen answered with her typical social grace as they heard her respond in her irascible tone, "I said I'd get you your rent next week, for Christ sake!

"Jen, it's Jill. Kate's friend."

"Who?"

"Jill. Kate said you'd be here!"

"What do you want?" she asked with an annoyed growl.

"Kate's in trouble and she really needs you."

"Business hours are over, *girlfriend*." I already gave to charity once this week."

"I don't care about that. Kate told me where to find you."

The TV volume fell to a low hum as footsteps approach the door. When it cracked open as far as the chain lock would allow, they saw darkness except for the flicker of the TV.

"Are you dense, I said…" Before she could finish, Gunther kicked the door in, smacking Jen square in the jaw, reeling her backward with such force he heard the sound of bone crunching. Jen took a swing at him but Gunther was quick to grab her arm at its apex and separating the crowbar, sending it flying and shattering the glass case holding the lavender candle. He grabbed her right arm and brought it around, immobilizing her while covering her mouth.

"Sorry, guhrl-frehnd!" Marina said in a thick Chechen accent. She raised the TV volume to an uncomfortably shrill level, then pulled out her pistol and pointed it at Jen's face.

Gunther said, "Now, you're going to tell us where Kate is. If you scream, she'll blow your face off."

When he moved his hand away from her mouth, she said, "Fuck you. I don't know what you're talking about."

He reapplied his hand over her mouth and said, "I truly think you do."

"Go ahead and shoot me, asshole," she said brazenly, but clearly in pain as she spoke.

"We'll find her without you," he said before Marina's pistol butt whacked her in the right temple. Gunther then kicked her stomach before Jen lost consciousness.

Gunther and Marina both bound her up with duct tape at the shins, wrists behind her back and gagged her with silver electrical tape. Blood had stained the tape where her jaw had broken.

They rummaged through the apartment, finding only Kate's clothes in the garbage. As Jen came to, Gunther looked down on her. "Your time is up." He'd thought it a fitting epitaph.

Then he opened his lighter and lit up the lavender candle that Marina placed on the counter, well out of Jen's reach.

"Don't worry," he said lovingly to Jen. "In ten minutes, you'll be dead… give or take a minute."

Gunther grabbed Jen's gun from the nightstand, then they left the apartment with Marina ever so gently shutting the door behind them. Soren and Sticks lay in waiting as they saw them leave the front entrance.

Jen had emerged from the darkness. She knew Roary had slept on her throne in the bathtub while Gunther and Marina were tying her up, and only awoke to find her owner sideways at her eye level. Roary climbed on top of her, nudging her chin and purring.

Jen's welcomed Roary's slobbering lick of her face. When she opened her eyes, she realized where she was. The tape muffling her screams, she smelled the gas and tried to wriggle free. The pain from the broken jaw made her cry.

Her blood had soaked the silver duct tape. Left alone with Roary, all Jen could do was squirm.

She found she could roll over onto her side. Shards of broken glass were only a few feet away. Two body rolls later, she tried to grab a palm-sized one with her fingers, but couldn't hold onto it at first. She felt the burning aftermath of a brand a new slice of blood on them. She couldn't have cared less about the blood.

She looked up at the stove to see the lavender candle still glowing brightly. Either she'd live to feel the heat of the explosion just before being roasted alive or she'd just pass out from the gas before then.

Shit.

She grabbed a smaller shard that had a smooth rimmed edge. She bent backwards in a bridge to reach the tape wrapped around her shins, thankful that the yoga classes may actually pay off. She dragged the glass along the edge of the tape between the back of her shins, now also soaked with her blood. She tried to simulate a sawing motion to sever the tape, but the angle just wasn't what she needed to be to do the job.

When she tried to bite the tape from the inside, a mouthful of blood forced her to swallow it.

Lightheadedness was coming on.

The tape loosened slightly as she dropped the shard. She rolled her way through the bed of glass toward her open bed, and tried to kick her legs up onto the mattress. She made it on the fifth try, hoping she could slide most of her body weight onto the bed making it easier to lift the rest of her on the mattress. Coarse glass shards were caught in her hair.

She looked to the false wall, then looked at Roary. Roary saw the wall and stared back at her. The tape around her mouth had slipped down to her chin.

Jen could speak, but not over the sound of the flat screen. So she used her eyes, directing Roary to the pull string dangling below the Cross. "Go get it girl!" She yelled even though the crunch of jawbone made speaking unbearable.

At least we'll go down together.

Jen thought to roll all the way around facedown onto her head. When she did, a bit more of her lower body angled onto the mattress.

Roary sprung up onto the mattress and tried to climb up the wall to the pullstring, but there was nothing for her to claws to grasp and it was well out of Roary's reach.

Having pulled herself onto the bed, Jen squirmed over to the wall and used her legs to form and incline, to form a staircase for Roary to follow.

Roary wrapped a paw around the string and tried to pull downward, while Jen choked when she inhaled more gas.

The explosion was deafening and fervid.

Chapter 41

May 2, 9:30 p.m.
The Lower East Side, New York City

Kate saw the assemblage of police cars, fire trucks and EMS vehicles parked on the street blocking traffic. Gawkers had congregated on the opposite sidewalk of onlookers craning their necks up at what a few moments ago was a fiery inferno. She asked a passerby enamored by the sight of what had been apartment 5B, now reduced to a smoldering shell of billowing smoke and soot raining onto the street.

When she asked what had happened, a young man filled her in "I dunno, some kinda gas explosion up there." Gloom turned to panic. Her world had died completely and nothing could revive it. Not only that, it was time for another one.

Again.

She ran to the end of the block where Delancey Street awaited. She saw visions of what her life would look like now on, which in cruel irony, looked just like it had in her childhood. The jostling of two pair of legs closed in on her from behind. Soren and Sticks were in hot pursuit.

Catching a breath, she stumbled and fell to her knees on the pavement, breathless.

Soren looked down on her. "It's over, Ms. Carrie. You come with us now." She looked up and noticed a bulge under his jacket that could only be a weapon.

Both bent down to pick her up. That's when she screamed. "Let go of me!" she pleaded, arms immobilized.

Passersby noticed what was happening, then one well-built man intervened. "Guys, what're you doing to her. Is she okay?'

"They'll kill me!" she responded with maddening ferocity.

Realizing this was awkward, Soren said, "She's crazy, mate. Bugger off."

The gentleman didn't back off, seeing the opportunity to rescue this apparent damsel in distress. "Dude, I think she wants you and your friend to let her go."

"Just mind your own business or I'll spill your guts all over the street!"

Hey!" the man said, extending both arms with open palms against Soren's chest, jarring him backwards but he impulsively withdrew his knife, pointing it at the man.

He froze, but the diversion allowed Kate to reach around with her right hand and dug her fingernails into Sticks' cheek. When he released his grip, she bolted up the street to the corner, both men gaining on her, Sticks holding his cheek. Soren speed dialed Gunther while in flight." We've got her. She's on Delaney, heading east," he puffed.

She ran east toward the Williamsburg Bridge approaching along Delaney Street, but chose to cross it, ignoring the red light, causing beeping horns and squealing brakes. One truck whizzed past her from behind and a car stopped just short of her. Panting, she almost lost her footing, but regained it once she reached the median.

Soren, knife in hand and Sticks, hand on face, converged on her again as she crossed the median. This time as she crossed, one car swerved into the left westbound lane and stopped, blocking their path for a few seconds as Kate reached the north side, then continued west, away from the bridge approach.

They had to run around the vehicles, slowing their pace. Soren speed dialed Gunther again in mid-stride, "Now she's heading west to the Bowery. We're almost on her."

This time, she couldn't improvise a useful scientific experiment on a moment's notice. All she had was the fanny pack and her withering legs.

She thought she wouldn't make it to the Bowery.

She looked for any kind of hiding place she could find and thought she found one. There was an alleyway before her, adjacent to the corner building, so she took it. The two story structure storefront was padlocked with corrugated metal rollers for the night. The sign above it said, "Gotham Restaurant Supply Co." painted on the brick exterior.

She scampered back to the rear using the wall to maintain her balance and saw that an eight foot fence sealed off any escape from the rear that abutted, from what she could make out in the darkness, a vacant lot. Cornered, she looked for a way to enter the building, but also had to slow down her assailants. A row of metal pipes lay vertical against the side of the building which she pushed onto the walkway, blocking their access, if only for a minute or two. Too weak to lift them, driven by pure adrenalin, she pushed them onto the ground.

In the rear, she wriggled through an open window. Hands and sleeves now covered in soot, she stepped into a darkened stock room illuminated only by exit signs and the dimly lit screen of her last burner phone. As far as she could tell, the room was filled with appliances on the ground level, some still in oversized cardboard boxes. A mezzanine hugged the wall of the upper level with metal shelves holding unidentifiable wares in smaller boxes.

She climbed up a set of what felt like 100-year-old creaky wooden steps with a flimsy metal railing and hoped there would be a way out, perhaps to the store front.

There wasn't.

Three jarring gunshots rang out, followed by the thud of a door being kicked in. She heard shoes stepping through crushed glass as they entered the darkened space that suddenly turned bright. They had found the light switch.

Kate fell and started crawling to the end of the raised walkway. Having the high ground as an advantage, she frantically pulled out small boxes of cutlery and tossing them down the stairs, slowing them down. She then pulled on an empty shelve with her body weight as it tilted over across the walkway. She had tapped into some kind of superhuman strength in a life and death situation.

With her fingertips, she swiped her forehead through a film of sweat. Soren climbed up to the mezzanine and approached, gun in hand. She'd wrapped an extension cord around some kitchen appliances on the rack, which when she pulled it, they came crashing down on him. Her scream was drowned out by Soren's as the entire section of mezzanine collapsed under their combined weight.

Sticks looked up as the room filled with dust from the collapse and didn't know quite what to do. Kate was still trapped in a corner.

"Let me go, please," she begged. When she thought her request futile, she jumped. A cardboard box broke her fall and Sticks moved closer to apprehend her, but she'd clutched her spray and aimed. Kate kicked him in the shin while he covered his face with both hands, then limped out to the rear.

Gunther reached the building within ten minutes, only to find Sticks on the ground clutching his face covered in read splotches.

"Where'd she bloody go?" Gunther shouted, grabbing Sticks' collar in desperation.

"I don't know. She sprayed me."

"Where's Soren, mate?"

"Under there," he said, pointing in the general direction of the fallen floor, still trying to open his eyes.

Gunther could see the still hand and leather jacket of his friend.

It took some doing, but he was able to push the loose flooring aside.

"That girl led him up there, he could reach her."

"Shut up."

There was no doubt. He would end her the next time he'd see her. Kate's usefulness on this earth would end, no matter what Vanessa wanted. Just a tight squeeze and deliberate twist of the neck would do it.

Gunther had let her slip through his fingers yet again and thought that if he'd actually believed in the power of prayer, he would do it to save himself. At that moment, his phone chirped with an anonymous text message.

"Come to 131 Claremont Avenue Bronx. The girl will be waiting."

The Almighty God shared his wish for vengeance.

Given a new life, Kate jogged eastward, limping. She was determined to run, no matter how much it hurt: away from people, away from the City, even away from herself, which she knew was only possible through death. The fear of doing nothing had dwarfed that of finding the unknown.

As she stepped across a narrow one way side street, a dark nondescript van swerved around from Delaney in front of her and braked, blocking her way. The last thing she remembered was movement from behind as a hand grabbed her arm and the sting of another needle jabbed ito her neck, a moment before her body went limp and kissed the pavement.

Chapter 42

May 2, 10:30 p.m.
The Bronx, New York City

The musty aroma of aged furniture and dust, the din of distant, urgent voices and the faint hum of a TV news report were the first things that registered in Kate's mind, but she was blind. Her consciousness was emerging from the void, but her own ability to validate herself and her world was absent.

Who am I? Where am I?

Lying face up, Kate opened her eyes to see a harsh, blurred light that made her cringe. Once her vision fully adjusted, she looked up at the elongated ceiling light with two parallel ballast tubes. Disorientation led to confusion and then to panic. With a start, she sat up to survey the room. Its walls were cloaked with porous white baffling tiles to absorb sound, save for the round, Seth Thomas clock with a black rimmed border and white face, the red minute hand softly pulsing its perpetual sweep over the numbers. The time was 5:10. a.*m. or p.m.?*

The door had an opaque wire matrix on its upper half. Kate then realized she was sitting on a temporary cot. A government-issue metal desk sat in one corner and a dated couch with a small, ripped cushion next to it. Above the desk was a mirror. On a metal coat rack next to the bed hung a navy blue woman's blazer with black buttons and a shiny black holster enshrouding a handgun. She stroked both of them gently with her right hand when she noticed her missing fingernail. She checked her left hand, finding the other index finger also de-nailed. From the recesses of her brain, a momentary memory flash of the pain appeared out of nowhere, and then quickly receded.

As Kate walked up to the desk, she looked into the mirror hanging above it. She stopped to stare at her own face and pressed both palms against her cheeks. She scanned the desktop where five items lay. One was a black rectangular plastic nametag, the name K BECKETT etched on it in white block letters. Next to that, she saw a shield shaped silver badge, an engraving across the top edge reading "City of New York Police". Her iPhone, the one she'd heaved at her bedroom mirror, lay flat with its cracked outer case. Next to them were horn rimmed glasses, the identical pair she had worn before Danny removed them from her face. But she didn't remember that or why she needed them. She just grasped them gently with the palm of her hand then set them down. And the outlier item—a small bottle of Frugeré perfume. She focused on that item with curious fascination.

Mounted on a rack in the upper corner of the room, near the door, was a flat screen Sony tuned to what she thought was CNN. The images were of an on-site correspondent standing in front of a building in some urban setting, talking about terrorists and potential casualties, but she couldn't quite focus on it while fighting through her haze.

She gasped when the door flung open. It was Danny, dressed in street clothes. "Oh, thank God! Kate, are you okay? I heard about what happened!" He moved to embrace her. She thought about pulling away, but just took in his warmth.

"Kate! They said you were hurt so I rushed right over. All hell's broken loose around here."

All she could do was respond with questions. "What is… this place? Who are you? I… don't…"

Before she could express a coherent thought, another officer walked in. It was Sabir. "Is she okay?" he asked in his Middle Eastern accent. "I'd heard that's she'd been in an accident." Dressed in the standard New York City police uniform, he wore a name tag on his left chest with 'T RIMETH' in black letters etched on it.

Barely a split second later, she felt a jarring hot flash of pain running upward from her fingertip up through her spine. An image of Sabir staring at her in the warehouse streaked across her mind, then dissipated long before she could grab hold of the memory. "Accident? I don't remember anything," she said, perplexed.

Sabir continued. "The captain was looking for you. She needs you, Kate. They brought someone in. One of the terrorists. A woman."

"I don't understand…" she said as if she were in a somnambulant state. She started swaying from side to side. "I feel dizzy."

Both the men caught her and sat her down on the cot.

Sabir looked at Danny and said, "The accident must have affected her. But there's no time, and no one's better."

Danny said, "No, just give her a few more minutes. She's been through so much lately."

"I don't remember anything," she admitted.

"Kate, don't you remember me? It's Eric. Eric Stone. Your husband."

"No, I don't. I'm sorry."

"Look, Kate, let me try to help. You were in a car accident, but when the paramedics arrived, you were able to walk away, even though you had some cuts and bruises. So you came back here… and fainted."

"Where is… here?

"The 12th precinct," a woman chimed in as she entered the room. This was Joanne, holding a worn manila file folder under her left armpit. She wore a dark pants suit, holster around her waist. Her name tag said 'V GATES'. "Is she alright? I heard about the accident."

Danny said, "She'll be okay but her mind is still hazy. She doesn't remember much at all."

"Well, she needs to, in a hurry," Joanne said impatiently. "You guys need to step outside so we can speak privately." Once the door shut behind Danny and Sabir, Joanne started in. "We don't have a moment to spare on this one, Kate. Thousands of people's lives are at risk and until a few minutes ago, we had nothing to go on, Kate. Listen to me. What do you remember? I mean, before the accident."

"Who are you?"

"God, this is worse than I thought. Look, Kate, I'm Captain Victoria Gates. Does that ring any bells?"

"I... things are starting to... It's like I remember... fragments of things, like memory flashes that don't mean anything to me."

"Kate, you've got to try to remember. While you were unconscious a terrorist group released an Internet message that they were going to release some kind of new toxic gas in three locations in Manhattan today." Kate was nonresponsive, so Joanne punctuated it with, "Do you understand me?"

"What can *I* do about that?"

"Everyone knows you're our best interrogator in the precinct, Kate. They just brought in the wife of one of the terrorists. She might be able to tell us where the locations are and what type of gas it is so we can neutralize it before they have a chance to release it."

"Interrogator? I've never..."

"Look, Kate," Joanne said, repeating her name, "She apparently has a background in biochemistry and we believe she has the requisite knowledge of how to create the toxin. If we could somehow get that information out of her in time, we could save thousands of New Yorkers with an antidote, to protect them before these guys make good on their threat."

Still at a loss as to who she was or how she got here, Kate turned her head downward, eyes shut at the floor as if admitting defeat. *I guess it must be true, right?*

"Here. You need to review this," Joanne said, handing the file to her. "We were able to create this file on this woman on short notice. You'll also see that I've written out a list of questions that you are to ask her to help you along. I'll leave you alone for a few minutes while you review it. Take your time to review the file very carefully. And let me know when you're ready, okay?"

Kate nodded and then Joanne left the room, shutting the door behind her.

Alone again, she had only herself, a gun, a badge and the file.

The file was a dark brown binder with two subfolders. A black and white mug shot of Adalet was already paper-clipped inside the inner flap of the file. The name entry was left blank, except for a handwritten summary of the woman's background: born in Lebanon but earned an advanced degree in biochemistry from M.I.T. There was also a surveillance color photo showing the woman from a distance speaking to a man. The man looked like the one whom she had just met after her 'husband' came in. Her heart raced. The photo was of Sabir before his Beirut makeover with a full head of hair, but that face hadn't changed.

Brief memory flashes illuminated the dark recesses of her mind, if only for a moment, like sharp daggers stabbing through the brain. They slid out whole, only to return again a few moments later. She caught a glimpse of Sabir's face, first as she'd just seen him a moment ago, then of Sabir in his own interrogation room withholding drugs from her. Then nothing.

Why can't I hold on to my memories!

*F*rustrated, she tried to focus on the file before her, which was very sparse with information. She read the long list of questions Joanne had mentioned, most of them typical interrogator how-do-you-do-prisoner questions.

Mentally exhausted, Kate dropped the file on the desk and cupped her hands to her face. This was too much and too fast for her to handle. All she could hear now was the news report, which strangely seemed to be on some endless loop.

"…I am standing here in front of City Hall where the mayor is currently holding a conference call with Homeland Security to discuss this most recent terror threat on New York City, where a terrorist group had issued a warning earlier today on its website that it plans to release hidden containers of a deadly chemical weapon planted in four Manhattan locations if certain demands were not met by 7:00 p.m. this evening. All police and fire fighter and hospitals are on high alert. Fay Rugeré, Channel 7 News."

That name stuck after the reporter signed off, but it was lost on Kate as to why. The picture then shifted to a studio where an on-air anchor engaged in a question-and-answer with an expert on chemical weapons, according to the identification key along the bottom of the screen.

Danny viewed the monitors with Phil, Jeff, Trae, and Devon. One monitor showed Kate's image, another, an empty interrogation room, and a third a hallway as Joanne walked through it on her way to the control room. Two false doors on either side of the hallway led to nowhere.

"So far, so good everyone. Just keep focused," she said as she entered. "She'll be starting to remember things as the drug wears off. We'll have to guide her to exactly where we want her to go." She turned to Danny. "A word."

The two of them left the control room and walked down the hall to another door, this one leading to the larger room where Joanne and Danny first met. Behind them was a stretch of diagonally placed wooden two-by-four support planks that supported the drywall 'set' from the exterior. They climbed up a metal staircase to a balcony where they surveyed the enclosed set.

"Danny, I just wanted to tell you again how well you performed during this whole operation."

"Thanks," he said as his neck stiffened. Danny could no longer bear being a part of a further stripping down of Kate's mental condition. Yet, that was exactly what Joanne was asking him to do.

"No, I mean it. I know how so emotional it must have been for you."

Danny wondered where this was going.

"I think it's safe to say that you are back to your old self. Your job is done here. Once she breaks—and she will—the only thing left to do is to expose Vanessa Carrie. The hard part will be over, soon."

"Katelyn was a special assignment," Danny agreed. "At least now she has a chance to start over and break her habit. It's not too late for her, Joanne. I always disagreed with your assessment."

"Danny, the DDCI..." Joanne began, but hesitated when her cell phone buzzed. It was Jeff calling from the control room. He told her that Kate had read through the file and was restless.

"Good. I'll be right down." Joanne turned to Danny and said, "Let's check on our good doctor to guide her through the finale."

She walked down the metal stairs to the landing and downward to the ground floor. Danny followed. Joanne popped her head into the control room, connected her cell phone to her charger, and set it down on the control panel. "Okay, let's bring out our suspect and strap her in." Then she turned away from the microphone to look at Danny. "Just be ready for your cue." Then she spoke into the microphone with the bravado of a Hollywood director and said, "This is the final act, guys. Lights. camera and action, people!" Then she walked out, heading toward Kate's office and leaving Danny to do nothing for the moment except to watch the show that was about to unfold.

Danny was transfixed on the monitors. One viewed the length of the hallway Joanne had just entered, another in the interrogation room and another in Kate's office.

He heard the purr of Joanne's cell phone. When he looked down, he eyed the lit display. It was a text from Scuro. A response to Joanne's text from not fifteen minutes ago. Joanne's said: *Compound confirmation imminent. Please advise on subject.*

Danny shuddered when he read Scuro's chilling response:

ok to terminate Carrie at will

Chapter 43

May 2nd, 11:10 p.m.
The Bronx, New York City

Gunther and his crew arrived at the warehouse and parked their two vans at the corner past the entrance. There didn't appear to be anyone guarding the festivities inside. Alleyways abutted the building on both sides leading to the back but as far as he knew, they were close enough to utilize the parabolic microphone. The range of this one extended beyond what was considered typical. He had Zak point it at the southwest corner of the two story windowless building. *What were they doing with her in there?* He had hoped the answer would come by listening in.

"No white noise detected," reported Zak.

"Good. It's always refreshing to know that American intelligence is as careless as it is stupid," Gunther quipped. "Keep scanning. Inch by inch."

It only took a matter of minutes.

"I've got something!" Zak switched the output from his headphones to the speaker on the front panel.

Gunther and the others listened intently to the sound of a television news report describing the terrorist threat. At first, he didn't know what to make of it. Then the microphone picked up random voices, several men and at least one woman, but the words were unclear.

"Zero in on those voices!" he ordered. Zak complied as if his life depended on it.

A woman's voice came through. "...leave her... a while... the drug's... she's still... amnesia state..."

Amnesia? Gunther's face crinkled, eyes squinting. He was unsure about what the woman was talking about but recognized that voice from his past. "There. Focus in on that area," he said, pointing to the window on the second floor.

The voice continued. "Tell Adalet she needs to be aggressive with her. Don't let up. The tougher she is, the sooner she'll break down and tell us what she knows."

Another male voice responded. "The identification with the aggressor?"

"Right. Given another hour or so, she'll give it to us without knowing why or how she knows it."

Gunther could hear everything loud and clear now.

"Oh, this is so good!" he said with a sneer, then relaxed the muscles in his face, returning to a serious scrutiny of the building. Gunther couldn't believe it. The pieces of the puzzle were coming together. He whispered to himself, the others still too dense to understand. "Bloody Hell! Don't you hear it? It's all just one big… mind shag. They're working her over."

Incredible.

"Whatever they're doing to her in there, it's pretty elaborate mates. I say, now we let them do the work for us and engage at the right time. For now, sit back and enjoy the show," he said, clasping both hands behind his head.

"Ready?" Joanne asked as she peeked her head around the door.

Kate stiffened. Panic infused her voice. "That police officer earlier. Where is he? I swear he looks exactly like this man in the photo."

"Who, Rimeth?" Joanne said, pronouncing his name with a short 'i' sound as she stepped inside the room. "Don't worry about him right now. Just focus on the suspect. They're bringing her in, now." On cue, the two 'police officers' played by Devon and Trae walked past the door down to the interrogation room, guiding Adalet, bound in handcuffs, between them. Kate viewed them through the door window.

"Okay," Kate said, trying to sound self-assured, but failing miserably.

Joanne motioned down the hall as Kate stood up, grabbed her glasses from the desk and followed out of the room, file folder in hand.

They entered the small viewing area as the police officers uncuffed Adalet and sat her down on a metal chair in front of a steel table. There was no other furniture to keep them company. Here, too, the walls were covered with baffling tile, even the ceiling.

"Remember, if you lose your train of thought, just read off the questions to get you back on track," Joanne said.

"Got it."

"See what you can do, kiddo. We're all counting on you."

After escorting Kate to the room, Joanne sauntered back to the surveillance room to watch. There she found Danny, standing with his gaze transfixed on the monitors. When she walked up to Danny, she noticed that all color had washed from his face, leaving behind a ghastly blanched hue. He would not turn to acknowledge her.

"You okay?"

He answered with a hard count. "I'm fine."

As officers Devon and Trae left the interrogation room, they held the door for Kate. From the doorway she eyed the suspect. Only a metal table separated them and there were no restraints. The staring match lasted a good thirty seconds or so.

Although not having done this before, she started off in command as if reading from a script. A familiar *Castle* episode no doubt guiding her though it.

Just be the ball. Be Kate Beckett.

A chair was provided for her, but Kate chose to stand. "You're in a lot of trouble, I hear. Serious trouble."

Adalet's apoplectic expression looked past her.

"Let's begin at the beginning," Kate said for lack of a better introduction. It deserved a good laugh but for the monotone deadpan cadence. "Tell me your name," she said calmly.

Still no response.

"I repeat. Tell me your name," she said with a tightened jaw.

"Vanessa Carrie," Adalet uttered.

She hadn't remembered it up to now, but when she heard that name, another memory jolt plunged through her brain for an instant, then withdrew before she could focus and retain it.

"It says here that you and your husband came here not more than three weeks ago. What is his name?"

"Sabir."

An image of his face streaked by, as well as a high angle view of him during her electrotherapy session.

Kate paced back and forth deliberately, skirting around the table and hovering over Adalet from behind. "So, you're a biochemist, is that right?" Hearing nothing. she whispered into Adalet's right ear. "Isn't that right, Vanessa?"

"I don't have to tell you anything, bitch," Adalet hissed.

That was all the confirmation she needed. Kate moved back behind the table facing Adalet again. She leaned forward with both hands on the desk for support and stared directly into her eyes. Kate ramped up the momentum with a swagger that even Jerry Orbach would appreciate. "I bet you know all about chemical weapons, don't you?" Then she raised her voice sharply, "Don't you?"

"I don't know anything about it," said Adalet.

"Well *I* sure as hell do. Let's quit the bullshit right now. I bet you even prepared it for them. No one else in your cell has anything close to your background." She was making it up as she went along. "Ready to share your little secret with me?" Kate said, gushing sarcasm.

"Fuck you!"

"We'll see about that," she said, adjusting her glasses. "They're nothing without you, are they?" Kate waited a beat, but drew no reaction. "Uh-huh. If you tell me the chemical compound, I promise you we'll give you leniency." Now she had no idea where this was coming from, it just seemed to flow. "Just tell me, or else it will get very uncomfortable for you."

This time Adalet cracked a smile, then chuckled. "You don't scare me. I would gladly walk through fire if it meant killing any more western infidels."

Astonished, Kate pushed even harder. "Don't waste my time. Focus on the compound. Tell me about its molecular structure."

"You won't find out until your people have died an excruciating death," Adalet gloated.

"Just tell me what it is! You feel pain. We all do." Kate paused, but quickly lost patience. "Answer me, Goddammit! Answer me!" And for a split second, she looked directly into the real Vanessa's eyes before Adalet's visage returned into focus.

Adalet wore a confident smirk on her face, gazing into a nonexistent void beyond Kate.

"Answer me. The compound! Answer me!" Vanessa reappeared before her, wearing the same clothes Adalet was wearing. "Do you hear me?! Are you deaf?!" Her heart was pounding in her ears with anxious frustration. "I said, answer me, you sick bitch! Answer me!"

Adalet's lips started moving, speaking in a low whisper, mouthing the word's 'answer me' repeatedly. She repeated it, increasing volume each time.

"Shut up!" she said,

Then Adalet stood up and mimicked her. "Shut up! Just answer me!"

Another image sliced through Kate's mind. Now Vanessa was sitting across the table for a longer period of time. Kate shut her eyes tight and clutched the hair on her head with both hands.

Adalet leaned forward with a mirror image verbal barrage of her own. "Just tell me what it is, sweetie. Answer me!" She said it over and over, repeating her request in full voice. Then she broke rhythm and demanded, "You've been doing drugs again, haven't you?"

Kate froze in place and gasped for air. She was drowning and tried to pull herself out of the ocean. "No, *I-I'm* the interrogator, not you!" A groundswell of unbridled rage consumed Kate. The memory of her last encounter with Vanessa took a firm hold. Before she knew it, she found herself lunging forward, her entire body in full extension across the table as she grabbed Adalet's throat with both hands and squeezed.

I remember doing this somewhere before!

Joanne clicked on the intercom. "Detective! Are you all right? Stop! Let her go!" Devon and Trae ran into the room, leaving Danny behind to watch the scene on the monitor.

The two agents pulled the women apart. Kate shut her eyes as hard as she could, as if that would squeeze out the memory assailing her. When she opened her eyes again, expecting to see Adalet, Kate instead saw a reflection of herself, wearing her glasses.

"Take it easy! Take it easy!" Joanne shouted. "Officers, take this suspect back to her cell, now!" They complied.

Adalet continued her rant. "Infidels die! I'll never tell! Never!" as they dragged her away.

When Kate looked up again, her vision of a former self had vanished. Her eyes welled up and she started hyperventilating. "I don't understand this! Someone please tell what I'm supposed to do!"

"Get a hold of yourself, Kate," Joanne said. "It's alright. She's gone, now. Come with me. You could use a break."

Joanne put her arm around Kate's upper back, guiding her out of the room and down the hallway, back to the other room. The TV was off, the room was dead quiet. But Kate was too distraught and wrapped in her own thoughts to care.

"Tell me. What happened in there?" Joanne asked. "You lost it. I've never seen you like that before. What's going on with you?"

"I just don't know. I thought I saw… someone." Kate hung her head in defeat while catching her breath.

"You look exhausted, but we're running out of time." Taking Kate's arm and guiding her from behind, Joanne said, "Here, lie down again and get some rest." She directed Kate to the cot. "I know you may not think so, but I truly think you've had an effect on the suspect. I think if you keep on her, she'll crack. Even though you lost it in there, I liked your tack in the beginning. How you pressed her on the locations of the canisters as a wedge to get her to reveal the compound. But we're not there yet."

"Thanks. I need some time alone," Kate mumbled.

Joanne held her hand, then left the room without saying another word.

When Joanne was gone, Kate glanced up at the clock. It told her 5:52.

What did she say? We have until 7:00?

Kate lay down, face up and closed her eyes.

Vanessa Carrie. I don't know who she is... but I don't like her.

Chapter 44

May 2nd, 11:30 p.m.
The Upper East Side, New York City

"So, when were you going to tell me?" Brooke said with the sting of betrayal. She had left no fewer than fifteen messages between Vanessa's cell, office, and apartment phones.

The apartment was mostly dark, except for the track lighting that illuminated Vanessa splayed out on her sofa, drinking Slivovitz, straight. A lone tendril of cigarette smoke rose into the air, curling up from the ashtray on the coffee table.

Vanessa explained what had happened and shook her head in frustration. "We'd lost all faith in each other. I don't think she'll try again based on what happened at Times Square." She inhaled two puffs in rapid fire succession before resting the cigarette in the ashtray. "I'm sorry. I panicked," she groveled. The chalky blue smoke encircled her. "God, it's awful. She'll destroy us all."

Brooke wasn't one to argue, but was infuriated at what she'd just learned. She grasped Vanessa's shoulders and shook her. "Damn it, Vee! What do we have here if we can't share everything with each other? In less than twenty-four hours, we'll need to come up with the toxin somehow. These are not people you want to screw with. They don't miss a trick."

"Gunther failed me on this one too but I have no one else to call on. He promised to find her by tomorrow morning."

"Promised? That doesn't work for me at all."

Vanessa grasped Brooke's face with both hands and squeezed, as if wanting to crush her. "I won't take that from you. From anyone! We both know I wouldn't be in this hell if it wasn't for you. You led me down this path. All those re-fis set me up for failure. So stop thinking about what doesn't work for you and focus on what will work for me!" Vanessa shoved Brooke away.

"Y-you're right. I-I'm sorry. I should have recognized the signs early on. I never thought…"

"No, you didn't!" Vanessa pontificated about the virtues of motherhood. She paused and took another swig of her brandy. "Oh, what does it all matter anyway? The creditors are set to put me into bankruptcy on Monday. I'll be nothing but a disgraced fool."

"My reputation's on the line, too. But being fools is the least of our worries if we can't deliver the Tri-Meth by tomorrow night." Brooke leaned in close. "We need each other to get through this."

The door creaked open and Danny saw Kate sitting at the desk, hands cupped to face. He grabbed the other metal chair in the room and sat down beside her.

She didn't move. "Here," said he said, offering a cigarette. He wanted to tell her to run as far away from as she could, but eyes and ears were on the both them.

She sat up and reached a hand out to him. "Thanks, Eric," she said as she accepted. He extended a butane lighter and lit the cigarette. Two puffs calmed her down.

"What are we like, together?" she asked.

Staying in character was excruciating. He too dealt with conflicting thoughts; intimate moments interspersed with how he would handle Joanne. "Bad day?"

Kate pushed her glasses up on the bridge of her nose. "Yeah, I'm still trying to figure things out." She shut her eyes for moment, trying to get a fix on something, until she lost focus. Turning to him, Kate whispered. "Eric, I don't remember you, or working in this place. But then something inside tells me I should. Why?"

He reached across the desk and caressed the back of her hand. "I know it's hard, but believe me when I tell you that you're not the only one who has a role to play. I do. We all do. And when you realize that, it'll be clear to you."

She gave him a blank look and slid her hand away. "This place is all wrong, but I can't tell you why. If you are my husband, then tell me what I'm supposed to do here."

"Exactly what you *have* been doing—your *job*." He wanted to slip her a note as if they were in high school English class.

"That woman's crazy. I'm not even sure I can face her again." She looked to the desktop and frowned for a moment, then turned to him. "But you know what's even crazier? I actually thought I saw someone else in that chair for a second."

"Who?"

Kate shook her head. "Someone I hate. A lot. But I can't even tell you why."

"I think you can." He leaned in toward her, only inches away from her face. "This thing you're going through here, just try to remember the moments we've had together, especially the last two weeks."

"Two weeks? What do you mean? What moments?"

"I mean this." He moved in and embraced her with a kiss. Kate tried to pull away at first, but then relented. He'd hoped something inside her told her it was okay.

They parted, but stayed close. "I thought I'd lost you, the only person who ever cared about me."

"I'm right here and not going anywhere."

Just then, Sabir walked in, still in uniform. "How is she?"

Danny saw her sit upright and noticed her breathing intensify. He grasped her hands to help her up, then addressed Sabir with a stern glare. "You know, I really don't appreciate how you guys are pushing her right now. Can't you see she's not herself?"

"Eric, you must go. I think you being here is making it harder for her to recover," Sabir replied.

"What the hell do you know about it?" Danny stepped toward Sabir, right fist ready to connect to his face.

Kate stepped between them. "Stop it, you two. Please."

Danny relaxed his fist and took a step back. He seethed at the presence of the man but had held the feeling in check.

"Don't you see? She can't handle it. Captain Gates should not have let her do this after the accident."

"I remember you!" she erupted as she approached Sabir, raising her arms ready to strangle him. "You asked me questions. You were there. In that room. With me. You… killed… Eric…"

It was Danny's turn to intervene, blocking her path. "What is she talking about?" Sabir asked with a shrug, looking to Danny. He tugged at his own nametag. "Look at my name. You know who I am."

T.Rimeth… T-Rimeth… Tri-Meth.

"Do you see what I mean?"

"Get out and leave us alone," Danny ordered.

Before Sabir could step out, Joanne entered. "Ready to give it another go? We have to do this now." Then she paused, eyes darting back and forth among the room's occupants. "Everything okay in here?"

"No problems here, Sir." Sabir looked off to Danny and made a quick exit.

Kate's forlorn eyes told Danny she didn't want to do this until she figured it all out.

Joanne's drill sergeant voice got her attention. "Kate. We have to go. The City is counting on you. We're *all* counting on you."

"Just watch your back," Danny warned.

The two women left, leaving Danny standing alone in the room, helpless as to what was about to happen.

Joanne led her into the viewing room with a one-way mirror looking into the vacant interrogation room. "Don't let her get to you. Remember, like you started earlier. Start asking foundation questions that lead up to the big one."

The door opened as Devon and Trae sat Adalet down. Kate saw Devon take a syringe and injected the woman in the left arm as Trae held it down on the table.

"Is that allowed?" Kate asked.

"Based on your last encounter, don't you think it'd be a good idea?"

"But the syringe? I've never seen that done. The police don't…"

"Officially, yes, but desperate times call for desperate measures. Until she makes a request to see a lawyer, we'll do whatever it takes under the circumstances and this is an emergent circumstance, so go for it." Kate nodded as Joanne slipped her the file folder and whispered in her ear, "Good luck, golden girl. You can do this."

Golden girl.

Danny spotted Javi outside of the control room." Let's get out of here," he whispered.

The two walked outside the set to the far side of the cavernous warehouse space, climbing up an exposed metal stairway to an exterior catwalk fifty feet high that ran the circumference of the room overlooking the entire set. "Joanne's going to kill her."

"That's sick. I'm gonna tell Joanne where to go."

"Forget it. You'd be in her doghouse. It's over. Joanne's going to break her, kill her and there's not a damn thing we can do about it."

Danny's phone buzzed for an inbound text message from Jay. It said: *Check your email.*

When Danny opened it, he saw the smoking gun he had been waiting for—the encrypted attachment confirmed that Gunther McGore had altered the ACO database.

Danny's phone buzzed with a call from Jay. Without Danny saying a word, Jay started talking. "Hey Danny boy, there's also something else you should know. I also found out who helped McGore cover his tracks at the COAC."

"Who?"

"Just check your email, Danny Boy." Before Danny could check, Jay's line disconnected.

The email contained an attachment of another email sent to Gunther himself, which merely said, "It's been handled. I expunged your database records breach. No worries."

The sender: JDawson.

Before Danny could share the shocking revelation with Javi, they both heard two explosions as the overhead lights flickered, then went dark. Gunfire erupted. There was nowhere to run.

Chapter 45

May 3, 12:10 a.m.
The Bronx, New York City

"Alright, so tell me how the toxin is stored," Kate demanded.

"Vials." Adalet offered. "Small vials." To Kate, the 'drug' seemed to be working.

"Oh c'mon, how much damage can one small vial do? Maybe cover the footprint of Bryant Park?"

"Try one mile, golden girl!"

"Don't call me that. Why are you—?" Kate halted midsentence and took in a breath before continuing. "So you must feel proud that you really created something so God-awful, don't you?"

Adalet was silent.

"Tell us where they are or we'll bring in your husband, too. We have his photo." She showed it to Adalet/Vanessa. "So, tell me…" Kate cut herself short when she saw the photo. It was Sabir's face, but with hair. She thought back to cop she knew as Rimeth and knew something didn't add up. Her brain was an open faced sandwich—flipped over onto a grill. Images sharpened in her mind but they were short bursts of memory, ephemeral jolts to the mind that didn't hang around long enough for her to figure out who or what they were.

She dropped the whole file down onto the table. "Look, I know something about chemical weapons, Vanessa. So don't think I won't smell your bullshit if you lie to me." She took a moment to organize her approach. "How do you plan to release the gas? Can I assume that whoever does will sacrifice himself?"

"No," Adalet said with a slurred and lethargic, almost serene voice. "Remote… control," she said.

"How? By whom?" Kate glanced up at the clock. The time was 6:28 p.m. "How do we neutralize the gas?"

"Can't… Can't be done."

"What did I tell you about lying to me? Any nerve gas has an antidote. You know it and I know it."

"Can't. No antidote."

"All right, so we're back. What is the molecular structure? Just tell me and we can all go home. You were doing so well."

"No. No, please no."

The stone wall had resurrected itself but Kate was determined to breach it. "Think about its molecular structure," she said thoughtfully. "The NH3 nitrous oxide rings have to bond together. How did you accomplish that?"

"Tri. Methyl. Phospho. Flour amine," Adalet said in a catatonic stupor.

T Rimeth. T Rimeth. Tri Meth. "No, it's not! Come off it! You and I both know that's the chemical compound for Sarin." *It's on the tip of her tongue.* "So stop insulting my intelligence and tell me the real one. Christ, I could almost figure it out for myself. So let's have it. Now."

Adalet's face turned ashen.

Kate repeated the same command, her voice steadily growing hoarse. She understood the stakes. She was all alone in a room with a murderer, or just maybe there were two in the same room. She looked behind her at the mirror looking for some kind of help, like Joanne would burst in and take over.

Just when Kate was about to give up, Adalet relented, suddenly aroused from her drug-induced state. "All right, I'll tell you. I'll tell you. The structure. It's…" Adalet's mouth moved, but the volume inexplicitly shut off.

Kate was baffled and tried to reign in her frustration. "What? Speak up. I can't hear you. Say it louder!" Adalet's mouth kept moving faster, nonstop, without a sound. She ran around the table and grabbed Adalet's shirt by the collar. "Just speak up! What's wrong with you?" Kate let go of her but was eyeball to eyeball with Adalet's face. "Tell me!" Her voice broke up into a pitiful rasp.

Adalet mimics what Kate was saying in a silent whisper. Then she slowly raised her voice with each repetition. "Tell me! What. Is. The. Structure? I know you know what it is!" Adalet rose up from her seat, circled around the table to Kate and continued her verbal assault.

The tables had turned.

"Stop it! Sit down! What are you doing? I'm the interrogator, not you!" Kate said, backing away, now on her literal heels.

Adalet kept slowly moving toward her. "No, *I'm* the interrogator! *I'm* Vanessa Carrie and you'll tell *me* what it is. You owe it to me!"

"No. I… Shut up!" Kate would have run out of the room had Adalet not blocked her way.

"You tell me what I want to know or I'll kill you!" Adalet shouted.

Trae and Devon burst in to restrain Adalet, but before they could, she moved on Kate, slamming her into the wall as she strangled her. The two men separated the two women and dragged away Adalet as she shouted unintelligible Arabic epithets, leaving Kate aghast.

Joanne entered. "Are you okay? We saw it all. You were great in there."

Breathless, Kate said, "What are you talking about?"

"The locations and the compound too! A big win for everyone. Congratulations."

"No, I… couldn't hear her at all. Did you?"

Joanne feigned surprise. "No, we couldn't. The microphone didn't pick it up, but you must have heard it, right?"

"Captain, her mouth kept moving but I heard nothing. She just mouthed it. Then you saw what happened."

Joanne pulled up a chair. "Have a seat, Kate. We have run out of time."

Joanne came in close and spoke low with a gentle guidance. "Do you want to know what I think? You didn't *want* to hear her. The accident must have brought up memories from within you, about your life. That's typical of an upbringing of abuse and abandonment. You'd always wanted to please people, but somehow let them down at the finish line. I thought that by giving you this assignment, you'd overcome that. Apparently, I was wrong," Her voice trailed off with a sigh.

"No, you weren't. I swear," Kate argued. "Give me a chance. Maybe I can figure out what she was saying if I concentrate."

"Fine. Here's a notepad. If you have any revelations, now is the time."

Although Kate hoped Joanne would stand up to leave, she didn't.

"You said in there that you knew the chemical compound for Sarin. Write that down, then maybe it'll jog your memory." Joanne slid the yellow lined notepad toward her with the word Tri-Meth written across the top margin.

Kate took it, but still drew a blank. "When I was in there. I had it. I thought I did, anyway. I swear it was on the tip of my tongue."

"You know what will happen if you can't remember. Those terrorists still have their chemical weapon and thanks to Vanessa, they know how to make it and expose the entire world to it. With no known antidote. Now, I want you to focus on Vanessa's mouth."

One moment, Kate saw Adalet's face, then Vanessa's, struggling to reach the recesses of her mind. Then she wrote out rows of chemical element symbols, attempting to unscramble them.

At first it was no use, but then she jotted down haphazard molecular notations of nitrous oxide rings and chlorine… *or was it fluoride?…* element symbols.

It occurred to her, like a Wheel of Fortune letter board solution, the answer was right there in front of her, with clarity leading the way. Eric. Sabir. Vanessa. They all meant something to her, she knew.

She wrote out multiple molecular notations that grew longer and made more sense. Then, suddenly, she realized that it was right there in front of her. It was done. Kate looked up at Joanne, saying the magic words, "I remember!" Kate slid the notepad across the table to show her.

Chapter 46

May 3, 12:25 a.m.
The Bronx, New York City

The ten interlopers scrambled silently into positions surrounding the warehouse. It was just like his SAS days; moments like these when Gunther was in his element. Few men were built for this kind of work, but it was the kind of work Gunther McGore was born for; the proper balance of brilliant planning and coldblooded execution.

He'd heard enough to move in. They divided into two groups. The first was led by Shane and Angolan merc, Nkiambi Abdourohimi, 'Kim' for short. They entered through the rear and cut the electrical power. The second, led by Demarco Walker with his brother Dion, hailed from Chicago's South Side, both men were Marine Corps veterans. Clean shaven and of substantial build, Demarco sported dreadlocks while Deion was bald, his covered by a brown skull cap. Seeing no perimeter opposition, each team affixed Primacord along the circumference of both outer metal door frames of the building.

Gunther directed them through his com-link. "Initiate your assault on my word but remember, Katelyn Carrie must be taken alive." Although they acknowledged, he well knew that as trigger happy mercenaries, it was always shoot first and don't bother to ask any questions later.

Zak stayed behind in the truck and received Gunther's signal to scramble any electrical listening and video surveillance devices inside, including the front entrance camera. Shane and company located the electrical demarcation point and simultaneously received Gunther's order to sever the electric cable.

Upon Zak's confirmation, Gunther issued the 'go' order. The Primacord explosive detonated with a wave of intense heat. It would have crushed anyone on the opposite side of either door. Wearing night vision goggles, his team confirmed that no one was on the floor. Gunther instructed them to hold fire as he caught up and entered through the rear entryway. What he saw was a wooden enclosure in the center of the room and noticed light bleeding through a drywall seam.

"They're in there, mates!" he shouted. They had a full view of the set, but no sign of any agents.

Danny heard the detonations fore and aft of where they were standing just before the room turned dark. He heard the commotion below them, but could not see the men enter through the rear entrance. Danny and Javi had to improvise a plan or die.

In seconds, Gunther's men had converged on the cavernous room, machine gun fire tracers electrified the air like amber spikes. The emergency lights mounted below the catwalk activated, illuminating some of the shooters in red while the two special ops veterans lurked in the rafters above them undetected.

"They'll find Kate if we don't do something," Danny said. "We need a diversion."

"The others," Javi reminded Danny, pointing across the room, referring to their colleagues in the second floor office overlooking the set.

Danny realized Gunther's men hadn't thought to look upward. Being in each other's line of fire told him they were undisciplined and not used to working as a unit.

Danny had to figure out how two Glocks could overpower seven, maybe eight submachine guns. Even if he and Javi were able to take out two each, the muzzle fire would make them sitting ducks for the remaining shooters.

Then Danny remembered as he pointed upward. "The sprinklers!"

Danny had noticed the matrix of steel water pipes suspended from the ceiling from earlier visits. Two catwalks traversed the room through the center. He turned to Javi and said, "Follow my lead. I'll run across and shoot out as many heads as I can. You do the same by taking the other catwalk. Don't make your run too predictable for them."

The good news: both of them still had their weapons. The bad news: they would be ripe for the taking because their own muzzle flashes would make them sitting ducks. One by one, they took out any sprinkler head they saw.

As water rained down on Gunther's men, the low roar grew steadily louder as more sprinkler heads popped. The effect was a momentary halt in gunfire. Danny heard one merc shout, "What the fuck!" before realization hit. "Hey, somebody turned on the sprinklers, man!"

Danny and Javi continued running along their catwalks, shooting out sprinkler heads, crouching, then repeating.

Another voice said. "Up there! Tracers!" and yet another one yell, "Get 'em!"

Several rounds of machine gun fire shot upwards into the darkness, some of them piercing skylights, followed by specula raining down.

As they approached the midway point, Danny said, "I'll double back to take out more heads. You keep going." He thought of an escape plan when he saw the angled skylight array lining both sides of the ceiling edge. Danny and Javi could reach them easily, if they weren't shot first. Mindful to conserve rounds, he said, "Shoot out a window and climb onto the roof when you reach the ledge."

Danny felt the heat of the bullets ricocheting off the metal catwalk grate behind him. He wanted to stop and shoot down at the mercs but remembered his own advice about conserving his rounds, leaving at least one to shoot through the window. Ten feet away, he felt a rumbling behind him. The catwalk was buckling. A bullet had struck one of the support brackets supporting the catwalk, which now angled downward behind him. He hit the deck, still gripping his gun, but had to grab onto something or else slide off the walk and tumble to his death below. Thinking quickly, he reholstered his gun with his right hand while grabbing a railing with his left. He only hoped their little diversion had saved the lives of the other agents as well. The fact that he had stopped firing would make it more difficult for the shooters to spot him and in fact, their gunfire had stopped but still, he dangled by a thread.

Less than ten feet from the edge, he used his upper body strength to slowly pull himself up. But then, his section of walkway collapsed, separating completely from the remaining walkway. His metal section of walkway hung a full 90 degrees off the edge; Danny heard the other part creak and fall to the floor with a metallic thud. Thankful for another diversion, he continued his upward crawl as his upper body strength propelled him, trying to breathe steadily to avoid any sudden grunt that would give away his position. When he finally reached the edge, he hoped that the collapsed catwalk would prove to the shooters that no one was still hovering above them, but he still needed to shoot out the window to the rooftop.

He waited one minute after the last shot had been fired, then took his own through the window, hoping the steady roar of the sprinkler-induced rainstorm would mask the sound. Once he did, he stepped through it and climbed onto the roof, hearing a few more shots below him fall short.

When he stepped onto the rooftop, he had to use the parapet as a guide in the dark. Javi had disappeared and Danny didn't know if his friend had even made it outside. He walked the perimeter of the roof until he found a rusty, wrought iron ladder that stretched all the way to ground level.

It wasn't until he reached the ground at the rear of the warehouse that he heard multiple shoes pounding on the pavement from the darkness. Unsure who they were, he decided to pursue them.

Joanne examined the drawing when the dual explosions shook the room. Rapid sub-machine gun fire followed. She told Kate to hide under the table as she did the same. Thinking quickly, she grabbed the notepad and snapped a picture of it with her cell phone.

"When I open the door, you crouch down, got it?" Joanne pulled out her Glock.

Joanne saw Adalet through the open doorway huddled on the hallway floor. "Just stay down!" she shouted across. Joanne remembered the side exit door on the far side of the set if they could reach it while under fire. The inexplicable drum beats of a rain shower pelted the wooden ceiling above them.

"Stay down and follow me!" Joanne directed. She grabbed Kate's arm and pulled her into the threshold. Deion had found his way inside and spotted them. Before he could aim his gun at her, Joanne crouched, protecting Adalet behind her and fired twice. Both bullets struck him square in the chest, thrusting him backward into the pressboard that gave way.

Gunfire reverberated in their ears, so she motioned to Adalet to help her drag the interrogation room metal desk into the hallway to use it as a barricade. Kate was too dazed to do anything.

Joanne saw the outer door burst open. Nils, seeing movement, opened fire toward the tabletop that had been turned on its side, effectively shielding Joanne and Adalet. When Joanne heard Nils change magazines, she rose up and returned fire. One bullet separated his rifle from his hands, the other caught him in the chest, forcing his legs out from under him and sending him falling to the floor with a *thud.* This was their opportunity to escape.

Joanne grabbed Nils's semi-automatic and the two flash bang grenades he'd dropped. "Follow me!" Joanne ordered. She returned to the room for Kate. "Get on all fours and crawl out of here. And stay down!" she added for emphasis. She led them to another door of the set that led to a side exit door of the warehouse.

As they approached the exit, she led the two others through the rain as three of Gunther's men approached. Joanne removed the pin from one flash bang and threw it at them. The sound was so disorienting she instinctively held her ears, but the flash disabled their NVGs, enabling the women to escape the building. Outside, they found themselves in complete darkness, save for some dimly lit alley lights. She was thankful that their ears would get a well-deserved break from the noise of battle.

Joanne knew the entire operation had been compromised, but she was relieved she'd secured the toxin's molecular structure. Now the only thing left was to close it out.

Kate, along with Adalet at her side, followed Joanne, who directed them down the alleyway through the back of the building. Dim lights led the way to a dead end where three garbage cans were lined up against the outer wall of the adjacent building.

"Stay against the wall while I look for any more shooters," she ordered.

A gunshot rang out and Kate fell forward as Joanne kicked her in the back. Kate looked up at her confused. "Captain, did you…?"

"Just stay on the ground, Kate," Joanne said, pointing the Glock at her face. Kate tried to crawl toward the garbage cans, seeing Adalet's lifeless body, blood seeping out onto the pavement from the hole in the back of her head.

"I didn't do anything! Please!" Kate begged.

"Sorry, Kate, but it's time for you to go."

The approaching footsteps distracted Joanne. Instinctively, she dropped to her knees and used Kate as a human shield, pressing the barrel up against Kate's temple.

It was Danny. "Drop the gun, Joanne. Now!"

"She has to die, Danny. I'm just sorry you had to watch it happen."

Chapter 47

May 3, 12:35 a.m.
The Bronx, New York City

Gunther stepped through the elaborate set, furious at his men for taking out zero targets. He'd let Kate slip through his fingers again. Deion and Nils were still on the floor, alive thanks to their Kevlar vest but dazed, trying not to show it.

"Did you see anyone?" he asked, unconcerned they'd both been shot.

"Yeah," Deion was the first to speak, clearly nursing his bruised ribs. "A sister plugged me in the chest. Definitely CIA."

Gunther took a moment to translate Deion's colloquial description "What about the girl?" he pressed.

Nils, also smarting from the bullet said, "They ran out that door. Three women. Couldn't see their faces but I think one of them was her. The blonde, right?"

They had shut off the water. Gunther had to appreciate the deception. The police station walls were held up by wooden struts, the break room, the hallway from which led to the contrived interrogation room, where he'd guessed they had worked Kate over. When he walked in, he saw it. The notepad lay on the floor. When he saw "Tri-Meth" written in the top margin, his eyes focused with curiosity, then lit up with recognition of Kate's handwriting and molecular diagram:

```
      CH3 OH
          |
CH3—N—P—OH
      |—|
      CH3 F
```

He smiled and ripped out the page, folding it in half.

He smiled and ripped out the page, folding it in half.

When he walked down the hallway, bullet holes everywhere, he joined up with Marina and Shane, who'd stormed into the surveillance room, trapping Phil and Jeff by surprise. The latter were prone on the floor at gun point. Gunther nodded. "Just do it."

Both men took bullets to the base of their brains.

"If you shoot her, you'll be next," Danny said with his gun cocked and aimed. He'd have to shoot Kate to take down Joanne. He drew closer. Adalet had been shot in the back of head, her blood pouring out onto the crumbling pavement.

Joanne snickered. "That's funny. If I were you, I'd better think very hard about it before pulling that trigger. I'll die knowing I saved our country from a WMD that this bitch—who you fucked—created. You kill me, you'll be running for the rest of your life. Langley will disavow you, and I'll get my star up on that wall."

"You really believe they'll engrave a star for you? Is that what all this meant to you?"

"We all have to do things that we can't live down, for the greater good."

"You knew. All along, you knew." It took all he had to control his rage and not to pull the trigger.

"Like you, I was doing my job. In war, there are *always* acceptable losses to preserve the status quo. You know that, and so did Kelly."

"Gunther deserves to pay for what he did, even if I have to kill him myself. You just let him walk scot free."

"That report would have poisoned US-British relations for good and do you know what the terrorists would have done then? Laugh while they escalated their shameless attacks. Is that what you *really* want?

"The terrorists got stronger anyway."

"Gunther was useful to us because he knew how to play the game. It was a risk worth taking."

His hand shook. "Kelly was *my* wife!" Kate shuddered and shut her eyes tight.

"You think it's a tough decision, do you? Well let me clear it up for you. I'm sorry about all you went through since you lost her. I really am, but trust me when I say our world will be much safer with Kate dead than alive."

"Just make her stop. Please!" Kate bawled.

"When this is over, you'll accept it as the way it has to be," Joanne said, her eyes never leaving Danny's.

"No, I *want* you to put your gun down, now," Danny demanded. "Kelly was *not* an acceptable loss to me and neither is she." He quickly did the calculus in his head as to whether his feelings for Kate were worth the execution of a CIA officer.

Joanne summed it up for him. "You can shoot me or not. Either way, Kate will die."

He wanted to shut his eyes at the moment Joanne's bullet would pierce Kate's skull. Danny made his decision. "She drops, you drop."

"So be it," she said as another shot rang out, this one slicing through the left side of Joanne's skull, the cell phone dropping to the pavement as she toppled over onto Kate, who shrieked as blood splattered over her.

Joanne never pulled the trigger.

Kate was splattered with blood across her face and blouse. Danny saw two arms emerge from the shadows, smoking pistol in hand. Then he saw the shooter wearing an NYPD uniform.

Kate opened her eyes and saw the face of malevolence. "The terrorist!"

Danny was ready to unload his remaining rounds but Sabir dropped his gun. He stepped toward Adalet, a lifeless corpse whose eyes were wide open.

Danny could have easily shot Sabir then and there. That would be one less terrorist to worry about. But then, Sabir's grief-stricken face touched something deep within himself. Instead, he ran over to Kate, who was very much alive. "Are you okay?" He crouched down to help her.

"I have blood on me!"

"But it's not yours."

He and Kate looked over as Sabir knelt down to touch Adalet's face. Caressing her cheek, he bent to kiss her. The soles of his black shoes were already drenched in the growing blood puddle surrounding Adalet. Sabir's face twitched. "I did this for her," he said solemnly.

Danny recalled the *acceptable losses* Joanne had fought so hard to justify. Joanne wanted to turn a seasoned terrorist to expose more of them. Joanne's cell phone lay next to the dead CIA officer.

"Please help me move her," Sabir said, still staring at Adalet's corpse.

"Sabir, I'm so sorry but there's nothing we can do for her," Danny replied.

Sabir eased Adalet's head down and walked over to Joanne. Before he could react, Sabir scooped up the cell phone and ran away into the darkness.

"Why did she call you Danny?" Kate asked. The drug had run its course, her fugue dream a distant memory. He wanted to tell her that it was all over but knew that would be just another lie.

"My real name."

"I thought you were dead." Kate said. Then she glanced over to what was Joanne. "I take it that wasn't Captain Victoria Gates and that this isn't an episode of *Castle*?"

Danny smiled, then said, "My now ex-boss. She assigned me the job of securing your Tri-Meth compound."

He reached out to help her up but Kate swatted his hands away, now fully alert. "Get away from me!" she said. "You tried to kill me. Why should I even trust you?"

"Kate, let me explain. I only found out tonight that the CIA wanted you dead. I would never let that happen. Ever."

"Go to hell," she said in disgust. "All I know is I saw you shot to death in a parking lot and now you tried to kill me!"

Danny froze, not knowing how to respond honestly.

"So that's why you fucked me, to get the Tri-Meth."

"No, it wasn't. I don't…" Danny fumbled his words while reaching out to help her.

"I said don't touch me!" She started punching him as if pounding on a locked door.

He grabbed both arms, thankful she didn't think to kick him. "I know you don't believe me right now but I do love you, I care about you, Kate. I want to help you. That's no lie."

"I just don't get anything anymore!" Her voice broke. Tears suddenly appeared. "And that… terrorist?"

He talked over her. "Listen, Kate. You may still be in danger. Did you divulge the chemical compound to anyone in there?"

Kate glanced at Joanne again. "She took a photo of it with her cell phone."

Danny now understood why Sabir took it and the ramifications.

"I'm sick of the fucking compound!" she said. "Why can't everyone just leave me alone? You're no better than Sabir or Vanessa." But Kate wasn't finished. "So, was it all about her? Your dead wife? I was just the rebound girl for you? Did you actually think of her face when we fucked?"

"It wasn't like that, Kate. You and I share common demons and common foes. I thought I'd found someone who could make me whole again."

Approaching voices made Danny reach for his gun, but then recognized them as the other agents.

"Over here!" Danny shouted.

The agents converged on the grizzly scene. Javi asked first. "What happened, man?"

"How did you all get away?" Danny asked.

"The second floor fire escape side entrance on the other side of the warehouse," said Lindsey. "That was too close. We heard a shot and… Oh my god!" Lindsey and the others cringed at what they saw.

"Both shot in the back of head. It was awful." Danny said, not offering up any sordid detailed.

"By who?" asked Javi.

"Sabir but he got away before I could stop him." He feared that some of them didn't buy his story. Yet they all looked haggard from their narrow escape. He asserted *de facto* leadership of the operation, now in disarray. "Are we all accounted for?" Danny asked, taking a silent headcount.

The agents looked around and realized who was missing. Javi finally said, "Phil and Jeff. They were still in the surveillance room during the raid."

"Shit." It was unlikely Gunther's men kept them alive if they found them. "Let's move."

The agents and Kate made a hasty retreat from the alley to their nondescript vans, both intact and sped away. Kate and Danny sat in separate vans.

Gunther's men rigged C-4 explosives around every visible column.

"No time to lollygag, mates. We've still got a lot of work to do, so get your arses in gear and let's move out now."

As their vans drove off back to Manhattan, the building imploded behind them with a roar, then a rumble. A huge cloud of smoke arose in the night air. Gunther thought the demolition a sweet punctuation mark to an evening of soundly obliterating an American intelligence operation. He looked down at the paper and chuckled to himself with giddy revelry.

Katelyn Carrie, you're a dead girl.

Chapter 48

May 3rd 2:15 a.m.
The Upper West Side, New York City

Kate retreated to her cold and lonely shell.

Exhausted, mentally and physically, she reflected during the car ride on what had been real about their relationship, sorting out fact from fiction. She couldn't deny Danny's effect on her, and yes, it had been special. Yet she still had doubts about his honesty. She thought she deserved more than a dark alley apology.

The SUVs drove up to Danny's CIA apartment. He got out first and walked over to Kate's window. "You're welcome to stay in my apartment for the night."

Kate was cool to the offer, but didn't feel comfortable staying in a hotel alone either. When they entered the apartment, she saw her purse was lying on the coffee table and recalled the untouched syringes buried deep within it. The urge to shoot up was omnipresent.

Danny broached the subject by speaking first. "I know you need space. I get it. My bed is all yours. I'll sleep out here," he said, pointing to the sofa.

She debated whether she should respond at all. "No," she replied, "*I'll* sleep out here. Thank you," she said with resolute assurance.

During the night, Kate awoke quivering and helped herself to another hit. What a pathetic human pin cushion she had become. She remembered their chat about breaking the pattern, but that happened right before they had sex.

She entered his bedroom and lay down fully-clothed beside him. He'd fallen asleep on top of the bedspread, a faint snore resonating. For a moment, she wanted to wrap her arms around him, but the heroin hit was overpowering, so instead she rolled onto her back and stared up at the light fixture.

She awoke first, but didn't want to look at him. She heard him awaken as he rolled over to her. "After tonight, I'm leaving the Agency," he said. "I won't let anyone hurt you again."

"How do you know if I even can be saved?" she said with pensive detachment.

He didn't address her question about her. He focused on them. "Let's get out of here. Leave the City. Both of us. Tomorrow."

Kate was high, yet he moved closer and kissed her on the cheek.

She did not kiss him back. "Where would we go? Why do you want to spend the rest of your life with a junkie, anyway?" she asked.

"Because I already know that's not what you want to be. Being with someone who supports and empowers you makes the path easier. Remember what I told you about that place in New Hampshire?"

"Yeah. I know it's time I break the cycle."

He caressed her palm gently. "If it weren't for all this, I'd want to leave with you right now. If you kept the vials buried, there wouldn't be any auction to stop and Vanessa would get what she deserves." He knew the proposal was utterly ridiculous once he said it.

"You know, a part of me wants to fly off with you, but I need to do this. Besides, burying a deadly toxin in the ground was just plain dumb of me. Looking back, I'm amazed I went through with it."

He didn't argue the point.

"I need to know, Danny," she said, still staring up to the ceiling.

"What?"

"That you've truly let her go."

"What Kelly and I had was special and nothing can ever change that. You would understand that if you were me."

Kate couldn't empathize no matter how hard she tried. "What happened to her that Joanne felt she had to hide it from you?"

"Gunther McGore had her killed."

That made her turn to him, meeting his gaze.

"Yeah, I know," he went on. "I've still got a score to settle with him."

"So, your now dead ex-boss got you to spy on me knowing that he destroyed your marriage?"

"I swear I didn't know. I only found out he was involved after Sabir got you. Then I didn't know the full story until yesterday," he added. "I never lied about my own addiction either. When Kelly died, I fell into the same dark hole you're in now. It took everything I had to climb back out."

She believed he was sincere. It was an intuitive feeling. Danny rolled on top of her and kissed her on the lips, stroking his fingers through her hair. She could feel him getting hard.

This was what she had always dreamed of, a man who was devoted to loving her without strings attached. But she couldn't reciprocate. Not now. He had to understand.

She pushed his shoulders from her. "Danny," she said as gently as she could. "I just can't.

I'm sorry, Danny. I just need more time but I believe you. It's just that everything is moving so fast. I need to take a step back and figure out what we have here. And you need to figure out what I truly am to you."

She had hurt him with her rejection and his ruffled forehead told her so.

"There's something *I* need to know too," he said. "What made you create it?"

"I was angry, at everything and everybody. I was angry at myself most of all. I was pissed that I was too weak to stand up for myself. The tri-meth thing started as a biochem thesis on a new pesticide to help the agri-business industry. When Mom brought me in to Frugeré, she found out about it and I guess told Brooke about it. At the time, I thought it was a way to focus on my science while shutting everyone else out.

"At the house, I told you that no one can control it if someone takes something you made for good and uses it for bad things.

The genie in a bottle thing." He nodded.

Danny smiled at her, indicating he understood. Yet she still had the urge to atone. "I have other ideas in my head I want to develop. Really. Good things."

"I know and you will."

Kate smiled back, acknowledging the validation. Suddenly, the burden of responsibility was something she thought she could handle.

"There's one thing left for you to figure out," he said.

She followed his lead. "Uh-huh. What I'm going to say to Vanessa when I see her. All my life, I've blamed the shit I've taken and blamed it on everyone else. I'm appreciative that you've taken risks to save my life, but now it's my turn to stand up for myself." She had the confidence to choose and lowered the boom. "I just haven't decided whether I want to start my new life with or without you."

"Will you decide that by tomorrow?" he asked.

She had no earthly idea if she could or would.

Danny's cell phone vibrated, for which he turned over to grab and listen. "It's game time. Are you ready?"

"I wouldn't have it any other way."

When Gunther arrived at her office at 10:30 a.m. to report on the compound's retrieval, Adele advised him Vanessa had left instructions that she would see no one.

If she was to sack me, who would she call to have me escorted out of the building?

Ignoring Adele, he entered the office, expecting a brush-off.

"Adele told you I didn't want to be disturbed, especially by you." She went on. "How could you let her get away for, what was it, the *fifth* time? Because of your total failure to fulfill your employment objectives, your services are no longer required here. Consider yourself terminated. Just see yourself out."

Gunther stood his ground. "I know it's your prerogative, Vanessa," he said, now ready to recite a humbling *mea culpa*. "You are correct. I failed to deliver Kate by the appointed time. You know I take this personally but you and Brooke will need protection if the meeting is canceled, and you know I am fully capable of providing that service to you. My men are at the ready to do it, but won't move without me."

That brought her anger down just a notch. "Having the chemical compound is all well and good, but I need those vials, yesterday. Just tell me how you're going to get them back by midnight."

"She will call. Trust me. Whether or not the CIA blokes still have her, Kate will want to make a deal just as before. You are not the only one with limited options."

Vanessa exhaled, acknowledging Gunther had outplayed her. "Fine. Stay, for now." Vanessa said, as the mid-morning sun brightened up the entire office. She, however, exuded dark-minded cynicism.

Shortly before 3 p.m., and Vanessa was well into her second pack when she got the text. It said to expect a call in one minute, so she quickly paged Gunther.

She activated the speakers. "Kate, how are you? We've all been so worried."

Kate dispensed with any pleasantries and plowed ahead, all business.

"No need to trace this call Gunther. I know you're there." Neither one surprised. "I'll be brief. I'm willing to give back the vials in exchange for my freedom—from you."

"What do you mean, dear?"

"Don't call me that. You'll never patronize me again like you just did. Just listen closely. I want one million dollars in cash or else no vials. Got it?"

"I can't come up with—"

"You and I both know you can!" Kate interrupted. "Besides, we both know that you'll get a nice share of the proceeds to save your business tonight at the auction."

Kate's accusation hung in the air for the moment.

Gunther cursed inwardly. They knew the time, but did they know the location?

Vanessa looked to Gunther, who raised his hand, to calm her down before he spoke. "Look, Kate, we know the CIA is with you right now, so don't think you'll be able to bait us into some bloody trap."

"Fine. I'll come alone. Vanessa comes alone. Understood?"

"That's fine, dear. Where would you like to meet?"

"Central Park, near Belvedere's Castle, along the path going south of the Traverse. Just bear right and follow the dirt path around along the fence."

"I know it."

"Come at 4:30 p.m. And Vanessa…"

"Yes, dear?"

"Come alone or else I'll walk away and the deal's off."

"That goes for you, too, Kate," Gunther responded, but the line had gone dead. He looked at Vanessa. "They were listening in, no doubt about it."

"She's got us!" she said bitterly. "I will *not* give that girl one million! For heaven sakes, Gunther, once I take the vials, they could arrest me! Tell me why did I agree to this?"

Gunther's mouth curled up into that familiar sneer of his. "Because I have a way out, but you'll have to make a decision."

Vanessa gazed out of her office window looking down onto the Fifth Avenue milieu. And then she knew.

Chapter 49

May 3, 4:30 p.m.
Central Park, New York City

Kate reached a milestone in her life. She would never go back. The chance to experience free will was new and exciting and she looked terrific, with golden yellow hair flowing down below her shoulders, the result of a fresh haircut. Wearing her brand new white tunic, Forever 21 black Capris and black flats, she looked quite the woman of leisure.

The cocaine heightened her senses to sky-high levels for sure, but it also brought out anxiety that pulsed through her like countless firecrackers. She just wanted to get this over with and move on.

She told Danny after the call that she had to 'tie up some loose ends'. That included her new hairstyle, closing out her bank account, and buying a suitcase and carry-on and that smart ensemble.

The truck, both a makeshift dressing room and surveillance van made to look like a closed food service truck was parked across from the Delacourt Theatre. Inside, Lindsey prepared her behind a floor length partition, adjusting the wire on Kate's bra, beyond the view of the other agents. "Remember," she instructed, "it will feel a little uncomfortable, but try not to move around too much. You don't want her to suspect that you're wearing this."

Then Javi had Kate recite a few words to test the audio levels. "Let's check with the guys."

She heard him confirm the positions of the other agents. Eddie would trail Kate until just before the bridge leading across the 79th Street Traverse highway. Shannon was stationed to the east of the meeting location, Monique slightly to the south. All retreats from the clearing would be covered.

"How far away will you be?" Kate asked Lindsey as she re-buttoned her tunic.

"Close enough to intervene should we hear any trouble."

As a touch of nostalgia hit her, she said, "Vanessa used to take me on walks here all the time. Did you know that there were hiking trails?"

"No, I didn't," Lindsey answered with mild disinterest. "Kate, I know you must be nervous right now, but please try to focus on the exchange"

She heard some rattling plastic bag and guessed Danny had piled in a mouthful of gummy bears. "That's a lot of gummy bears you got there, bro," Javi quipped after which his lips turned upwards in a lighthearted smirk, intimating Danny's reference to Kate.

"Problem?" Danny said, after one gulp.

"No, no problem. I'm just sayin'."

Danny's face was in mid glower, when Kate decided to pull back the curtain. Danny motioned her to step outside.

"Are we good?" he asked Javi.

"All set, man."

They stepped over several bags of newly bought clothes in periwinkle shaded Bergdorf Goodman shopping bags. Danny rested his hands on both of her hips. "Are you ready?" he whispered, meeting her blue-eyed gaze.

She hugged him, resting her head on his chest, taking in the warmth. "I'm sorry," she said. "I believe what you said. It was hard after all I've been through. Vanessa's the one I should be angry with, and believe you me, I've got a few choice words for her."

Danny kissed her on the forehead, being almost a head taller than she. "Just don't let her get to you, okay?"

"I won't. Never again."

Danny locked eyes with her and just said, "Let's get her."

She smiled back at him before stepping outside and strolling with deliberation in the direction of Belvedere Castle.

Kate arrived at the clearing. Under the rock, she dug out the vial case, then climbed up on top of the boulder, setting the case down beside her. At the opposite end of the clearing, Vanessa appeared first, with Gunther following close behind her holding a briefcase. Kate balked at the sight of him, her face showing loathing distrust.

"We agreed you'd come alone!" she said standing atop the rock, with arms on hips, Akimbo style, like a general overseeing his newly conquered lands.

Vanessa inched forward, giving Kate no verbal acknowledgment.

"Stop or I'll shatter them on this rock. Then where would you be?" Kate warned.

Vanessa waved Gunther to stand down.

Kate made her descent from atop the rock, taking the short dirt path down to Vanessa's level. They stared at each other from twenty paces as if anticipating a duel.

Vanessa smiled. "Kate, it's so good to see you, again." Her voice sweet as maple syrup, with that comforting maternal charm. "I must say, you look… different."

"In more ways than you'll ever know," Kate said proudly. She wasn't fooled.

At that moment, Kate saw Gunther reach down to his belt buckle and press a button on a small cube-shaped device.

In the van, the conversation fizzled into a crackling sound.

"I've lost the signal," Javi said in a panicked voice.

"We've got to move in, now, "Danny demanded.

"No. The operation will be blown."

Danny's chest stiffened.

"I don't care!" He said, but Javi grabbed his arm. "No, man! Gunther can make you. If he does, it's over."

"Thirty seconds. That's it," he said, looking at his friend with frustration.

"Sweetie, I know you really don't want to do this, so let's just stop all this nonsense and go home. Together," Vanessa said.

"Not a chance. I don't need you to validate my existence on this planet."

Cumulus gray clouds enshrouded the sun as Vanessa's face grew dark. The smile disappeared. "No Kate, you're wrong. Someday, you'll come to realize that we're all pawns to be played at the pleasure of the king. But as far as you and I are concerned, I always win, and that will never change." Her voice reverted to a steady calmness. "Now, Kate, Brooke and I need you at that auction. This is your night to shine"

"So that the world will know I was the one who created the Tri-Meth? No way."

Just as quickly, Vanessa's fangs returned with a vengeance. "Well you're one to talk, you little shit! I trusted you and what happens? You betray me and stand to destroy everything we've worked for. And after all I've done for you!"

"By making me a murderer? I'll never forgive you for that."

"But the Tri-Meth is *your* creation."

"Well let me tell you something," Kate said, fists clenched by her side. "It wasn't worth all this."

"But it's worth a million dollars to never see me again?"

"That's right. No money, no vials."

"No vials, no money," Vanessa retorted with dead calm precision. "Besides, it doesn't matter. Foreign governments, terrorists, they'll be chasing you down for the rest of your days. Your life will be a living hell. And don't kid yourself, they'll find you."

"Don't act like you care about me. You always cared more about your empire than you ever cared about any human being."

Visibly, seething, Vanessa unleashed the most hurtful thing a parent could ever say to a child. "You know, most days I wish I'd never even met you!"

"And there it is," Kate said triumphantly. "I guess there's nothing more to say, is there? We're done here. Now where is the money?"

Vanessa motioned Gunther forward, who lifted up a briefcase with gloved hand on either side and opened it. "It's all yours Kate," he said with a smirk. "You may count it if you wish."

She did. Then Kate lifted the vials from the case for Vanessa to view, maintaining her distance. "Let's do this," she said coldly. "Now drop it in the middle of the clearing." Gunther did exactly that, then stepped back behind Vanessa.

True to her word, Kate carried the vials and placed them next to the briefcase. She grabbed the briefcase handle and turned back toward the rock.

"I made a big mistake trusting you," Vanessa hissed. "But mistakes can be erased."

"Are you done?" Kate said, indignantly turning back.

"No, but you are," Vanessa said wearing an ugly sneer.

She looked down and knew it was already too late. Her grip on the handle weakened, the briefcase falling to the ground and opening up on impact, the bills falling out. The toxin raced through her doing its deadly work. Helplessness was the only emotion she felt as she trembled and broke out in a scalding sweat. She would die in three seconds.

This is how it went.

Three seconds.

She thought of the enduring pain as a child: the rape, the physical and mental abuse and tears of hopelessness. That little girl, now a distant memory, called out to her now, but she could only say, 'I can't help you anymore. My time has passed'. Kate thought of her adult life ravaged by drug abuse and what could have been. The hours spent in euphoric isolation, so satisfying in the moment, now an angry charge for the lost time living. *How could I have let it rule me?*

A place where God's gift of scientific acumen became a deadly curse in the end. She asked questions she couldn't answer. Why did I think that science would embrace my discovery? Was it arrogance, delusions of grandeur, the lure of Vanessa's money and lifestyle? Was it that being female assured her of claiming some sort of moral high ground? Kate never experienced it. She remembered Vanessa's visit to Zion, the scent of Frugeré No. 3 etched in the memory, then of Vanessa's fading interest in raising her as a teen.

Two seconds.

A life with Danny that would never be. The hope of future happiness through intimacy she experienced for however brief a time, unattainable. She thought of the places they wouldn't see, the sex they wouldn't have, the restaurants they'd never try and the children she'd never have. She regretted her decision to pull back from the relationship. For a fleeting moment, science meant nothing. She had come to accept her role as creator of the most powerful nerve toxin on earth.

One second.

Her nervous system sputtering to a halt, Kate's mind bubbled over with random non sequitur thoughts. I hate her. I hate her. Don't stop, Danny. You fucking bitch! Must get the perfect chemical mixture. He's so good to me. Fuck you, bitch! I'll have the Niçoise salad. More needles bring more pleasure. Where are those damned amber lights? Aren't my new shoes so cute? Her last second of consciousness then focused on the hateful Vanessa, who Kate swore she wouldn't give the satisfaction of seeing her suffer. But she couldn't control the convulsions.

She willed herself to wheel around and charge Vanessa in one last desperate burst of energy. She fell just short falling into her shouting, "How could you do tha—!"

She never finished. In a fluid motion, Kate grabbed Vanessa's jacket, which ripped open as Kate's last triumphant expression of rage. When her bowels released, she lost her lunch, vomit spewing onto the jacket. As Kate fell into her, Vanessa whispered in her right ear, "Say goodbye to hell, my golden girl."

Kate expelled a grotesque withering moan as her breathing stopped cold. With

Kate still gripping the jacket, Vanessa heaved her to the ground as if she was a lifeless ragdoll, the corpse hitting with a hard thud.

There was nothing left of Dr. Katelyn Carry to save.

Vanessa saw Gunther withdraw a hypodermic needle filled with enough heroin to kill a full grown thoroughbred and injected it into Kate's right arm, leaving it there to dangle. He picked up the briefcase with his two gloved hands, while Vanessa held the vial case to her chest.

Then she dropped to her knees, staring at the corpse with morbid fascination at what she had just done.

Gunter snapped her out of it. "Vanessa, we need to leave immediately."

She stood and unzipped her now-torn, vomit-covered jacket and flung it on the ground in disgust. "Get rid of it," she said blankly.

"The case, Vanessa." She set it down on the ground gently, then straightened her blouse as if she was about to leave the ladies room.

"We'll meet at the rendezvous point?" she asked.

Gunther nodded as Vanessa walked west. He pulled out an unadorned Jansport knapsack and placed the soiled jacket in one compartment, the case in the other. Strapping it on his back, he mounted a bicycle that had been hidden from view and rode east.

Eddie reported in after Vanessa walked right by him "Guys, Vanessa Carrie just left the Park *without* the vials. Repeat, *without* the vials!"

"Jesus," Javi said.

"Shit, let's move!" Danny exclaimed, throwing open the doors as Javi and Lindsey trailed after him.

Past the theatre, and wanted to cry out for her. He glanced across the traverse to the metal fence, but saw no one standing in the clearing. They sprinted past the Castle, then hung a right over the footpath across the Traverse and another right past the metal fence to the clearing at the bottom of a slight slope to the boulder.

Kate was splayed face up on the dirt, her head twisted to the left, mouth and eyes wide open; her face awash in bubbles of vomit.

Danny was the first to reach her as he dropped to his knees. "No! No! What did they do to you?" Danny wasn't ready to let her go and was about to grasp her poisoned hand when Javi grabbed his arm to intervene.

Javi grabbed his hand. "Careful. Don't touch her." The skin of her palm that had touched the Trimeth-laced briefcase handle was beet-red.

Danny wrapped his arms around her tightly, feeling for a sign of life, but her breath had stilled. He turned back to Javi. "Help her! Mouth to mouth! CPR! Something!"

Javi had just checked her pulse as he dropped the limp wrist and shook his head.

Her soul had entered the world of the forgotten.

Danny shut his eyes to hold back tears of dread and anguish as he clung to her still warm body. The world around him was dead. He had loved her, he was certain of it now. This tortured soul of a woman, who opened her heart up to him during her darkest hours, ultimately accepting the burden of her creation.

Danny's grief then swelled into vengeful anger. "They did this to you! McGore did this!" His voice trembled, thinking he was powerless to do anything about it. Gunther McGore had shattered his life to pieces for the second time. His mind raced to find a way to gather up those pieces and finally give Gunther what he deserved. He gently laid Kate back down on the ground, face up, arms by her side still staring down at her.

The three agents just sat there in silence for an extended moment in time, trying to make sense of what they had just witnessed. Javi approached Danny and tried to console him. "I'm so sorry, Danny. Her secret, it died with her."

He knew it hadn't but Sabir had disappeared with the knowledge on a cell phone. Suddenly, he gained the strength to focus. Maybe, he wasn't as helpless as he'd thought only a moment ago.

He broke their silence with a sobering assessment, "Carrie still has the toxin, so we still have a job to do."

Taking his lead, Javi said, "Carrie and McGore will get what's coming to them."

Danny wanted to concur but heard the sound of talking passers-by from above them past the rock. "Let's get out of here now."

Javi nudged his left shoulder and added thoughtfully, "I think you're supposed to shut her eyes."

After doing so, Danny gently kissed her on the forehead. "Call the police and tell them…" speaking through grief stricken unsteadiness, he said "tell them a young woman was found dead in the park."

Chapter 50

May 3 8:45 p.m.
The Upper East Side, New York City

Twilight ceded to nightfall over the City. The pleasant spring daylight a distant memory as a sharp chill ruled the nighttime air.

Gunther had found the homing beacon in the vial case and deftly removed it at the clearing. An agent found the device under the vial case in a garbage can by the Great Meadow restrooms. All the time and effort planning this operation amounted to nothing and the most virulent nerve agent know to humankind was going to find its way into foreign hands when the clock would strike twelve. On top of that, the operation was headless, its leader now dead in a Bronx alley adjacent to a nameless warehouse that was reduced to rubble.

Gunther assembled the nine men left at his disposal in a vacant East Harlem parking lot underneath the Metro North elevated rail tracks. Three cars pulled into the lot and he waited for the rumble of a Bronx bound train to dissipate. "Mates, I just received security protocol direction and the location of the meeting." He looked over at Shane, saying, "I want to see our hardware."

Shane opened one of the car trunks to show him. Inside were disassembled M-4s and Uzis, as well as some grenades and protective armor.

"Good. You and Zak drive the rest of them to the location. I'll be sending you an encrypted text with the address after I leave. Under no circumstances are you to use GPS. Figure no more than three hours to get there."

The cars pulled out of the lot, Gunther heading south toward Brooke's apartment building.

From the same safe house on the Lower West Side from which Kate made the call, the team regrouped and prepared for a combined surveillance and assault operation. The storage facility kept a healthy cache of weapons and military hardware. The homing device software Devon loaded onto Brooke's cell phone was active. The signal linked to a geosynchronous satellite and could track her to the ends of earth. Danny had agents surveilling the two women's apartments and offices. It was shaping up to be a long night, regardless of the outcome.

Trae radioed in that Brooke was on the move, crawling northward up Park Avenue in what they surmised was a nondescript vehicle driven by one of Gunther's men.

Danny and Javi positioned their Toyota Highlander across the street from Vanessa's apartment building. A black Mercedes soon pulled up and Vanessa came out and quickly got in. It turned east, then south on Second Avenue to the RFK Bridge approach. The outbound traffic was heavy but Javi kept close enough, about 500 feet separating the two cars.

The indicator on the GPS suddenly lost the signal.

"Gunther," Danny said.

Vanessa stepped inside without so much as an acknowledging gesture, looking forward.

"Where's Kate?" Brooke asked. "I thought she'd be coming."

"She couldn't make it," she said in a deadpan monotone. Her brown eyes were stone cold.

Brooke said, "That's a shame, but we'll still be okay."

She started talking about the mechanics of the auction, when Gunther interrupted. "Ladies, I would advise not to say anything until my signal. Ears may be listening."

As they sat in silence, Brooke placed her left hand over Vanessa's right, who cracked a slight smile as she looked at her. "You won't have to wait much longer."

Zak driving, Gunther turned around and spoke to them. "Cell phones, ladies."

They handed them to Gunther, who removed the batteries, opened his passenger side window, nonchalantly tossing them out into the night. Queens-bound lane closures flowing off the bridge slowed traffic to a steady crawl on the Grand Central Parkway. The westbound lanes leading back into Manhattan were clear.

"Take care and follow me out at my signal," Gunther said.

They drove into the left lane as they approached the LaGuardia Airport exit, then slowed to a stop adjacent to a gap in the guardrail. "Exit on the left side."

The three occupants stepped out and hustled through the gap, switching to a Cressida with flashing blinkers. Its driver had timed the stop perfectly, then headed west, back into the City. The switch occurred quickly enough not to draw any horn noise from trailing drivers.

"They've switched cars!" Danny said.

"Shit! We're fucked," Javi said, held hostage by the stalled traffic ahead.

"Back to the City? I'm sorry but it doesn't make any sense." The bidders wouldn't want be seen anywhere near the City. It had to be somewhere secluded. Danny thought about his time with Kate, groping his mind for something she may have said. Then the answer became clear to him.

Going on pure instinct he said, "Maybe not. When we get to the exit, turn around. And head north on the FDR."

"Why?" Javi asked.

"I just have a hunch," Danny responded.

Until they were an hour away from the secret location, both women had been silent. Brooke began to impart detailed instructions about what would happen tonight. "The bidders collectively hired an impartial chemist to verify the potency of the Tri-Meth, so you'll need to present that test vial to him. We'll sync their laptops up with mine to start the bidding process. But expect a lot of tension in the room up until a winner is determined. I've run several of these things before and can tell you that emotions can run high. That's why we need Gunther's security."

Vanessa nodded without saying a word and thought of what she had done while looking out into the darkness.

Minutes later, she said, "I tried to be the best mother I could be."

Brooke reached over and squeezed Vanessa's bone-chilled hand gently, as if to warm it.

When they arrived at Monticello at about 11:30, Gunther's men were waiting.

He stood outside, greeting them as they entered the house. "Our guests are due to arrive at midnight, so you ladies have time to prepare."

Brooke assumed the leadership role, Vanessa still in a pensive mood. "We have to put these men in their place from the very start. We run the meeting. No smiles. Be gracious of course, but light on small talk. It'll be a very orderly, tightly controlled process."

"Gunther will be in the room with us, too?"

"Absolutely. There'll be three rounds. They'll enter their bids through their cell phones. Make sure you keep that vial case out of sight. Once we have a winner, all the money transfers will take place:" Brooke referred to the winner wire of payment and the return of the initial deposits to the losing bidders. "It shouldn't last more than half-an-hour."

Chapter 51

May 3, 11:45 p.m.
Monticello, New York

As planned, the first car drove up the circular driveway to the front entrance right before midnight. Four more followed within minutes. Each bidder brought their own bodyguard along. They had traveled from the Canadian border in separate nondescript cars. This transaction, they all agreed, was worth the risk. Gunther had guaranteed them security, but these men were not the trusting type. They would return to Canada well before daybreak.

Stationed out front, Kim and Zak brandished their semi-automatics like sentries posted at a castle drawbridge. They motioned the bidders' vehicles to park on the grassy area abutting the perimeter of the circular driveway, creating an impromptu make-shift parking lot. They would continue to stand guard at the front door and warn Gunther of any unwanted visitors.

Naturally, Gunther had all the security detail positions mapped out. Even though he'd been reasonably certain that he'd shook off the American agents' tail, he would leave nothing to chance tonight. Besides allaying the concerns of the honored guests, the security presence was to demonstrate that their hosts for the evening meant business.

Each man was armed with Sig Sauers, M-16s and knuckle knives, plus any additional personal items each thought to be helpful, or bring them good luck, depending on their individual superstitions. To his knowledge, no one brought a rabbit's foot with them. Nevertheless, Gunther encouraged such creativity so long as it kept them focused on the matter at hand.

Nils stood inside the doorway at the bottom of the staircase that led up to the den while Dion was stationed at the top of the stairs to welcome them. He would also stand guard outside of the den during the auction. Sticks was assigned to the hidden stairwell on the garage level. This was done more for Vanessa's and Brooke's protection in case the testosterone level bubbled over. Of course, Gunther was more than capable of handling that. He'd be right there alongside them and the only one with his Sig Saur at the ready ensconced in his left corduroy sports jacket inner pocket.

Marina lay prone on the west side of the rooftop gable with the barrel of her sniper rifle perched over the rooftop pointing eastward, covering all automobile access. Child's play as she had taken out Russian soldiers from well over 300 meters away. Dressed in black, as they all were, it would be virtually impossible, absent a floodlight, to detect her. To eliminate any rifle flashes, she covered the barrel with a pair of panty hose.

The others were scattered about the mansion as the guests gathered by the front door, Zak turned away and spoke into his wrist com-link. "They're all here, mate."

Everyone, including Gunther received the message through an earpiece and stood at the ready. When Brooke gave him a nod for 'go', Gunther spoke into his com-link. "Alright blokes, it's show time."

The first to arrive was Nasser al-Khalishem, by far the oldest of the group. Syrian born, he pocketed millions starting in the late 1970s selling arms to any country that had been subject to an U.N. arms embargo. It didn't hurt his bottom line that he also engaged in drug trafficking.

Pavlos Niasakos of Greek origin, and sporting a well groomed mustache to compensate for his receding hairline, was infamous for providing arms to Saddam Hussein in the 1980s war against Iran, as well as to various Lebanese militia groups during their civil war.

Dale Kendrick, the lone American of the group, with cropped brown hair and a goatee, was the most mentally imbalanced one there. He wore a military blouse, blue jeans, and Dockers without socks. Dressed appropriately for the occasion, he thought. His refusal to shower beforehand complemented his disheveled appearance. The former mercenary frequently supplied Iraqi and Afghani resistance militias during their most recent conflicts.

Next came Sergei Leonidski, the Ukrainian-born arms dealer, a heavy-set man with uncombed black hair whose bangs curled up just above his eye line. He made his name by supplying African and Balkan nations with illegal arms.

The last of the bidders was Shamir Basar, a youngish Israeli whose clean cut demeanor and stylish choice of clothing exuded confidence. Physically the shortest of the group, he answered only to one power: the Chosen People.

The final guest of the evening to arrive was the chemist who drove up alone in a late model Hyundai. He was a withering septuagenarian who was escorted inside.

The group of bidders and bodyguards climbed the staircase, passing DeMarco and entering the den where Gunther greeted them. As they assembled outside of the den, he said, "No guns, gentlemen." Within minimal grumbling, the bodyguards all complied by removing their pieces and placing them in the metal box, which Gunther locked.

Behind the oak desk, Brooke wore a black sweater, sitting before her open laptop. Vanessa stood with arms folded, wearing a black pants suit, rainbow herring bone scarf and Stuart Weitzman boots.

As the group entered, Brooke established control, standing before them in her navy blue power suit and pumps "Good evening gentlemen. I trust all of you have left your guns or any other weapons you had brought with you at the door."

Gunther scanned each man with a metal detector. "Just a precaution gentlemen." Each bidder sat in one of five cushioned chairs surrounding a glass coffee table.

"Please have a seat, gentlemen."

All of the bidders complied, their bodyguards stepping back toward the far wall.

"I know each of you have traveled a great distance to be here tonight, and we appreciate that. You all know who I am." Brooke acknowledged Vanessa with a swift arm movement. "Please welcome Vanessa Carrie, the reason we are all here. Without her guidance and investment into this project, this evening would not have been possible." Done with pleasantries, Brooke continued with the business at hand. "Your mutually agreed upon chemist will verify the item. Once each of you is satisfied, on my signal, the auction will begin. A short recess will be afforded after the first and second rounds to permit any of you to make the necessary calls to whomever you would need to contact regarding additional funds for the next round. Each round will conclude when no one submits a bid within one minute of the last one. After the third round, I will declare a winner. Brooke took a moment and scanned the group. "Except for the winner, all of you will have your deposits wired back to each of you, then will promptly exit the room and leave the premises. Are we clear, gentlemen?"

Each of them gave silent nods while Gunther stood behind them, guarding the double doors.

"Let's begin with verification." She nodded to Vanessa, who withdrew the test vial from her handbag on the desk.

The chemist sat himself down in a chair next to the desk, facing the bidders. Vanessa gave him the test vile. From a black doctor's bag, he withdrew a small metal board, litmus paper and a syringe from his bag he had laid on the floor. In very clinical terms, he explained the procedure in a steady professorial voice. "The strength of the nerve toxin will be verified by a red mark on this litmus paper. The darker the red, the stronger the substance."

He then injected the syringe into the rubber topped vial and withdrew less than 1cc of it. When he injected what was maybe two drops onto the paper, the color turned from light pink to crimson red, to almost black in less than ten seconds. When the color had stopped changing, the chemist's eyes widened in reaction and he held his breath in amazement for a split second before he announced. "Gentlemen, what you have here is the most virulent nerve agent on earth, bar none."

Vanessa and Brooke had just witnessed the validation of Kate's life work.

Chapter 52

May 3rd, 11:55 p.m.
Monticello, New York

This operation was not unlike Danny's Black Ops days. He had been assigned to a Special Reaction team that carried out various assignments, including the rescue of political figures, the execution of terrorists, and the securing of enemy targets such as airfields and hidden munitions caches.

Shortly after midnight, the team drove up the dirt road in two vans along the ridge, but on Danny's direction they stopped about ¾ mile from the home. Each agent was equipped with Semi-automatics, M-4 submachine guns, flash bang grenades, crossbows, pistols, and night vision goggles. The plan relied on the team taking out the power source in the home, giving them an edge in the nighttime engagement. They all wore black baklavas, fatigues and flak jackets and com-links to maintain constant communications with each other. They needed to encroach deliberately in order to estimate the strength and number of Gunther's security detail. In essence, they were flying blind.

Only 200 meters from the home, they laid in wait amongst the towering pine trees, confirming that one of Gunther's goons was not scoping out the perimeter for intruders. Danny's familiarity with the layout would give them a decided advantage in their attack. He recalled the trails extending north and south from the home along the western facing ridge.

Danny devised a three pronged attack, employing a deliberate assault strategy, taking out any sentries along the property's exterior, with either cross bows or silenced pistols, depending on the proximity of the target. Then, once the meeting location was confirmed, it would shift from a covert raid to a dynamic 'shock and awe' attack.

Although he remembered the second floor layout, they could just as easily be holding it in the living area, basement, or one of the open air balconies for all he knew. If it was in the den, Shannon would infiltrate it and secure the toxin. Danny divided the eight remaining agents into three attack teams of three agents, designated North, South, and East. Two in each group would press forward, guns blazing, while the third would cover the rear flank.

They all crouched low to the ground as they surveyed the home from the south. They saw the light shining brightly through the drawn shades of the den. The other second floor bedrooms were left dark, the first floor living room glowing brightly.

They saw two sentries, Kim and Zak, machine guns drawn, walking back and forth along each side of the front doorway.

"Alright guys. Group North, circle around the foliage on the eastern perimeter to the north access point. There's a kitchen entrance there. South group, listen up. Shannon, go ahead and approach from the southeast and scale the exterior to the balcony at the point of attack and stand by for my signal. After he crashes the party, I'll give the command for all out, dynamic encroachment.

"Once all targets are eliminated, we'll meet up at the second floor, with Brandon and Trae as cover, just in case we've missed anyone, then recover the article. Devon, once you're inside, monitor the stairwell from the garage that leads up to the den and take out anyone who tries to try that escape route."

Danny paused a moment, noticing the heavy sound of crickets and cicadas grating around them. "Devon, if Carrie or Sato comes down that way, you are to apprehend them. Do not shoot to kill. Got it?"

Devon answered in the affirmative. "But if Devon's magical software does what he said it'd do, they might be dead before we can reach them, anyway."

He was positive the ensuring grins would be the last he'd see tonight.

NVGs at the ready, the agents spread out as instructed. Danny, Brandon and Trae hung back. Brandon assembled the parabolic microphone. Within seconds, he could hear the voices.

Bingo.

The pit in Danny's stomach reflected his fear that some of his team wouldn't survive this engagement. He'd already experienced enough death in the last several hours. The only question that remained was when the right moment to strike would come.

The first round was underway.

Brooke monitored all of the incoming bids from her laptop screen. It was very neat and clean.

One minute after the last bid of round one, Brooke spoke up. "Gentlemen, round one has concluded. You are now permitted to make calls, emails or texts you need to make. You have five minutes."

Brooke noticed three of the bidders typing out emails to whomever they required authorization from.

Pavlos Niaskos spoke with disappointment. "I'm afraid I will have to withdraw."

Brooke noted it on her laptop.

The second round saw the bid price rise once again. This time, it was Sergei Leonidski who decided to bow out.

Shamir Basar stood up and walked over to a corner on the picture window side of the den to make his call. Speaking in Hebrew with a soft but audible tone, he paused for about one minute waiting for a response. Then he disconnected the call with a 'Shalom' and returned to his chair, prepared to continue.

As the last round drew to a conclusion, Brooke looked at Vanessa as if to say, 'don't smile'. She knew that in five minutes, Vanessa's problems would be over and their relationship would take precedence.

When the final round expired, Brooke stood up. "Gentlemen, after three rounds, I have confirmed that Mr. Basar is the winner at $123 million." She looked over to him with gratitude and extended her congratulations, then addressed the other men. "I regret that it was a winner-take-all proposition. However, you are welcome to come again when more product will become available."

The moment had arrived as Brooke signaled Vanessa with a look. For the first time tonight, Vanessa spoke. "I also wish to thank you for coming this evening. Mr. Basar, please come forward." Brooke sat back down and proceeded to enter the necessary codes to make all of the transfers from the escrow account. She knew the losing bidders would not leave the room until they verified the return of their deposits from their cell phones.

But when she typed in her account number, what she got was a bright red error warning box filling the screen with the message, 'ACCOUNT CLOSED. CONTACT CUSTOMER SERVICE FOR MORE INFORMATION'.

At first, Brooke assumed that she had mistyped the codes. But after she made four more attempts, she reached up and slid her finger through a slippery spot on her forehead.

Vanessa picked up on it and walked over. Brooke remained transfixed on her screen.

This has to be a mistake.

The account had been wiped clean. That was irrefutable from where she sat. So Brooke deftly spoke to give herself more time. "Gentlemen, I'll make a call to my office to release the funds in short order." She stood, walked over to a corner and tried accessing the account from her cell phone, but got the same result. Then she made a call to the Pan Asian overnight desk. She was perspiring.

Thankfully, Sanjiv Aggarwal, the night desk manager answered immediately. After exchanging pleasantries, Brooke said in as monotone a voice as she could muster, just above a whisper, "I need you to check an account number for me. It's for an escrow account I have to dish out now." She recited the number to Sanjiv.

After only a few moments, he said, "It's closed out, Brooke."

"Are you certain?"

"Positive."

Brooke thought she was about to keel over. "Sanjiv, I need you to find out why. Check the records and find out who authorized that the account be closed out."

The bidders, in the meantime, had checked their accounts and found that no transfer had been made. They turned to her with looks of suspicious bewilderment.

Again, after only a few moments, Sanjiv returned to the line. "Brooke, I'm a bit confused."

"Why's that?" she asked.

"Looks like that account was wiped clean and all the funds were transferred to another one."

Her anxiety level just skyrocketed, turning away from the others. "Whose account for Christ sake?" she whispered.

"Yours, Brooke."

Her head was throbbing.

"That's impossible! Who authorized this! I want to know, now," she said with clenched teeth.

Then came the deathblow. "You did, Brooke."

Chapter 53

May 4th, 12:30 a.m.
Monticello, New York

Group North had the longest distance to travel as they had to sweep around to the northern exterior of the home until they got a visual of the kitchen and dining room. All Group South had to do was continue up the trail to the three car garage illuminated only by two sconces above and between the closed doors. Group East, led by Danny, had the toughest job. They would be the easiest to spot, so they traveled along with Group North and stopped halfway, then turned west making their way through the brush and stopping just short of the tree line. They had an unobstructed view of the home. Eliminating Kim and Zak would put his group on the front doorstep.

Trae contributed to his assessment. "They make predictable walks back and forth along the house, so team North and South could take one out each."

"Could work, but let's wait until both groups are in place."

Brandon chimed in next. "We could use those cars and vans as cover. In case we take fire from the second story." He echoed Danny's concern. If he were in Gunther's shoes, he'd add shooters above.

Danny then saw the south group with Lindsey, Shannon and Devon close in on the southwest corner of the house.

Javi, Eddie and Monique on team north were poised to eliminate Shane and Demarco with kill shots through the dining room windows, but Danny ordered them to stand down. He thought that the breaking glass would tip off Gunther's men too early in the raid. Danny instructed Lindsey and Devon to converge on the fuse box in the garage from the rear.

Danny paused to rethink the operation out loud. "Let Shannon take care of business, then converge when we hear his gunfire." Shannon would have the quickest access from the inside after he broke up the party.

Trae checked him. "But if South Group doesn't cut power before then, we'll be sitting ducks for any shooters."

"No," Danny decided, "When they hear the gunfire, all the targets should divert their attention to the second floor, and won't even think about us. Then we'll take them out from behind."

Meanwhile, Shannon threw up his rope toward the second floor balcony. With the agility of a cat, he pulled himself up. He knew he had to keep his climb as quiet as possible as he approached the rear floor length windows, which thankfully were covered by an equally long curtain. Inside, he could hear the murmur of voices, seeming to grow in volume and intensity.

After he lowered himself on the balcony, Shannon whispered into his com-link, "Sweeper in position. Ready for kill shot." He then raised his M-4 and waited.

That was all Danny needed to hear. "It's go time, guys!" Danny had clear visuals Kim and Zak still walking along the front of the home in opposite directions.

Danny said, "North target approaching." He knew Monique, with crossbow at the ready, stood in the shadows as Kim reached the northeastern corner of the house by the kitchen.

She stepped forward from where the tree line was and let fly. Kim had turned to eye her, but before he could react, Monique's arrow caught him square in the neck with a *thwup,* spearing his trachea. He crumpled to the ground instantly without a sound.

"Target eliminated," she said.

For Team South, Lindsey had the honors, taking Zak in the back of the head just below the skull after charging him from behind with her own crossbow. After the same reverse sucking sound, he too fell forward to the ground with a thud.

When he saw the second kill, Danny said, "South, proceed to next position." He knew this was the side door to the garage in the rear beyond his view. "Wait for gunfire, then proceed."

"Roger, that," Devon responded."

Danny directed Brandon and Trae to make their frontal encroachment in a prone position, careful to stay in the shadows. The problem before them was a twelve yard open patch of lawn separating them from the cars they'd use as cover, then another twenty meters beyond that to the front doors.

For Danny, it had gone well, but he also knew the path to the toxin was heavily guarded.

Brandon then turned and touched Danny's shoulder, as if to brace himself while concentrating on the audio. "They've just concluded the auction and I think Carrie and Sato have a big problem."

Danny then made the call that would change everything. "Shannon, execute now!"

Barely able to stand, Brooke pressed the disconnect button and stared down at the floor, having no earthly idea what to do next.

Nasser al-Khalishem was the first to protest. "Ms. Sato, we'd really appreciate it if you told us what the holdup is."

Vanessa, confused about what was happening walked over to Brooke and mouthed the words, 'what's wrong?'

Brooke ignored it and walked past her to her seat and started typing away to access her personal account. None of the escrow account monies had been transferred in.

No longer able to contain her curiosity, Vanessa stood in front of the desk facing Brooke, blocking the view for the others and whispered. "What's wrong, dear?"

She looked up at Vanessa. "Someone closed out the escrow account."

"I don't understand."

"Don't understand what, ladies?" pressed al-Khalishem, who had walked up to the desk.

"Where are the vials, Brooke? Basar asked as he approached her.

Brooke saw Gunther slowly reach inside his jacket pocket.

Brooke rose up to put an end to the rumbling. "Gentlemen, there appears to be a glitch in the wire transfer server at this time. You all can rest downstairs in the living room while I resolve this inconvenience."

"What the hell is going on?" asked Dale Kendrick, who stormed up to the desk and grabbed the laptop to flip it around to view it. "Open the account now, Ms. Sato. I don't have time for your bullshit."

She reluctantly returned to the Pan Asian bank account ledger, Kendrick saw that the account had been closed.

"What the hell did you do with our money?" he said throwing her laptop to the floor. All of the bidders with their bodyguards were now up and converging on the scene. The chemist was the only one who remained seated off to the side.

"I... I don't know," she stammered.

Leonidski pulled out a plastic gun and pressed it against Brooke's left temple. "We want our money, now!" he growled, then grabbed her collar and slammed her head and torso face down onto the desk. Her cheek lay square on the desktop.

Gunther had his Sig Saur aimed at Leonidski.

"I swear, I don't know! We don't know!" Brooke pleaded. "We've been set up. Just give us a chance to fix this."

"I'll say," Kendrick said to her, then turned to the rest of the group. "They *both* set us up!" Dissatisfied with her answer, he moved around the desk to where Vanessa stood and put her in a chokehold before pulling out a brass-plated letter opener from the desk and pressing the point against her neck. "Give it back to us Ms. Sato or I'll cut your friend to pieces!"

"No!" Brooke said. "Please. Let her go. She never handled any of the money." She instinctively played the role of martyr. When it came right down to it, her commitment to Vanessa was real.

Kendrick ignored her and instead dragged the letter opener along Vanessa's left cheek, carving a jagged but deep diagonal line just passed below her left eye, then threw Vanessa down to the floor.

Vanessa's shrill scream filled the room, her left face dripping with blood as she fell to the floor and whimpered.

Gunther, with the stone faced look of anger, said with a subdued British-like politeness, "Please stand down, gentlemen. No one has to die here, tonight."

The room that moments before had concluded a well-orchestrated business meeting, became an unmitigated chamber of horrors. A chilling moment of tension froze in time until the shots rang out.

Chapter 54

May 4th, 12:35 a.m.
Monticello, New York

Brooke felt Leonidski's bullet-riddled body fall on top of her. She could twist around so that his body rolled off her onto the floor. She fell to her knees, Leonidski having spared her the bullets, becoming a human shield.

Shannon's stream of machine gun bursts followed laterally across the room, about four feet from the floor, cutting down almost everyone except Brooke and Vanessa, both of whom now huddled on the floor by the desk. The lone male survivor was Gunther who by virtue of having stayed by the double doors had avoided the swath of bullets by a hair. He too dropped to the floor.

The tattered draperies were beyond repair.

Brooke saw Vanessa trembling with fear, hands cupping her ears. Her own ears rang out, so she screamed to get Vanessa's attention and directed her eyes to the fireplace.

"Run ladies!" Gunther shouted. "I'll take care of this!" He dropped to a prone position facing the window with his pistol drawn.

Brooke crawled over to Vanessa. "Open it!"

Vanessa looked up and pointed to the desk. Brooke knew what she meant. The vials were hidden from view in one of the desk drawers. Brooke opened the right one and took the case.

Nodding, Vanessa reached up to pull the ensconced latch in one of the bricks at the fire place edge. When it cracked open outward, Brooke guided Vanessa out to the stair well. Against her better judgment, Brooke turned back to see a wall-to-wall human carpet of bloodied bodies and groaning men. The last thing she saw was Gunther open fire on Shannon after he'd kicked in the remaining window frame and drew back the curtain. She watched in horror as Gunther's repeated rounds thrust Shannon backward, mercilessly propelling him over the balcony into the frigid night as his NVGs fell to the balcony floor.

On the other side, they saw Sticks on the first floor landing waiting. He ushered them to the garage level door. But before they could reach it, the stairwell went dark.

Danny heard the gunfire followed by a crackling sound of an electrical explosion from the garage. Devon and Lindsey had just destroyed the fuse box. Danny shot out one of the car windows, grabbed a grenade, released its pin, and threw it inside to rest on the front seat. After five eternal seconds later, the grenade erupted, creating a fiery wall between Danny's group and the house.

Trae then threw another grenade, striking the front door. The resulting explosion blew out the doors and adjacent windows. Brandon, Danny and Trae fanned out, running for cover behind separate cars. Seeing movement behind the inferno, Marina's first bullet caught Brandon half the distance to his car cover. The bullet took him at a seam under his mask, taking out a chunk of neck. As Trae and Danny reached their cover, Marina fired again twice at Danny, one shot destroying a rearview mirror above him. Two more shots shattered windshields, resulting in an invisible shower of jagged raindrops. Two more bullets found car metal.

Danny spoke into his com-link. "East Group under fire from rooftop sniper! Priority, take out! Talk to me guys!"

Lindsey volunteered Devon and herself to take care of it. "On it," she said.

Monique radioed back to report on North Group's location, still stationed outside the kitchen entrance.

Another barrage of bullets flew in Trae's direction as he hunkered behind a battered a car, which caught fire. It exploded in what seemed an instant. Just like that, Trae was gone.

"Dammit!" Danny hailed Shannon, but got no response, fearing the worst.

Hearing gunfire from the southern end of the house, Javi and Eddie saw that both Shane and Demarco were standing guard outside the kitchen along the rear turned toward the stairs. When the scene went dark, Javi and Eddie entered first as Monique covered their sixes. Javi breached through the dining room and Eddie the kitchen.

Inside, Demarco and Shane's backs had turned away, but Nils and Dion saw Javi and Eddie in the darkened living room by virtue of their muzzle flashes.

Nils shouted to them, "*Pass auf*!"

It was too late for DeMarco, who caught Eddie's barrage in the back and toppled over the Ma-Jong table. Shane had dropped to the floor below the dining room table as Javi's gunfire sailed overhead. Monique trailed Eddie through the kitchen.

Below, Nils fired across the living room at no particular target, but screamed across to Shane, "*Blendgranate*!"

Shane reached for his flash bang stun grenade and threw it over to Eddie's direction. The ensuing explosion effectively caused blindness and hearing loss for a few valuable seconds. When it detonated about five feet from him, Eddie crumpled to the ground, groaning in agony and holding his ears. Javi crept up on Shane but before Javi was able to fire off any rounds, Shane spun around, dropped to the floor and unloaded his semiautomatic at him. The bullets struck a row of hanging cookware as Javi dropped to his knees for cover behind the kitchen counter. Shane took the opportunity to run over to Eddie, where he unsheathed his knife and sliced open Eddie's flak jacket, then his bowels.

Gunther rose to his knees as machine gun fire erupted from the living room. Gunther scooped up Shannon's M-4 and his spare magazines. It sounded as though the enemy was pouring in from all directions. He'd never shy away from a fight but he had to protect his employer above all. His instincts told him to shepherd Vanessa and Brooke down the stairwell though he'd told them to flee on their own a moment earlier.

He reached the landing as a jarring explosion below him, from the garage, followed darkness. A battery powered light activated and a green tinge illuminated the stairwell.

"Sticks!" he yelled.

Gunther crouched low when he heard a short burst of gunfire directly below him, harsh gasps, then the telltale sound of a body striking a metal floor landing.

Gunther peered down. Devon was pointing his flashlight at the two women and told them to move through the doorway to the garage with his back to the open door. As he stepped over Sticks' body, Gunther took advantage of the distraction and ran down the stairs, tackling Devon from behind. All it took was two seconds with an arm stranglehold and quick twist of Devon's neck to sever his spinal column.

With blue smoke billowing out and over them from the still crackling fuse box, Gunther grabbed the vial case that Vanessa had dropped. Gunther found the two of them beyond the threshold, huddling together, Vanessa trembling as the blood from her cut dripped down onto her blouse. He realized that neither of them had ever seen him—or anyone else as far as he knew—kill a man with his bare hands.

Drawing breath, he said, "This end of the house appears secure, ladies." They were too frightened to speak. He extended his arm to give Vanessa the vial case. "Head outside and take the trail down to the main road. I'll meet you there." He held up his hand, then ran back to Sticks' body and removed his knife which he handed to Brooke. "Take this," he said, not caring whether or not they knew how to use it. "Go!"

Without a word, they complied.

He then took Devon's semi-automatic, along with Sticks', and ran upstairs through the den, back out to the mezzanine. Deion, Shane, Nils and himself were all that stood between the enemy and the den.

Using Shannon's rope that still hung from the rafter, Lindsey scaled the rear side of the house. She reached the second floor balcony mere seconds after Gunther had run through the den for the mezzanine

This sniper had to go.

Not knowing what she would encounter on the roof with the NVG to guide her, she hoped her position on the southwestern corner of the roof in the dark of night wouldn't attract the shooters attention. Danny and Trae were still taking fire. She whispered into her com-link, “In position.”

She hoisted herself onto the roof, using her upper body strength. If the shooter had turned to her direction, she would die. But Lindsay saw the shooter focused ahead, now under return fire, bullets upending shingles. Still undetected, Lindsey lay prone on the roof and crawled toward Marina.

As Lindsey shifted her position, her Glock fell from her holster. Marina turned toward her and a hand appeared out of the darkness and grabbed Marina’s trigger arm from the opposite direction. Javi had scaled up the opposite side. Before Lindsay could reach them, the butt of Mariana’s rifle found Javi’s forehead. He rolled down the rear gable helplessly and fell off the roof. Lindsey heard the clatter of metal lawn furniture, then the thud on the wooden deck.

As Lindsey and Marina fought for the rifle, the both started to roll down the front gable with the acrid smoke from the fire below caused them to cough.

Marina ripped off Lindsey’s NVGs and pinned her to the roof, both hands clamped down on her neck. Lindsey heard the echo of a single bullet, then Marina fell backward, rolling down toward the lip of the gable. A bullet had entered through her upper back. Marina's body fell directly into the front door fire.

Lindsey spoke into her com-link, “Sniper neutralized. Javi fell off onto the deck.”

“I had your back Lindsay,” said Danny, whose bullet it was who saved her.

“Thanks.”

Lindsey repelled down from the roof and saw Javi, face up on the ground, a sun umbrella having broken his fall. Javi was barely conscious. She couldn’t tell if he’d broken anything. Lindsay heard footsteps behind her from the house. She was a sitting duck. More machine gun fire erupted as the bullet sailed over her head into the valley. She looked back to find two lifeless bodies, Nils and Shane, who were cut down from behind.

Danny saw Marina fall to her death and burn in the fire that blocked the front door and had spread up the front of the house made of wooden beams. But he had to enter the house and find Gunther, unsure how many goons were still standing. Behind him was the inferno of cars, swallowing Brandon and Trae with them. He felt the searing heat of the explosion behind him and stench of gasoline, the flames spewing up above the rooftop.

“Talk to me, damn it! Anyone!” he pleaded. Monique and Eddie reported they were under fire from the mezzanine level. One, maybe two targets.

Then he heard Javi’s tepid voice through the speaker. “I’m down, man. Hostiles coming at me,” referring to Nils and Shane who had shot through the rear window and converging fast. Danny heard semiautomatic machine gun rounds. For one excruciating moment, he shut his eyes, accepting that he’d just lost a good friend. In that instant, Danny had forgotten where he was.

The click of the com-link brought him back as Lindsay broke in. “I’m with him, Danny. On the deck.”

Danny exhaled but said nothing.

"Javi fell but one of ours took them out. Not sure who."

Trae and Monique had done their job.

Danny surveyed the inferno before him, then quickly ran to his left around to the rear through the garage entrance, up the staircase and into the darkened smoke filled den. His nostrils flared at the pungent aroma of death striking him square in the face. He was thankful it was too dark to see what he had to trudge through. The only saving grace was the howl of a fresh, cool night air blowing in from the balcony.

Chapter 55

May 4th, 12:40 a.m.
Monticello, New York

From behind, Danny saw Gunther and Deion take cover behind the mezzanine wall which withstood gunfire from across the living room, no doubt from Monique and Eddie. Although made of solid oak, the barrage of bullets soon would pulverize it. Deion, who also took cover along the mezzanine railing, was spared the sight of DeMarco's end.

Danny saw Gunther speak into his com-link for status. He turned to Deion. "We're it, mate."

Before he could reach them from behind, Deion heaved a grenade. Danny heard a blast from the far side of the floor by the kitchen.

"They're gone," Gunther said, gritting his teeth with satisfaction.

Danny clenched his fists in anguish, but squatted low on the floor behind the door and tossed his last grenade the two of them.

Gunther heard the *clunk* of the grenade on the floor behind him and instinctively rolled away from view. Deion wheeled and returned fire before it detonated, taking out the entire mezzanine and Deion with it, leaving only one escape route through the garage stairwell.

More smoke billowed from the hallway into the den overhead. He couldn't see Gunther and prayed the grenade had taken him out too. Eerie silence was broken only by the crackling flames of multiple fires throughout the mansion. Danny could have escaped the inferno through the garage, but chose to locate Gunther's body to confirm his demise.

His satisfaction deflated when he heard machine gun bursts and shattering glass from the rear bedroom ahead to the left. Gunther was on the balcony. Danny thought he could take down Gunther from behind before then, who was brandishing a machine gun in each hand. Danny held his breath as he stepped through the threshold, aimed and pulled the trigger.

Click.

Out of rounds, he cursed the tragic error he'd made to stay and fight. He'd die in seconds if he didn't take evasive action.

The dark image of Gunther froze. Danny heard the chilling voice. "I know it's you, Strong. There's nowhere to hide."

He wondered why Gunther didn't turn and fire instantly, but used his hesitation to back out and flee to the office through the smoke-filled hallway.

Danny could have exited through the bookcase exit, but chose to face Gunther. He took refuge behind the bullet-riddled desk, nearly stumbling over bodies as he gagged at the aroma of smoke melding with multiple blood-soaked corpses. Stepping on one torso, Danny heard a post-death exhale squeak from one and the squishing sound of exposed entrails as he stepped on another.

The balcony was now an open air extension of the room, the chilly night air a welcome respite from the billowing smoke above him. He heard Gunther's footsteps stop and pick something up from the floor, then continued his march in his direction amidst a carpet of broken glass.

"It's over for you, mate," Gunther taunted.

Danny thought he'd have to use the advantage of his NVGs as Gunther only had the moon's light from behind. He scanned the floor close to him and immediately noticed the shattered laptop on the floor. He realized he could use his machine gun as a make-shift club. But Danny was down low to the floor and if he'd try to use either of them, Gunther could get his shots off and end it all. Scanning in the opposite direction, he saw within his reach the blood soaked letter opener Leonidski used on Vanessa. He also saw that the stairwell entrance was ajar, but knew Gunther would either cut him down instantly if he'd made a break for it, or be cut down on the stairs as Gunther fired down upon him. He remained in a crouch position under the desk. Waiting.

Gunther opened fire on the oak desk, in controlled bursts. Some bullets penetrated and wisped by Danny's neck and left ear. He lay prone, facing the exit.

"I know you're out, or you'd have used them by now," Gunther said, creeping even closer.

Danny presumed Gunther wanted to look him in the eye before the kill. He'd have to wait until the last possible second before Gunther could take aim. *Stay put.*

He heard Gunther circle around the desk to his left, Danny's right, like a vulture ready to swoop down on its prey.

One more second.

As Gunther's leg came into view, Danny struck, ramming the opener through the sinews of Gunther's calf. There was a growl of pain, then, in what seemed like one fluid motion, Danny rolled, leaped and thrust the laptop against Gunther's forehead. He intended to repeat the move with his weapon, but saw Gunther still holding one machine gun, having dropped the other as it clattered on the floor.

The attack surprised Gunther, but nothing more. He wore the NVGs that Shannon had worn, the same item he'd picked up moments earlier. Gunther swooped his gun over toward him like a baton, catching Danny's floating ribs. But when Gunther took another swing, Danny blocked it with both hands. He pulled away, releasing a side kick to Gunther's gut. The gun sailed across the room, landing with a thud on one of the bodies.

Gunther responded in kind with a bulrush that slammed Danny hard against the desktop. But in leaning back, his foot caught Gunther in the groin. Too weak to disable Gunther, all it did was enrage him even more.

Trying to squeeze out the pain in his ribs, he rolled off the front of the desk, the fall only broken by another body. Gunther quickly reached down and pulled out the letter opener from his leg and plowed ahead. He made a preemptive kick that just missed the kneecap, while ducking under the knife arm and moving left, looking to take him down in the process.

Gunther dropped the letter opener, but used his larger body weight to pull Danny to the floor with him, landing one kick of his own into his gut.

Both were heaving, eying each other in crouch position.

Gunther charged again, but this time, he used his lower body strength to limit the blow, both of them grappling arm in arm, grabbing what they could of each other, shifting and tumbling in the darkness through the doorway onto the second floor landing.

Fighting like a man half his age, Gunther was winning the brute strength battle, inching his opponent closer to the stairs, where Danny wouldn't have anything to break his fall. His head lunged at Gunther's ear, mouth wide open and snapping close shut like a bear trap. Danny dropped to the ground, taking a piece of earlobe with him. He leaned backwards over the stairs. His groans as his back struck the stairs were only exceeded by Gunther's scream as he sailed overhead.

That should do it.

But it didn't. Defying gravity, Gunther was able to twist in midair and flip to fall front ways, rolling downward onto the first floor landing, braced only by Sticks' corpse. A crunching sound told Danny that Gunther had just broken a few ribs of his own on the way down as well.

Finish. Always finish. Danny was about to end his foe with a knee stomp on Gunther's solar plexus when Gunther swung his legs up and succeeded with a reversal.

They rolled downward to the landing, both eying Sticks' machine gun.

Danny grabbed it first, looking to finish Gunther off for good, but Gunther leapt on top of him, also getting a hand on it. Both grabbed for the trigger, causing a three-round burst to fire into the walls and again up into the ceiling as they rolled.

Gunther managed to wrest it away from Danny's grasp, but before Gunther could aim and fire, Danny used his full body weight and pounced both knees into his chest. He heard the crunch of more broken ribs, but somehow Gunther was able to throw Danny off.

The gun clattered against the stairwell wall, so all Danny could do now was escape in one direction—the basement. He darted down the stairwell as Gunther rolled, grabbed the gun, and rolled back to fire two more bursts where Danny had been, chipped paint and dust flying.

Danny closed in on the open basement area's only refuge—the lab floor cabinets. With no weapon, he was merely prolonging the inevitable.

Then he saw the three heating pad switches and flicked them on.

He wasn't sure how many rounds Gunther had left and started going through futile calculations. *If I could just get him to use up his rounds. At three round bursts... Fifteen? Twenty?*

As Gunther entered the darkened room with only moonlight to illuminate it, he walked toward the glass doors to the balcony. Danny peered over the counter, seeing that they were still shut, knowing Gunther would turn the other way, having assessed that Danny was still there somewhere, cowering like a cornered animal. Danny grabbed a few test tubes and threw them at Gunther as if they were grenades. No sooner did he hear them shatter to the floor, than a hail of bullets sprayed the open cabinets above him, shattering the neat racks of beakers, flasks and test tubes hanging above him.

"I told you it was over for you, Strong."

Danny then looked up and noticed the beaker, just over the lip of the counter. The same one Kate had filled with potassium chlorate and gummy bears. Somehow, it had survived Gunther's last barrage.

"Get up so I can get a clear shot of you."

But Gunther had to get closer.

Head down, Danny said. "You'll have to climb over to get me, McGore."

Guessing right that Gunther would appreciate the sport of the moment, he saw Gunther climb onto the counter, prostrate.

Danny retreated back to the wall. He'd done everything he could do to give Gunther McGore what he deserved. But his efforts would fall short.

Gunther climbed up onto the countertop resting on his knees, hovering directly over the beaker. Bubbles started forming, but Danny could see Gunther was focused on him.

"Just do it. You know you want to," Danny said.

Gunther raised an eyebrow. "You weren't easy. I'll give you that."

The grotesque attempt at a compliment was lost on Danny. "You set up that whole platoon. You fucking killed my wife. Even after you kill me, everyone will know."

Gloating, Gunther took aim and rested his finger on the trigger, staring down at Danny. "Oh yes, and while we're on the subject of lost loves, your girlfriend cried like a scared little girl when she died!" Gunther laughed with the sick revelry of satisfaction,

The upward explosion of heat and light speared Gunther square in the face, his beard, hair, and face caught fire, causing him to fall backward off of the counter onto the floor. Gunther's reflexive burst of bullets barely missed Danny.

Though able to stand, Gunther's entire head was aflame like a lit candle. He dropped the gun as he instinctively grabbed at his face, but his hands started burning, too. Through high-pitched screams, Gunther staggered backwards toward the balcony.

Danny stood up and walked slowly forward, eying Gunther's insufferable cries, then leapt over the counter, grabbed the gun and took aim.

"Did she sound like that, asshole?" Danny demanded.

The remaining rounds propelled Gunther backward, the merc convulsing with every bullet that struck him. Gunther crashed through the shattered sliding glass door and over the balcony.

Amidst the smoke and flames, Danny collapsed to his knees and vomited. The overpowering stench of blood and guts and his own adrenaline fell off, both responsible for the sudden evacuation. Recovering as fast as he could, Danny raced back up the stairs through the garage. He heard the basement ceiling cave in and felt the scorching heat of flames behind him.

Danny had to circle around the front of the house to access the deck. A mangled shell of metal and rubber raged where cars once stood.

When he reached the deck, he saw Lindsey hovering over Javi. "How is he?" he asked.

"Very lucky," said Lindsey.

Javi was conscious but Danny could see that his body ached all over.

"What the hell happened to you, man?" Javi asked.

"I slayed an old dragon. Is anyone else alive?"

"I doubt it," Lindsey answered, confirming Danny's worst fear. The house fire would envelope the wooden deck in a matter of minutes, so they helped Javi up. The three of them trudged past the house, now reduced to kindling.

Danny noticed something on the ground by the garage and limped over to pick it up. It was a ladies' scarf with streaks of blood on it. "Carrie and Sato are still out there somewhere."

When they reached the van and eased Javi down, Danny collapsed alongside him. After Lindsey attended to their wounds, Danny recounted his confrontation with Gunther. Nearly an hour later, Javi was able to sit up. Remarkably, he suffered no broken bones.

"What about Carrie and Sato?" asked Javi.

Before Danny could answer, Lindsey posed another question. "Danny, do you think they took the vials with them?"

"We have to assume they did but they couldn't have gotten very far," Danny reassured them. "Let's go get 'em."

Chapter 56

May 4th; 2:30 a.m.
Monticello, New York

Walking on the footpath in darkness, Vanessa and Brooke were nothing more than wanted criminals on the run. As they put distance between themselves and the inferno that was once a picturesque summer home, Vanessa clutched the vial case as if her life depended on it.

With only moonlight to guide their way, they had to struggle to make sure they never strayed from the path. The trail was rife with stones and roots. Both had kept themselves in decent physical shape but Vanessa had the better of it, having worn boots. The seven mile trail down the mountain would take at least average hikers less than four hours at a steady pace, but at night, somewhat longer. Vanessa was fighting back tears during their descent.

More determined, Brooke was wracking her brain about damage control. "Once we make it to the main road, we can approach the police, explain who we are and get transportation back to the City before anyone discovers what had happened. We were never there." Of course, she also knew it to be a pipe dream, a last hope for both of them to salvage anything out of the whole affair.

"I need to rest, dear," Vanessa said, short of breath. The blood from the jagged wound had clotted. To look into a mirror would have killed her. Her hip muscles seized up, causing her to trip over a root and fall to the dirt, scraping her knees.

"We have to push on, Vee," Brooke urged. "There's no turning back."

Danny predicted they would have taken the south trail, the only one that led to the main road and had Lindsey drive them down to the trail heading off the main road. The three of them fanned out and made their way back up the trail. Lindsey followed on the trail and the two men flanking thirty feet to each side of her.

"There's nowhere else they can go, right?" Lindsey asked.

Danny answered. "We'll eventually run into them on the way up. I doubt they'll have any firearms with them or know how to use them"

"Yeah, but remember, Sato knows judo," Javi interjected.

"That's not what I'm worried about," Danny warned. "As long as they still have the vials, consider them armed and dangerous."

The eastern sky had brightened shortly after 5:00 a.m. Vanessa and Brooke could only hope their fortunes would do the same.

They heard the trickling sound of running water up ahead and to the left. Their path paralleled the access road 120 feet away. Vanessa knew this to be the halfway point of the journey. Both were cold and spent, yet they trudged the short distance through the pine trees to the bridge. Underneath it, a metal corrugated drain pipe provided a welcome respite from the mountain wind. The pipe was wide enough so they could sit without touching water. Brooke laid the knife down in one of the metal grooves.

Brooke cursed. "Damn it. Did I not say 'no guns'? I still can't believe it."

"Tell me what happened with the escrow account," Vanessa said.

"My access codes were compromised. Someone closed out the escrow account, leaving no trace of where the money went."

"What can we do now? This wasn't supposed to happen," Vanessa finally said in desperation.

"I don't know. I won't be able to do these deals again once it comes out I was involved in this disaster."

Vanessa reacted as if she had been insulted. "You? What about me? My company's finished."

Brooked answered with irritation. "You know I care about you, Vee. We can get through this together."

Vanessa attacked her with vicious sarcasm. "'Everything will go according to plan.' That's what you said."

"Someone fucked us. I don't know who, but whoever it was, they knew exactly how to hit us."

"But you guaranteed it. You promised me," Vanessa continued, sounding like a spoiled child.

"Like I said, we were set up and very cleverly tricked. There was nothing we could have done, probably by the same group that attacked the house last night." Brooke groped for a silver lining. "Look, when the Frugeré's Chapter-11 plan is confirmed, the sale of company assets will be enough for you to retire on. You'll be fine. You always keep saying you want to devote more time to Kate."

Vanessa looked at Brooke and had a *mea culpa* moment. "Kate's dead."

"What?"

"I had to. The vials."

"Jesus! What are you talking about, Vee?"

"She was going to turn us in. I couldn't let her do that."

"My God," Brooke said, her mouth hanging in disbelief. With her career and world collapsing, she understood the implications of being an accessory to murder. "You're right. I failed you in every way imaginable. I should have intervened. Instead, I turned the other cheek, acting like it wasn't part of my job description."

Exhausted, they sat there and stewed silently to themselves. Within minutes, Vanessa fell asleep while Brooke remained awake, tormented by the thoughts of the kind of person Vanessa really was, how she deluded herself that she could love such a person and how she was going to explain this to the Board—all to the sound of early morning larks.

A thick early morning fog set in on the mountain as the three agents continued their search in a fanned out formation, their com-links still active. The ground was still very muddy from the April rains, which made for slow going on either side of the trail.

Stepping through the brush, Danny's thoughts were a jumble of questions. How he would handle Vanessa? What he would he say to her? Could he restrain himself from ending her on the spot?

He thought of the night before when he could have killed Joanne, but didn't have the wherewithal to do it. He tried to focus on riddling Gunther with bullets in a fury to relive the satisfaction, but he was already dead. Kate's abandoned experiment was what had killed him. He questioned if he still had the stuff of a Delta Force soldier, or if he'd become pusillanimous in the way he'd conducted his life. Then he cringed inwardly over his own gross miscalculations about the raid and the loss of most of the crew.

Danny heard the trickling water flow of the creek ahead as the bridge came into view.

At about 6 am, Brooke heard the sounds of rustling leaves. It was Lindsey, walking the bridge directly above them. Brooke nudged Vanessa awake, then hushed her with a silent finger to the lips.

Vanessa and Brooke trembled in fear and cold.

"Oh my God, Brooke," Vanessa whispered before Brooke could cover her mouth.

It was too late. They heard a woman's low voice. Someone said, "Targets ID'd." Then they heard the rustle of more leaves and twigs as the woman made her way down to the bank of the shallow creek before stopping. "Come out, slowly!" the voice said.

Vanessa leaned in and caught Brooke's eyes, which softened instantly, their lips inches part. "I don't ever want you to leave me," she whispered. "Promise me you won't tell anyone about Kate."

"Your secret's safe with me."

"I know you're in there. Come out slowly with your hands up!"

Vanessa's yearning eyes suddenly turned to a stone cold stare. "I know you'll keep your promise, sweetie," she said, stroking her left hand through Brooke's hair as their lips met.

Brooke felt the cold hard metal sheer through her throat as blood splattered on Vanessa. Brooke uttered a gurgling scream from her slit throat as she collapsed in the shallow water. Swirling crimson strands flowed downstream. Brooke writhed, holding her throat, while her eyes turned upward, glassy and dull.

Just as the butt of the gun appeared from the lip of the pipe from the mist, Vanessa ran toward it screaming, holding the blood-soaked knife. As she stumbled forward, the knife pierced sinewy flesh. She pulled the knife out and fell on and the woman, grabbing a red ponytail and dragging her back inside under the bridge with new found strength.

Lindsey cried out, "She's in here! She's in here!"

Danny jumped into the water, following Lindsey, who seemed to disappear through the haze. When he reached the lip of the pipe, he saw Vanessa on her knees, her left hand clutching Lindsey's ponytail, her right hand held fast against her neck.

"Let her go, Vanessa!" Brooke's corpse lay sideways facing him, her blood discoloring the running water flowing by his boots. The vial case was well within Vanessa's reach, partially soaked in red.

"I'll kill her. I swear!" Vanessa shrieked.

Javi approached from the other end of the pipe. Danny knew if he could keep her talking, Javi could take her out from behind, but Lindsey could be hit by any bullet that passed through Vanessa at such close range.

"It's over, Vanessa," Danny said.

Lindsey shouted, "Do it, Danny! Just do it!"

"It wasn't my fault!" Vanessa screamed.

"Like Kate's death or hers?" he said, glancing over to what had been Brooke.

Vanessa wavered, but still pressed the knife firmly against Lindsey's neck.

"I'd like nothing more than to put you out of your misery right here and now, but if you let her go and let us take you in, you'll still live. Your choice."

There was a frightening moment of silence. No one moved.

Vanessa lashed out, "I brought her up to be a lady. She was nothing, and look what she became. Look what she created. That was my girl!" Her statement was prideful. She glanced down briefly at the vial case.

"That's not the real toxin, here, Vanessa. You are! Your sickness destroyed her. It destroyed everyone you ever touched," Danny said.

The irony was that Vanessa had not hesitated at killing the women in her life whom she loved—allegedly loved—but when it came to Lindsey, someone she'd only known for less than one minute, she couldn't make the fatal cut. When Danny stared her down, she lost the nerve and dropped the knife and let go of Lindsey's ponytail all at once. She went for the vial case when she heard the loud click of Javi's automatic machine gun behind. The muzzle pressed against her skull. As Javi held her at bay, Danny rushed in and kicked the case out of her reach.

It was over.

"There is no lower life form on this earth than you, Vanessa Carrie!"

Vanessa whimpered like a child, disarmed and disgraced before their very eyes. Danny took over while Javi attended to Lindsey's wound.

They led Vanessa up to the bridge and handcuffed her to one of the railings. Then

Danny spoke loud enough for Vanessa to overhear it, "Local law enforcement will be thrilled to make the news when they discover this piece of shit."

Vanessa shouted epithets, then tried to bargain as a last gasp. "Don't leave me here, please! You'll be sorry you ever fucked with me! You won't get away with this! I'll squash you like a bug!"

Danny removed one of the vials from the case and examined it at eye level, the morning rays shining through it. "Incredible. What a waste. All the misery this thing caused."

They started their hike down to the main road, never turning back while Vanessa continued her frenzied rant.

Chapter 57

May 4th, 10:30 a.m.
Poughkeepsie, New York

They drove Danny to the Metro North station in Poughkeepsie, with no other mid-day riders in sight. The rural drive helped to quell their collective anxiety, but as soldiers, they refused to show or admit it.

"She could have made something of her life." He'd truly miss his time with Kate. He still had to man up to the hard fact that he'd failed to protect her. He'd never met anyone so brilliant—and so flawed.

"You gave her hope," said Javi. "I have to move on. I thought New York would be a place to start over but I can't stay." He shuddered inwardly about walking the streets and being constantly reminded of what had gone down.

"I hear you. I wouldn't mind a change of scenery, too, but I want to stay with the Agency. I mean, we can't go back to Delta, can we?" Javi asked rhetorically.

Danny smiled. "Don't give me any ideas. Although, it sure was something we went through last night. Recover the item and eliminate the bad guys."

"Yeah, it was, except the falling off the roof and almost breaking my back part."

They exchanged brief laughter.

When they pulled into the station, Danny and Javi stepped out, leaving Lindsey to wait.

Javi took the opportunity to confront Danny about his future, and the recent past. "Where you gonna go, anyway?"

"Today? Just grab a few things from my apartment and do just like I was going to do when Kate was still alive: disappear for a while." He paused for a beat. "They're going to ask a lot of questions down at Langley about what happened."

"You were the one with the balls in this operation, Danny. Everyone should know about it. You were a real hero, man."

Danny couldn't have disagreed more. He knew that Kate was the one who'd saved *him*. She'd literally risen from the grave to help him end Gunther. If she hadn't invited him up to the house, he'd never have been able to plan the final raid and scuttle the auction. Thanks to her, he'd be addicted to gummy bears for the rest of his life.

And then there was Sabir. If he'd ever get the chance, he'd track him down before…

"No. You damned well know Langley will think I killed Joanne," he said, breaking from his reverie.

"But, I thought—"

"Just know that I know who did, even though they'd never believe it in a million years."

"Tell me where you're going, then. You're a brother."

"No. I told you. I gotta' disappear for a while. When the time is right, I'll call you, to sneak up on you from behind or whatever."

They embraced, then Javi opened the car door.

"Hey, you should try these," Danny said as he threw a small bag of gummy bears at him. "They're pretty good."

Javi smiled back at him through the car window as he and Lindsey drove off.

Danny walked the Brooklyn Bridge from Manhattan to the Heights and the Promenade, where he and Kate walked just before her nightmare began that fateful evening. The sky was a gray overcast. It looked like rain today, yet the place was bustling with joggers, loving couples, and kids.

Was it fair to have Katelyn Carrie go through all this to save the world? Was she just another so-called 'acceptable loss'? He knew it would be only a matter of time before someone else would' improve' upon her deadly discovery. And they wouldn't bother with the formality of an auction either.

He pulled out Kate's eyeglass case and inside that, the glasses. The same ones he removed from her face the first time they made love. The night they connected. When he removed them from the case, he clenched them in his hand as if he were holding her for the last time. Wedged in the bottom of the case, he noticed a folded piece of paper. It was a handwritten note:

Danny,

It is really hard for me to write this.

At first, I couldn't deal with the fact that I was the subject of some grand manipulation to get the Tri-Meth from me. Then I had to accept that you were just doing your job.

You made me realize that I had the strength within to break free. I once had dreams of doing great things with my gift, but I was a slave to my own self-indulgence.

I realize now that for my entire life, I was living someone else's dream. Now, I'll be free to follow my own.

But before I do, I need to know how I came into this world. Whoever that may be, I want them to know that I made it through the rough part and that now it's time for me to be my own woman.

I just want you to know that whatever happens today, whatever I decide to do and

direction I want to go, I'll always love you.
Kate

P.S.: If you'd wanted the Tri-Meth the whole time we'd been together, all you'd had to do was ask!

He smiled as he reinserted the note and glasses in the case, returning it to his jacket pocket. The sound of a news radio station announcer with the teletype beat in the background wafted through the air. The news reader reported on accusations of corruption at the Mayor's office. He then rattled off the previous day's police blotter report of various muggings, thefts, and murders. One report caught his attention.

"Yesterday, a young woman was found dead in the Ramble section of Central Park. Although the cause is alleged to have been a drug overdose, police are still investigating as the official cause of death is unknown. They received the location of the victim from an anonymous source."

The announcer then discussed the lead international news item in which foreign ministers of several nations were gathering in Geneva today—of all places—to discuss the worldwide proliferation of chemical weapons.

He walked half way across the bridge expanse and stopped to take in the view of the downtown Manhattan skyline. *This is as good a place to do it as any other.*

He gripped the glass case with its contents and paused. There was one more item to add.

Opening his wallet, he carefully slid out Kelly's photo from its plastic insert. She deserved one last look before he closed the case. Then in one fluid motion, he threw it all into the river. Burial at sea.

Epilogue

August 30th, 4:30 p.m.
The Lower East Side, New York City

Brenda Lipschitz would make a killing today. A recent duplex co-op on Avenue D caused her voicemail to max out. The bidding wars had commenced. The Lower East Side was the place to be and she knew it was going to be a good commission year.

This particular co-op had the latest conveniences, high ceilings and a hip brick interior wall, with a fireplace no less. And it was 'bright'. Her client had paid top dollar, outbidding the second-highest bidder by $25,000.00. All that had to happen was for the client do a final visual inspection and sign the contract. Brenda made sure to bring it with her.

She showed the client the first floor with its modern kitchen and spacious living area. The second floor had three full bedrooms and two baths. Brenda was curious why this client needed such a large living space, being single.

She led the way upstairs. Her client followed, but very slowly up the natural wood staircase. The sound of a cane clicked on each stair, as if Bluebeard the Pirate himself was buying the place.

"Do you need help?" she asked.

"No, I'm fine," the woman's voice responded.

As the client stepped on the second floor, Brenda smiled, relieved her client survived the climb and therefore preserved her commission.

The woman's face was badly burned and bruised. The client had 'hit it big' over the summer and used the cash windfall to buy the place.

After walking through each room, the woman said, "It's perfect. I'll take it." Her voice sounded awful. It sounded like sandpaper on wood. She was dressed in newly acquired Goth clothing. At least that hadn't changed.

"Great. I'm so glad you like it. I told you it'd be perfect for you," Brenda said. "I've brought the contract for you to sign."

"You can send it to my lawyer to look over, but I think everything will check out."

Disappointed at the missed opportunity of making the quick kill, she said, "No problem at all."

They walked to the staircase to start the climb downstairs when Brenda asked, "May I ask what business you're in?" Because the woman had left the occupation space blank on the application, Brenda had assumed she was an independent consultant or something of that nature. Confirmation of a bank account balance was all that was needed to enter her bid.

The woman hesitated for a moment, then said, "Oh you know, I provide happiness to all sorts of people. And let me tell you, happiness is in very short supply these days."

"I see. So, how's that going for you?"

"To tell you the truth, business has never been better."

THE END

ACKNOWLEDGEMENTS

My heartfelt gratitude goes out to a virtual army of individuals who helped to shape this book into what it is today. First off, I thank all those individuals at my nanowrimo.com writers group and forum who honed my writing skills with many more miles to go. Their guidance cannot be overstated. Thank you Alexis, Carlos, Avi and many others whose comments definitely improved by writing and storytelling abilities. I acknowledge author E.J. Rand for his invaluable advice and encouragement. I thank my editor, Clyde Wolfe, who put me on the right track early on with his invaluable developmental editing critique. There are also my consultants who added realism to the story, namely chemists Rodney Bannwart and Evelyn Libertelli and Demarest police officer and special ops veteran Kirt Glynn. And finally to my family, who put up with my incessant fishing for compliments along the way. A special thank you to my eldest daughter, Leah, whose initial motivation and endorsement of my story set me on my way through this incredible journey. Good luck at Vanderbilt U.! Most important of course, is my loving wife, Sharon, who suffered through countless nights of having to fall asleep without me at her side as I obsessively typed away on my laptop. I love you so much! I hope you are ready for the sequel.

ABOUT THE AUTHOR

Alan practiced as a lawyer in New York for more than 20 years in the entertainment and high technology space. Three years ago, he knew it was time to step back and write what he liked reading: gripping international thrillers that focus on relevant geopolitical issues of the day. Over the years he published legal articles, but *The Chemist* is his first crack at fiction and has enjoyed the experience immensely. He grew up in Moorestown, New Jersey, a suburb of Philadelphia, and graduated with a music degree from James Madison University in Virginia. He lives with his wife and four children in Demarest, New Jersey, a stone's throw from the George Washington Bridge.

CPSIA information can be obtained
at www.ICGtesting.com
Printed in the USA
BVOW08*0815160217
476198BV00014B/9/P

9 780998 050829